BETH BOLDEN

PROLOGUE

It was the very best part of Tate Ward's week—and also the worst.

Some people—Tate was not going to name names—took Home Economics to boost their GPA during their senior year so it'd look better on college apps, and initially, Tate had added it to his schedule for that reason, too. But his initial apathy had faded away, and he'd discovered that he actually *loved* to cook. Nobody was more surprised than he was. But it turned out that his mother popping frozen meals into the oven and using box mixes wasn't technically cooking, which was why he'd never been particularly interested in either the process or the flavors before.

But his unexpected discovery of how much he loved to cook took second place to the *other* reason that Home Economics had become his favorite class.

The other reason was waltzing into the classroom now, five—no, *six*, Tate corrected after glancing at his watch—minutes late and was taking his sweet time to walk across the room towards the kitchen station that he and Tate shared.

Several high fives and a chest bump later, Chase Riley stopped next to Tate and gave him a bright, wide, absolutely winning smile. Tate's heart flipped in his chest, and then flopped.

His crush had come on like a freight train, unwanted and yet undeniable.

The best thing about it: Chase seemed game to flirt as much as Tate, at least in the relative anonymity of the Home Ec classroom. The worst? Tate had never heard even a single whisper that the great Chase Riley, star of the Petaluma High School Thunderdogs, was anything other than straight.

So he basked in Chase's attention twice a week, and the rest of the time, mourned the thought that all he would ever get was one hundred and thirty-two minutes a week. Nothing more, and nothing less.

"Hey, dude," Chase said, tapping him on the shoulder. Everything seemed to move slow and sluggish when Chase touched him, like his blood coagulated, congealing until every body part simply froze up. "How's it hangin'?"

Tate had known *of* Chase Riley for most of his life. Had always thought he was kind of an idiot. Chase was friendly with everyone in a low-key, laid-back way, not a snobbish bone in his body, but he was insanely good at sports, and well, Tate *wasn't*. Their lack of friendship could be explained easily by Tate's complete inability to be one of the cool kids. And Chase Riley had always been so damn cool.

Even before he'd become a five-star-college recruit, and had committed to Oregon as a wide receiver in their high-powered offense.

Even before he took the Thunderdogs to state twice, and won the state football championship the second time.

But none of those cold, hard facts could keep Tate from falling and falling hard for the funny, irreverent, incredibly hot guy that he spent a hundred and thirty-two minutes a week with.

"You're late," Tate hissed under his breath. "Six minutes late."

But Chase just kept smiling at him. Like he actually wanted to be here. Like he enjoyed their time together just as much as Tate did. Thinking that way kept Tate up at night, so he pushed it aside.

"If I knew you'd be that happy to see me, I'd have rushed," Chase said.

"I'm not," Tate claimed. Except he was. Every traitorous cell in his body leapt the moment he saw a glimpse of that too-long honey blond hair out of the corner of his eye.

"What are we making today?" Chase asked, leaning closer to Tate. He smelled like sunshine and freshly cut grass, and Tate was swamped with it.

"Biscuits and gravy," Tate said, trying to drag his attention back to the recipe sitting in front of them, away from the tanned, muscular forearm that Chase was resting so casually right there on the table. It was hard, because he was so utterly irresistible.

Utterly unattainable, too.

"Oooh, breakfast. You hungry, Ward?"

Tate swallowed hard. He was so goddamned hungry, and there was no way he would ever satisfy this particular craving.

"Sure," he said.

Chase crossed his arms over his chest, which didn't make anything easier. His biceps, in that tight t-shirt, bulged, and Tate *ached* with everything he couldn't ever say. Couldn't ever do.

"You guys all set?" Mrs. Mary, the Home Economics teacher, stopped by their station, probably because she noticed they hadn't even started cooking yet. "You better get going. Biscuits need a special touch."

"Right, okay," Tate said, but didn't move, even after she moved on to the next station.

"You alright?" Chase said, and took another step right into Tate's space.

Tate told himself that the only reason he'd keep doing that was because Chase didn't know 1) he was absolutely, totally gay, and 2) he was head over heels for the guy.

Maybe he'd still get so close. Chase didn't strike him as a particularly homophobic asshole, but it was impossible to say for sure, and Tate had already decided that he didn't want to come out now. Not til college. Not til he'd left this small Northern California town behind.

He was going to NYU, and in New York City, home to millions, he would find some guy who made Chase look like *nothing*.

Except that Tate already knew that was impossible, and that Chase would probably haunt him for the rest of his life.

"I'm fine," he said shortly. "Go get the butter from the fridge, and I'll get the dry mix for the biscuits started."

"Sure," Chase said. "But don't think we're done talking about this."

"Yeah, we are," Tate muttered, as he began to measure flour out into a big bowl.

"So," Chase said, when he returned with the butter, "you got the magic touch, Ward?"

Tate. Call me Tate. He yearned for so many things, but high up on the list was Chase calling him by his first name. Whispering it in his ear. Groaning it as Tate sucked his cock.

"Better than you," Tate said as he dropped in the chunks of butter into the flour and began to crush them into the pea-sized pieces called for in the recipe.

"Nobody's got a more magical touch than me," Chase said confidently. And not for the first time, Tate wondered if he realized that he was flirting. And flirting *back*.

Surely he couldn't be that obtuse?

But Chase didn't seem to realize it; just did it instinctively. The two of them, lost in their own little world, twice a week.

"Someday we should compare," Tate said, voice not quite steady. He took these risks, even though he knew they could backfire.

"Yeah?" Chase's grin was wild and bright. "Yeah, we should. You might be the underdog, but you'd definitely bring it."

"Damn straight," Tate said. "Measure out the buttermilk, okay?"

"Is that all I'm good for?" Chase wondered. "Fetch this, grab that, pour this thing into this other thing."

Tate rolled his eyes. "When you actually learn to *follow* the recipe, you can take the lead."

"I follow the recipe!" Chase insisted, all innocent outrage.

Except he didn't. The one disastrous time that Tate had let his crush make the decisions and do the majority of the cooking, their pot pie had turned out half-raw, half-burned.

Since then, Tate had been in charge.

Despite his protests, Tate had a deep, unshakable feeling that Chase *liked* it that way.

"You're a terrible liar," Tate teased him. "Just absolutely fucking terrible. If your lying is anything like your magic hands, you're in real trouble."

"With you?" Chase asked silkily, and Tate swallowed hard. *God*, there were some days, some moments, when it was a real struggle to not grab Chase by that golden, perfectly muscled forearm, and drag him to the big walk-in pantry, shut the door, and push Chase against it. Make him eat every single word. Kiss him until neither of them could even stand.

"Of course with me," Tate ground out. His cock was already hard—all it took was a whiff of Chase, and the wild taunting teasing that drove all his fantasies—but thankfully it was hidden by the countertop.

"Sounds like a good time," Chase said. "I'm already looking forward to it."

Tate gritted his teeth together. "Have you managed to measure that buttermilk yet? You pour it . . ."

"I got it," Chase interrupted, and leaned in, hair brushing the side of Tate's head. It was silky and Tate dug his fingers into the flour and butter, trying to resist the urge to turn into it. Rub against it. "You're awfully impatient today, Ward."

"Not really." Except he *was*. One month left of high school, and Tate never could have imagined in a million years that he wouldn't want it to end. He and Chase would only spend a handful more classes together, and then they'd go their opposite ways, to opposite ends of the country, and Tate would probably never see him again.

He was impatient to change a fate that couldn't be changed.

Chase poured in the buttermilk, as Tate gently incorporated the biscuit dough into one big lump. They worked great together—another nail in the coffin of Tate's heart.

"It doesn't look very appetizing," Chase observed. "Did we fuck it up?"

"You mean, did *you* fuck it up," Tate pointed out. "I don't fuck stuff up, remember?"

Chase nudged him with an elbow. "Of course you don't. You're perfect."

When Tate glanced up in surprise, Chase's dark eyes were serious.

"Hardly," Tate scoffed.

"But you're good at this. You should do this." Chase waved around Tate's head. "Like as a job."

Tate dumped the bowl of biscuit dough onto the floured counter. "Seriously? I told you I'm going to NYU. Probably for business."

"But you love *this*," Chase argued, like he really actually cared what Tate did with his life, even if he wouldn't be part of it. "That grilled cheese you made me last week, when I told you I was hungry? It was the *best*. I could die happy, eating that grilled cheese."

"Yeah, and?" Tate grabbed the rolling pin from the utensil drawer and began rolling out the dough. "Becoming a chef isn't exactly practical as a life choice."

"And football is?" Chase wondered.

"Football is when you're *you*," Tate said.

"You're not wrong." Chase smiled bright and wild again. "Or so everyone keeps telling me."

"Modest, too," Tate muttered. Except that defying the odds, Chase kinda *was*. Even though people all over, from the kids at their school, to their coaches, to the coaches at so many universities across the country, to the sports media who were already following him, were constantly telling him how drop-dead amazing he was.

It would give anyone a big head, but all the attention hadn't changed Chase Riley.

"I meant it," Chase said firmly. "You should do this."

"I'm going to NYU," Tate said. Like if he said it enough times, he could rediscover the joy he'd once taken in that accomplishment. "Not cooking school."

"But you *could*. You know you could do anything you set your mind to," Chase continued. "You're smart."

Tate glanced up at him. Somehow Chase had ended up with a smear of flour on his cheek, even though the closest he'd come to any actual cooking had been to spend the entire class hip to hip with Tate.

His fingers itched, wanting to brush it off. But his fingers would only leave more flour in their wake. At least that was what he told himself.

"Hey, find the biscuit cutter, if all you're gonna do is lecture me on what I should be doing with my life."

"It's just . . ." Chase sighed as he dug through the drawers at their station. "It's just you . . . fucking light up when you're in here."

It's not just cooking. It's you.

"How do you know what I'm like when I'm not in Home Ec?" Tate challenged. They didn't really acknowledge each other outside of this classroom. In Tate's head, it was because that was safer. He'd assumed that Chase didn't really notice him. Tate knew he wasn't exactly the most striking guy on the planet. He was shorter. He'd managed to put on some muscle mass between his junior and senior year, but Chase's muscular frame still dwarfed his. His brown hair had a reddish-brown tint but was unremarkable otherwise. He wasn't a spectacular golden god, like Chase was, and he'd made his peace with that fact.

Chase shrugged. "I notice," he said cryptically. The butterflies in Tate's stomach fluttered.

"Did you find the cutter yet?" Tate demanded. He didn't know how to deal with any of this. So he focused on the task at hand. *Get the biscuits in the oven. Get the gravy started. Avoid fantasizing that Chase Riley might feel even a fraction of what you do.*

"Yeah, it's right here." Chase set it on the counter. "I'll get the oven preheated."

"Make sure you hit *Bake* and not *Broil* this time," Tate cautioned.

Chase shot him an unrepentant grin. "That wasn't my fault. I was distracted."

"By what?"

"You, of course. You were talking and I just . . ." Chase shrugged. "I listened."

Ugh.

Tate's movements were jerky as he grabbed the baking sheet and began to plop the biscuits onto it. "Can I trust you to mix up an egg wash?" he asked.

"What's an egg wash?" Chase wondered.

Tate sighed. "Never mind. I got it. Can you at least gather the ingredients for the gravy unsupervised?"

"You got it, boss," Chase drawled, and yeah, there was a frisson of *something* that went up Tate's spine at his words.

Maybe Chase was straight. Maybe he wasn't. Maybe he knew he was flirting. Maybe he didn't. But Tate *knew* how good it might be between them. That was why all of this sucked so goddamn much.

By the time Chase returned, juggling all the gravy ingredients in his big hands the same way he juggled footballs, Tate had whipped up the egg wash, brushed the tops of the biscuits and had them in the oven with only a few minutes to spare.

"I'll grab a pot too," Chase said, reaching into the cabinet and picking one out, setting it on the stove. "I know you like this one."

"I do?" Tate had never told him that. It had seemed like such a silly thing to mention, so he hadn't.

Chase shrugged. "I told you, I pay attention."

Not for the first time, Tate wondered how much was going on beneath Chase Riley's easygoing, laid-back exterior. A lot, he thought. More than anyone else realized.

But Tate knew, and he was lucky enough to see at least a little of what lay underneath.

They got the gravy started, Tate doing the bulk of the work, but Chase competently assisting him, for once.

Tate was almost done frying up the sausage, when he looked around and realized that Chase had forgotten to grab the cornstarch.

"Hey, you forgot the cornstarch," Tate said, nudging him with his hip. The first time he'd ever done that, he'd felt electrified. It still sent a thrill up his spine, that Chase let him do it. That Chase did it back. He wanted to curl his hand around Chase's muscular thigh, his waist, his abs, and pull him in closer. But he didn't, because that way lay disaster and almost certain humiliation.

"No, I didn't." Chase looked around on the counter. "Damnit, I thought I did." He took off for the pantry.

Tate turned the heat down on the stove, and then followed him, because despite how stupid and how pointless it all was, he still *wanted* to.

Chase hadn't turned the light on in the big walk-in pantry, so it was still dim. Quiet. Tate could barely hear the class noise coming from outside. "Hey, did you find it?" Tate asked.

Glancing over at him, Chase shook his head. "I don't know where it is, that must be why I missed it the first time." He grinned, bright in the dim light. "Or maybe I was just distracted, again."

"Again?" Tate raised an eyebrow. Then he caught a glimpse of the container, buried in the back, its familiar yellow packaging catching his eye. Right behind Chase's head.

Tate shut his mind down, closed it tight against the way it was screaming *danger, danger, danger*, and reached behind Chase, practically pressing up against him as he grabbed for the container.

He was one hundred percent sure that Chase would flinch away. They'd pushed each other's buttons and each other's personal space plenty of times. Almost every single time it was Chase who started it.

Maybe he had today, too, but goddamn it, Tate was going to finish it.

He pressed his body against Chase, fingers barely brushing the edge of the circular yellow container. Leaned in a bit closer. Imagined that it wasn't just his own beating heart he could feel, but Chase's too.

"You got it?" Chase asked slowly. Softly. Reached in and steadied Tate's body by wrapping his fingers around Tate's upper arm.

"Yeah, yeah, I do," Tate said breathlessly as he finally grabbed the container. Didn't pull back immediately. Thought he could see something similar to his own intense longing reflected in Chase's dark eyes.

"Tate," Chase said softly, gaze flicking to his lips.

Tate knew his heart was beating in double time. Triple time.

Was Chase going to kiss him? He might die of a heart attack before their lips actually touched.

"Tate? Chase?"

The light came on sudden and blinding, and Tate sprang back from Chase. Panicked. Paranoid. But it was only Mrs. Mary, staring at them with a confused expression on her face. "Did you two need any help?"

Did they need any help? Tate needed more than just *help.*

"No," Chase said firmly. "We're good. Ward was just looking for the . . . uh . . . the uh . . ."

Tate held up the container in his hand. "The cornstarch," he said weakly.

"Well, your sausage is burning. I turned the burner off."

"Shit," Chase said, but when they got back to their station, Tate realized that for the first time all semester, Chase wouldn't look him in the eye.

He sighed and picked up the spatula, halfheartedly stirring the sausage which, just like Mrs. Mary said, was beginning to look a little crispy around the edges.

"You okay?" he asked Chase, panic still churning inside of him. Had he ruined everything? Their friendship? Their easy camaraderie? He'd wanted *more*, goddammit, not *less*.

"No, I'm good," Chase said easily, giving him a smile. But it was not quite as bright. Tate might not have noticed, but the problem was he'd made a study of Chase Riley. He knew him, probably way too well. Stalker-well, in fact. And Tate had a horrible sinking feeling in his stomach that he'd just destroyed everything by pushing way too hard.

A month later, Tate graduated.

Chase did too, of course, but the difference was he was surrounded by a crowd of already adoring fans. Tate, standing outside the gymnasium, watched as Chase's friends and family congratulated him. Watched as he threw his head back and laughed. And wondered, horribly, how long it was going to take him to mend a broken heart once he reached New York City.

"You're staring," his sister, Rachel, hissed at him.

"Yeah, well, it's probably the last time I'll ever see him again," Tate said, moping, because how could he not?

He'd had another month of Home Economics classes, but even though Chase had eventually relaxed with him, he wouldn't flirt quite as readily as he always had before.

It was almost like, Tate thought, when he was alone in his bedroom late at night, consumed by too many thoughts that wouldn't stay silent, he'd *almost* realized exactly what he'd wanted and been terrified by the brush with reality.

But even that hypothesis didn't help Tate feel any better now.

"You could," Rachel claimed. "There's no reason you can't like . . . connect online or something. That happens. All the time."

Except that Tate was Tate, and Chase was still Chase. And they'd never actually been friends. Not really, anyway. Not in any of the ways that mattered.

"Maybe." Tate grimaced.

"Come on, Tate," his mother cajoled. "Let's take some pictures."

He took one last look at Chase, assuming it would be the last.

Later he would look back on this moment and realize just how fucking wrong he'd been about not just this, but *everything*.

CHAPTER ONE

For the last ten years, Tate had expected seeing Chase on TV would eventually get easier.

Tate had been through multiple collegiate football seasons, then five professional seasons, including two Super Bowls, and now this third playoff run, and he always expected to feel somehow *less* of a jolt every time the camera panned to Chase, dark eyes intense, but usually with a smile on his handsome face. Usually because they were winning.

They were not winning today, and Tate's stomach cramped. He'd agreed to come watch the game with Tony and Lucas at the Funky Cup because he didn't know how to say no. Didn't know how to say, *You know Chase Riley? Yeah, he's the one who got away.*

Except he wasn't. Not really. *Nothing ever happened between you,* he told himself firmly, *and it was never going to, because Chase is straight.*

At first, when Chase had become close friends with the *not*-straight circle on his team, the Los Angeles Riptide, Tate had waited, expectantly and with a terrible hope, that Chase might also come out of the closet. But even though he remained close with Heath Harris, Sam Crawford, Neal Fisher, and now Jamie Wright, Chase had never expressed any interest in being anything other than a staunch ally.

"You look tense," Tony said, patting him on the back. "Maybe you need another drink. These guys'll be fine."

Tate had proclaimed himself to be a very casual Riptide fan, in an attempt to hide his ten-year obsession with the team's number one wide receiver.

"I'm just concerned about the truck," he said. It wasn't really a lie. He *was* concerned. Sales had been sluggish during the fall and winter, normally times when his food truck, Say Cheese, did really well. He sold grilled cheese and macaroni and cheese, in many different specialty variations, and people liked to carb load when it got cold. Even though "cold" for LA was often seventy degrees.

He'd become even more concerned about sales when Tony and his brother-in-law, Ryan Flores, who played for the Los Angeles Dodgers, announced their plan to open a food truck lot, where trucks could park semi-permanently. There'd be outdoor seating, lights, music, and a festival-like atmosphere that Tate knew his particular menu would do well in. However, when Tate had expressed an interest in joining the collective, Tony had pulled him aside and let him know they were vetting the trucks and everyone had to reach a certain sales threshold to be allowed in.

Tate was not even close to the threshold that Tony had mentioned.

He sighed.

"There's stuff you can do," Tony suggested. "You could always bump up your social media. Overhaul your menu . . ."

"Or you could find a famous brother-in-law," Lucas leaned in and suggested.

Tony smacked his boyfriend on the shoulder. "Don't listen to him," he said.

Tate didn't have a famous brother-in-law. He had a famous ex-crush. Unfortunately that was not the same thing.

"You know very well that Ryan rarely ever mentions What a Catch," Tony said defensively, referring to the food truck he shared with his brother—and Ryan's husband.

"Except everyone and their neighbor knows that Ryan's associated with it," Lucas said with a shrug. "It's natural marketing."

Tony turned to him. "I don't suppose you know anyone famous you could convince to give you a boost?"

Yes, but I'm never using him. Using him would mean actually *connecting* with Chase Riley again, and Tate had zero intention of ever doing that. He was too smart to keep dreaming about a straight boy who wasn't going to love him back. And if Tate ever ran into him again, he knew that was exactly what would happen.

"No," Tate said, shaking his head. "No, I don't."

"Maybe we could get Ryan to give you a quote or something. Or mention Say Cheese in one of his interviews . . ." Lucas suggested, before Tate shook his head even more firmly.

"No," he repeated. "No, I don't need the help, though I appreciate the advice."

"Hey, man, we want you with us," Lucas said, getting up. "I'll grab another round of beers. It looks like the Riptide might rip our hearts out again."

It did look like that was becoming a possibility. The Riptide was down fourteen points, with only six minutes left in the game. The camera kept panning to shots of Sam Crawford, the Riptide quarterback, sitting on the bench, a frustrated, agonized expression on his face. Chase was sitting next to him as they flipped through a tablet together, probably trying to come up with one last miraculous play to save the season and win the AFC Championship.

Tate knew better, had spent the last ten years trying to know better, but he ached for him anyway.

"You know Lucas means it, right?" Tony said earnestly. Which was a little scary, because Tony was the kind of guy who did not do earnest very often. "We really do want you with us at the lot."

"Yeah," Tate said. Feeling extra super-duper guilty that on top of letting himself down, he was letting his friends down. "I'll . . . try some new things. I've got some good placements coming up; I think it'll help."

"Good," Tony said warmly, clapping him on the shoulder again. "You're awesome, you know that? And I can't wait for the rest of LA to know it too."

Just one person in LA, Tate thought. But he would take professional success too. Because while he hadn't exactly written off the possibility that he'd find someone who looked at him like Tony and Lucas looked at each other, he'd had way too long to come to terms with the fact that it wasn't going to be Chase Riley.

Lucas returned with a trio of beer bottles in his hands. "Not lookin' good," he said as he flopped down into the chair next to Tony's. "Shaw's crying into his bourbon."

"Two Super Bowl appearances in three years is kinda unheard of," Tony pointed out.

"Yeah, and they *lost* one," Lucas retorted.

"That kick was . . ."

"Yeah, yeah, it was deflected, I know it. Everyone knows it by now."

Tate had heard a version of this conversation a hundred times since the last Super Bowl. Not just between Lucas and Tony, but between dozens of customers at his truck, in the grocery store at least twice, and incessantly in the sports media. It had finally started to die down, but then Neal Fisher, who'd missed the kick—*it was deflected*, he could hear Lucas arguing, even in his own head—had retired as a member of the Los Angeles Riptide and announced he was dating the new kicker, in the same press conference.

After that, Tony had started gathering his friends together at the Funky Cup to watch the Riptide games. "We need to be supportive," Tony had said firmly. "These are fucking queer icons, and we're gonna do our part, okay?"

And that was how Tate had come to watch the Riptide, not in the privacy of the loft apartment he shared with his sister, Rachel, but in the company of his friends.

In some ways it was easier because he didn't want any of them to know he knew Chase, and of course, Rachel did. Usually shot him one or two painfully sympathetic looks before retreating to her own room.

"Ugh, what a disappointment," Tony said. "Maybe we jinxed them by watching every week."

"Of course we didn't," Lucas said, leaning in and brushing a kiss across his boyfriend's mouth. "You did a good thing."

The game slowly, painfully ticked to an end. The Riptide tried a last-minute drive, trying to salvage the game, and Tate watched as Sam and Chase connected for one last long pass, Chase throwing his big body in the air to catch the ball.

But even that wasn't going to be enough, and Tate found himself chugging his beer as the game clock hit zero, and the camera decided instead of panning to the other team, celebrating obnoxiously, they'd do a nice close-up of Chase's disappointed expression.

Tate swallowed hard, finishing his beer. He wondered what it would be like to watch the games and not imagine what Chase was feeling.

"Come on, let's get out of here," Tony said. "That's it for this season."

"There's always next season," Lucas said. "Crawford and Riley are still young. They've got tons of good years ahead of them."

"As do we," Tony said, throwing an arm around his boyfriend's shoulders. "Catch you later, Ward?"

"Yeah," Tate said. "Thanks for the beer."

Tony stopped right next to him. Put a reassuring hand on his shoulder. "You've got this, you know? I know you do. And I meant it about Ryan. He'd love to do a quote for you, if you needed it."

"I've . . ." Tate cleared his throat. "I've got an idea, but thanks, anyway."

"Sure thing," Tony said. "See you later."

When Tate got back to the loft, Rachel was sitting on the sofa, working on her laptop, her concerned expression illuminated by the screen.

"I saw they lost," she said, glancing up at him as he collapsed down on the couch. "I'm sorry."

"Sorry for me?"

Rachel shot him a look. Younger sisters were pretty good at that, and she was better than most. "Yeah, *you*, because Chase Riley is a multimillionaire and already has a Super Bowl ring."

"That's fair," Tate conceded.

"I was working on the books," Rachel said. She owned Say Cheese with him. When their grandmother had died, she'd left them both some money, and it had been Rachel's idea for Tate to move back to California and start a food truck together—a dream he'd been nursing since his early twenties.

Was it always awesome working so closely with his little sister? No. But he wouldn't trade it for anything else, either.

"How bad is it?" Tate asked with a wince.

Rachel's concerned expression had already said everything he needed to know. "Not good," she admitted. "Did Tony have any suggestions?"

"Not really anything we can use." They'd already been hitting social media hard but with so many food trucks in LA, and no *really* good hook for Say Cheese, sometimes it felt like they were screaming into a void. "He did suggest I ask Ryan Flores for a quote."

"His brother-in-law?" Rachel looked pensive at this idea. "You could always . . ."

"No," Tate said in a hard voice. "No, I am not going to ask him. I don't even *know* him. I didn't really know him back then, and that was ten years ago."

"I wasn't going to suggest you ask Chase because you're already a mess over him," Rachel retorted. "I was going to say we don't even *need* to ask Chase."

"What do you mean?" Tate was afraid he understood what she was suggesting. But they were kind of desperate. He already knew what kinds of stupid things desperation could make him do. Like press himself against Chase in a dark pantry, hoping for something that would never happen.

"I mean, you don't have to *ask* him," Rachel said. "We're so small, do you really think he'd notice or complain if we said Chase Riley loves our grilled cheese?"

"What if he does notice?"

Rachel just shrugged, like this wouldn't be the worst scenario in the universe. "So we take it down. But by that point, we've gotten what we needed out of it, which is better traffic and increased sales."

Tate groaned. "You're a terrible influence, you know? I can't believe you want us to *lie*."

"Are you ready to talk to him again?" Rachel challenged.

"You know I can't do that," Tate said.

"You don't want to lose our truck either. Which is a very real possibility right now. *And* you want to get into Tony's food truck lot. This gets all of that done, without you actually having to deal with Chase." Rachel sounded pretty proud of herself.

"You've been thinking about this for awhile," Tate said with disbelief.

Rachel stared at him, her gray eyes wide in the dark room. "A few days, maybe," she admitted. "We've got to do *something*."

Tate didn't like it. He didn't want to lie. But then, faced with the possibility of asking Chase for a favor, ten years after he'd tried to kiss him in a darkened pantry during Home Economics, fudging the truth definitely seemed like the better option.

It was impossible not to remember how, so many years ago, Chase Riley had once loved his grilled cheese. Had even said he could die happy eating one.

How much of a lie was it to use that quote now? If it could be considered a lie, at least it was a little white one.

"Fine," Tate said. "But we're gonna be careful how we do this. Only a few mentions on social media, and we *will not* tag him."

"I was thinking we'd do that, and we'd alter the menu, maybe point out his favorite choices," Rachel said.

She really *had* been thinking about this.

"I am going to regret agreeing to this," Tate said.

"No way, you're going to be super glad, in the end," Rachel insisted. "You'll be in the lot, our sales will be up, and you'll be able to stop stressing. It's high time that Chase gave you something back, after you've mooned after the stupid guy for the last ten years."

"Chase Riley doesn't owe me anything," Tate said.

Rachel shot him another look that made it perfectly clear that she didn't agree with that assessment at all.

Chase Riley shoved a stray chip around his plate and tried very hard to ignore what his agent was saying.

Actually, the words themselves weren't so bad. It was the decidedly lecture-like tone Alec was giving them.

"I know that it was a tough loss, following a tough loss the year before, but I've received several messages about your behavior at the . . ." Alec paused. "Well, I guess it wasn't really a victory celebration, was it?"

Chase rolled his eyes. "Not really." It hadn't been particularly victorious, that was for fucking sure.

"Okay, your behavior at the . . ." Alec was still searching for the right word. Any other time Chase would have been amused at seeing his very put-together agent so tongue-tied. "At the consolation event?"

"You had to work way too hard for that," Chase said.

"What I have had to *work hard at* is making sure that your sponsors don't drop you, Chase," Alec said firmly. "That video of you dancing around on the empty stage? It's making the rounds. It's not a good look, especially when it's been added to all the other crap you've pulled over the years. The silly stunts on the sidelines. The ridiculous quotes to reporters. The photo shoot you did with the porn star."

"The porn star? Oh, that guy," Chase said. He'd met him at a friend's house and he'd seemed nice and funny and taking a picture with him hadn't seemed like a big deal.

Here was the thing: Chase had every intention of taking responsibility for the shit he did that was genuinely his fault. Like all the times when it felt like his head was going to boil over, like an overfull teapot, and he did something dumb? He always regretted it later.

The dancing on the empty stage at the "consolation event" after the Riptide had lost the AFC Championship had been a prime example of this. He'd known the moment he stepped on that stage that it was a mistake, but he'd done it anyway.

"Yeah, *that* guy," Alec said. He wasn't a judgmental prick, or else Chase never would have picked him to be his new agent, but sometimes he drove Chase a little crazy.

"That was nothing and you know it," Chase argued. "It wasn't a big deal."

"Not by itself," Alec agreed. "Except that this irresponsible behavior is a pattern for you. And even worse, I *know* it isn't even you, and it isn't what you want people to think of you. We talked about spending the off-season working on your image. And now instead of doing that, we're dealing with this video."

Shame roiled through Chase in a nauseating wave. He hadn't wanted to go to lunch with Alec, because he knew exactly what his agent was going to be upset about, but somehow it felt even worse than he'd expected it to.

"I was bummed," Chase said defensively, "and I wanted to take my mind off how much losing sucked. You can't be bummed when you're dancing."

Alec's sharp gaze made it clear he didn't ascribe to Chase's theory.

Originally, Alec had been his friend Neal Fisher's agent. When Neal had praised him to the skies, Chase had decided that maybe what he needed to try to smooth over five years of semi-foolish public behavior was a new agent. He'd been in a better emotional place. He'd believed that he'd left that part of his career behind. And he had . . . *mostly*. Occasionally, he still felt out of control. Occasionally, he still messed up.

"You think you can confuse me with this ridiculous dancing stuff?" Alec said, leaning forward, his pale blue eyes sharp and intelligent, ready to prick all the balloons Chase regularly deployed to confuse people. "You can't. I know just how smart you are. When you decided to hire me as your agent, we negotiated, remember? You even recognized before I did that your image needed a makeover."

Chase pushed his plate of tacos away. Halfheartedly he considered busting out some moves now, because he was currently very bummed out. But if it was the kind of bummed out that tacos couldn't fix, then dancing was probably a no-go too.

"Fine," he said mulishly. "Did you come here to do anything else than lecture me on how I fucked up?"

"Yes. I actually came here to tell you to keep your head down."

Not surprisingly, that had been Chase's therapist's advice too, when she'd called him yesterday. *And*, Moira had added, *please remember all the coping strategies we've worked on.*

His friend and ex-quarterback Heath Harris had recommended he see her, after the Super Bowl loss last year. He'd felt out of control and reckless, even for him, and Heath had pulled him aside, reminding him that it wasn't wrong to admit you needed help.

He'd gone to see her for almost a year, and then decided, a few months back, that he had a good handle on his own shit.

Then the AFC Championship had happened, and another successful playoff drive had evaporated into defeat and failure, and he'd lost his mind again. Chase wasn't stupid enough to pretend he didn't know why: his therapist had called it emotional overwhelm. Sometimes he could feel it coming. Sometimes it crept up on him. He wasn't always good at controlling it. Not yet, anyway.

Maybe that was why he'd actually *come* to the meeting today, instead of following through with his first instinct, and canceling.

Had he *wanted* Alec to yell at him?

Maybe. Just a little.

"I can keep my head down," Chase said. "I'm . . . I can do it."

"Can you?" Alec's gaze narrowed in on him. "You have to *want* to."

"I . . ." Chase did want to change, but what he'd also discovered was that it was harder than anticipated to change years and years of patterned behavior. Thanks to Moira, he had a whole list of coping mechanisms and they usually worked, but when they didn't, he didn't always know how to handle things. "I do. I really do."

"Okay, then." Alec's serious expression slipped for a moment, and Chase thought for a split second he might've seen the man *smile*. "That's good news, then."

"The sponsorships?" It wasn't like Chase necessarily *cared*, but it also didn't look very mature to get fired.

"I can salvage them. But only, *only*, if you do what I'm telling you to."

"I can."

"Good," Alec said, and he was actually smiling now, and not even trying to hide it. "I thought so. But I still had to check."

"So, what other plans do we have?" Chase said. He pulled his plate of tacos back. He felt a little better. Better enough that a taco might help. Dancing was probably the only thing that could *really* help, but he had a feeling that Alec would skin him slowly if Chase decided to bust some moves out in the middle of this too-fancy Malibu restaurant.

"Plans?"

"To make me look . . ." Chase waved around his head. "You know. Mature. Like an adult."

Alec sighed. "We're working on that. I think I might have a company interested in you that might help, a lot."

Chase munched his taco. "What is it?"

"It's a company called Happy Health. They sell online therapy services," Alec said.

Chase nearly choked on his bite. "What?" he exclaimed.

"I know you talked to someone, after the Super Bowl loss last year," Alec said.

"I did," Chase admitted. "But . . ."

"But?" Alec questioned. "That's not something you want to publicly share? That sometimes even Chase Riley's feelings overwhelm him and he needs someone to talk to?"

Chase glowered at his agent. He was regretting asking. Scratch that. He was regretting coming to this lunch at all. Even the tacos were mediocre.

And if there was anything Chase hated, it was food that had the potential to be spectacular, but just *wasn't*.

"Right," Alec said, before Chase could even answer. "So we'll think about that one. But it'd be a good look for you."

"They should get Harris. He doesn't like . . . well, he doesn't like publicity but he's the one who referred me to the therapist."

Alec looked at him. "Heath is already on board. They're filming some marketing spots this month."

"Oh." Chase felt ashamed, even though he knew he shouldn't be.

"Heath was a good choice," Alec said. "But you're a better one, and they know it."

"I'll think about it," Chase said, which was just about as good of an answer as he could give. He was doing better. But admitting something inherently private, like that he'd needed a therapist—that maybe he *still* needed a therapist—was a step further than he was currently willing to take.

"Good, that's what I told them," Alec said.

"What?" Chase couldn't believe it, but Alec's slightly smug expression told him the whole story. "How did you know that I'd tell you I'd think about it?"

"You know, I've been doing this for a long time," Alec said. "You are not my first rodeo, Chase Riley."

CHAPTER TWO

TATE LEANED BACK, STRETCHING out his stiff back. It had been a long morning and an even longer afternoon. Not that he would or *could* complain. He and Rachel had been dying for exactly this to happen, so it'd be dumb to whine when they'd actually gotten exactly what they'd wanted—the craziest, busiest week they'd had in *months*.

The toughest part about being a food truck in LA and not having a permanent or semi-permanent home was finding places to do business that actually *led* to sales. And the spots that did exist? The highly coveted ones at breweries and festivals and in front of the skyscrapers downtown for the lunch crowd? They were extremely competitive, and Say Cheese's inability to land some of them had made changing their fortunes even harder. It was why Tate wanted the opportunity that Tony was offering so badly. It would give them stability and hopefully a more even income he and Rachel could come to depend on.

"I think . . ." Rachel sounded pleased and a little surprised as she rested a hip against the stainless steel counter that ran the full length of their Say Cheese truck. "I think that's actually everyone for the day."

"Crazy," Tate muttered. "That was just crazy. I thought you said you just offhandedly mentioned it on social media."

"I did," Rachel said, a little defensively. "A couple of times. But it was almost all variations of 'Come check out Chase Riley's favorite sandwich in LA.'"

"And yet all these people came." Tate would trust Rachel with his life, but he also wondered just what else she'd posted. All these people had come from somewhere, and while a lot of them had ordered other things, Tate had a feeling if he checked the sales records, the thing they'd sold the most of was the so-called "favorite" sandwich.

"Chase Riley is super popular," Rachel said, giving him a knowing smile. "I can't imagine why."

"I just . . ." Tate took a deep breath. "I keep waiting for this to backfire."

"How can it?" Rachel said blithely. "We've got business. Almost more business than we can handle. Maybe we should consider picking up a temp for next week. At least someone to take orders."

"It could totally fall apart tomorrow. What if we get a cease and desist from Chase's lawyer?"

Rachel rolled her eyes. "Didn't you see that video of him after the AFC Championship? Actually, scratch that, don't answer that question. I know you saw it and I really don't want to know what you did while watching it. What I'm trying to say is that he's got a lot more problems to deal with than his old high school crush using his name to sell grilled cheese sandwiches."

"He never had a crush on me," Tate said stiffly.

"Right," Rachel said, sounding totally unconvinced. "Of course, because Chase Riley is straight. How could I forget?"

"He is," Tate said. He hated to say it, but what other conclusion could he possibly come to?

"You're making a hell of a lot of assumptions about him," Rachel reminded him. "And you know what they say about assumptions . . ."

"I'm going to get some fresh air," Tate said. He loved their truck. He loved his sister. But sometimes they conspired together to push every single one of his buttons. "I'll be back in a few and we can get cleaned up."

"Sure," Rachel said, with no judgment in her tone. But the look in her eyes made it perfectly clear that she knew he was running away.

Tate climbed down the little set of stairs, pushed open the door to the outside and took a breath of air. It was Los Angeles, so it wasn't exactly *fresh*, but at least it was different air than the same closed-in, overly heated air he'd been breathing for the last five hours.

He leaned back against the side of the truck and closed his eyes. He was worn out, and not just from the huge crowd of people they'd served today. He was tired from worrying—both because he was afraid their truck wouldn't make it, and also that the risk of using Chase Riley to sell sandwiches might backfire.

He heard a car pull up to the side parking lot they were currently set up in, and opened his eyes, ready to tell whoever had just shown up that they were about five minutes too late to enjoy the best grilled cheese that LA had to offer, when he realized, with a deep, unshakable certainty that the risk *was* greater than the reward. Because that wasn't just any person looking for a late lunch, it was someone who drove the same custom bright turquoise Audi roadster that Chase did. Who had the same shoulder-length honey blond hair that Chase did.

It might actually *be* Chase Riley.

Tate's breath caught in his chest as the car parked. Tate's knees wobbled as the man unfolded himself from the small car and stretched, his t-shirt riding up for a split second, revealing abs that Tate had tried not to fantasize about.

"Hey," Chase said—because it was undeniably Chase Riley—walking over to where Tate stood, struck speechless by shock. "Hey, Ward, I hear this is a great place to get a grilled cheese sandwich."

Tate stared. Somehow, unbelievably, Chase Riley was not only even better looking in person than he'd been ten years ago, he was *brighter* in person. So bright it was hard to even look straight at him, except that Tate couldn't quite look away. He'd forgotten that, after spending all these years only watching him on a screen.

Chase smiled.

"And also," he added, his eyes shining with sincerity, "it's great to see you, man."

Chase Riley is here. Chase Riley remembers who I am. Chase Riley thinks it's great to see me.

Rachel had been one hundred percent wrong. One *thousand* percent wrong. Not only had this backfired, it had backfired in the worst and most spectacular way possible.

It had brought Chase Riley straight to his doorstep.

Chase should've forgotten all about that semester of Home Economics that he'd spent with Tate Ward. A lot of things had happened in the last ten years that would make forgetting about it totally understandable. He'd gone to college and played four years of ball at Oregon, before graduating and declaring for the draft. He'd been lucky enough to be drafted by one of the best teams in football, the Los Angeles Riptide. He'd won a Super Bowl with them and lost another one.

And all the while, he'd kept waiting for the same feeling he'd experienced during those months he'd spent with Tate. That prickling of awareness at the back of his neck. The churn of butterflies in his stomach. The way Tate's face often popped into his head unexpectedly when he was jerking off. But he'd never found another guy that had done anything for him. Not the way that Tate had.

Over time the memories had begun to fade, and ten years in, Chase had *almost* been sure that his attraction to Tate had just been a figment of his imagination. That he'd just dreamt up the whole thing.

But the moment his mom had forwarded him the Say Cheese tweet last night, everything had come roaring back.

Tate was in LA. Tate had a food truck. Tate was using his name to sell grilled cheese sandwiches.

Maybe another man would be pissed off that Tate was trading on his name to promote his business, and if it was anyone else, Chase probably wouldn't have been very happy about it. Especially considering Alec's admonitions to keep his head down.

But Tate Ward? Tate Ward could take anything of Chase's that he wanted.

Anything.

Tate was still staring at him, shocked into silence, probably. Chase thought that was kind of unfair. After all, did Tate really think that he could use his name in the same city where he lived and Chase wouldn't find out about it?

Apparently he thought exactly that, because Tate had an expression that could either be total shock or abject terror. Chase wasn't sure which.

What *was* clear was that Tate was not nearly as happy to see Chase as Chase was to see him.

That stung, more than he had expected it to.

"Good to see you too," Tate finally mumbled as Chase stopped in front of him.

The truck behind Tate was just as cute and quaint as it had looked in the pictures Chase had found of it. He noticed that they'd even altered the menu to identify which sandwich was Chase's "favorite."

And Tate? He was just as cute as he'd been in high school. Cuter, actually. He'd grown up, but his eyes were still that cloudy, dreamy gray, his hair covered up by a bright blue beanie with the "Say Cheese" logo embroidered on it. He was scruffy and looked like he needed both a nap and a shave, and somehow, nobody had ever looked better to Chase.

"I thought I'd stop by because I thought it'd only be the right thing to do."

Tate looked at him, uncomprehending. "Right thing to do?"

Chase smiled. "I need to make sure you've got it right. Don't want to get caught out with false advertising."

He watched as Tate swallowed hard, his Adam's apple bobbing underneath a layer of soft-looking reddish-brown scruff. "Are you going to sue us?"

That was the whole problem, wasn't it? Tate thought he was in trouble. And maybe other players might've been assholes about this, but Chase couldn't be.

"No?" How could Tate think that he would even *dream* of it?

"No?" Tate repeated right back at him.

"Seriously, I came here for lunch. Does that sound like someone who's gonna sue you?"

Tate eyed him suspiciously. Really, it should've been the other way around. Chase knew that. But the problem was that Chase had always had a huge soft spot for this guy in particular. It had started in high school, and then afterwards, he'd tried not to be interested every time he heard something about him from one of his old high school buddies. But he'd never been able to convince himself that Tate didn't matter.

Probably because he always had.

"You want a sandwich?"

Chase looked at the menu. Shot Tate a grin. "Maybe not *just* a sandwich. Maybe I want a grilled cheese, *and* the roasted tomato soup, *and* the short rib mac and cheese."

"We're closed," Tate said, but even he didn't sound convinced by it. "We're actually closed. And I'll have Rachel delete the posts. I . . . I didn't mean to create a problem for you."

Chase rolled his eyes. "I'm here to eat your food, man. That's all. You wanna keep this up?" He gestured at the notations on the menu—indicating which items were his special "favorites." "I don't give a shit. But I'm hungry, and you should remember well enough how I get when I'm hungry."

"Fine," Tate said tightly. "Fine. I'll be right back."

There was a handful of worn wooden picnic tables set out through the thin green strip of grass next to the sidewalk. Chase plopped down on one and watched as Tate walked inside the truck. He heard raised voices but couldn't quite make out what they were saying. Someone wasn't happy. He wondered who Rachel was. Hoped, even though it was terribly unfair, that Rachel wasn't Tate's wife or his girlfriend. He'd heard a rumor from one of his old high school friends that Tate had come out as gay on social media about a year after high school had ended, but he'd never been able to confirm that for himself.

Why? Because he'd been too much of a chicken shit to actually friend Tate himself.

He'd wanted to, but what would they even talk about? Would they even talk? Or would they just become one of those social media friendships that claimed closeness but in reality meant nothing? Tate didn't think he could let that tenuous, but strong, connection they'd formed in Home Economics devolve into something like that. He'd held on to it for so long, he'd wanted it to mean *something* when they reconnected.

That was probably why, when his mom had forwarded him the tweet, with a note attached—"didn't realize you and Tate had become friends again"—he hadn't hesitated. He'd done his research, and then waited to see where the Say Cheese truck would show up today. As soon as he'd gotten out of his meeting, he'd driven straight here. Hoping that Tate would still be around. Not sure what he'd say to him if he was, but knowing he *needed* to say something.

A few minutes later, Tate re-emerged from the shiny silver truck, carrying a paper plate in one hand and a bottle of water in the other.

He headed in Chase's direction, and without saying a word, sat down opposite him and slid the plate across the table.

"Rachel's heating up the mac and cheese. It'll be out in a second."

"No soup?" Chase wondered.

"We're out." Tate shrugged. "Busy day. Shouldn't have come at the end of lunch hour."

"I had a meeting," Chase said. One he probably could've canceled, but he also knew what would happen if he'd shown up when there was a crowd here. It'd have become a circus, and he wouldn't have gotten a moment alone to talk to Tate.

The grilled cheese was perfectly browned and crispy, glistening at the edges with butter and melted cheese. It looked just as good as Chase remembered, and when he bit into it . . . *bliss*.

He chewed and swallowed. Wished he had about a thousand other bites. "This is even better than I remember it," Chase said.

Tate drummed his fingers against the worn wooden grain of the tabletop impatiently. "It's been ten years. I was a kid. I've refined the recipe since then."

"I don't suppose you'd tell me your secret ingredient," Chase wondered.

Tell me all your secrets. Please.

"Secret ingredient? Time? Patience?" Tate seemed annoyed he was here, and maybe it was his fear of being found out but, deep down, Chase was worried it was something else. Maybe it had only been Chase who'd been so affected by their classes together twice a week. He hadn't wanted to believe that was true, because he knew flirting and Tate had undeniably flirted with him. Had always responded, even when Chase hadn't really known what they were doing.

Honestly, he *still* didn't know what they'd been doing.

Chase finished one triangular half with three more big bites. "Well, I thought about this sandwich a lot," he said.

I thought about you.

Tate looked incredulous. "I made you *one* grilled cheese sandwich, in high school, and you've been thinking about it ever since? For *ten years*?"

It sounded ridiculous when Tate put it like that. "Well, it was a good sandwich," Chase retorted. "And so is this one."

"Does this mean you're not going to sue us?"

Chase groaned. "I *never* planned on suing you. I just wanted . . ." What *had* he wanted? He hadn't let himself contemplate exactly what it was that he wanted from Tate, hadn't given himself the chance, but now, even with Tate seemingly annoyed, that indescribable tension hummed between them.

He'd wanted to know that he hadn't misremembered or imagined it after all. He'd wanted to know if it had been *real*.

"No? You just came here to intimidate me?"

"Oh for God's sake," Chase said. "I'm not here to sue you or intimidate you or any of that crap. Is it so hard to believe I just wanted to see you again? See how you're doing?"

Tate stared at him. Those gray eyes—usually so warm but opaque now—had always unnerved him. Before, in the best possible ways. But now? Chase didn't know what to think.

"You really aren't here to demand I stop talking about you?"

Chase shrugged. "You posted that you make my favorite sandwich in LA. Technically, it *was* true. You did, just ten years ago. And now I've confirmed, officially, that you *still* do."

Tate tugged off his beanie and ran his hand through his hair, the auburn strands of it shining in the mid-afternoon California sunshine. "I'm sorry, it's just hard for me to believe that you're not pissed."

"I could pretend to be pissed off if it'd make you feel better," Chase offered.

Tate chuckled. "No, no, that's okay. I'm . . . I guess I'm just surprised. I'd have thought you'd hate people who use your name."

"Most people, yeah," Chase admitted, biting into the second half of his sandwich. "But you're not most people. Never have been."

Tate looked surprised by this, and Chase couldn't figure out why. Sure, they hadn't kept in touch, but there was still that last semester—hadn't Home Economics been the brightest part of Tate's day, too?

The door to the food truck opened abruptly and then slammed shut, and a young woman with bright red hair pulled back in a ponytail stomped over to where the two of them were sitting. She set a plate of mac and cheese topped with a delectable-smelling meat mixture in front of him. "Here," she said. "I hope you enjoy it. Please don't sue us."

Chase rolled his eyes, but it was Tate who responded. "He's not going to, Rach, it's alright. Why don't you get a head start on the cleanup and I'll help in a few?"

"Sure," the woman said, and stomped right back to the truck.

"Rachel is my sister and the co-owner of Say Cheese," Tate said, almost apologetically. "I'm afraid she's feeling kinda guilty that she pushed me to mention you to drum up business."

Chase plucked the fork stuck into the middle of the plastic dish and dug into the thick, caramelized meat that topped the creamy goodness below. "Why did she want to?" he asked. There was clearly a story there, and just as he figured, Tate didn't want to tell him.

"It's . . ." Tate hesitated. "Does it matter?"

"Of course it matters." Tate was a smart guy, but sometimes he could be really stupid, too. Chase would be lying if he said that wasn't one of his more endearing attributes. It had been that way in high school, and he honestly wasn't that surprised that nothing had changed.

"How much do you know about food trucks?" Tate asked.

Chase moaned around a bite of short rib in his mouth. Tate had offset the richness of the meat and the gooey cheese with a handful of pickled red onions, flecked through the dish, and it was genuinely *to die for.*

He swallowed, reluctantly, and started fishing around for another perfect bite. "That they're trucks and they serve food."

Tate was drumming his fingers on the table again. Chase wondered if that was a new nervous tick of his—he'd never done it in high school—and then realized delightedly that he made Tate nervous.

Maybe Tate wasn't pissed off at all. Maybe Tate was actually flustered.

"There's kind of a hierarchy, here in LA," Tate said. "The popular trucks, the ones with a special or unique concept and lots of good reviews, with all the 'buzz,' get the prime parking spots and invites to the best festivals, the breweries and the distilleries in the evenings. If you're not getting that kind of attention, you're scrounging for a good place to park. Alternatively, an even better option is to get into a community lot with other food trucks. But rent in LA is crazy, and that's hard to do, unless you're selling a lot."

Chase had suspected something similar to what Tate was working around to telling him. The recent spike in Say Cheese's social media numbers—which weren't all that high to begin with—was telling. They'd been struggling. That was why Rachel had pushed Tate to use Chase's name to promote their business.

"I have a friend," Tate continued, "who actually is putting together one of these food truck collectives, and he wants me to join, but there's a threshold for sales and well . . . I'm not there yet. We need to be and . . ."

"You thought I'd sell some sandwiches," Chase finished for him.

Tate looked surprised. "Yeah. Yeah, I thought you might."

"And have I?" Chase already knew the answer, but he wanted to hear Tate say it. Out loud.

"It's gotten better," Tate admitted. "A lot better. Which is why we sold out of a lot of things today, actually."

"Would it help if I posted something?" Chase asked.

When Tate looked confused, he added, "On my Instagram. I've got a lot of followers."

"You'd do that?"

"Of course I would. I just . . ." Chase knew he was taking a risk. They'd never talked about it. They'd definitely not talked about it in the last ten years. "I just don't get why you didn't ask in the first place."

"Oh. Well. Huh. I guess I didn't think about it." Tate stared at the table. Wouldn't meet Chase's eyes. It was only one indication that he was lying, but even without it, Chase would've known.

"Well, I can now, if you want me to," Chase said. "And I'd mean it. That was definitely my favorite sandwich in LA, and this is now my favorite mac and cheese, too."

In fact, even though the dish was already half-eaten, Chase reached into his pocket and grabbed his phone, snapping a quick picture. With a few clicks, he'd uploaded it to Instagram, tagged the Say Cheese profile, and had typed a quick, raving review.

"There you go," Chase said, setting his phone down and picking his fork back up. "You're welcome."

A cute little frown, a crinkled wrinkle, appeared between Tate's eyes, that Chase wanted to smooth away. "You just did it. You mean . . . *just now*?"

"Yeah," Chase said, like it was no big deal. And for Tate? He'd have done much more. There was a part of him he was burying deeply that was bothered Tate hadn't just *asked*. But there was another part that understood exactly why he hadn't. It was the same part that had never tried to seek Tate out again, even though he'd wanted to.

He'd kept his own distance; could he really blame Tate for doing the same?

"I mean . . . I'm still trying to reassure myself you aren't going to sue us," Tate said, cracking a smile, and it did things to Chase's stomach that he wasn't quite ready to admit to.

Tate Ward had been a seriously cute eighteen-year-old, but Chase hadn't just been attracted to him because of that. He'd been smart and quick and funny and just the right kind of bossy. And that wasn't even taking into account the strange and inexplicable chemistry that had bloomed between them doing those Home Economics classes.

But Tate the man? Tate ten years down the road? He'd gotten cuter. Grumpier, too, and somehow that was a turn-on that Chase hadn't ever realized he'd be into. But he was. *God*, he was.

Just sitting across from him made Chase squirm, and he couldn't remember a time when anyone had made him feel this way.

He was afraid if he thought about it more deeply, the last time would be ten years ago.

"Just stop with the suing thing," Chase teased. "It's not as easy as you think to do it. And it takes work. Why would I want to work to harass you?"

"Well, thanks. I guess I *should've* asked you," Tate muttered. Then, to Chase's chagrin, he stood up. "I've got to help Rach clean up," he said. "But thank you again for not suing us, and for posting that photo. It's going to make a huge difference for us."

Chase had to grip the bench so he wouldn't leap up and catch Tate and hold him in place. Keep him from escaping. After ten years, this wasn't all he wanted. He wanted . . . he didn't know exactly what he wanted, but he knew, deep down, that it was more than a ten-minute conversation and a social media recommendation.

"I can do more," Chase said, before he could stop himself. "I could do a whole series. Chase Riley eats Say Cheese, or something like that."

Tate frowned. "But why would you want to?"

"Because you didn't go to NYU and get a business degree?" Chase felt like he was walking on a tightrope—one foolish admission away from confessing way too much truth, but he couldn't help himself. Or maybe it was because he couldn't let Tate just walk away again.

"I *did* go to NYU," Tate said slowly. Chase noticed, of course, that he didn't mention the business degree. Wondered what he'd done instead. Wished that Tate would tell him, but afraid that he wouldn't. Afraid he'd never get the chance to learn all of Tate's secrets.

Chase waved a hand. "It doesn't matter. I just . . . I want to do it."

"Okay," Tate said. "I guess I'd be dumb as a rock to stop you."

"And you're not." It was one of the many things that had made those Home Economics afternoons glorious. The brilliant, lethally attractive intelligence lurking in Tate's brain.

"No, I'm not." There was another glimmer of a smile. "Enjoy the rest of your mac and cheese."

"I'll be back tomorrow." He shouldn't. It might be the off-season but his trainer would shit bricks if he discovered that Chase was eating grilled cheese every day. But Chase decided he didn't care. That he'd work twice as hard to compensate for all the extra fat and calories. After all, Tate didn't look like *he'd* been eating nothing but grilled cheese. His smaller frame was still compact, and even though Chase had tried to ignore it, he'd noticed just how well Tate filled out the Say Cheese t-shirt he was wearing.

"Really?"

"Really," Chase said. "Where are you gonna be?"

"Here for lunch, and I think we've got one of the breweries booked for dinner," Tate said cautiously. "They had a cancellation and called us, unexpectedly."

"Because you had such a good week." *Because you told everyone that I loved you.*

Your food truck, Chase reminded himself. *You love his food truck.*

"Yeah, probably." There was that glimmer of a smile again. Chase wanted him to smile deeper and broader and without the hesitation. Like he used to do ten years ago.

"Alright. I'll meet you guys there."

"For dinner? At the brewery?" Tate seemed surprised, and Chase couldn't blame him because he'd surprised himself. He'd come today, as late as he dared, because he hadn't wanted to face a ton of people. But there was nothing that would get buzz going like people actually *seeing* him, in the flesh, at the truck. Social media posts could only go so far.

"Yeah, at the brewery," Chase said. "Better have more food, tomorrow."

This time Tate's smile was *almost* what Chase wanted it to be. "Yeah, yeah, we can do that." He turned to go, but then unexpectedly turned back. "I can't thank you enough for this. Really. It's . . . you didn't have to do it."

"Yeah, I did," Chase said. "After all, I told you to do this with your life, didn't I?"

"That's right," Tate agreed, "you did."

CHAPTER THREE

"You're in deep shit," Rachel said to him, as they were prepping for service the next day.

It wasn't like Tate didn't already know it.

"Yeah," he said. "But at least he isn't going to sue us."

"I'm more worried about you falling for him all over again." She paused. "Actually, scratch that. I'm worried about you falling *harder* for him, since I'm not sure you've ever really gotten over the guy."

There was nothing more that Tate wanted than to disagree with her. But the way his heart had accelerated? The sudden buzzing of butterflies in his stomach? The energy that had crackled between them despite ten years passing?

Tate knew his sister was right.

"He's going to make sure we get into Tony's lot, and that's the most important thing," Tate said, changing the subject.

Chase had retweeted their daily tweet referencing the truck's daily schedule. He hadn't said, specifically, that he'd be coming to the truck, but Rachel had pointed out that based on the social media chatter she was seeing, it didn't even matter. Everyone was assuming he'd be stopping by, and because he hadn't specifically said *when*, they'd probably be swamped for both lunch and dinner.

It was a good thing. A *very* good thing. Tate kept telling himself that. So why did he feel so goddamned apprehensive?

Probably because he was afraid that after this good deed, Chase would disappear again, and Tate would have to reconcile himself to the realities of the situation all over again.

It hadn't been very easy the first time, and he had a feeling that it would be way harder the second.

At least this time Chase was going to give him something vitally important. He was under zero obligation to do it, but he'd obviously decided to help Tate achieve his dream.

"Believe me, I'm thrilled that he's been so cooperative and willing, but what does he get out of this?" Rachel wondered as she finished prepping the garlic butter they used on their grilled cheese sandwiches.

It was exactly the question that Tate had spent all night lying awake, asking himself, and that he hadn't been able to answer. "The satisfaction that he's done his good deed for the month?"

Rachel shook her head. "That doesn't sound anything like Chase Riley."

"He's not a selfish idiot like everyone thinks he is," Tate argued. It never made him more frustrated than when people spouted off about what they thought Chase Riley was like. Especially when he *knew*, even though it had been so long ago, what Chase Riley was really like.

"I'm not saying he is; I'm saying that *you're* an idiot if you think that he's doing this out of the goodness of his heart," Rachel said.

"I don't care why he's doing it, only that he is," Tate said, hoping that he could stop Rachel from going where he already suspected she was headed.

"Liar," Rachel teased, laughing. "But that's okay. I get it."

"You do?"

"Yeah," Rachel said. "If Megan Rapinoe showed up at the truck and wanted to promote it, I wouldn't exactly tell her no."

Rachel's crush on Megan Rapinoe was legendary. Maybe not quite as legendary as Tate's on Chase Riley, but then she'd never gotten lucky enough to actually meet the soccer player.

Tate's crush was a hell of a lot more complicated.

He was about to tell her that *yeah*, she was right, when she nudged him. "Is this really right?" she asked, pointing to the quick list of prep that Tate had jotted down while sipping his first cup of coffee this morning.

"Yeah," Tate said, nodding.

Rachel gave him a worried look. "If we don't sell all of this . . ."

"I know, it'll set us back. But the last thing I want is to have Chase show up with a ton of other people and sell out of everything. Can you imagine how disastrous that would be?"

"I guess," Rachel said. "You're taking a risk."

"*We're* taking a risk, but at least we aren't going to get sued," Tate said, grinning.

"So Chase says," Rachel said.

"I . . ." Tate took a deep breath. "I trust him. He's not going to fuck us over."

"No, just you," Rachel said. "If you're really lucky, anyway."

Chase was officially pathetic, and after sitting around his house all day, trying to keep busy and occupied, he finally gave in and climbed into his car, driving to the brewery that Say Cheese was scheduled at for the dinner hour.

The brewery was one of Southern California's most popular, and as it was a late afternoon on a Thursday, it was already packed.

Chase wondered what it would feel like to walk up to a place like this and not see every single head in the whole place swivel in his direction. He told people that you got used to the attention, but the truth was, he never had.

Chase stopped in front of the bar, and read the list of beers on tap. "Hey," he said, as the bartender approached. It was a young guy, in his early twenties, and his face was flushed red. Chase smiled. "Do you guys have a sampler of stuff I could try?"

"Yeah," the young bartender stammered. "A six . . . a six-taster flight, if that's what you wanna do."

"That's perfect," Chase said. "What do you recommend?"

The bartender looked at him like he'd just grown a second head. "What?"

Chase inwardly sighed. Once he'd complained to his good friend Heath Harris how frustrating it was to deal with strangers' starstruck behavior and Heath had merely replied, his humor as dry as it always was, "Would you rather have been boring and ugly, then? Not famous? Not rich?"

Chase understood what Heath was saying. He was absolutely fucking lucky. He'd gotten better at dealing with people who looked at him like he was some kind of god, but at the same time, he didn't think he'd ever consider it *easy*.

"Yeah," Chase said, even more gently. "You must know all the beers like the back of your hand. I like a wheat style, but nothing too hoppy."

The trick was always to use a language that the person understood. In this guy's case, once Chase started talking beer, he calmed right down.

"Yeah, we've got a few that will definitely fit that description," he said, setting a plastic laminated menu in front of Chase, indicating a few options with his finger. "Why don't you pick two others while I pour those?"

Scanning over the list, Chase selected two other beers that he thought he'd like, and when the bartender returned with the tasting sampler, added to his order.

When the guy settled the last two glasses on the little wooden tray, Chase asked, "I saw there was a food truck here tonight."

"Yeah," the bartender said enthusiastically. "They make the *best* grilled cheese."

"I've heard that," Chase said dryly.

"Well, they're parked around the side," the bartender said. "You should check them out."

"I think I will," Chase said, and picking up his tray, slid down to the end of the bar, and took a seat. Picked up his first beer and like clockwork, someone appeared in his vision.

"Hi," the woman said, smiling charmingly, "you're Chase Riley, aren't you?"

"What gave it away?" Chase said in a mock shocked voice.

She laughed. "Your hair is kinda a dead giveaway."

"Yeah, I've heard that once or twice before," Chase said wryly. There was even a whole website devoted to proving that this wasn't really his natural hair color and that he augmented the blond with highlights.

Chase pleaded the fifth.

"I was wondering if I could take a selfie with you," she asked.

It was inevitable that if he said yes, he would spend the next several hours doing it with everyone else in the brewery.

And while he wouldn't mind doing that normally—he'd met some pretty damn awesome people that way—tonight he wasn't here to promote the brewery or himself. He was here to bring Tate's food truck some much-needed attention.

"Sure," he said, and then lowered his voice conspiratorially, "but I need you to do one favor for me, after."

"Of course. Anything." The way she fluttered her eyelashes at him made it clear that she really meant it. She'd do *anything*. The only problem with that was that the only person Chase was interested in getting into bed was Tate. And if he actually managed to accomplish that feat, he wasn't sure he'd know what to do with him.

Lie. He'd watched enough gay porn that he knew exactly what he wanted to do. What he wanted Tate to do to *him*.

"I have a really good friend, and he's got a food truck here. Fucking amazing grilled cheese and the best mac and cheese you've ever put in your mouth, guarantee it. I'll take a selfie if you get something to eat from his truck later tonight."

"Oh, yeah, that's totally doable," she said in a fake excited voice, but he could see the lie in her eyes. He'd been looking for it for enough years that it was easy enough to identify. Chase had been shocked to discover how many people were totally comfortable lying to his face. "Your really good friend?" she wondered.

"His name's Tate," Chase said, and he knew that Alec had *meant* it when he said to keep his head down, but he was annoyed that she was lying to him. Annoyed that, like so many other people, all she wanted was a piece of him, but never actually part of *him*. The only thing she cared about was that he was hot and famous and rich. And then there was the whole boatload of assumptions she—and so many others—had already made about him.

The assumption that he was straight. The assumption that he was just a piece of meat to be used and then bragged about.

Chase could feel the frustration welling inside of him, and knew he was walking on the razor's edge of losing his self-control.

"Actually," he confessed, before he could swallow the words back down. "He's kinda my boyfriend."

The problem was that he *wanted* it to be true, so he'd said it out loud. Like he could magic genie his fantasy into reality.

He knew he shouldn't have said it. Shouldn't have given in to the clamoring in his brain. But the shock on her face as her jaw dropped was worth it.

"Your boyfriend?" she squeaked.

It wasn't revolutionary, at least not anymore. He'd be one of more than two dozen players in the NFL who had come out of the closet in the last three years. A lot of people already thought he was gay because he hung around Heath and his boyfriend, Sam, and their other friends, Neal and Jamie.

The truth was, Chase didn't know what he was. He'd been wondering, since high school, when he would meet another guy that would make it as obvious as Tate had, but that had never happened. He was also definitely attracted to women, though not this one in particular.

But honestly, it didn't bother him if she thought he liked guys. The shocked expression on her face was worth it. Besides, who was she going to tell who might actually believe her?

"I didn't know you were . . ." She hesitated. "That you had a boyfriend."

"It's new," Chase said. "Do you still want to take a pic together?"

She looked at him blankly.

"A selfie?" he repeated.

"Oh, yeah. *Yeah*." She pulled out her phone and they posed together quickly as she clicked three or four photos.

"Thanks," she said. Hesitated, then her face turned from the fake smile to something a lot nastier. "I'd always heard but, you know, I didn't believe it."

"Heard what?" Chase had heard so many times about people being shitty to his friends because they were professional athletes and not straight. He'd never assumed they were exaggerating or that it sucked any less than they said it did. But he'd also never imagined just how infuriating it could actually be when it was *you* the random person was insulting.

"That you were gay." She sounded annoyed. Like he had personally ruined her evening. "What a fucking waste."

She turned around and walked off, not even giving Chase a chance to respond. To tell her she was a dumb homophobic shit.

But the biggest problem was that now, Chase was pissed off, the emotions swirling through him. Controlling him, instead of the opposite.

He pulled out his phone. Typed a quick tweet, and posted it before he could rethink or even wonder what kind of crap Alec was going to give him.

He was definitely not keeping his head down.

It had been an exceptionally busy day for Tate, and even though he was glad there was a never-ending line, he was also tired and he wanted a break more than he wanted just about anything. He just needed five minutes without noise or sound, where he could try to relax and try *not* to think about either the next order coming up or Chase Riley.

But based on the huge line he'd seen outside the truck, the somewhat frazzled way that Rachel was calling out orders, and the way Chase never seemed to leave his thoughts, even when he tried to dismiss him, it didn't seem like either possibility was going to be happening anytime soon.

"Two Riley specials," Rachel called out.

That had been her idea, and it was working brilliantly. They'd put a small sampler of everything that Chase had tried the other day. Half of one of their standard grilled cheese sandwiches, a small cup of their famous roasted tomato soup, and a half-portion of the short rib mac and cheese.

It was a lot of food, but then Chase was a lot of man. But it hadn't really stopped *everyone* from ordering one of the samplers.

They were more work, but also cost more, and for that, Tate was grudgingly grateful. If they could keep this up and continue this pattern of sales, it wouldn't take long to reach Tony's benchmark, and he could finally tell his friend that Say Cheese was in.

"You okay?" Rachel asked as Tate flipped two grilled cheese sandwiches on the flat top grill, spooned up short rib mixture and pickled onions onto plastic plates, ladled soup into cups.

"Fine," Tate said. "Busy, but that's good, right?"

Rachel's forehead was creased with concern. "Someone just asked me if he could meet Chase Riley's boyfriend, and I didn't know what to say to him. Stared at him like a real idiot."

"Probably just someone thinking they're funny," Tate said, distracted with the rapidly browning grilled cheese. He turned his grill down a tad, and after slathering two pieces of bread with garlic butter, slapped them onto the surface.

"I don't think so." Rachel was still frowning. "He seemed pretty serious about it, actually."

"Maybe they realized I was gay, and you know how everyone is always trying to make Chase gay, because he's friends with the other guys on his team? They just stuck us together in their head."

"I guess." Rachel did not sound convinced. But Tate was too busy to worry about it.

"Here you go," Tate said, sliding two finished Riley specials toward her.

"When you're done with that, I've got two grilled cheese BLTs, a chicken fajita ranch, minus onion, and a full-size short rib mac and cheese."

"This crowd is hungry," Tate said. "Must be the beer."

Rachel shot him an unimpressed look as she turned back to the window to take more orders. "I don't think it is."

For the next ten minutes, Tate focused on getting order after order out, the line in front of the truck never seeming to dwindle. Even though it was crazy busy, he would absolutely take it. Hopefully some of these people would be back without the extra motivation of spotting Chase Riley.

The truck shell insulated him from a lot of the crowd noise outside, but he still heard the cascade of noise that started and hadn't stopped yet.

Tate glanced up from where he was mixing a new batch of cheese sauce and noticed Chase's telltale mane of hair, still shining in the setting California sun, as he moved around the group of people gathered outside the truck.

For a split second, Tate considered sticking his head out the side door and waving hello, but then remembered that weird thing Rachel had said, about him being Chase's *boyfriend*—it was so unbelievable that Tate couldn't take it seriously—and so he didn't. Not that he thought anyone would actually *believe* it. But at the same time if they did, he'd be a real fucking disappointment, wouldn't he?

Nobody would ever look at him and think, *that's totally Chase Riley boyfriend material.*

Even if Chase Riley *had* boyfriends!

Which he didn't. Right?

"Hey," Rachel said, turning around, "why don't we swap for an hour or so? You look exhausted."

Great. He looked exhausted, just in time for him to meet all the fans who apparently suspected he and Chase Riley were dating.

"Don't give me that look," Rachel said. "You've been working your ass off back there. Anyone would look worn out."

"Well," Tate hissed under his breath as he grabbed a clean towel and wiped his sweat-damp brow, "the issue is that I'm not just anyone anymore, right? I'm supposedly Chase Riley's new boyfriend. As if anyone who saw me would actually believe the rumor."

Rachel rolled her eyes. "Supposedly? Stop your mouth. You are totally adorable. Now, get that cute ass up there and sell some grilled cheese."

Tate grinned. "If you insist." He pulled off his stained apron, brushed down his t-shirt and approached the window, where a nice-looking couple was examining the menu. "Hey," he said, "welcome to Say Cheese. What can I get for you today?"

The woman glanced up at him in surprise. Like she'd been expecting someone else. Rachel maybe, or possibly a much hotter guy who had the ability to turn Chase Riley gay.

"Oh yeah," she said. "Um, what do you recommend?"

The guy she was with nudged her. "Just get the special!" he muttered under his breath. "It's what Chase likes!"

"Does Chase like it?" she asked him, her words accompanied by a very direct look. Tate had to wonder if Rachel was getting asked all these uncomfortable questions too, or if it was just him. But then, how could he complain about it, when they'd literally created a Chase Riley special? With all the things he supposedly liked the best? When they'd put signs up on their menu? And shamelessly posted about him on social media?

If anyone was to blame for all this, it was definitely him and Rachel.

"He does," Tate confirmed. "It's a combination of his favorite dishes."

"Well, then," she said, suddenly smiling brightly. "We'll take two."

Tate ran her credit card for the machine, and after calling out the order to Rachel, glanced over at where Chase was standing, holding a pint of beer, laughing and smiling with a whole circle of fans surrounding him. Like he could sense Tate's attention, Chase looked over, and their gazes collided. Had he been waiting for him?

Don't be ridiculous. He's not waiting for you. This isn't a fairy tale. This isn't a romance novel, and Chase Riley is not breathlessly anticipating you looking at him.

Except the moment stretched out, and snapped tightly between them. And Tate was reminded, viscerally, of all those moments they'd shared in Home Economics. *That was ten years ago*, he reminded himself. *Except, it doesn't feel like ten years ago. It feels like right fucking now.*

The problem was, Tate didn't have time for it.

His greeting to the next set of customers was more distracted and perfunctory than normal, but the good news was nobody seemed to notice. They all seemed way more interested in staring at him like he was a particularly fascinating bug under a micro-scope, and almost all of them ended up ordering the Riley special. And even more weirdly, at least *three* separate people winked at him as they did it.

By the end of the hour, the line had finally started to slack a bit, and that was when Chase meandered over, trailing people after him.

"Hey," he said, smiling up at Tate like he was the best thing he'd ever seen.

"Hey yourself," Tate responded. Unsure of what he should say, especially when there were a lot more people waiting and watching than he'd anticipated.

"I've been trying to decide what to get," Chase mused as he stared at the menu. "At first I thought, well, *duh*, gotta get the special, especially because of how you named it, but then I thought, maybe I should try something else."

Another few people walked up, but didn't get in line behind Chase. Just stared at Tate, who tried not to squirm. Tried not to demand an answer from Chase on why everyone was acting so strangely.

"You want a recommendation?" Tate asked. Maybe if Chase got on with it and actually ordered, instead of taking his sweet time, these people would finally leave and stop acting like he was famous too, and somehow worth watching. Six months ago, he'd have thought he was crazy, because all this business was everything he'd wanted, but something about tonight was making Tate more uneasy with everything than he'd been yesterday.

"I'm always open to your suggestions," Chase said, the slant of his smile turning sly and knowing.

"You'd like the lasagna grilled cheese," Tate said. "Or the meatball mac and cheese. I remember you liking Italian food in high school."

"Always carb loading before the big game." Chase laughed effortlessly. Tate didn't know how he could do it with so many observers. Maybe Chase was just too used to it for it to bother him anymore. But it was definitely new for Tate.

"Right," Tate said.

"Yeah, I'll give those a try," Chase said. "And make sure to give me a little of that soup too, it's getting chilly out here."

Tate eyed him suspiciously. "It's at least seventy degrees."

"Then maybe I need you to come keep me warm," Chase teased.

It was a step further than either of them had ever gone in high school. And it was definitely not high school now.

Tate stared at him, incredulously. "Uh, okay," he said, barely registering as Chase shoved what looked like it might be a fifty-dollar bill into their tip bucket.

"Think about it," Chase said, and walked off.

The problem with that statement was it assumed that Tate had *stopped* thinking about it in the last ten years. And he hadn't. Not by a long shot.

An hour later, Chase was still holding court near the brewery, under the strings of twinkle lights that crisscrossed over their expansive patio. But the line at Say Cheese had finally died down as the dinner hour passed and people started drinking their carbs instead of eating them.

Rachel flipped the sign on the truck and leaned back against the counter, watching Tate carefully.

"You seem jumpy," she finally said.

"I felt like everyone was watching me," Tate said, more than a little defensively. "I should've stayed in the back, and not started taking orders."

"I swapped with you because you needed a break, but also because people wanted to see *you*, not me."

"How do you know that?"

Rachel shot him a frank look. "Do you know how many people asked me if you were Chase Riley's boyfriend?"

"You said three," Tate said, flipping the flat top grill off. "And that was definitely three too many."

"How about thirty?" Rachel challenged. "I think . . ." She hesitated. "I think you need to talk to Chase about what he's saying about you."

"He's promoting the truck," Tate said, even though a bad feeling was crawling up his neck. He wouldn't . . . *would he?*

"But what is he doing to promote the truck?" Rachel said. "We don't know."

"Maybe we should look," Tate said, pulling his phone out of his back pocket. He stared at the screen, which was overloaded with notifications. Notifications numbering not in the teens, but in the *thousands*. The kind of attention that Say Cheese had never dreamed of getting in its entire existence.

"Uh," Tate said, hesitating. He almost didn't want to know what Chase had done to promote the truck. It was obviously *something*, and he already had a feeling that it was a something he wasn't going to like.

"Holy shit." Rachel had pulled out her own phone and was scrolling through social media with a shocked expression. "Did you ask him . . . *no,* I know you didn't, because you wouldn't. Not in a million fucking years."

"Did I ask him what?" Tate's voice was calm, but he didn't *feel* particularly calm.

"Chase tweeted about three hours ago that you're . . . that you're *dating.* He said, *come check out my boyfriend's food truck.* He didn't tag us or the brewery but . . . from what he's been posting about in the last few days, it's not exactly difficult to connect the dots."

Tate felt the air rush out of his lungs. "He did *what,*" he said dumbly. "He wouldn't. He got . . . hacked. I don't know. Why would he do that?"

"Attention, likely," Rachel said cynically, "but as to why he would do it and not ask your permission first? I don't know. But you need to talk to him."

Tate eyed all the people still milling around the brewery, spilling onto the concrete patio. "Not with all these people around," he hissed. "But . . . *why.*"

"I hate to even *ask* this question," Rachel said reluctantly, "but are you sure he's straight? That he hasn't come out before? I know he hangs around with . . ."

Tate glared. "Don't you think I'd know?" he demanded. "I mean, *my god.* I've only wanted Chase Riley to be into men, more specifically *this man,* for almost half my life. I'd *know.*"

"You'd know," Rachel agreed. She shot him a knowing little smile. "Well, maybe this is his way of telling you."

"It's not. It's . . . I don't know, a big dumb stupid prank," Tate said. "I'm going to tell him that it's not happening, and it's definitely not funny. I'm not doing it, whatever it is he thinks we're doing."

Rachel was still looking at her phone. "Holy shit," she repeated, as she tapped the screen. They had a handy app that connected to their point-of-sale system. With a few clicks, they could see, real-time, how much money they'd banked during the day.

She turned her phone towards Tate. "Look at this," she said slowly. "Have we done this in a day before? *Ever*?"

Tate stared at the number. It was a fantastic fucking number. He'd known they'd had great sales today. How tired he was proved it. But that kind of sales? He was shocked.

"Whatever he wants," Rachel said insistently. "Tell him you'll do it."

"You were *just* warning me away from him this morning," Tate pointed out.

"I was, but clearly I was stupid," Rachel argued. "This is the kind of shit you can't make up."

"I know, but what about . . .?" Tate took a deep breath. "What about me?"

Rachel set the phone down and put her hands on Tate's shoulders. Looked him straight in the eye. "How much do you want in that lot of Tony's?"

"A whole fucking lot," Tate said with a resigned sigh. In most of the ways that counted, he'd been working towards that goal since he was eighteen. Ten years was a long time to want something and not get it.

"You can do anything, for any amount of time, for that. But still, you should totally give him hell for not asking you first. That's not cool."

"Can I really complain if he came out of the closet for me?" Tate wondered.

"Hell yes you can. He could've done it any day of his life, in any way he wanted to. Pulling you into it . . . *well,* it was lucrative, I can say that much, but it was shitty timing. And it was shitty to do to you, specifically."

"Right." Tate couldn't disagree with her.

"Go talk to him," Rachel said, gesturing outside. "I'll get started on the cleanup."

CHAPTER FOUR

ALL EVENING, CHASE HAD been waiting, half-terrified and half-thrilled, to hear what Tate was going to say when he'd found out what he'd done.

Alec had called him about twenty straight times, had left several voicemails, and had sent a whole load of text messages. Chase had read them, but then ignored them, because they were all questions he couldn't answer.

He'd sent one each to Heath and to Neal, and he'd said, simply, **it was just something I needed to do,** when they'd expressed their disbelief that Chase wasn't straight.

He'd never told them about high school and about Tate. How could he, when he didn't even know what it all meant?

He'd talked to his mother, *briefly*. She'd always known how he felt about Tate, because he hadn't ever been able to hide anything from her. She'd sent him a demanding text, wanting to know what had finally happened between them, and he'd had to tell her the truth.

The truth. Both more complicated and so much simpler than one tweet could contain.

Well, you've just gone and told the whole fucking world, that annoying voice in his head reminded him, *so we'll see how well that works out for you.*

From the way that Tate was stomping over, a frown on his face, it seemed like it wasn't going to work out very well at all.

"I need to talk to you," Tate said.

Chase had imagined, more times than he cared to consider, what it would feel like to finally be honest with Tate about his feelings. That he *had* feelings. He could admit that it had *never* looked like this, not in any fantasy he had ever had. But truthfully this was better than anything he'd dreamed up because it was real.

The people surrounding Chase, that he'd barely been listening to, melted away, several of them shooting him knowing grins. Chase thought he might've heard one of the guys even tell him he could *get it.*

They weren't exactly alone, but close enough that they could talk frankly. And it really looked like Tate wanted to talk *frankly.*

"I kind of figured as much," Chase said.

He felt shy, suddenly. Exposed, with Tate staring at him like he was seeing him for the first time all over again.

"You," Tate said, suddenly crowding into his space. Chase's heartbeat accelerated. *Was he going to kiss him? Had he been waiting for Chase this whole time, and now that Tate knew, he wasn't going to waste a minute?*

Except no. That dreamy bubble burst, almost immediately, and with force.

Tate shoved a finger into his chest, and up close, his eyes were flat and gray, hard as stones. Just as hard as his voice. "You are a fucking idiot," he said.

"Sadly, not the first or the last time someone's gonna tell me that," Chase said wryly. Hoping it would cover his disappointment.

What did you expect? You threw this out without talking to him, without even floating the idea. You totally suck at this.

"If you faked . . ." Tate said.

But Chase couldn't let that stand. Tate didn't think he was being honest? Tate thought he was lying *now*?

"No," Chase said. "It's true . . . I'm not straight. I'm . . . not sure what I am. But I *know* I'm not straight."

Tate's gaze softened. Not by much, but enough that it didn't feel like Chase's heart was being squeezed until it exploded.

"Okay," he said. "Still, you should've told me," Tate said in a low, angry voice. "You should've told me ten years ago. And now? You definitely should have told me *first*, before I had to find out with the rest of the world. Especially since we're apparently dating now?"

That was rich. Chase had suspected about Tate back in high school—the flirting was kind of a dead giveaway, and that wasn't even counting the way that Tate had looked at him—but it wasn't like Tate had been honest back then either. And when he had been? Chase had had to hear about it from mutual friends.

However, Tate wasn't wrong. He probably shouldn't have suggested to his millions of followers that they were dating without clearing it with him first.

And Alec? Alec was probably having an apoplexy.

Chase could already imagine what he was going to say: *we talked about this, about you going off half-cocked and not thinking through major life decisions first.*

"I thought it would help," Chase said. Which was a little bit the truth. But mostly he had just been really frustrated. He never made the best kind of decisions when he was caught up in a pissed-off whirlwind.

Tate stared at him, apparently still shocked. "You tweeted that we were dating . . . *no*, scratch that. You tweeted that you liked men generally—me, *specifically*—because you thought it would help sell more fucking sandwiches?"

When Tate put it that way, it sounded even worse. But the damage was done now.

Chase shrugged. "A lot of people thought I wasn't straight before this. And it's not the big deal it was, like it was a few years back."

"That doesn't matter. You can't just . . ."

"I can't just what?" Chase hadn't expected that Tate would be *pleased*, exactly, but this was not going as planned.

"You can't just call yourself my boyfriend. What if I had a boyfriend already?"

Chase's heart leapt traitorously. "I didn't call *you* my boyfriend." He'd thought at least *that* through. "I didn't tag you. I didn't tag the truck. I never said what your name was." He took a deep breath. "And, do you?"

"Do I what?" Tate's face creased into an adorable frown. "Think you are absolutely batshit crazy? Yes. One hundred percent. One *thousand* percent. You've been posting nonstop for days about Say Cheese, and now this? It's not exactly going to be hard for people to make the connection."

Chase couldn't quite meet his eyes. It was funny how he didn't really care that Tate thought he was crazy—probably because he knew he could change Tate's mind—but he absolutely, totally cared if Tate had a boyfriend already.

Because you want him to be yours.

Chase ignored that voice. "Do you have a boyfriend?"

"*That's* what you're focusing on?" Tate threw up his hands in frustration. "I cannot fucking believe you. But *no*. I don't. Though I guess for all intents and purposes, I do now."

"What?" Chase wasn't quite sure he was following.

"*You.*"

Chase didn't know what to say. "Oh."

"Without asking me first," Tate stressed.

"Oh," Chase repeated again. He knew he'd been reckless, but he'd rarely dragged anyone else into his chaos. But in trying to help Tate, he'd done the opposite. "I'm sorry. I really didn't mean . . ."

"It's alright," Tate interrupted. "I can't exactly complain, can I?"

"Well, you *can*," Chase teased, feeling his heart lighten a little. He hadn't totally fucked up. Not *totally* anyway.

"But why would I? Look at this fucking *crowd*," Tate said, and the success in his tone, and the smile on his face made Chase happier than he could remember being. That was because of *him*. He'd done that.

"That's what you were doing, wasn't it? And it worked," Tate continued before Chase could figure out how to just ask: *would you go steady with me?* Why was that question so easy the rest of the time, and so fucking difficult with Tate.

"It worked?" Chase wondered. Not quite sure at what Tate was getting at.

Tate rolled his eyes. "You were trying to get people to come visit the truck. And it worked."

That had never been the point. He'd wanted to tell Tate he wanted him, and he didn't know how to do it. How to even say the words. With women, it had never been difficult. Probably because they'd always thrown themselves at him. But Tate? Tate with all his suspicions lurking behind those gray eyes? Tate, who seemed like he couldn't dismiss him fast enough as some NFL playboy with zero serious thoughts in his head? Who wanted to use him for a social media recommendation, pat his head, and shove him on his way?

Was it any wonder that Chase had fucked this up?

"I guess it did," Chase said, resignation swamping him.

"No guessing about it," Tate said dryly. "We had the best day, by triple, that we've ever had. So yes, I'll do it."

"You'll do it?" Chase knew he was just repeating back Tate's words like an idiot, but he couldn't quite make his brain cooperate. Was Tate recommending what he thought he was? *Oh god, this was not what he'd had in mind and yet how could he turn Tate down?*

Tate shot him a look. "You told people I was your boyfriend. I assumed that you wanted to do some kind of fake relationship. You know, for the marketing angle?"

He'd wanted to date Tate *for real*. But Tate thought he wanted to fake it. For *grilled cheese sandwiches.*

No, Chase told himself firmly, *no. This is for Tate. This is for him, because you want him to succeed. Just think what he can do with even a little of your spotlight.*

"Alright," Chase said. "That's . . . yeah, that's good."

Tate smiled then, and the way it made Chase's heart beat faster almost made it worth it. "You are absolutely fucking crazy, for the record," he added. "I can't believe you'd come out of the closet for a fake relationship, just to help me boost the food truck." His smile was lopsided, and he seemed charmed in spite of himself, even though when he said it like that, Chase looked legitimately nuts. "It's a lot, but it's a lot that means something to me."

"Yeah, yeah, well . . ." Chase said weakly. Inanely. What could he even say to that? *God, Tate, I've wanted you for ten years. Let's date for real.* All he had to do was say the words.

But how could he? When Tate was so sure none of this was true?

The only legitimate conclusion that Chase could come to was that even though the spark between them felt as real and immediate as it had ten years ago, it was over for Tate. Faded, over time. Probably because he'd had plenty of chances to hook up with lots of guys. Chase was the one who'd just pathetically hung out in the closet, waiting for the right time. Waiting for the right guy.

Meanwhile, the right guy hadn't exactly waited for him.

Chase couldn't even be angry about it.

"I seriously thought . . . I mean . . . I really thought I was just embarrassing myself ten years ago," Tate said wryly as he leaned against one of the picnic tables. "I was sure that at some point, you'd figure it out, and decide I was some kind of freak."

I still haven't figured it out, and you're not the freak. That's me.

Chase's fingers slipped along the condensation beading on the side of his beer. "You're not a freak."

"I know that now, but back then?" Tate chuckled. "I was a *mess.*"

"Hormones," Chase said weakly. What would Tate say if he admitted he was just as much of a mess today as he had been all those years ago?

It didn't matter, because Chase couldn't tell him. Not now.

"Seriously though, *thank you*," Tate said enthusiastically, pulling him into a tight, quick hug that Chase wanted to last. But before he could think to grab Tate back, he was already moving away from him. "It means a lot. I'm . . . I can't wait to tell Tony about this."

"Tony?"

"He's a friend, a good friend. He's the one running the food truck collective. He . . ." Tate's expression broke into an unexpectedly bright grin. "Have you ever met Ryan Flores? The baseball player?"

"A couple of times, yeah," Chase said. Not sure what Ryan Flores, the Dodgers' second baseman, had to do with anything.

"Ryan is, well . . . Tony's brother is his husband."

"Tony's brother is Wyatt Flores?"

"You've met Wyatt too?" Tate sounded surprised.

"At a few LGBT fundraisers," Chase said. He'd always gone, pretending to be an ally, wondering when he would be honest about who he really was. Wondering when he would *figure out* who he really was.

Maybe he'd known all along. Maybe he'd just been waiting to see Tate again.

"Well, Tony and Ryan are running the lot, taking the applications, etcetera. They'll probably be pretty happy about this. It'll boost the lot exposure, too."

"When does it open?" Chase wondered.

"Four weeks," Tate said. Hesitated. "Maybe we should make a timeframe. You don't want to be fake dating me forever . . . I mean . . . why would you?"

The question was so clearly inane that Chase just stared at him. "You want to call it quits in a month?"

"Yeah," Tate said, nodding. "Right after the lot opens. Does that work for you?"

It's horrible. How am I supposed to convince you to do this for real in only four weeks?

But Chase nodded anyway. "Yeah, that's fine. I'm not really up to much, before the summer, when training camp starts. Until then, I'm totally yours."

Tate looked surprised. "Oh, I'm sure I won't need you that long," he said.

"We'll see," Chase said. He had *no* intention of letting Tate go after only four weeks.

"I guess we will," Tate said, suddenly sounding unsure. "I should really . . . I should really get back to the truck. Help Rach with the cleanup."

Yeah, Chase could tell now. Tate was nervous. Definitely nervous. If Chase still made Tate nervous, that was a good sign.

Be smooth, be cool, Chase ordered himself.

"Yeah, but all these people are watching. If I had to guess, I'd think they're waiting for you to ravish me," Chase said, grinning at Tate. "You gonna disappoint them?"

Chase watched as Tate swallowed hard, his Adam's apple bobbing under all that scruff. Chase wanted to rub his face all over it—it looked soft, and he bet it felt even softer.

He'd never wanted that before. Not once in his whole life. Probably because eighteen-year-old Tate hadn't had scruff. But it was still a reminder that while he might be particular about the man, he *liked* men.

"What did you have in mind?"

Chase took a deep breath. "Just this," he said, and reached out, pulling Tate into his arms. Tate had already given him the briefest hug in history, but he let himself sink into this one, loving the way they lined up, Tate's head fitting just under his chin. For a single heart-stopping moment, they didn't move, pressed together, Chase's arms wrapped around Tate's waist. Then, he finally felt Tate touch him, run his hands, so tentatively it was almost like they weren't there, up his back. Like he was afraid to get caught touching. But everyone here knew. Everyone in the whole world was probably going to know soon.

Chase felt those feelings he'd always imagined would come back, if he ever met another guy like Tate, stirring to life again. Tate's cap was scratchy against his chin, but he didn't move, because he didn't think he could.

It took Tate a few moments longer to pull away than Chase had predicted. He didn't run, though. Just stared at Chase, eyes big and wide.

"That's better," Chase said, with satisfaction. Tate might not be sure what he was feeling, but he wasn't unaffected. And Chase knew he definitely wasn't.

It was only a hug, but it was the kind of hug that stayed with you, that stuck to your bones, and warmed you even when it was only a memory.

"It is?" Tate licked his lips. Chase wished that he could've kissed him. But not here. Not now. He'd waited for so long, it needed to be right.

"If you were my boyfriend," Chase said with a certainty that felt new, "and I was letting you go, I'd want at least that much."

"At least?"

Chase drained the rest of his beer. "I'm a touchy-feely kind of guy," he said quietly. "And I'd want to touch you all the time."

"If you were my boyfriend." But Tate still didn't sound that sure.

"Right," Chase said. "If you were my boyfriend."

"Uh, I guess I should go," Tate said. "But . . . I'll DM you my number. I guess we should get a story together, right? Because people are going to talk about this."

"Yeah," Chase said. "People are definitely going to talk about this."

Chase definitely expected that he'd have to face his friends—and his agent.

He hadn't expected to have to deal with Heath Harris first.

He was almost home when his phone rang. His first and second and third instinct had been *not* to answer it. There was almost nobody he really wanted to talk to, especially after what he'd done tonight. But after glancing at the caller ID flashing onto the dash display in his car, he hesitated.

Heath had told him once that he hadn't realized that he was queer until he was twenty-eight years old and he'd met Sam, the quarterback who would both replace him and become his boyfriend.

If anyone might understand Chase's struggle to identify his sexuality—and his long-term obsession with Tate—it might be Heath.

"Hey," Chase said, answering the call, hoping that he wasn't making a mistake.

"You picked up." Heath sounded surprised. And not much surprised him. Chase mentally cringed.

"Am I going to regret it?" Chase wondered as he pulled into his driveway, and shut the car off. Leaned back in his seat and hoped that Heath wasn't about to lecture him.

After all, he had Alec for that.

"No," Heath said. "I just . . . we just . . . I don't understand, Riley."

"Don't understand what?"

Chase knew he couldn't play stupid with Heath Harris—but for some inane reason, he was doing it anyway.

Heath made a sound halfway between a growl and a laugh. "You know what. You stood by when I came out, with Sam, three years ago. You stood by Neal. You defended Jamie. And the whole time, you had a boyfriend and you never told us."

"I didn't have a boyfriend the whole time," Chase said.

"So it's new?" Heath's normally serious voice grew sterner.

"No, it's . . ." Chase hesitated. "I've known him for a long time. But it's not . . . it's not exactly like that, though . . ."

"He's not really your boyfriend."

"He . . ." Chase swallowed hard. "Not exactly, no."

There was a long silence.

"You really should call Moira," Heath finally said. "She said she talked to you a few days ago, after the AFC Championship, but maybe . . ."

The rest of Heath's sentence was so obvious that Chase didn't know why he hadn't bothered to finish it. *But maybe you need more help if you think that stunting on Twitter, pretending to have a boyfriend, is okay.*

"I'm . . . I'm not straight." Chase could say that much. At least. Unfortunately in this moment, it didn't feel like very much at all.

"I wondered," Heath said. "Before. But you never said a word."

That stung because there was almost nobody that Chase respected like he respected Heath. But then, it wasn't like Heath had gone out of his way to have a serious, respectful coming out.

He and Sam had kissed in a flurry of confetti during the Super Bowl celebrations, right over the Vince Lombardi Trophy.

And yet, because Heath had a history of taking everything so seriously, everyone had assumed that Heath was *still* being serious. Tonight? Everyone probably assumed Chase was just being Chase.

Including all his friends.

Chase swallowed his apology. He was so damn tired of apologizing when he lost control.

"Maybe I will call her," Chase said. Because what else could he say? *I've only liked Tate since we were in high school and I couldn't do anything about it then, so I decided to do something about it now?*

He *could* say that. Heath would even understand. After all, there had only ever been one guy for Heath too, and Sam had been the worst possible person for him to fall for.

"You should," Heath said, his voice growing softer, kinder, the slight Texas twang in it growing more pronounced. "We're worried about you, you know."

"I'm fine," Chase said. *I'm elated. I'm terrified. I'm . . . a whole bunch of things, wrapped up in a buzzy anticipation that's only been ten years in the making.*

"You'll call if you need to talk?" Heath paused. "I know what it's like . . . everyone thinks they know who you are, and when you turn out to be something else, it's hard."

Chase let out the breath he'd been holding. Heath *did* understand. "It was the wrong way to do it," he confessed, "but now that it's done, I don't regret it."

"I never did, either," Heath said. "But seriously, call Moira. That's what she's there for. Supporting you, during a difficult time. You don't have to do it alone."

And Chase knew that Heath wasn't just talking about Moira being there for him—Heath was saying that he was, that Sam was, that Neal and Jamie were. That every person that Chase had protected and sheltered and defended during his years on the Riptide were ready to return the favor.

After Chase thanked Heath and said goodbye, he thought about it, and wondered when he would ever feel like he truly deserved that kind of support.

After several insistent text messages, Chase had agreed to meet Alec for breakfast. An *early* breakfast, because according to his agent, "You've created a situation and now we need to deal with it."

He had not expected to walk into the restaurant, one of his favorite diners in LA, and see Neal Fisher sitting across the booth from Alec.

It was one thing to get read the riot act by Alec, especially when he definitely deserved at least *some* of Alec's frustration. But Neal? Neal who had always been his friend? Neal who had always been honest with him about his sexuality?

Chase swallowed hard and fought the urge to run back out the door and drive home.

You did this. You can own up to it.

He approached the booth. Alec and Neal glanced up. "I can go home if you guys wanna have a one-on-one?" Chase said, even though he knew the joke was terrible.

Neal frowned at him. "You know that's not why I'm here."

"No," Chase said, sighing as he slid into the booth next to his friend. He put his arm on Neal's shoulder. "You're here because you made a spectacle of yourself. A press conference, wasn't it? Didn't you do it by making out with your boyfriend in front of a whole bunch of sports media? I'm only surprised Alec here didn't drag in Harris and Crawford. Nobody will ever top their coming out story. Me, I just sent an innocent little tweet. Kind of anticlimactic when you think about it."

Alec shot him a glare.

Yeah, he probably deserved that too.

"You are *insane*," Alec said between clenched teeth. "What happened to keeping your head down?"

"It wasn't very fulfilling," Chase said. "Though, really, I didn't mean for this to happen. It was kind of an accident."

"What?" Alec demanded. "You tripped and fell out of the closet?"

"Sort of?" Chase shrugged.

Alec looked over at Neal, who was smiling now. "I brought you here as a witness so I don't murder him. Remember that."

"I thought you brought me here as moral support," Neal said, chuckling.

"I *did*, and also because I thought our most beloved idiot over here could use some moral support of his own."

Neal glanced over at him. "Do you?" he asked Chase. Suddenly turning serious. "Because I have to admit, I didn't know this about you."

"And I could've told you?" Chase said, ignoring the pulse of guilt. He knew enough to know that closets were tricky, complicated things, but he also knew his friends would've had his back, no matter what. The same way that he'd always had theirs. Being queer in the National Football League wasn't easy, even though a lot more players were being honest about who they were. There was a certain safety in numbers, but that still didn't make it *safe*.

Chase had helped to form a loose association of players, coaches, and staff—both allies and representatives of the queer community—who were trying to make the NFL even safer for everyone who wanted to come out.

Yet, during all that time, he'd never told his own truth.

"Yeah, but this isn't about me," Neal said. "You know Jamie and I support you, no matter what."

"That isn't why I never said anything," Chase said. "I just . . . it's just been this one guy. Forever. I kept waiting to run into another one, that made me . . . well, *you know*, but it never happened."

"Sexuality isn't as clear cut as people want to believe it is," Neal said, putting a comforting arm on Chase's shoulder. "It's awesome you found him again."

"And this guy, he's the one who runs the food truck?" Alec wondered.

Chase nodded. "But it's . . . well, it's not what you think it is."

Alec frowned. "Do I want to know? Actually, I *do* because it's the worst when you don't tell me things and I'm surprised by them later. But honestly, for once, it would be really fucking great if everything was exactly what it seemed."

"You'd be bored in a minute, and you know it," Neal said, laughing. "You live for things not being what they seem."

"I know what I said," Chase said, twisting his napkin. "What I tweeted. But well . . . it's not exactly like that."

"You're not actually dating him," Neal guessed. "But you'd like to be."

"He needed my help. Higher profile for his food truck and all that and well, I *do* like him. Or I did. Though I'm not sure that's the kind of thing that can change, even though it's been so long."

"Oh my god," Alec said. "You're fake dating him but want to be real dating him. Someone get me a drink."

"It's not even nine in the morning," Neal said, clearly amused.

"There is not enough alcohol in the world for this," Alec said. "At least last year when you and Jamie started dating, you weren't actually *playing*. I was just trying to get you on Sunday Morning

Football so you could crack some jokes with Terry Bradshaw. This is . . . I don't even know what this is."

"Neither do I," Chase said quietly.

Alec's annoyance softened. "I know, kid, and it's gonna be okay. We're going to make it okay. First thing, I need to meet this guy, and then we need to make your arrangement official. Believe it or not, I have way too much experience with this fake dating shit. But not for awhile, because players don't feel as much pressure to find a girlfriend to cover for their boyfriend anymore."

"We can thank O'Connor for that one," Neal said, referring the first NFL player who'd come out of the closet, Colin O'Connor.

"Right," Alec said.

"What do you mean, make it official?" Chase wondered. He had a feeling that Tate was going to freak out if he wanted him to sign a contract. He was already uneasy about the whole thing—even though he clearly liked the way sales were picking up.

But the last thing he needed was to scare Tate away with a *contract*. Fuck.

He'd known this meeting was a mistake, but there was no way he could keep dodging his agent. One of the things Neal had said to him when they'd discussed Chase switching agents was that Alec was the most persistent, stubborn person he knew. *It's a blessing, and it can be a curse, too,* Neal had said. *But he's always going to be on your side, even when it doesn't seem like it.*

It was those words that had convinced Chase. He wanted someone who was loyal, even when he fucked up.

Well, this was the very first test. The drunk dancing after their AFC Championship loss looked small in comparison to a sudden coming out via Twitter and a brand-new fake boyfriend.

"You know what I mean, Chase," Alec said patiently. "We can't just have him running around saying and doing whatever he wants. You have a brand. A valuable brand. In two years, we're going to start negotiating a new long-term deal with the Riptide. You said when you signed with me that you wanted to play with them for the rest of your career. This kind of stuff? Impacts that possibility."

"I'd think they'd like me *more* now," Chase grumbled. The Riptide were rather notorious for having the largest percentage of "out" players in the NFL.

"Maybe, maybe not," Alec said. "I'm serious about this."

"We have an agreement," Chase argued. "We agreed to do this through the next four weeks—that's when this food truck lot that Tate wants into opens."

"A verbal agreement?" Alec raised an eyebrow.

"Yes," Chase said. Hating how defensive he sounded.

Alec shook his head. "You've been doing this too long to be naive about this." He turned to Neal. "And *this* is why you're here. Help me talk some sense into him."

Neal sighed. "Riley, I know you like this guy. It must feel like a freaking miracle that you ran into him again, after all this time. But Alec's right. You can't jeopardize your career for him."

"You did, for Jamie. Fuck, Jamie definitely did, for you."

"I know. And it was stupid. I won't argue with that. But we were in love and well—" Neal paused, grinning. "—you do really stupid things when you fall in love."

Alec groaned. "Don't you dare encourage him."

"Hey, I'm just telling the truth. You wanted me here, you deal with the consequences," Neal said with a shrug.

For the first time since he'd sat down, Chase felt the tension inside him begin to unwind.

The waitress arrived at their table, and they all ordered, and after pouring another round of coffee, she disappeared, leaving Chase to figure out how to convince Alec that he and Tate didn't need a contract.

But Alec started talking before Chase could figure out where to begin. "How about we just start with me meeting him," he suggested.

Chase opened his mouth. But Alec held up a hand. "I'm not saying I'm okay without a contract. I'm an agent, remember? But I'm also a pretty good judge of character—and so are you, honestly, despite all the things you do that make me question that opinion. But first, before that, you are going to tell me the whole story. Starting at the beginning."

"The beginning?"

"The beginning," Alec confirmed. "I want to know every-thing."

Chase squirmed. There was a reason he hadn't ever told anyone about this. "Uh, well, I guess it started in high school. It was our senior year, and we had Home Economics together, and ended up partners. Tate really liked—*likes,* I guess I should say, considering his profession—to cook, and we got to be friends."

"And you liked him." Alec said it unequivocally. Like it was really that simple.

If it had *ever* been simple, Chase wouldn't have waited to act on it. Chase wouldn't have ever let Tate out of his sight, no matter what that took.

"I guess," Chase said.

Neal elbowed him in the side. "You just told the world he's your boyfriend. You're helping his food truck succeed. You *like* him."

It was so weird to actually *admit* it, but Chase knew he should. He *did* like Tate. Had liked him ten years ago, and so far, didn't think that anything had changed. If anything, he was at least more prepared now to do something about it.

"Yeah, I do," Chase said. "I like him." Couldn't believe how much lighter he could feel, finally saying it out loud.

"Good." Alec was smiling too. And Chase was reminded again of what Neal had said about his agent. *He's always going to be on your side, even when it doesn't feel like it.* "What else?"

"What else is there?"

"How did you meet him again? Did you seek him out?"

Unbelievably, it seemed like Alec was actually making notes on his phone. About Chase and his ten-year-long crush. It was both a little embarrassing and also kind of gratifying. Like what he felt actually *mattered*. It had never really felt like it mattered, before, because in all that time, it had never happened again, but here were two queer men who didn't care that Chase hadn't ever been attracted to another guy after Tate. There was a refreshing lack of judgment—and even though he'd never imagined that either would condemn him for it, it made it easier to keep talking.

"Actually, he started posting about me on social media," Chase said. "That his truck served my favorite sandwich in LA."

Alec glanced up, his busy fingers pausing. "I thought you said you hadn't been talking to him."

"I hadn't," Chase said.

"So, he needed to boost sales, and thought, *why not invoke this famous football player I knew ten years ago?*"

"Uh, something like that, I guess? Anyway, my mom found out about it, and sent it to me, probably thinking it was sweet that we still knew each other, and I thought, well, if he's saying it, I should make sure it's actually true."

Neal laughed. "This is why I love you, Riley," he said, patting him on the back. "Someone's using your name and all you think is, *I gotta make sure they're telling the truth.*"

"Well, with anyone else, I might've just sent it to Alec and let him deal with it? But Tate? Yeah, that was something I was addressing hands-on," Chase said, grinning.

"Oh, I just bet you were," Neal teased.

"So I went to see him, and *yeah*, he actually is telling the truth about the sandwich thing. Plus, he needed the help, so I shared some pics on Instagram, and then I thought, why not do some more?"

"Why not," Alec muttered.

Chase turned to Neal. "Don't you ever get tired of people hitting on you, even though everyone knows you're both gay *and* very taken?"

"I mean, *no*," Neal said with a laugh. "Because it doesn't happen very often, actually, and it's a nice boost to the ego when it happens. But Jamie? It happens all the fucking time, and it makes me a little murderous. However"—Neal paused—"in your . . . *defense,* I guess? You're young and hot and notoriously single. So yeah, you're gonna get a lot of women hitting on you."

"There was one there, last night, who just . . . wouldn't quit," Chase said, "and maybe it wouldn't have been so bad. I could deal with it. But to get her off my back, I told her I was there for my boyfriend, just offhandedly, and she told me what a waste it was. And god, that really pissed me off."

"Yeah, people suck," Neal said with a frown. "I'm sorry you had to deal with that. I keep thinking, *we're getting better,* but then I'm usually reminded that we've made progress, but we're not nearly there yet."

"And that's when you tweeted, wasn't it?" Alec wondered. "When that woman told you that it was a waste you had a boyfriend."

Chase nodded.

"Well," Alec said, with a resigned sigh, "that makes a hell of a lot more sense."

"Tate wasn't very happy about it either, at first," Chase said. "But he came around. Probably when he found out that it wasn't me just making shit up to sell sandwiches."

"Was he surprised?" Neal wondered.

"Uh, well, I think we kind of knew about each other, back in high school." Chase felt himself flush. "The nonstop flirting probably gave it away."

"Probably," Neal said with a smirk.

"And that's when you agreed to fake date for a month?" Alec asked.

"Yeah," Chase said. "Like I said, his friend Tony, who it turns out is related to Ryan Flores? Dating his brother? Is Ryan's husband's brother? I couldn't keep it straight. Anyway, they're starting up this food truck lot together, and Tate wanted in, but he wasn't meeting the minimum sales threshold, so he needed help."

"Now, is he?" Alec asked, making more notes.

"Well, of course he is," Chase said, feeling more than a little proud. "I showed up, didn't I? And told everyone that he was my boyfriend. He's going to have more sales than he knows what to do with."

Alec gave a resigned sigh. "I'd call that a rather egotistical assumption, but we both know you're right, so I'll let it slide."

"Damn straight. Or not straight?" Chase burst into laughter.

CHAPTER FIVE

TATE DIDN'T KNOW WHAT to expect when he met up with some of the guys at the Funky Cup the next night. Say Cheese had been slammed all day, and Tate was having trouble even keeping up with the avalanche of email invitations, never mind the insane number of social media notifications he was getting. Their Yelp reviews had gone up to seventy-three and their average had even improved, Rachel excitedly telling him that many of the new reviews had talked about seeking out Say Cheese initially because of Chase's recommendation but promising they'd be back because the food was so good.

That was exactly the boost Tate had been hoping to get, and yet, it was a *lot*.

For the next month, you're getting both everything and nothing that you really want, Tate reminded himself as he pulled the door to the Funky Cup open.

Shaw was behind the bar, like he usually was, and his brother, Jackson, was on one of the barstools, a laptop in front of him. Jackson's boyfriend, Alexis, was sitting next to him, nursing a glass of clear liquor. Probably some kind of vodka, if he knew Alexis at all.

"Hey, look at who's decided to grace us with his presence," Shaw said, reaching into the big under-counter fridge and pulling out a bottle of his favorite beer, flipping off the cap and setting it on the counter. "I thought you might be too busy being a big shot to show up for the meeting."

Tate grabbed the bottle and took a long sip. Maybe he was predictable, but it was also really nice to be able to walk into his favorite bar and have Shaw instantly know what he wanted. "Not this meeting," he said.

"Yeah," Jackson said in a teasing voice, "maybe you could get your new boyfriend to buy you your own lot."

Tate rolled his eyes, flipped off the two brothers, and sauntered off towards the back patio, where Tony had told him they were holding the meeting.

Everyone else was already there. Gabriel and Sean were glaring at each other from opposite sides of the bench by the main fire pit, Ash sitting between them. Probably trying to keep the peace, because that was what Ash did.

Tony and Lucas were deep in some kind of hushed discussion, papers spread out on the other bench between them.

There was a point, only a week ago, when Tate had worried that he wouldn't be able to join this meeting. And now, because of Chase, he could walk in with his head high, and not worry that he was dragging the group down with his lower sales.

He'd worked really hard to get here, and the fact that he was *here*, hadn't quite sunk in just yet.

"It's a good group."

Tate looked up, and Alexis was standing next to him, grinning. "Yeah," Tate said, "yeah, it is."

He really liked Alexis, who ran a Greek-themed food truck. His hummus was to die for, and just thinking of it made Tate's stomach grumble. It was funny how he could still be hungry even after being around food all day.

But you didn't eat any of it, a voice told him reproachfully. Tate ignored that it sounded way too much like Chase. He'd been busy helping Rach clean and close the truck up, before getting to this meeting tonight, because the last thing he'd wanted was to be late to the *first* meetup. The vague idea that he'd grab something quick on the way hadn't actually materialized.

Because you don't take care of yourself, the voice continued.

But before he could give in to the voice—to *Chase*—and ask Alexis if he happened to have any hummus lying around, Tony walked up. "Hey," he said, clasping Tate in a quick, tight hug. "It's so good that you're here."

Tate knew Tony well enough to know that he really meant it. He'd never *wanted* to leave Tate out.

"It's a relief," Tate said. Alexis gave him a last shoulder nudge and went to talk to Gabriel and Sean, who were now pressed up together on the bench.

Tony raised an eyebrow. "That you got in, or that you suddenly have a hot new boyfriend, a *famous* boyfriend, that none of us knew about?"

Tony was also an asshole, but that was part of his charm.

At least that was what Tate told himself.

"Uh," Tate said. Suddenly he realized that he and Chase hadn't discussed whether they were going to be honest with the people they were close to. Rachel knew the truth about their relationship, but should he tell Tony? If he did, everyone in Tony's circle would find out eventually.

The plus side of that was that Tate wouldn't have to pretend in front of people he knew and liked. The downside? How convincing was the sham going to be if he kept telling everyone the truth?

"Really, when I was going on and on about Ryan and how you needed to get someone famous to endorse you, you could've said, *oh, by the way, I'm dating Chase Riley,*" Tony teased.

And *yeah*, Tate couldn't do it. Maybe it was that he'd wanted those words to be true—really, truly, true—for so long that he couldn't just sit by and listen as someone he respected and admired and downright *liked* talked about it.

This is going to be a very long four weeks.

"I'm not," Tate said in a rush. "I'm actually not dating him."

Tony raised one dark eyebrow. "But . . ."

"I know what he said," Tate said. "We knew each other in high school, and well, he agreed to do me this favor. I didn't think he'd go as far as he did, but well, he's Chase Riley. He doesn't always do what you expect."

Tony grinned. "Even coming out of the closet to help you sell grilled cheese sandwiches?"

"He didn't even tell me first," Tate complained.

Tony patted him sympathetically on the shoulder. "Someday, when I'm not dealing with this feat of organization, I'll tell you about my brother and Ryan's 'fake' relationship."

Tate did a double take. "Wait," he said. "Aren't they married?"

"Yep." Tony sounded delighted. "But that's definitely not how it started out."

"If this is your way of saying that Chase Riley and I are going to end up married, I think you're crazy," Tate said, even as his stupid heart leapt traitorously.

"You never know," Tony said with a shrug. "If you'd told me that I'd end up moving in with the new guy I hired for the truck, I'd never have believed you. Sometimes fate works in mysterious ways."

"Not that mysterious," Tate said, scoffing. "This is *Chase Riley* we are talking about. You know, the guy we watch every Sunday on television."

"And?" Tony looked confused.

"Chase. Riley," Tate repeated slowly. Just in case somehow all the loved-up action Tony enjoyed with Lucas had destroyed one too many brain cells.

"I know who Chase Riley is. I guess I'm confused why you think it's so crazy that you might end up dating for real?"

Tate threw up his hands. "I don't know? Maybe because I run a food truck called Say Cheese that before this week was barely scraping by. And he's *Chase Riley*."

"You keep saying his name like it's some kind of mystical incantation," Tony said, smirking. "What's that about?"

I've only been saying it that way for years, because Chase is magical.

"Maybe I'm a little starstruck," Tate admitted. Even though he knew it was a hell of a lot more than that. Rachel was right about one thing; he was in serious danger of having more than just a little spot of weakness for Chase. His whole body felt weak. Especially when he thought about that hug they'd shared yesterday. The way Chase had tugged him closer, and had held him for that long-drawn-out moment, like he hadn't wanted to let go either.

"A little?" Tony questioned. "I think you're underestimating yourself. Well, and Riley too, but that's between the two of you. I meant it—I'm so glad you're here. Relieved, a little, because I really didn't want to bend the rules and I considered it."

Tate couldn't believe it. "You'd have done that for me?"

"No," Tony said with a laugh, patting him on the shoulder. "But I would've *wanted* to, and I'm glad you didn't make me debate with myself over it."

"Or get you in trouble with your brother-in-law?" Tate asked.

"More like my brother *and* my brother-in-law, and probably my boyfriend too. They're all sticklers for the rules," Tony said with a resigned sigh. "I'm definitely the rule breaker of the group."

"Tony," Tate lied unapologetically, "I don't believe that at all. But I'm relieved it didn't come to that."

"Me too," he said. "Come on, let's kick this shit off."

There were going to be six trucks to start—Tony and Wyatt's truck, What a Catch; Alexis's The Big Fat Greek Food Truck; both Gabe and Sean's On a Roll trucks; Ash's truck, Leaf it to Us, which focused on chopped salads; and last but not least, Say Cheese.

Tate was a little surprised—but not as much as he had been before he and Tony had talked—to see that Good and Planty, the new vegan truck he'd started with Lucas, wouldn't be included, and neither would Granny's, the coffee and baked goods truck he'd started with his brother. Both of those were very new and still establishing themselves, so Tate guessed that Tony and Ryan were pretty serious about their sales requirements—even other trucks they owned that didn't make the cut hadn't been invited to participate.

"Lucas is passing around the contracts," Tony said, gesturing with his beer bottle. "We used Ryan's fancy, expensive lawyer, so they're *probably* sound, but if you'd like to go over them, even hire your own lawyer, be my guest."

Tate took a copy from Lucas, and flipped through it briefly. Rachel had a friend who'd gone to law school, that he could probably ask her to call in a favor with. The contract outlined the monthly rent that each truck would pay, as well as requirements for group promotion and marketing, and guidelines on how often the trucks were allowed to be closed for a day or not parked at the community lot.

The restrictions seemed reasonable—and also left Say Cheese free to do what it wanted once a week: either close down for what might be a much-needed break or accept one of the many invitations that had arrived in his inbox recently.

Rachel had expressed concern this afternoon before Tate had gone to the meeting. "We said we needed in the lot because it would get us a steadier clientele," she'd said, "but maybe with what Chase has done for our bottom line and our visibility, maybe it's a mistake to commit to anything right now." Tate had told her that she was crazy, because this was the opportunity they'd been working so hard for, but then as he'd driven over, he'd wondered too what they were potentially giving up.

Truthfully it felt weird to have options, because in the two years that he and Rachel had owned Say Cheese, they hadn't had very many of them. But now? Tate felt like the sky might be the limit.

But he was reassured that they wouldn't be forced to give up everything they'd just gotten a crack at for the first time. They could still do the breweries, the specialty festivals, the lunchtime crowds. They'd just have to be pickier about which opportunities they took, that was all.

His stomach grumbled again, as Lucas took over, talking about group promotions, focusing on holidays and special occasions, especially game days.

"We're only a few blocks away from the Coliseum," Lucas explained, referring to the famous Los Angeles sporting field, "which means that on USC game days, we are going to be *packed*. Those days, if you'll notice, are specially marked in the contract as being days you are required to be open. That's for you," he added wryly, "and for everyone, honestly. Nobody wants to deal with more business than we can handle just because you decided to fuck off."

"We were thinking of cool names," Tony said, "and we thought . . . if we're by the Coliseum, why not be warriors? Food Truck Warriors."

It was kind of a stupid name. Tate would be the first one to say that, but Tony looked so excited about it, that it was hard to burst his bubble.

Luckily, his boyfriend had no such qualms. "Yes, it's kind of dumb," Lucas said, shooting Tony a fond glance, "but Tony was watching *Gladiator* one night and got all pumped about it. We're willing to entertain other ideas, but I'll admit, it's grown on me."

"Hey, if Tony likes it, I do too," Gabriel said.

Tate watched with complete non-surprise as Sean shot him a look that bordered on a glare. "I think Tony liking something isn't a good reason to pick it," he said.

"How about we vote?" Ash suggested. "We've got an odd number."

"We all know how that's gonna turn out," Sean complained. "Lucas is gonna vote with Tony. So will Ash—and we know Gabe likes it, because he likes *everything*. There's no point. Food Truck Warriors it is."

"What about you, Tate?" Lucas asked. "Alexis? Your thoughts matter too."

Alexis shrugged. "I don't have a preference either way."

For a split second, Tate considered telling Lucas and the rest of the guys that he'd accept Tony's delusional name if everyone left him alone about Chase.

But the truth was, Sean was right. Tony already had a majority, and he obviously was aware of that fact, which explained why he hadn't suggested a vote in the first place. Lucas making sure everyone was okay with the name was more of a formality than anything.

"Food Truck Warriors it is," Tate said.

Tony gave a fist pump, and Lucas rolled his eyes.

They went over a few other things, and blessedly, the meeting broke up before Tate's stomach decided to eat him alive.

He headed back into the bar, grabbed another beer from Shaw, put in an order for a burger and sweet potato fries, and headed to a table in a peaceful corner to start reading over the contract.

Tate had made it halfway through the contract, making notes in the margins, when his burger arrived. He'd taken exactly two delicious bites—Jackson and Shaw knew too many foodies to ever have crap food at their bar—when his phone vibrated in his pocket.

It was an unknown number, so he hit decline and went back to his burger.

The number rang *again*, and he repeated his earlier action, finishing his burger in a few more undisturbed minutes.

He was just wiping his hands on a napkin, getting ready to dive into the best sweet potato fries in the city when a series of texts began to appear on his phone.

Answer your damn phone, Ward, the first one read.

You're ignoring me? ME? read the second text.

I can't believe you, Ward, the third text said, **I'm gonna have to track you down.**

Tate glanced up in concern. He could guess who the texts had come from, and he wasn't really naive enough to believe that if Chase really wanted to find him, he could stay hidden. Los Angeles adored Chase, and would give Tate up to him in a minute.

Had *already* given him up.

Tate sighed as he spotted Chase leaning against the bar, a bottle of beer in one hand and a smirk on his face. He'd covered his distinctive hair with a beanie—*no,* Tate insisted to himself, *he is not copying your signature look, it's probably just handy*—but nothing could disguise Chase's height or the intimidating breadth of his shoulders.

He sauntered over, flopping down in the chair opposite Tate as Tate glared at him.

"What are you doing here?" Tate asked.

"You closed early, and I didn't get my fix," Chase said. "I stopped by and Rachel was cleaning up."

"I had this meeting," Tate said testily. They were only fake dating. It wasn't like he needed to tell Chase Riley everything that was happening in his life.

"Yeah, Rachel told me all about it," Chase said. He leaned back in his chair, his eyes never leaving Tate's face. "Your first food lot meeting. I think some appreciation is in order."

"I'd be happy to buy you a beer," Tate said stiffly. Money wasn't as tight as it had been only a few weeks ago, but he certainly wasn't as rich as Chase. Still, that was the least he could do.

"How about something else?" Chase said. He lifted his hand, with the still mostly full bottle in it. "I've already got a beer."

It occurred to Tate way too late that he'd already fallen into the trap, and Chase already had something in mind. Something that Tate wasn't going to like much.

"What did you have in mind?" Tate asked, sighing.

Chase reached over and snagged a handful of sweet potato fries. "I want you to go to dinner with me and my agent this weekend."

"Why?" Tate asked suspiciously. "I'm busy. I've got work. Which, thanks to you and your wild and unrestrained fingers, is crazier than ever."

"I know. But Rachel said you were thinking of hiring part-time help for when you open at the food truck lot, and well," Chase added with a lopsided, entirely too charming grin, "there's no time like the present."

Tate stared at him with disbelief. "You realize it takes longer than a few days to find, hire, and train someone?"

Chase shrugged. "You've got lots of friends with trucks, right? It can't be that hard to find a friend of a friend who wants a job. Or someone who could pinch hit for you."

Chase was spot on, which was the annoying part.

"And," Chase added, "I bet you can even find one of those many friends to sub for you this weekend."

Chase was also right there; but Tate had no intention of letting him get away with strolling in here and dictating terms for their "relationship."

"Why do I need to go to this dinner again?" Tate asked, refusing to acknowledge that Chase had been right on either of his assumptions.

"Why?" Chase looked surprised, like people didn't usually turn down invitations to dinner with him. And frankly, they probably never did.

But Tate had already resolved that he was going to have to figure out a way to protect his heart from falling for Chase all over again—and key in that was to not get too close. Sharing a dinner? Faking dates? Meeting the people in Chase's life? That was getting way too fucking close.

"Why? Because I'm going to have to rearrange a lot of things and leave Rach shorthanded with someone who isn't familiar with our system, just to do this dinner. So *why* do I need to go?"

Chase sighed. "Because my agent wants to make things more official, like contract-official, and I don't want to deal with that, and I don't think you do either. But if he meets you and doesn't think you're going to fuck me over . . ."

"Then there's no . . . what? No contract?" Tate gestured to the papers in front of him. "I mean, that makes sense. I've got about all the contracts I can handle right now."

"Alright, then you'll look for someone?"

"I'll ask Lucas," Tate said. "The vegan truck doesn't usually work nights and sometimes he helps out with Tony's truck, but they've got staff now, so he can take an evening off to help Rachel."

He didn't usually *like* asking for favors, but Chase was right, one of the benefits of being in this tight association with other food truck owners was that they could help each other out. He and Rachel weren't alone in this. Chase was right; they had friends.

"Good." Chase sounded pleased with himself. "So, how did your meeting go? Pretty good, if the way you've been absorbed in that contract is any indication."

A terrible thought occurred to Tate. "How long have you been here?" he demanded.

"A little while," Chase said nebulously. "Long enough to be impressed at the way you demolished that burger."

Ugh. Definitely the way not to impress Chase Riley was to eat like he was a wild animal. "I hadn't had dinner," he retorted. "And the meeting went fine. There's going to be six trucks, at first. I'm really happy I got in, honestly, so I guess I should thank you for that."

Tate wasn't so stubborn that he couldn't acknowledge that Chase's help—even the more extreme angle he'd taken—had made the difference for Say Cheese.

"Of course," Chase said, grinning. "But now that you're in, we need to talk about your plan going forward."

"I don't have a plan going forward," Tate said. "Continue doing what we're doing, that's the plan."

"But I've got one," Chase said, leaning forward, his dark eyes sparkling in the dim light of the bar. It was insane to still be so goddamned charmed by someone so many years after an originally ill-fated crush, but Tate found himself drawn to Chase like a moth to a flame.

Or a bug to a blowtorch.

"You have a plan?" Tate told himself that it was silly to be suspicious when he didn't even know what Chase had in mind—*and*, his brain added, *at least he's telling you about it up front this time*—but he couldn't help but remember what had happened the *last time* Chase had come up with a plan.

"Don't sound so paranoid," Chase said. "It's gonna be great."

"The last time it was a 'great' idea, you came out of the closet on Twitter by invoking a grilled cheese sandwich," Tate said warily.

"True," Chase said. "But I think you're going to like this plan. It has a nice symmetry."

"What is it?" Tate asked, finally giving in. The more Chase insisted he'd like it, the more Tate knew he wouldn't.

"You said you needed help, right?" Chase said. "I could work at the truck! Think of the crowds that would bring in."

Tate stared at him. "You want to . . . *work* at my food truck?"

"Yeah!" Chase sounded very enthusiastic.

"Okay, to clarify a few things. You realize that the only reason Rachel and I do this is because we really, really love it and most people would hate it, right? Including you."

"I wouldn't hate it. I think it'd be fun to take orders. Talk to people? Make recommendations?"

Tate had been right; he really hated this idea. He wasn't sure why, exactly, but he was secretly convinced it had something to do with being crammed in a tiny, hot space all day with *Chase Riley*.

"Except that the thing is . . . Rachel and I don't *just* take orders," Tate said. "There's prep and finish work to be done."

"I can do that." Chase shot him a confident smile.

"You really can't," Tate muttered. He remembered Home Economics better than just about any class he'd taken in high school, and the one thing he felt sure of was that Chase was a nightmare in the kitchen.

"Then, teach me," Chase said.

"Why do you even want to do this?" Tate asked. "Surely, you're not doing it for the money. Also, by the way, am I *paying* you to do this?"

"Of course not," Chase said. "You couldn't afford me."

"Exactly," Tate said. "So, *why*?"

"It's the off-season and I'm bored," Chase said with a shrug. "There's only so many crazy workouts my trainer can come up with."

"But you want to spend your time off working . . . *working*?"

"Is it so crazy that I might want to help you?" Chase sounded perturbed by Tate's incredulity, but Tate thought he was being just the right amount of incredulous. Why would someone who pulled in millions and millions of dollars a year want to cram himself in a tight, confined, hot, space, and do the kind of work that barely paid above minimum wage?

"You've already helped me," Tate said steadily.

"Listen," Chase said intently, "I know you're going to end up hiring someone and training them for when you join the food truck lot. Just . . . think of this like a temporary arrangement."

"Like our 'relationship,'" Tate retorted.

"Yeah, sure, I guess," Chase said. Then smiled brightly. "Just think of the attention you'll get when people realize that I'm working at your food truck."

"They'll think you're doing it because we're dating," Tate said.

"Right, it makes total sense. Why would I ever let you out of my sight if we were really together?" Chase sounded very confident about this. Tate stared at him.

"Wouldn't it be the other way around?"

Chase just laughed. "You really don't see yourself very accurately, you know. You never did."

Tate considered asking Chase how he saw him, but that way lay insanity and madness and the point of no return. So instead, he nodded. "Okay, fine, you can work at the truck. I will teach you the *bare minimum*, and I mean the *bare minimum*, and you can take orders. It'll be . . ." He paused, envisioning it, and hating and loving the image in the same moment. "It'll be good. I'm not going to complain about extra help."

"Awesome." Chase sounded so excited that he clearly had no idea what it was really going to be like.

Hell, Tate thought, *it's gonna be hell. Being so close and not being able to touch . . .*

"And if you want to do this," Tate added, "that doesn't mean you can show up whenever you feel like it. We have a schedule and we keep to it."

"You do realize I keep to a schedule all the time," Chase said. "I know how it works."

"This is my business, not your personal playground," Tate reiterated. Maybe he was being unfair to Chase; it was undeniable that he worked hard. Of course the kind of hard work that he was used to wasn't anything like the hard work he was going to be experiencing when he climbed aboard Say Cheese.

"Sunday is a day we don't usually schedule," Tate said. "We'll do some basic training then. Our schedule's packed next week and, honestly, some additional help might be nice."

"Maybe you *should* buy me another beer," Chase said with an unrepentant grin as he finished the one in his hand. "Since I'm apparently going to be slaving away for you."

"Okay," Tate said.

"Besides, we're supposed to be dating," Chase said. "Why am I sitting all the way over here?"

"We are *not* doing this here," Tate hissed as Chase dragged his chair over, right next to Tate's.

We're not doing this at all.

Chase slung an arm around Tate's shoulders, and it felt like a reassuring weight and also a terrifying one, dragging him and all his unruly thoughts to a place he really didn't want to go.

"We're not?" Chase asked.

"I . . . these are my friends," Tate said, struggling to figure out how to say what he knew he needed to. "I'm not going to lie to my friends."

Chase glanced around the bar. "All these are your friends?"

Technically, his friends were still all outside, except for Shaw, who was manning the bar as he usually did. But he was busy enough with the Thursday evening crowd that he wasn't exactly paying attention to who Tate was canoodling with.

But he also didn't want to lie to Chase either. Not after what Chase had done for him. Out of what? The goodness of his own heart? To what? Honor a friendship that neither of them had done anything about in ten years?

"No," Tate admitted. "They're outside."

Chase's arm settled more fully onto Tate's shoulders, and his own body betrayed him by leaning into the warm firm touch. He couldn't help but remember all those times he'd dreamt in high school of how they would fit together. Remember how they'd fit together two days ago, when Chase had hugged him.

"See?" Chase said. "That's kinda nice, isn't it?"

It was more than "kinda nice," and that was going to be a problem, because Tate was never going to be okay settling for a dim echo of the real thing. He was always going to want all of Chase.

Both ten years ago, and today. Nothing had changed.

"Yeah," Tate said. He already knew he couldn't lie.

"Guess we'll have to forgo that second beer after all," Chase said in a low, intimate voice, the edges growing gruff. "'Cause I'm not moving. Not now. And neither are you."

Like he'd gotten exactly what he wanted and now he wasn't going to take the chance that he'd lose Tate.

If only he knew just how easy Tate was for him.

Tate reached over and patted Chase's broad, firm chest. His fingers tingled at the ripples of muscle he could feel under the thin, worn material of Chase's t-shirt. "Can't let yourself go," he teased. "Now that I've finally got you."

Chase smiled slow and sweet, the warmth of it spreading through Tate until he felt light-headed. "Don't have to worry about that," he said. "I'm gonna be real good for you."

Tate swallowed hard, remembering all the times they'd flirted and nearly crossed the line before. This was going to be a *real* problem, because crossing it now? Came with the territory.

"So what super fancy place are you taking me to on Saturday?" Tate wondered, because his brain-to-mouth filter was wearing down and too many things he'd craved forever felt a little too close.

"I was going to let Alec pick," Chase said seriously. "He's got good taste. Better taste than me, and I don't want . . . I want to treat you right." Like that really mattered to him. Even though none of this was real.

"You've got good taste," Tate argued. "You picked me, didn't you?"

Technically, Chase had picked *Say Cheese* and not Tate, but Chase's intimate smile at his words made Tate's insides quiver.

He's not straight. He told you he wasn't straight. There doesn't have to be any line anymore.

Except it was more important than ever to keep the line intact, because even if Chase wasn't straight, that didn't mean he was interested—or could ever be interested—in Tate.

"I did," Chase said. "I guess I do have decent taste. But this is a big thing. Our first date. I wanna do it right."

"It's not really . . ." Tate wanted to tell him that it wasn't real, that this wasn't their first date or anything even remotely close to it, but something, maybe that soft glow in Chase's eyes, stopped him.

Or maybe it was the exultation cresting through him. Maybe it wouldn't ever be real, but he'd know now what it was like to date Chase Riley.

"I'll get in touch tomorrow about the details," Chase said. Nudged him playfully. "Answer your phone, next time."

"I'll add you to my contacts," Tate said, and his fingers shook a little as he typed in Chase's name.

"Good," Chase said. "Now, are you gonna tell me more about your meeting?"

And to Tate's surprise, he wanted to, so he did.

CHAPTER SIX

Under any other circumstances, Chase had known Tate would never agree to a date. He'd already decided that Chase couldn't possibly be *really* interested, so there was nothing to stop Chase from pulling out every single stop in order to win Tate's heart.

And step one was the Big Date.

"Now remember," Chase said to Alec, juggling his phone as he slid into his car, "you meet him, you decide he's not crazy and that he's not going to use me for fame and fortune and then stick a knife in my back, and then you *leave*."

"I got it," Alec said. "I'm almost at the restaurant. I'll make sure the table is what we discussed ahead of time."

"Private," Chase said. "That's the most important thing."

"It shouldn't be an issue. And don't worry; I have no intention of being a third wheel tonight." Alec sounded amused, like he wasn't used to Chase being so worried about everything being just right.

Truthfully, Chase couldn't remember the last time *not* in a football game that it had mattered at all.

"Okay, I'm just getting ready to pick Tate up," Chase said. "We'll see you in about twenty."

Chase hung up the call, tossed his suit jacket on the seat next to him, and setting his GPS for Tate's building, backed out of his driveway.

Tate had sounded uncomfortable when Chase had offered to pick him up and had tried, several times, to insist that they could just meet at the restaurant. But Chase knew what a real date was, and he was determined to deliver.

Alec had picked out not just the "fancy restaurant" that Tate had assumed, but somewhere that was classy and elegant and yet laid-back, and then had called in a favor to make sure they got a really good table. A *private* table.

"I can't believe I'm spending my time playing matchmaker for you," Alec had said ruefully.

"Just think of all the other crazy shit that clients make agents do," Chase said. "I'm practically doing you a favor."

If everything went to plan, Alec would duck out after the first few minutes, and that would leave Chase and Tate alone.

On a date.

Chase grinned at himself in the rearview mirror, congratulating himself on a job well done.

He pulled up at Tate's apartment building a few minutes early, and stepping out, he smoothed his white button-down shirt, open at the neck, and made sure his hair was perfect, before he walked in. Normally he'd take the stairs—a trick his trainer had taught him to work fitness into an everyday routine—but he was dressed up. He didn't want to get too creased or sweaty, so instead, he pushed the elevator button.

It was a nondescript building. Not fancy particularly, but not a dump either.

Tate had said he was on the third floor, fourth door down.

He knocked on the door—it was just as plain as every other door on the floor, though he heard some commotion immediately behind it. The door opened and to Chase's disappointment it wasn't Tate; it was his sister, instead.

Rachel crossed her arms over her chest, and looked him up and down. "Wow," she said, which was pretty gratifying. Chase knew he was hot; knew that he cleaned up well, especially when he made the effort, but the truth was, the person he most wanted to impress was Tate.

"Is it too much?" Chase asked.

"No," she said critically, eyeing him again. "But he's going to melt through the floor."

"A good kind of melting?"

Her expression softened. "Yeah, but since I love him, I've got to say it. Don't hurt him, okay? He seems tough and put together and he is, but well, he's always been hung up on you."

Chase stopped himself from a victory dance complete with fist pumps just *barely*. He couldn't help the big smile. "I've always been hung up on him too," he admitted.

"Yeah, exactly," Rachel said. Unimpressed. "That's the whole problem. You two can't seem to get out of your own damn way, and now this whole fake dating thing?"

"It'll turn out fine," Chase said. Reassured her. Reassured himself.

But he couldn't hear Rachel's response, because Tate appeared in the doorway.

"Hey," Tate said breathlessly.

Rachel had said Tate would melt through the floor at the way Chase looked, but she'd neglected to mention that Tate could look like *that*. He'd left the beanie off, *finally*, and his hair shone a deep reddish brown, the lights picking out all the highlights that Chase knew were natural because he'd spent way too much time in Home Ec looking at them. He wore a pair of slim-cut dark gray slacks, that hugged his waist and hips in all the right places, and a dark navy polo, the sleeves tight around his surprisingly muscular biceps.

Chase felt his mouth go dry. Words, words, he was supposed be saying words right now. *Impressive* words. But the problem was that his brain had gone totally blank.

"Hey," Tate repeated again, tucking a strand of his hair—god, Chase hadn't realized it was that long, since he always wore it covered—behind an ear. "Are you ready to go?"

"Yes," Chase said. Rachel was still standing there and she looked deeply amused.

But how could Chase look at her when Tate was right there, just his presence sending shivers of arousal up his spine? Nobody had ever affected him this way—definitely not another man.

"You two have fun," Rachel said dryly. "Not that that's up for much debate at this point."

Tate turned to his sister. "Enough," he hissed under his breath, and stepped into the hallway, the door shutting behind him.

Chase wished he could've been a fly on the wall while Tate had been getting ready. He wanted to know more about the *he's always been hung up on you* subject.

"You look great," Chase said. It was amazing how easily those charming platitudes used to fall out of his mouth. Now it sounded practiced and rehearsed and well . . . *dumb.*

Maybe Chase hadn't cared before if people thought that, but he couldn't handle Tate thinking that.

"Really?" Tate turned to Chase as they waited for the elevator. "Because honestly . . ." He trailed off.

"Honestly?" Chase wondered.

But instead of answering, Tate just laughed, shaking his head. "Just, geez, dude, warn a guy."

"About?"

The elevator dinged and they walked in, the doors closing behind them. Tate jabbed the first-floor button with enthusiasm. "Warn a guy when you're going to show up looking like a wet dream, that's all."

"Really?" Chase was hoping that he'd feel that way, but it was gratifying to hear that it had worked.

Everything's going according to plan.

When they exited the apartment building, with Chase's car parked in front, Tate whistled under his breath when he saw the shiny black Maserati that Chase had picked especially for tonight out of his collection of way too many fast cars. "I thought you'd bring the obnoxious turquoise one," Tate said as Chase opened the door for him.

"This one was a little more subtle. More the speed I'm going for tonight," Chase said, then shut the door.

When Chase settled in the driver's seat, the engine quietly roaring to life, he flexed his fingers against the leather steering wheel in an attempt to get them to stop trembling so damn badly.

It was like the last ten years hadn't happened, and he was back in Home Economics, those way too bright lights shining on them, making it hard to deny the obvious: that he was attracted to guys, and *very* attracted to one guy in particular.

You're totally past this freak-out, Chase told himself firmly. *You got past this freak-out years ago. It's gonna be fine. Everything's gonna work out.*

Still, he couldn't quite convince himself as they drove into the heart of the city, towards the restaurant that Alec had selected. Chase had prepared a whole list of small talk ahead of time, but his mind, shorted out by Tate's unbelievably hot appearance, had yet to make any kind of comeback. So they were stuck in an uncomfortable silence.

"This looks nice," Tate said, as Chase pulled up to the sidewalk and the restaurant's valet station.

The dark opaque windows, trimmed in gold, with the restaurant's name subtly picked out in a similar gold font, *did* look nice. Chase gave Alec a mental high five.

The valet opened the passenger door before Chase could get there. The guy did a double take when he saw who it was getting out of the driver's side. "You're Chase Riley," the man said, his voice a stuttering mess.

"Yeah," Chase said, tossing him the keys, which he promptly dropped and had to stoop down to pick up. "Baby it, yeah?"

"Oh yeah," the valet agreed with a worshipful expression.

Tate glanced over at him as the other valet opened the door for them. "Was it necessary to make him so speechless he could barely function?" he asked under his breath.

"Believe it or not, it's not something I *try* to do," Chase said. Well, most of the time he didn't. He'd totally, one hundred percent, been desperate to take Tate's breath away tonight.

"Yeah, right," Tate retorted, but he sounded wryly amused, not upset. "You know the effect you have on people. Rich and famous and hot."

"Am I hot?" Chase couldn't help but grin as they approached the host station.

"Oh my god," Tate said. "I can't even with you."

"Is that a yes?" Chase wondered.

"Oh, Mr. Riley," the host said deferentially. "I'll show you to your table."

Tate shot him a look that said, loud and clear, *yeah, you totally know it was.*

They followed the host through the darkened, candlelit restaurant, and even though he couldn't see Tate's face, Chase could see apprehension tightening his shoulders. He was nervous, because yeah, the romantic candlelit alcoves were totally date-like.

On purpose, dude, so you might as well embrace it.

Their table was all the way in the back, not quite in a private room, but close enough, with an ornate wood-carved screen on one side and a large, towering flower arrangement on the other. Alec stood as they approached.

"Hey, you must be Tate. I'm Alec," his agent said, and they shook hands. Tate still looked nervous, and Chase sympathized with him, because his own stomach was churning.

"I took the opportunity to peruse the wine list already," Alec said as they settled down at the table. "And I ordered an excellent bottle of red. I hope that's alright with you, Tate."

Chase watched as Tate glanced at the side of the bottle and his eyes bugged out of his head. He knew Alec had really good taste—really *expensive*—taste in wine and he suspected that Alec had shown it off here.

"Uh, yeah, this looks amazing," Tate said. "I've always wanted to try this winery."

"Excellent. I didn't bother asking Chase because as I'm sure you know, he doesn't have much of an appreciation for good wine."

"Actually, I didn't know, but I'm not surprised," Tate said wryly. "He always struck me as more of a beer type." Chase, who really *didn't* like wine, was tempted to push his empty wineglass towards Alec and prove both of them wrong. But then he remembered something that Neal had told him once, when he'd asked him how he and Jamie had fallen in love. "I was myself," Neal had said. "I was myself and Jamie loved me—loved me *anyway*, I think sometimes—but he always says he loves me *because* of who I am."

That conversation had made Chase think, not just about the few women he casually saw, but a lot of other things too. It had made him want to be a man that someone could fall for. A man who could be proud of being authentically himself. Even if that man was someone who drank beer over wine.

"So," Alec said, very casually as he poured wine into Tate's glass. So casually that Chase knew something was up and couldn't help but tense. "I hear you two knew each other in high school."

"We did," Tate said, swirling the wine in his glass. "We actually knew each other for a long time, but I'd say we more . . . *knew of* each other. But senior year, we had Home Economics together, and we ended up partners."

"Oh, I bet that was interesting," Alec said, chuckling. Chase wondered how quickly his agent could invent an excuse and leave the two of them alone, *but* it seemed Alec was enjoying himself too much to do that right away.

Chase was sure that Tate was going to break into one of the stories of him burning something, or ruining it, or that time he'd crushed the tomatoes in his hands and they'd ended up all over the ceiling. He had a good memory, and he knew there was a lot of material for Tate to pick from. But instead, Tate just smiled. "No, he was great," Tate said, glancing over with a fond glance. "The best partner a guy could hope to have."

"I can see why you reconnected," Alec said. "I only wonder why it took so long."

"Sometimes fate just intervenes," Chase inserted, because this conversation had already gone on too long. Alec had gotten a look at Tate. Could see that he wasn't sketchy. And could surely figure out that if Tate wouldn't even sell Chase out on how terrible he'd been in Home Economics, then he wasn't going to betray him now.

"Yes, it does," Alec said with a smirk as he sipped his wine. "I still have to ask, because Chase is working on improving his reputation, how this . . . *association* . . . is going to help with that."

Chase opened his mouth, because this had never been part of the plan—at least *his* plan—but it clearly had been part of Alec's the whole time. But before he could interrupt and tell Alec that he was *fine*, thank you very much, Tate said, "I think it's already helped, don't you?"

Before Alec could ask how it had, Tate continued. "Maybe it wasn't in the playbook to have Chase come out on Twitter, talking about his boyfriend's food truck, but here's the thing about the

LGBT community—we embrace our own. And Chase, who's been an ally for years, revealing his own sexuality? Makes him inherently more likable."

Alec leaned back in his chair, regarding Tate. "You are not what I expected," he said.

"You thought I'd be some kind of idiot that uses the name of some guy I knew in high school to promote his food truck?" Tate said with a laugh. "I'm that, too. But I care about Chase. I don't want to make him look bad. I promise."

"Tate's incapable of making me look bad. We both know I do that all on my own." Chase finally managed to get a word in edgewise.

Alec drained the rest of the wine in his glass. "*That* is true," he said, and stood, holding out his hand to Tate. "It was really good to meet you," he said, "but I'm actually double booked, so I've got to run. Still, enjoy the wine. Have a nice meal. Maybe you can take a trip down memory lane together."

Tate shook Alec's hand, and when the agent walked away, he shot Chase a betrayed look. "You knew he was leaving," he said.

Chase shrugged. He didn't want to lie. "He's double booked a lot," he said. "Got a lot of clients."

"I've heard so many horror stories about agents, but he seems . . . reasonable?" Tate said, like he was as surprised as anyone that Alec had turned out less like a shark and more like a human being.

"Yeah," Chase said. "He's a good guy."

"He even seems to care what happens to you." Tate still sounded slightly mystified. "Don't get me wrong, it's a good thing, but . . . I didn't really expect him to ask what he did."

"Me either," Chase said, a little darkly.

"I guess we should enjoy this dinner, anyway," Tate said, his expression softening. "After all, I took the night off and got dressed up and so did you, and I'd hate for all that . . ." He waved at Chase. "To go to waste."

"You would?"

Tate rolled his eyes. "You know just how fucking hot you are, so there's no point in pretending otherwise."

"That's me," Chase teased. "A total wet dream."

Tate smiled. "Exactly. I'm going to enjoy it while I can."

"Whenever you like, whatever you like, it's all yours," Chase said. He knew Tate didn't really believe him, because this wasn't supposed to be real, even if it was feeling increasingly real for him.

What would Tate do if Chase leaned in and brushed a kiss across his mouth? Felt just how soft his scruff was for himself? Figured out if Tate smelled just as good as he looked? Chase felt a frisson of nerves crawl up his spine. He knew what he was doing with women—kind of, anyway, he'd never pretended to actually be anything other than a total goofball—but with a guy? With *Tate*? God, he felt so out of his element.

He wanted everything, and he didn't know how to even begin getting it.

The waiter appeared then, and even though they hadn't ordered yet, set two appetizer plates in front of them, as well as a glass of what looked to be Chase's favorite beer, whisking away the wineglass Alec had known he wouldn't be using.

"What is this?" Tate asked.

"Mister Alec, he did you the favor of ordering ahead," the waiter said, winking. "The tasting menu."

Tate glanced over at Chase when the waiter departed. "Does your agent usually do stuff like this?"

It was hard to say, because Chase hadn't dragged his agent on a quasi-date before. He shrugged. "He knows this place well, if he thinks we should try the tasting menu, then I trust his judgment."

"I don't usually trust anyone but me when it comes to food but . . ." Tate's eyes fluttered closed in ecstasy as he chewed. "But this is really fucking amazing."

Chase hadn't even looked at the food in front of him. He'd been way too busy looking at Tate. He didn't know much about gourmet meals, but even he could admit that the jewel-toned food, scattered across the plate, looked more like a work of art than a meal.

He picked up his fork and spearing a few bites, had to admit that he might have been wrong. This was absolutely delicious.

"I think Alec is ordering for me from now on," Chase admitted. "Though . . . I'd trust you, too. You know your way around food."

"Not usually in places like this, but yeah, I've got training . . ."

"Training?" Chase's ears perked up. He wanted to know what had happened to a business degree at NYU—and how Tate had ended up running a food truck in Los Angeles instead—but he hadn't known how to ask. Especially when Tate hadn't seemed particularly interested in sharing details of the last ten years.

"You were right, in the end," Tate said, his self-deprecating smile unexpectedly charming. Or maybe it was just Chase who was unbelievably, unexpectedly charmed. "I didn't want to go to New York and get a business degree. I did go to New York, but I didn't stay. By the spring semester, I was more interested in learning all about the city's hole-in-the-wall restaurants and finding the best food I could, and then recreating it at home. I left after that."

"Where'd you go?" Chase wondered.

"Cooking school," Tate said nebulously. Chase wondered why he was being so stingy with the details, but this was supposed to be a date, not an interrogation.

"And then you started the food truck?" Chase asked, as he cleaned his plate.

"A few years after I graduated, my grandmother died, and left Rachel and me some money. We agreed to pool it and use it as seed money for Say Cheese," Tate said.

"So you've been in LA for awhile, then," Chase said. He was beginning to put together a better idea of how Tate had spent the time after they'd parted ways the first time. And he couldn't help but wonder one thing in particular. "You could've looked me up."

Tate looked at him incredulously, his gray eyes darker in the candlelight. "You were a superstar in college. By the time you got to LA, I didn't think you even remembered who I was."

Chase had been afraid of that. "I never wanted to be that kind of guy. The one who craved . . ." He trailed off. Knowing exactly how his years in the NFL made him look.

"Craved attention?"

Chase nodded. "I guess it goes along with the territory. You're good and people pay attention to you, because you've got these freaky athletic gifts, but it's not like I ever sought it out. I wouldn't have wanted it to keep anyone at arm's length."

"I didn't want to be one of those people who decided that since I'd known you in high school, I had any right to you," Tate said quietly.

God, if he only knew.

"You've got all the rights when it comes to me," Chase admitted.

"Even using your name?" Tate wondered.

"Did I sue you?"

Tate shook his head. Like he still couldn't believe it.

"Then, there's your answer. I'm glad we reconnected now, though. Really glad."

"If only because I gave you an excuse to ditch your closet?" Tate joked.

Chase had to wonder what Tate would say if he told him that he was the only reason *for* his closet in the first place. Maybe he still wouldn't be straight, but in the ten years since high school, he'd never met another man who'd made him feel the truth of his sexuality so viscerally.

"That's one reason," Chase admitted.

"I *am* proud of you, you know," Tate said, and the look in his eyes was undeniable. He *was* proud. Chase still wasn't sure of why. He'd just told the truth. More of the truth than either of them was probably comfortable with, but in the end, it was still just the facts.

He wanted Tate to be his boyfriend.

"For coming out?"

"It's never easy, even when you're a superstar. Probably *especially* when you're a superstar," Tate said.

Chase shrugged. "Everyone thought I was anyway, because of who I was friends with."

"I don't care," Tate disagreed. "You should still be *proud*."

"Out and proud?" Chase joked, taking a drink of his beer. "Yeah, I think I've got at least one of those covered."

"Did your friends know?" Tate asked, pouring himself more wine.

"Uh," Chase said.

"I'll take that as a no," Tate said. Regarded Chase like he was one of the most interesting specimens he'd ever encountered. "That must've been a surprise."

"They don't care that I'm bisexual," Chase said.

"I didn't think they would," Tate said. "And someday, well, I guess it seems crazy that I'm even suggesting this, but someday I'd like to meet them."

It had been a given in Chase's mind that Tate would. He'd wanted it to happen not just because his friends were important to him, but because Tate was important to him.

"I think we can arrange that," Chase said.

Tate smiled. "Tony, my friend who's running the food truck lot, he makes a big deal out of Riptide games. He talks about how your team is leading the LGBT community, and he's right. We always meet up to watch, at that bar we were at the other night."

"You watch the games?" It had somehow never occurred to Chase that Tate might have been watching him this whole time. He found that he was . . . *jealous?*

Yeah, definitely a little jealous. He'd have given almost anything to be able to tune in, once a week, to Tate. To see what he was up to.

"Not every single one." Tate sounded almost apologetic, when the truth was, Chase was thrilled he'd watched even *one* game. He knew that in high school, Tate hadn't been much of a sports fan. He'd been smart and driven, and while Chase would admit to a different *kind* of drive, he'd been more than a little intimidated by everything that set Tate apart. He could do anything. What could Chase do? Catch a ball insanely well? Run really fast?

To a lot of people that was everything that was important, even though Chase's abilities had begun as innate skills that he'd developed over time, but he'd always seen Tate's keen intelligence as something of much greater worth.

Which was why it was so unfair that Tate was struggling to make it, and Chase was a multimillionaire.

The waiter appeared again, carrying two plates, which he set in front of Chase and Tate. "Unless there's anything else?" he asked. "Another beer, sir?"

"No, thanks. Just water, please." He was driving and he'd seen and heard way too many horror stories of athletes who thought the rules didn't apply to them. Plus, even if he wanted to endanger himself, he wasn't going to endanger the man sitting next to him.

Tate gestured with his wineglass. "Letting me do all the drinking, huh?"

"Is it good wine?" Chase asked, but he already knew the answer because Tate's eyes, already that dreamy gray, grew even dreamier whenever he took a sip.

"It's fucking amazing wine," Tate said, his voice dropping to just a rough murmur, scraping over Chase's already-sensitive nerves. He dug his fingers into his fabric-clad thigh and tried to remember why he couldn't just climb over the table and pin Tate to the chair, taste the wine on his tongue.

You're not the one who's drinking, he reminded himself, *get a hold of yourself.*

But then Tate took a bite of the short rib on the plate, studded with pomegranate seeds, and moaned quietly, and Chase could genuinely not remember when he had ever wanted someone more.

In so many ways, Tate had always been the man for him—but Chase was beginning to realize it was more than that. They'd formed a connection that had endured, that every person he ever met couldn't quite measure up to. This whole time, when he'd been stuck in fleeting relationships, dates that never went anywhere, he'd wondered if there was something wrong with him. But the truth was, he'd been waiting for Tate.

"Let me guess, that's fucking amazing, too," Chase said, taking a bite of his own. And it was undeniably incredibly delicious, but he was reminded of Tate's own short ribs, and frankly, he thought he liked them better. Maybe that was because of who made them.

"Did you know that pomegranate seeds were considered to be an aphrodisiac?" Tate asked. He was slightly flushed now. With wine? With something else? *God*, Chase's fingers itched to touch him.

Chase's throat went dry. "They were?"

Tate's fork skewered a shining red seed from his plate and he chewed it thoughtfully. "Even now," he said, "pomegranate juice is rumored to increase virility in men."

Chase cleared his throat. He wished the waiter would get back here with his water. He also wished the waiter would take a permanent hiatus and never, ever come back. He couldn't even decide which he wanted more. "I wonder if that's true," he said inanely. With anyone else, he could flirt up and down, frontwards and backwards, but with Tate, who really mattered? He was fucking *hopeless.*

It was a good thing he was hot.

Tate nodded. "Though," he said, his voice lowering even further, his eyes glowing, "I don't think either of us probably need the help. Do you?" His gaze was intent on Chase. So intent Chase suddenly really wanted to know how much he'd had to drink. Was he drunk? Was that why he was flirting again, like they'd never stopped? Chase wanted it to happen, but suddenly he wasn't sure he wanted it to happen like this.

It had been maybe six months since Chase had had sex—he couldn't be quite sure, because it hadn't been particularly memorable. Truthfully, he hadn't even really felt the lack, but right now? Six months felt a lot like ten years.

"Uh," Chase said.

"I didn't think so," Tate said, returning to his food.

The short ribs, which were undoubtedly tender and delicious, tasted a bit like sawdust in his mouth as he ate them, scooped up with tidbits of pomegranate and smears of the sweet potato puree flecked with spices.

Tate poured the rest of the wine into his glass. A bottle of wine, even minus what Alec had drunk, was a lot for one man, and Chase wasn't sure whether to call Alec up and yell at him for ruining the evening by getting Tate drunk or thank him for at least making sure Tate wasn't uncomfortable the entire time.

Because Tate was definitely not uncomfortable, but the way he kept looking at Chase? Like he was starving, and not for food? It was not only making Chase's pants even tighter, it was making him regret the fact that he wasn't going to get the big kiss he'd planned for the end of the night. The last thing he wanted was for Tate to be drunk and not remember it. Not *want* it, especially not the way that Chase did.

The waiter whisked away their plates, replacing them with a tiny little pot of chocolate . . . was that *pudding*?

But before Chase could comment that he'd expect a lot better for dessert than *pudding*, Tate was moaning around the spoon in his mouth again.

"This is *the best thing* I've ever put in my mouth," Tate said.

Chase prayed for fate, for God, for some kind of miracle. "Maybe you're not putting the right things in your mouth," he suggested, because he was unlucky and heavenly intervention was a fleeting thought that, of course, didn't actually materialize.

Tate regarded him thoughtfully, like with all the wine flowing through his system, he was actually considering that suggestion. "You know," he said seriously, "I think you might be right."

Chase was about to damn himself and all his good intentions to hell, when the waiter appeared again. "Any coffee? Cappuccino?" he asked smoothly. Like he wasn't interrupting the hottest moment that Chase had experienced since high school.

Tate laughed, a little self-consciously, and the tension between them broke. "I should probably have something," he said, scrubbing his face with one hand. "That wine . . . that's potent stuff. A cappuccino for me, definitely. Strong, if you can do that."

"Of course, sir," the waiter said, and then turned to Chase.

"Just more water," Chase said. "Thanks."

Chase watched as Tate picked up the thin cookie next to the little cup and took a bite out of it. "This was an incredible meal," he said. He looked like he wanted to say more, but was afraid he'd already said too much.

"I'm glad you enjoyed it."

"I did." Tate hesitated. "And the company."

"You sound surprised," Chase said. And it took his ego down another peg.

"Not surprised, because well, you're *you*," Tate said.

Chase took a bite of the pudding, and discovered that it was dense and rich and absolutely nothing like any pudding he'd ever had. "What does that mean?" he wondered, licking every bit of chocolate off his spoon.

"I thought you'd be bored to tears in a second, and I was worried about well . . . preventing that from happening," Tate confessed.

"Seriously?" Chase couldn't believe it. Bored to tears? "Not likely. Not even close."

"I believe you," Tate said with a smile. "It was . . . it was really nice. We shouldn't wait ten years to do this again."

"I don't think we ever did it ten years ago," Chase said wryly. "Yeah, you fed me, but we never . . ." He'd almost said *we never went on a date*, because that was what this was, wasn't it?

"We never went out like this," Tate finished for him, shooting Chase an amused look. "We didn't. I *wanted* to."

Maybe he was just saying it because of the alcohol in his system, but Chase knew that wasn't true. He'd known back then that they'd had mutual crushes on each other; but it had never gone anywhere because Chase had been way too chickenshit to ever do anything about it.

Now, he wasn't, but Tate had already decided that what they were doing wasn't real.

Well, it felt damn real to Chase.

The waiter brought Tate's coffee, and he drank it down in a couple of gulps.

"Feeling better?" Chase asked as he finished his dessert.

"I wasn't feeling *bad*," Tate teased. "I was feeling maybe a little too good. But I'm fine now, thanks."

Chase paid the bill, and he found himself wondering, as they stood and walked out of the restaurant, if maybe he'd made a tactical error in letting Tate sober up.

But then, when the valet brought the car around, and Chase nimbly stepped in front of him so that this time *he* could be the one to open the car door for Tate, the slightly goofy edge to his grin made it clear that either he *wasn't* entirely sober yet, or maybe this tension, stretching out tight between them, had nothing to do with the wine.

Tate was quiet as Chase drove back to his apartment. "So," Chase said, trying to dig through his memory for his list of small talk subjects he'd compiled. He hadn't tried any of them yet, and it seemed like a waste to let good preparation go unused. "What kind of stuff are you going to teach me this week?"

Tate glanced over at him. "Teach you? Oh, that's right." He grinned. "You're my new employee."

"I can't believe you forgot."

"I was a little distracted," Tate said wryly.

"By tonight?" Chase couldn't believe that even though this had been a very good evening, it had been *that* distracting. Tate was so committed to his food truck, it was hard to see anything else getting in the way.

"Well, yeah," Tate said. "It's not every day that a hot guy picks me up in a hundred-thousand-dollar car and takes me to a high-end restaurant and we share an incredible meal."

"It should be," Chase said firmly. "You deserve that." He'd thought it ten years ago, and he still thought it now.

"Yeah, but it'd get old, right? You want this kind of thing to be special. Besides, there's nothing like a good night of Netflix and chill on the couch."

"Is that still a thing?" Chase wondered.

"It was always a thing, even before it had a name," Tate said firmly. "Next time, popcorn and a really terrible action movie and my couch."

It wasn't that Chase was surprised that Tate was talking about a *next time*, but it certainly made him feel braver as he pulled up to Tate's building. "Here," he said, unbuckling, "let me walk you up."

Tate's smile was wry as he opened the passenger door for him again. "You're more of a gentleman than I expected."

Chase laughed. "I'm going to try very hard not to be offended by that."

"You know what I mean," Tate said, as he hit the button to call the elevator. "You're just . . . well, I don't imagine you dressing up and taking someone out to dinner like this. At least I didn't when I was just watching you on TV." The elevator doors opened and they walked in.

"That's not . . . that's not all of me," Chase said quietly. "I hope you know that."

Tate's eyes were soft, even under the harsh fluorescent lights of the elevator. "I'm beginning to," he said.

The elevator dinged open on the third floor, and they walked out, Chase's heart rate already beginning to accelerate. Should he try to kiss Tate? Should he leave the decision in Tate's hands? He felt torn, and confused, and suddenly they were at Tate's door, and he'd pulled his keys out of his pocket.

"Rachel goes to bed early. She wouldn't leave the door unlocked," he said and glanced up at Chase's face. Was that hope in his eyes? Chase couldn't tell.

He knew what he wanted, but he also didn't want to push. Didn't want to scare Tate away, who'd believed that the only reason Chase had tweeted that was to "help" him.

Chase knew he should say something. Or maybe words were unnecessary, and he should just . . .

"I'm not, I don't . . ." Tate said, but before he could turn away, Chase gave himself a split-second pep talk. The kind of pep talk that on the football field, always resulted in a touchdown.

The kind of pep talk that resulted in Chase's mouth landing squarely on Tate's.

For a second, they both froze. Chase dimly thought, *this isn't what I thought it'd be like, kissing a guy, kissing Tate. It doesn't feel* . . .

And then Tate exhaled, sharply, right into Chase's mouth, their lips slid together again, the angle better, and suddenly it wasn't just another person and another kiss, but this was *Tate* he was kissing, and it was fucking everything. All the fireworks, all the explosions, all the fire racing up his veins and all that other nonsense that he'd kept expecting to feel all these years, except he'd never quite gotten there.

He was there right now. His arms snaked around Tate's torso and yanked him firmly against him. Right where he should've been ten years ago, if Mrs. Mary hadn't interrupted them in the pantry, and right where he belonged *now*.

Dimly he heard moaning, but he wasn't sure if it was Tate or if it was *him*. Chase didn't know, and he didn't want to stop kissing Tate to find out. Instead he pressed him closer, pushing Tate up against the door, finding another angle and then another, each one more incandescent than the last. Tate's foot snaked up his leg, aligning them and suddenly, *yes*, that was Tate's cock he felt, a hot, hard line against his thigh, and it was like a bomb went off in his brain. Self-control, already slipping, went totally fucking AWOL.

"Fuck," Chase groaned as he shifted Tate a little to the right and their cocks lined up, rubbing against each other. This was everything he hadn't quite understood that he wanted but it was undeniable now. He wanted this, and he wanted this man. Badly.

Yes, they were now dry humping in a semi-public hallway, where anyone could walk by and see, but Chase's *give a fuck*, already mostly gone, had been totally incinerated by the feeling of Tate's mouth on his.

But then, abruptly it wasn't.

Chase opened his eyes, and Tate was looking away, breathing as hard as if he'd just run a marathon.

Chase didn't think his own breathing was very steady either.

"Well," Tate said, and his eyes caught Chase's. They were wild, the pupils almost swallowing the gray.

Chase swallowed hard. He didn't know *what* to say, only that he should say something. Could he say, *that only took ten years?*

He was still considering it when Tate said, "Well," again, followed by the worst words in the human language. "Good night."

Chase opened his mouth, about to say *what?* when abruptly the door opened, swallowing Tate, and leaving Chase staring at the wood, wondering what the fuck had just happened.

CHAPTER SEVEN

"So how was the big date?" Rachel smirked at him over the rim of her coffee cup as she sat at their little kitchen table. Tate shuffled into the kitchen, grabbed a mug of his own—the biggest they owned—and poured himself a cup, leaving it black as he slumped down in the chair opposite his sister.

It had been the best date of his life, and a restless, sleepless night after, because he hadn't been able to stop himself from going over every second of it. Every soft look, every flirtatious glance, even how Chase had sounded so incredibly interested in what Tate had been up to. There had been so many things that Tate wanted to ask Chase about—but he'd been terrified of giving away just how closely he'd been following him over the years. It wouldn't even be a stretch to imagine that Tate knew more about Chase's career than Chase did.

And then there was the kiss. *The* Kiss. The best goddamn kiss he'd ever had in his whole life.

"That good, huh?" Rachel teased. "I would ask why you look like hell, but either it went *really* well and that's why you didn't sleep, or it went horrible and you stayed up all night angsting about it."

"It . . ." Even after his sleepless night, Tate still wasn't sure *how* it had gone. He'd had a really good time. The wine and the food had been spectacular, and the company just as amazing. Why was he feeling dissatisfied?

Probably because a date that great deserved a kiss that blew the top of your head off, altered your entire world, and left you thinking about it for months—for *years*—afterward. He'd actually gotten it but instead of enjoying it, he'd freaked out.

"It was good," Tate finally said. "It was really good. I mean . . . you saw him."

Rachel smiled. "Oh, I did. I'm impressed you didn't turn into a puddle right there at the doorway."

"I considered it." *Twice.* When he'd first seen Chase, and then after dinner, when Chase had walked him to his door and he'd sworn they both wanted it so bad it had felt like the air between them was sizzling with it, and then it had actually happened, and reality had dwarfed every single fantasy he'd ever had.

"But then," Rachel said thoughtfully, "he was pretty puddle-like when you showed up, too."

Should've seen him after we kissed.

"Sure," Tate said, but even despite that incendiary kiss, he still wasn't sure he believed that Chase Riley could be into *him*.

She rose, elbowing him in the side, as she got up to get more coffee.

"Ouch, what was that for?" Tate asked.

He could feel her eye roll from across the kitchen. "For not thinking you're worth that kind of attention. You were, and you are, and if Chase Riley can see it, then he's smarter than I gave him credit for."

"We're *fake dating,* remember?" Tate said. Reminding her. Reminding himself. That kiss sure as hell hadn't felt *fake.*

"Oh, I remember. But do you?" Rachel asked.

"I'm trying to," Tate said. *But,* he thought, *it's not like you're trying very hard.*

"Yeah, you and him both, for some ridiculous reason," Rachel said. "Are you really going to have him work with us?"

"He offered and you know we could use the extra help," Tate said weakly.

Rachel looked dubious. "If this is an excuse to flirt with each other all day, I will hurt you, slowly."

She was totally capable of it. Tate gulped some more of his coffee. "I know," he said. "And we won't be. He just . . . he wants to help. Is that so wrong?"

"It's not wrong," Rachel said. "I just don't want to end up holding the short end of the third wheel stick."

"You won't. This isn't a romantic thing. Not even close."

Rachel didn't look convinced. Which made sense, because Tate hadn't even managed to convince himself.

"I'm meeting him at the truck today," Tate said, glancing at his watch. "We're going to do a little bit of training."

"Aw," Rachel said. "Another date!"

"It's not a date," Tate stressed. "It's work *training*."

"You tell yourself whatever you need to," Rach teased. "But we know the truth. You finally got what you wanted, and now you can't wait to get a little more."

"That isn't true at all." And that actually *wasn't* a lie, because he might've gotten a taste—and a damn good taste it had been—but he hadn't even gotten close to everything he really wanted.

"Sure," Rachel said in a singsong voice. "Well, you enjoy yourself."

"I will," Tate ground out. But as he finished his coffee and stood, stretching, to go take a shower, he found himself smiling in anticipation. Because even if he convinced Chase that they couldn't indulge in more kisses that re-adjusted time and space as he'd known it, he'd still enjoy his time with Chase.

Because he was Chase.

They typically parked the Say Cheese truck a few blocks away from their loft in an industrial parking lot, and Tate liked to walk there most mornings. He also had the good fortune that there was a fantastic coffee shop on the way, which encouraged him to get the exercise on mornings he didn't want to. After picking up a pair of large coffees, Tate made it to the truck with a few minutes to spare. Just as he was unlocking the truck's door, he saw Chase, distinctive blond hair flowing out from under his helmet, pull up next to the curb, riding a sleek matte black motorcycle that looked like it cost more than Tate saw in a year.

Chase pulled his helmet off, shaking out his hair, and Tate's mouth went dry.

He'd been so ready to forget the kiss, to move on, but it was hard, especially when Chase looked like *that*.

"Hey," Chase said, jogging over after tucking his helmet under an arm. "Am I late?" He grinned. "Don't wanna be late for my first day. Good impressions and all that bullshit."

Tate knew he was standing there, staring at Chase, with one hand still on the door and the other juggling the two coffees.

Move, you look like a star-crossed idiot, Tate barked at himself. *And whatever you do, don't kiss him again.*

The problem was he *was* a star-crossed idiot and he also desperately wanted to kiss Chase again.

"Hey," Tate said when he unstuck his mouth. He fumbled with the door, finally getting it open. "No, no, you're not late. I'm . . . well, I'm early, I guess."

"A little eager, huh?" Chase said, his eyes crinkling with the brightness of his smile. "I can understand that."

"What?" Tate stuttered. He had been but was it that obvious? *Oh, god.* Was Chase going to bring up the kiss already? It had been less than sixty seconds.

"After . . . well . . . after that kiss and you just . . . evaporating, I wondered if we would still be on," Chase said, and he was still smiling. Like he already knew *why* Tate had done his little disappearing act.

"Why wouldn't we be?" Tate said.

"I thought you might be over-thinking everything. I just thought . . ." Chase shrugged. "I wanted to do that ten years ago in the pantry, but Mrs. Mary walked in. Last night, I thought, why not try it?"

"Try it?" Tate knew he was repeating everything Chase was saying, like a total moron, but there were no other thoughts currently in his head. Or blood in his brain, for that matter.

"Yeah, well, I came out of the closet. I figured I should at least know what it feels like to kiss a guy." Chase looked bashful now, like he hadn't wanted to be caught out.

"You hadn't kissed a guy before?" Tate inhaled sharply. He'd been the first. The very first. "I guess I can't really blame you for wanting to see what it's like."

Before he could ask Chase how it was—if he'd loved it, if he'd hated it—he set his own coffee down and handed the other cup to Chase. He needed something to do with his hands and his mouth that wasn't putting them all over the man in front of him.

"Coffee?"

"Oh, you're a fucking star," Chase said, taking a long sip. "This is good, too."

"There's this little coffee shop on my walk here, and well, it gets me out of bed some days," Tate admitted.

"There's two things that wake me up," Chase said, his voice dropping, his eyes glowing sugary brown in the morning sunlight. "Good coffee and good sex."

"Uh," Tate said. *I can give you both. So much coffee you're wired for a month. Enough sex that you wouldn't ever want to leave the bed.*

"Guessing you only brought one of those today," Chase said with a knowing smirk.

"Uh," Tate repeated helplessly. There was that *no blood in the brain* problem again.

"Thought so," Chase said smugly. "It's okay. I forgive you."

"Well, it'd be weird to be carrying sex around," Tate said dryly, finding his voice.

Chase tipped the coffee cup at him. "Might get you arrested," he said, and then they were staring at each other again.

Was Chase thinking about the kissing? Tate sure as fuck was. And now thanks to Chase, Tate was thinking about sex, too.

He remembered how Rachel had promised him a slow and painful death if he and Chase spent all their work time flirting with each other. If she could see them now, he'd be in major danger.

"Well, we should get started," Tate said awkwardly. "I'm sure you've got lots of things to do today . . ."

Chase shrugged. "Not really. It's the off-season. When my trainer isn't torturing me, I'm kinda at a loose end. I think you're actually doing *me* a favor."

Climbing the stairs, Tate threw a dubious look over his shoulder as Chase followed him. "I sincerely doubt that," Tate said. "And if you really think that, you are about to be re-educated about what working in a food truck is really like."

"Oh wow," Chase said, looking around the truck like it was fantastic and wonderful. Like Tate hadn't just issued a warning. "I didn't realize you could fit so much stuff in such a small space. This is fucking great."

Tate nearly told him to stop, to pay attention, but he was already paying attention, just to everything else around him, picking tools up, and putting them back down, examining everything. Finally, he looked back at Tate. "You've really built something here," he said. "I'm proud of you."

"Thanks, but it wasn't just me," Tate said, even though Chase's words sounded so sweet. "Rachel was a big part of it too. She deserves at least fifty-one percent of the credit."

"Fifty-one?" Chase was smiling again. It had always done something to the base of Tate's stomach, to see that smile, but now? The fluttering butterflies had become a whole goddamned flock. Or maybe a raging inferno.

Tate shrugged. "It was her idea."

"She gets one percent for the idea?" Chase laughed with delight.

"In my defense, I'd been making grilled cheeses for a long time," Tate said, all too aware that suddenly they were flirting again, and they weren't in front of his door after a spectacular date, they were crammed together in his food truck, Chase not even two feet away as he leaned against the back counter.

"Since high school. I think I ate your very first grilled cheese sandwich," Chase said. And maybe he had. There was a reason Tate had spent so many years perfecting it. Not only was it the best food in the world, and could have a thousand different variations, every time he made one, there was a tiny corner of his mind that thought: *Chase Riley*.

"Maybe we should add that to our marketing," Tate said wryly.

"Anything you want," Chase said, his voice eager.

If *everything* was on the table, Tate definitely wasn't going to stop at marketing sound bites about the long-ago past. He'd be *doing* something he hadn't been able to do back then.

"What I want is an employee that knows what he's doing." *Work now, play later*, Tate told himself firmly. He set his coffee down on the front counter. "First thing, put your hair back. I think I'll let you forgo the hairnet."

"Hairnet? Yuck," Chase said, pulling his hair back and twisting it up as competently as Rachel did.

Chase's hair was easily one of his most glorious assets, but without it as a distraction, his chiseled features got all the attention, and Tate felt his breath catch as Chase smiled. "Better?" he asked.

Tate nodded. "And an apron, you always have to have an apron." He pulled out the one he'd grabbed from home and rolled up, shoving it in his back pocket for the walk over.

Taking it, Chase unrolled the apron, eying it suspiciously. "I thought you'd want me to serve shirtless or something," he suggested, shooting Tate that addicting teasing smile.

"Yeah, no," Tate said. Imagined Rachel's reaction. Imagined his *own* reaction. He shook his head. "That wouldn't be safe. We've got hot oil back here. Wouldn't want to leave any permanent scars."

"Have to save it for a safer place, then," Chase said. He stretched out the apron—Tate had bought them originally for Rachel, who was small-boned and short—and on Chase it looked like a kid's apron.

"Well," Tate said, trying to hold back his laughter. "Maybe it won't get you *positive* attention . . ."

Chase laughed too, obviously good-natured about the whole thing. Which, *duh, Tate,* that voice reminded him, *he's working here during the off-season, when he makes millions of dollars a year.*

"Maybe we can find a bigger one?"

"I'll order one," Tate said, chuckling. He imagined that Chase would give the apron back then, but he persisted in maneuvering the much-too-small apron over his head and, to Tate's amusement, tied it around his waist, even as he dwarfed the rest of it.

"My very own apron!" Chase sounded delighted. "That's so kickass."

"The things you find exciting baffle me," Tate said, turning to make a note on his running to-do list.

"It's like a uniform, though, and we all know what a uniform means."

"That you get paid millions of dollars? I hate to disappoint you, but that's not happening here," Tate pointed out wryly.

"No, though that's a nice bonus." Chase's voice went serious. "A uniform means that you *belong*."

Tate had a hard time imagining a place that Chase didn't belong, maybe because he'd seemed so comfortable in his skin back in high school, when the rest of them had been only passingly familiar with who they really were. As the years had passed, that confidence had only grown, until Chase seemed comfortable everywhere. Scoring touchdowns on the football field, in a children's hospital doing charity work, on a Hollywood red carpet posing for a thousand cameras. Even dancing drunk, by himself, at the victory party that hadn't been very victorious.

But Chase's words had been grave and very, very sure, and Tate couldn't help but wonder if he'd been guilty of what so many others were guilty of: seeing Chase and therefore thinking that they *knew* him.

Then he thought: *Chase Riley is almost thirty years old, and he's just now kissed a guy for the first time. Even though he wanted to.* And suddenly, Tate thought maybe he hadn't known Chase as well as he'd thought he did.

"It's like this," Chase said, leaning closer, his fingers brushing the edges of Tate's beanie, embroidered with the Say Cheese logo. "Means we're part of a team. *Together.*"

There was a very persistent part of Tate's heart that leapt at his words. He pushed it back down again. This was not the time to start thinking that there was more to their fake relationship than there really was.

This is work time, Tate reminded himself. *Think of the gagging noises that Rachel's gonna make if Chase starts talking sappily about teamwork while she's around.*

"Okay, so first two items. Hair back, apron on," Tate said. "Third item. Orders." He pushed a printed sheet across the counter, and Chase came even closer, right into Tate's space, to examine it. "This is the menu. Be familiar with it."

"It's my playbook. I got it, Coach," Chase said, flashing him a set of very white, very even teeth. "Can I borrow this?"

"It's yours," Tate said. "Now, part of taking orders is actually *taking* the order. The other part? Moving people along efficiently. Even though the menu is on the side of the truck, big enough anyone can read it, I can't tell you how many times people will get to the front of the line and have no idea what to order."

"People are idiots," Chase said succinctly.

"You have no idea," Tate said. "Unfortunately, we've got to serve them anyway. The trick is to move them along without it seeming like you're rushing them."

"You'd be really good at that," Chase said, shooting him another disarming smile.

"I would?" He *was* actually. Rachel was a touch too impatient sometimes, and knew it, but showed zero interest in actually getting better at it. Tate told himself her brusqueness was part of her charm.

"Yeah," Chase said, nodding. "You've got a knack for making everyone think they matter. Obviously they don't *all* matter, but every single person who ordered from you the other night, at the brewery? They all came away with a smile on their face."

"That's because I was feeding them grilled cheese and macaroni and cheese," Tate pointed out. "Two items that not only contain *melted cheese* but are basically impossible to eat while being disgruntled."

"It's not just that," Chase insisted. "You're giving them a little bit of happiness each time they order. They might be coming to Say Cheese to see me, but they're going to be coming back for *you*."

"They're going to be coming back because they liked the food," Tate said dryly.

"Yeah, and *you*," Chase said firmly. "So teach me your ways, oh magical one."

Tate rolled his eyes, but as he went through his regular process, step by step, with Chase, he couldn't help but be pleased by what he'd said.

"So I enter everything into the iPad and that sends it to your screen over there?" Chase asked, pointing to the second screen set up above the back counter.

"Yeah, but I don't always look at it," Tate confessed. "So, it'd be helpful if you called out the orders too."

"You can keep track of that? In your head?"

"You keep track of an entire playbook, right?" Tate asked.

"Well, *yeah*, but that's different. I've got months to memorize it. You've got what, a few seconds?"

"I worked in a lot of high-end restaurants in Portland after I graduated from culinary school, and you either figured that shit out or you got fired," Tate said.

Chase's eyes grew big and that was when Tate realized that he'd just said the one thing that he'd sworn to himself he would *not* say.

"You were . . ." Chase swallowed, and Tate watched as his Adam's apple bobbed. "You were in Portland? That's where you went to culinary school?"

Yep. He'd gone straight from New York, a place that after a little while, he'd discovered he didn't really belong, to Portland, Oregon. To the same state that Chase was in. Not the same city, because Eugene didn't have the kind of training he was looking for plus Tate had decided that he was already stalking his high school crush enough as it was.

But going to Portland had been good. He'd loved the food culture there, and though that had been the best part, Tate had also loved how much Oregonians loved their football, and how much they loved their University of Oregon football. And they'd loved Chase most of all. Sometimes Tate hadn't been able to walk down the street without seeing a Chase Riley jersey out of the corner of his eye.

It had made him feel like Chase was there and close enough to touch, instead of a couple hundred miles away, with no idea that Tate was in Oregon.

"Yeah," Tate said tightly. He hadn't wanted Chase to ever know, but he could see now that probably it was inevitable that he'd find out his big secret.

"You were in Oregon, and you never told me." Chase sounded disbelieving. Hurt. "You . . . I can't believe you wouldn't tell me."

"I didn't really think we were that close of friends." That was the truth, but it had stung back then and it still stung now.

Chase stared at him. "But we could've been."

"Yeah, no," Tate said. "What was I supposed to do? Reach out on Facebook? Say, Hey, by the way, I happened to end up down the road from you. We should hang out."

What he didn't want to say was, *I didn't want to just be friends, and back then? That's all we could've been.*

"Yes." Chase's gorgeous face was creased in a frown. "*Yes.*"

Tate turned away, because everything was hurting, and he didn't know if he could hide it, and he didn't want Chase to see.

"I was so stupid. I kept hoping . . . this thing between us might *be* something, even though I knew better, even though I knew you were going places. And I was too, but *different* places," he said.

"But then, we never ran into each other again, and nothing ever came of it, and it took a long time, but I finally sort of got that through my head. Then you show up here and want to know why I didn't . . ." Tate took a deep breath, and then looked up at Chase, who'd taken another step closer. His eyes were still warm. As warm as they'd been last night, a soft amber brown that Tate had spent the last ten years wishing he could get lost in.

"I didn't look you up when I moved to Portland because I was afraid this would happen. And I was afraid it wouldn't happen." Tate cleared his throat. "Now we should . . . get back to work."

"You wanted to know why I kissed you last night; that was why. I thought of Mrs. Mary, and that stupid dark pantry, and I thought, *I should've done it anyway.*"

There was a part of Tate that wanted to inform him—clearly and with no chance for misunderstanding—that he shouldn't have done it at all. Because now he knew what Chase tasted like, and Tate couldn't imagine a world where he didn't want more.

"Well, it happened," Tate said. "You did it, and it happened, and we can . . ." He didn't know what they could do now. His mind was still fucking blank.

"We can move on?" Chase sounded amused, like he already knew that there was no moving on from that kiss. And there wasn't. Tate had already realized that. "Sure."

"Sure. Right. Yes." Tate turned his attention back to the menu. "Let's talk about serving."

Chase leaned against the counter. "I get to serve the food too?"

"I told you that you weren't going to love this job," Tate said. "It's a lot of work."

"Oh, I'm not upset about it. I'm . . . well, best way to describe it: fucking *thrilled*." Chase was grinning again.

Tate rolled his eyes. "Tell me again how thrilled you are when we have a line of fifty people waiting for their food, and your feet hurt and your back hurts and you wish that everyone would just go away."

"Awww, you really *do* need help," Chase said. "Now, what's this about serving? How do I do it?"

Tate went over each item on the menu, what it got served *with*, and then he got to the last item, which was the roasted tomato soup. "This is the soup carafe," he said, indicating the large metal warmer that kept the soup hot. "You'll dish up the soup into one of these bowls, leaving an inch from the top, and then sprinkle the parmesan parsley mix on, we keep that in this small container here," he said, pointing to a small translucent plastic container, currently clean and empty. "Then, it'll go on the tray with the rest of the items, when those are ready."

"Hold up," Chase said. "I get to make the soup?"

"Well, you're not *making it*, we've already done that, but we're just keeping it warm here, and you get to ladle it up and put the topping on, yeah," Tate said.

A huge grin broke out on Chase's face. An excitement that Tate wasn't sure *anyone* could fake. "This is so cool."

But even if it was hard to pretend that level of excitement, Tate couldn't quite believe it. Maybe because he'd been doing this job for the last three years, and while he wouldn't trade it for anything, because all of this was *his*, it was also back-breaking, sweaty, painful work sometimes.

So is playing football, Tate reminded himself.

Still, he had to ask. "You're . . ." Took a deep breath. "You're serious, right? You actually really want to do this? You're not putting me on?"

Chase's handsome face creased into a frown. "What?"

"You're just . . . so excited. That's not my usual experience with food service," he added wryly.

"Shouldn't we always be passionate about what we're doing?" Chase wondered.

Chase had always been a little bit naive—his way paved from youth, the golden boy who could do no wrong, who was destined for all the great things. Tate couldn't say it wasn't an accomplishment that he'd done all of them, and more, but his way had always been paved.

"We should, yeah, but sometimes we have to pay the bills, too," Tate said.

"You think if I had to do this for work, like for actual money, day in and day out, I wouldn't like it as much," Chase said, eyes shrewd.

A lot of people assumed Chase Riley was some big dumb jock. They would be wrong—and it would be their risk to underestimate him.

"No, I don't think you would," Tate said.

"Well, I don't know about that. I know how goddamned lucky I've been. Don't worry about that. I'm not . . . like one of those guys who thinks they should get everything they want just because they're rich and famous and catch a ball for a living," Chase said, and suddenly, those sparkling eyes were hard, like rocks. "I'm not like that."

He was here, wasn't he? Tate thought. He'd shown up, during his time off, and was willing to do this job because while yes, he might have a slightly optimistic view of it, he was doing it because he could, and because he knew Tate needed help. It wasn't the most selfless action in the world, but it wasn't the most selfish, either.

Tate could live with it, if Chase could.

"I know you're not," Tate agreed. "If I thought you were, you wouldn't be here. I wouldn't have . . ." *kissed you.* The problem with moving past the kiss was that he just couldn't. He'd known that, even as he'd said it, and Chase had known it too. That much was obvious.

"Wouldn't have kissed me?" Chase asked, his voice dropping low and taking on a gravelly edge that made Tate light-headed. He knew from Chase's voice and his nearness and his face: they were going to do this again. They were going to do this twice. Three times. A hundred times. A thousand.

Maybe he'd even figure out how not to run away afterwards.

CHAPTER EIGHT

IT HAD BEEN EASY enough to let Tate wind himself into knots over the whole kissing incident last night, because even though he claimed it was done, and they were moving past it, the way Tate's eyes followed his every movement, the way he couldn't stop looking at him, made it obvious that he didn't believe it any more than Chase did.

He'd known they'd kiss again. He'd hoped it would be today. He hadn't known it would be so soon—or so sweet.

Chase tucked his hand around Tate's neck, astonished at the smoothness of the skin just below his hairline, the softness of the hair peeking out from under his beanie, and tugged Tate against him. Reveling in just the feeling of closeness, when he'd wanted it for so goddamned long, before he dipped his head and their lips brushed again.

It was softer and sweeter, the second time. Instead of just being shocked that it was happening at all, Chase could enjoy it, could savor the way Tate melted against him, the way he moaned when Chase yanked his beanie off and threaded his fingers through his hair.

It wasn't like kissing a woman, but Chase had a feeling it wouldn't be like kissing any other man, either.

Tate groaned again and suddenly the kiss went from soft and tentative to something much hotter, much wilder, as Tate pushed him against the counter and his mouth moved urgently, desperately against Chase's.

This time it was Chase who broke away. He felt overwhelmed. Dizzy, almost, with the possibilities. *Want* had somehow evolved into *need*, and that was so unusual—so unusual that Chase couldn't remember the last time it had happened—that he felt like he needed a minute to breathe. To figure his shit out.

Tate stared at him. Licked his lips. Chase almost leaned in and kissed them again but reminded himself that they couldn't just go at it here in Tate's food truck. Well, they *could*, but he had a feeling that would be a bad idea that Tate would absolutely regret later, and if Chase had any plan here, it was to make sure that Tate didn't regret a single thing.

Could never turn to him and say, *I wish we hadn't done that.*

If that ever happened, Chase was terrified that he'd lose Tate, once and for all.

No, they needed to keep this light, keep this playful, keep it on Tate's terms, until he came to the realization he couldn't live without Chase in his life.

"We did that again," Tate said. Not accusatory. Just . . . contemplative. Like he'd surprised himself.

"I have a feeling we're going to keep doing it," Chase offered up along with a wry smile. Like he was also surprised—though nothing could be further from the truth. He'd felt that pull between them ten years ago, and seeing Tate last week again had only proven that it had never really passed.

Tate sighed. "I think you might be right." There was an uncertainty in his gray eyes, questions that Chase never wanted him to ask.

"I might be new at this . . ." Chase said, waving between them, "but I know enough to know that it's not a bad thing."

"If it feels good, we should do it?" Tate asked, even though Chase was pretty sure it was just a rhetorical question. Of course it felt good—why else would they keep doing it?

Chase nodded. "Yeah, something like that."

"What about . . ." Tate took a deep breath. "What about the whole fake relationship thing?"

"That's for them, for the rest of the world. Why can't this be for us?" Chase wanted Tate to want this just as much as he did, so he had to push back his desire to charm Tate into agreeing.

"I can think of a lot of reasons it shouldn't be," Tate said, still hesitant. He was gripping the edge of the stainless steel countertop, the white cast to his knuckles betraying how anxious this conversation was making him.

"How about this, instead. I've never been with a guy before, and I want to know what it's like."

"You want to know what it's like?" Tate's voice sounded strangled.

"Well, I've got some of the basics down. Porn came in pretty handy," Chase teased. "But maybe I'd like to experience them for myself."

Tate was still looking at him like he was crazy. And he might be. Maybe he should just be honest and put all his cards on the table. But if he did, what would Tate say? Maybe he'd just run away, the way he'd run away last night.

"So you want us to be in a fake relationship for the public, and fuck in private?"

"If fucking is on the table, then *yes*," Chase said. It wasn't even nearly everything he wanted, but he was willing to take what he could get, for now. Some of Tate had to be better than none of him.

"Okay," Tate said. "But only because we can't stop kissing each other, and that might be a problem."

Chase didn't think it was a problem at all, but he wasn't about to say that now, especially not when Tate had actually agreed to the plan.

"When can we start?" Chase asked, because his cock was hard and he wasn't even going to try to pretend he wasn't eager to get his hands on Tate and feel his hands in return.

Tate rolled his eyes. "Not right now. I have to work here, long after you're gone, and I don't need to be assaulted by images of us fucking in my truck."

"Assaulted?" Chase grinned. "I kinda assumed they'd be good memories."

Tate smiled back, and something hard and uneasy in Chase's chest began to unwind, slowly. "Okay, the assault would almost definitely originate with Rachel, if she found out that we fucked in the truck."

"Noted," Chase said. Reached up and smoothed down a tuft of Tate's hair that he'd twisted around his fingers. Had no idea where Tate's beanie had gone. He'd lost it, along with the rest of his mind, apparently.

"But . . ." Tate looked like he was wavering. Right on the edge of giving in. It was tough not to push for exactly what he wanted, but Chase could see some advantages to waiting.

For example, there was a total lack of comfortable surfaces in the truck.

"Why don't we get some lunch after we're done with this?" Chase suggested. It wasn't the sexiest suggestion he'd ever made, but maybe taking some of the pressure off might relax Tate some.

Made it feel more natural. More *right*.

Less like practice for some other guy.

Tate looked surprised, which just proved Chase had come close to nearly fucking this up, after all. "Lunch?"

"Lunch. More eating and drinking and less . . ."

"Less sexy metaphors?" Tate said, chuckling. He leaned down and plucked his beanie from the floor. "I guess we could do that."

"But first," Chase said, "I came here to be trained, and I don't think I've been properly trained unless I know how to make a grilled cheese sandwich."

Tate looked dubious, probably remembering all the times in Home Economics when Chase had set food on fire.

"That's not what . . ." Tate hesitated, like he really didn't want to tell Chase no, which warmed his heart.

"Don't worry, I know. I'm not going to be actually cooking anything for anyone. I get it. I just . . ." Chase shrugged. "I want to learn how. And maybe I want the master to teach me," he added in a teasing voice.

"Oh, I'll teach you alright." Tate smirked. "Get your virgin ass over here," he said, gesturing to the griddle. He fiddled with some controls, and Chase felt the wide surface begin to heat up. "First thing," he said, "get the griddle hot but not too hot—we don't want the bread to burn." He reached down and grabbed a loaf of bread from a drawer underneath the flat top griddle. "Here," he told Chase, "open this while I get the rest of the ingredients."

Chase did as he was told, carefully opening the clip and taking out two pieces of bread, and then re-sealing the package back up. "Here you go," he said, handing Tate the bread after he'd set two food storage containers down on the counter next to them.

"Perfect," Tate said. He opened each container, and grabbing a spatula, smeared one substance over one side of both pieces of bread. "This is usually kept at room temperature, but it's a combo of a couple of different things—butter, for one, and a little mayo, and a little olive oil to keep it spreadable. Plus, seasonings, herbs, garlic. That kind of thing. We wanted something that would give the bread flavor and would melt and crust up perfectly, and Rach and I eventually came up with this."

Tate slapped one piece of bread onto the griddle. "Now, this is yours," he said, passing the spatula to Chase, who took it uncertainly. He was comfortable with a football in his hands, but definitely not any kind of kitchen utensil. *But you asked for this*, he reminded himself, *you want to learn. You want Tate to teach you. So many different things.*

"Where's the cheese?" Chase asked, wondering why he would need this rubber implement to deal with Say Cheese's distinctive and famous grilled cheese filling.

Tate opened the other container, and to Chase's surprise, it wasn't just shreds of cheese, or slices. It was another mixture. "We experimented with the filling too. Well," he said, shooting Chase a lopsided smile, "actually that was me, long before Rachel suggested starting the truck. I discovered that shredded cheese melted better than sliced cheese, but it also got everywhere, so I used cream cheese to keep it all together, and it also gave me the opportunity to mix a bunch of different kinds of cheese in." He passed Chase the container. "Just slather it all over the bread that's on the grill."

Hesitatingly, Chase used the rubber spatula to take a big scoop and discovered that it was harder than it looked to smear it all over the bread that was already toasting.

"Yeah, get to the sides." Chase glanced over at Tate, who was smiling. "You got it," he finally said approvingly.

Chase was not sure of that—he was fairly certain he'd torn the bread in at least one spot with his overly enthusiastic spreading technique—but he also hadn't set anything on fire yet, so he'd take Tate's praise.

"Now, we put the other piece of bread on," Tate instructed, and Chase carefully set it down on top of the cheese mixture. Tate had confiscated the spatula and used it now, sliding it expertly between the hot cooktop and the bread. "It needs another minute. The trick is to get the bread perfectly browned and crisp, and the cheese melted. When this is hot and we're going through twenty, thirty grilled cheese an hour, that's usually right after I get the cheese spread on, but this isn't quite hot enough yet."

"Is making sure the grill is preheated some kind of sexy metaphor?" Chase wondered, nudging Tate's shoulder with his own.

Tate's smile was brilliant. "No, but it *could* be."

"Noted," Chase said, smiling back. God, he *loved* this.

"Okay, time to flip," Tate said, handing him back the spatula.

Chase looked at it suspiciously. "You want me to do it?"

"You said you wanted to learn how to make a grilled cheese, this is a big part of making the *best* grilled cheese. The perfect flip."

"Geez, no pressure," Chase muttered.

"Feeling a little performance anxiety?" Tate teased. "I know you can do it. You've got a good follow-through."

"Do I?" Chase wondered as he slid the spatula underneath the bread. He flicked his wrist and, thankfully, the sandwich landed on the other side, just a little crooked.

"See, nothing to worry about," Tate said. "You did great."

A minute later, the cheese was oozing out the sides, and Chase was getting hungry. And not just for grilled cheese.

Tate expertly flicked the spatula, the sandwich landing on a cutting board, and he whipped out a knife, slicing it diagonally.

He took a bite, chewed and swallowed, smiling the whole time. "Delicious," he said. "You're an expert now."

Chase took the other half and demolished it in two bites. He was *definitely* hungry now. "Closer than I was before, maybe," he acknowledged. "Thanks for teaching me."

"Hey, it's for me too. It's not outside the realm of possibility that we'll get slammed and need more help. You knowing how to do this is a good thing."

"What about knowing how to do this?" Chase wondered and leaned down, kissing Tate again because he was close and *there* and ultimately irresistible.

Chase could taste the sandwich, the sharp tang of the melted cheese, the butter from the bread, and underneath it, something darker and richer. *It's Tate*, he thought, before the heat flaring between them sucked him under.

"Yeah," Tate said breathlessly after they'd pulled apart. "Yeah, you don't need any help with that. None whatsoever."

"Ready to go grab some lunch? 'Cause I'm *starving*," Chase said, nudging him again.

"Yeah, let me just clean up a bit and lock up, and then we can go."

"Good. I'll get the engine heated up," Chase said, and left before Tate could squawk in protest that he wasn't going to ride that death trap motorcycle anywhere.

But to Chase's surprise, when Tate walked outside after locking up, he eyed Chase on the motorcycle, holding out the helmet in Tate's direction, and smiled so wide that it hit Chase right in the solar plexus.

"I can't believe you've convinced me to do this," Tate said wryly as he took the helmet and strapped it on. Chase had half-expected him to argue, to insist that if Chase wasn't going to wear one, that he wouldn't either, but he hadn't.

"Ride a motorcycle with me?" Chase slung a leg across the seat and felt rather than saw Tate do the same, in a surprisingly expert motion.

"No," Tate said, his voice muffled from the helmet. "Take the afternoon off."

"You've turned into a workaholic, you know?" Chase said. He hesitated, wondering how he should tell Tate to hold on tight. But before he could even compose the words, Tate's arms were snaking around his middle, holding on firmly to his waist, pressed hip to shoulder. It was still warm even though it was February, and Tate was wearing a light jacket, but he could still feel the warmth of him through it and his own t-shirt.

"I kinda had to be," Tate pointed out.

As Chase pushed off from the curb, the engine roaring to life underneath him, he found himself making a vow—that he would do what he could to make Tate's life a little easier. And not just for the next month, either.

He drove up the hilly roads towards the taco stand, and noticed that Tate seemed completely comfortable and relaxed, his arms holding tightly but not flinching or tightening when Chase went around a particularly sharp turn.

Pulling the bike into the gravel parking lot, Chase parked it in an empty spot, and finally got to ask the question that was on his mind. "You've ridden a motorcycle before, haven't you?" Chase asked, smiling. Why had he expected that Tate would be clinging like a damsel in distress? Even when he'd taken Chase's name and used it to bring attention to his food truck, he'd been willing to accept the consequences. He hadn't even wanted to tell Chase why he'd done it. Tate was one of the most fiercely independent people Chase knew.

"Yeah, I owned one when I lived in Portland." Tate's voice held a note of regret. "Sold it when I moved down here."

"That's too bad," Chase said as they walked towards the taco stand. It was a sunny Sunday afternoon, still a little chilly considering how Los Angeleans liked their warmer temperatures, but nice enough that a whole flock of people had turned out for lunch.

"Wow, this place is packed," Tate observed as they took in the long line.

"Best tacos in LA, no offense to your friend Tony," Chase said.

"Hey," Tate said, squinting in the sun. "Isn't that . . ."

Chase had wondered how Tate would react when he realized Chase had brought him here for more than just the admittedly fantastic tacos. Would he freak out? Insist they leave? Embrace the opportunity to meet Chase's friends? He hadn't been sure.

"Oh," he said, deciding to play it casual, "look at who happens to be here. Heath and Sam and Neal and Jamie." They were sitting at one of the picnic tables near the edge of the lot. Chase watched as Sam Crawford, the Los Angeles Riptide's starting quarterback, signed an autograph for someone and then took a selfie with them.

Tate shot him an unimpressed look. "You mean to tell me that we *accidentally* ended up here today with not one, but two current Riptide players and two ex-players, who all happen to be your friends?"

"Whoops?" Chase said, shrugging.

Tate rolled his eyes. "You are a terrible liar, and I will extract some kind of retribution for springing this on me unannounced, but you can stop sweating about it. Let's go over."

"Okay," Chase said. Ignoring the part of him deep inside that fluttered at Tate's words. Would he exact the retribution in some kind of incredibly hot sexual way? He kind of hoped so.

"Hey," Tate said, before any of them could introduce themselves, or before Chase could say anything. "I'm Tate Ward, and I'm Chase's fake boyfriend."

Sam laughed, his blue eyes full of amusement. "Hi, Tate, I'm Sam. And *fake* boyfriend? Really? That's the best you can do, Riley?"

Chase shrugged. "I guess," he said.

"Don't let these guys pretend they aren't thrilled that Chase has a boyfriend, fake or not," Heath said, speaking up. He stood and extended his hand towards Tate. "We're really happy to meet you. I'm Heath, and this is my boyfriend, Sam, and that's Neal, and that's Jamie." He pointed out the *ex*-Riptide kicker and the current Riptide kicker.

"Hey, Tate," Neal and Jamie said in concert.

"I'm really glad that Chase called us," Jamie added, shooting Tate a lopsided grin. "I've wanted to meet the guy who made Chase realize he was more like us than he wanted to admit."

Chase had anticipated that Sam would give him a whole load of shit. It was *Sam,* and he even gave his devoted boyfriend, professed love of his life, *and* his quarterback coach a whole load of shit on a regular basis. Sometimes he could hear them yelling at each other on the practice field, usually when they were working on fundamentals—Heath's favorite, Sam's *least* favorite—but he'd also caught them after one of those practices making out in the shower. Chase figured that nobody understood a relationship like the people in it, but there was something in the way he caught

Heath staring at Sam sometimes that had always made him uncomfortably envious.

On top of that, it had *always* made him think about Tate. Even when Tate had only been a distant memory.

But Jamie, confessing Chase's long-held secret? Chase was not amused, and shot him a glare, except his friend just kept grinning.

"I guess that would be me," Tate said, not sounding particularly perturbed by Jamie's revelation. "Home Economics was sure a lot more exciting than I thought it would be."

"Oh, I just bet it was," Sam said slyly. "Come sit down, guys. We already ordered enough food for an army. Well, probably the five of us, *and* Chase, which is a ton of food."

Chase slid in next to Jamie, and gave him a hip nudge. "You're a real punk," he muttered under his breath, but Jamie was still grinning. Tate could've picked the open seat next to Heath, but instead, he sat next to Chase, snuggling in closer than was entirely necessary. Chase felt his heart stutter in his chest.

"Did you get the carne asada tacos?" Chase asked Sam. "Because if you didn't, I'm going to have to go order half a dozen."

"Half a dozen?" Tate asked, raising an eyebrow.

"Hey, I'm hungry," Chase said. He was starving actually, and not just for food, but he wasn't going to talk about that now, because Tate had already announced they weren't *really* together. Would they be "together" when Chase gave him a ride home after this? *God*, he really hoped so. He was all ramped up, with nowhere to go, and nothing to do. Even if he went and worked out for hours in his weight room, he didn't think he'd be able to burn off all this tension. He wanted Tate, and he'd wanted him for years.

"You're always hungry," Heath said. "It's a special talent of yours."

"Remember when he ate that *huge* pan of pasta and garlic bread before the last game of last season and then chucked it all over the endzone?" Sam said, obviously delighted at this new subject of conversation.

Chase mentally groaned. Nobody was going to want to have sex with him if his friends kept dragging out every embarrassing story in their repertoire.

"What?" Tate exclaimed. "What? I was watching that game. You didn't puke."

"Uh," Chase said. "I kinda did, actually. And yes, it was gross."

"It was actually so disgusting that I wouldn't be surprised if the camera panned away," Heath said. He pinned Chase with a sternly fond look. "And I *told* you not to eat all that."

Chase shrugged. "Usually telling me not to do something doesn't work very well," he said. "You *know* that."

"Yeah," Sam said heartily, shooting Tate a sly grin. "I bet that you're now extremely familiar with that habit of Riley's."

"So, Sam," Chase said, changing the subject. "How's your contract extension coming?"

"It's coming," Sam said. "I think we're actually pretty close on a lot of points. With any luck," he added, shooting his lover a fond smile, "Heath and I will be around LA for a few years longer."

"Good," Chase said with satisfaction. He didn't want his friends going anywhere.

Tate really thought when he'd come face to face with Chase's friends—the guys he'd watched on TV for years—he'd be a nervous wreck. It helped that Chase had surprised him with it, because he hadn't had any time to get nervous. It also helped that they were as down-to-earth as Chase himself was, and seemed genuinely glad to meet him.

But he also hadn't wanted to face them under a false impression, so he'd made sure to clear that up right way. He'd kind of assumed that Chase already had told them the truth—which was confirmed when nobody had seemed particularly surprised at Tate's words. He didn't need any additional reasons to like Chase, but the fact that he'd been honest with his friends, not only about their relationship, but the way they'd liked each other back in high school? Tate knew he was edging closer to dangerous territory.

Not just crushing on Chase, but seriously, deeply, irrevocably crushing.

And, Tate screamed at himself, *you told him you'd help him figure out how to have sex with a guy! Are you insane? You are absolutely going to love every moment of it, and probably end up loving him, as part of the bargain.*

Loving Chase Riley, no matter how low-key he was, no matter how chill his famous friends were, was a catastrophic situation.

"So, Tate, you own a food truck, right?" Heath asked him.

It really didn't help that Chase's friends were all so friendly and welcoming, asking him questions about where he'd gone to college, what Chase had been like in high school, and now questions about his truck. As they'd demolished the delicious tacos, they'd all peppered inquiries in, making it as clear as day that they accepted him.

Just the way they all accepted Chase.

Tate's heart was already straining for a conclusion that wasn't ever going to happen. He chewed and swallowed. "Yeah," he said. "That's going to go on your Wikipedia page, you know," he said, nudging Chase with his foot. Chase nudged it back and then, suddenly, they were playing footsy, underneath the table.

"What's going to go on my Wikipedia page?" Chase asked, all innocence. And maybe he didn't have any experience with guys, but Tate *knew* he wasn't innocent. Not even close.

"That you came out to sell grilled cheese sandwiches."

"On Twitter," Neal added with a teasing glint in his eyes. "I know *I'm* never gonna let you live that down."

"Neal is hopelessly old and hates social media," Jamie explained, even as his gaze made it clear just how much he loved the guy. "Please tell me you have Instagram."

"Oh, I do," Tate said. He gave Jamie Say Cheese's Instagram, because he had long abandoned his personal one in favor of promoting the truck.

"Wikipedia is supposed to be a reflection of the facts," Chase said primly. "So yes, I am sure it'll end up on there eventually."

"Oh hey, you were *not* kidding," Jamie said to Sam across the table. "Chase is *all over* their Instagram."

Tate couldn't have held back the blush even if he'd wanted to.

"Yeah," Tate said. "Chase has been really, really great about it. He's . . . well, he's our best advertising."

"Oh, I bet," Sam said with a teasing edge to his voice. "I just bet he is. So selfless."

"Are we talking about Chase Riley? That Chase?" Heath wondered.

"Hey!" Chase exclaimed. "I do good stuff for people."

"Of course you do," Sam said, patting him on the arm. "We're just really enjoying giving you shit."

"Yeah," Jamie echoed. "It's *your turn*."

Chase turned to Tate, smiling helplessly, and Tate felt his heart flip and then flop.

Rach was right; this was going to be a real problem.

CHAPTER NINE

Chase knew that Tate expected him to drop him back off at his apartment building after lunch. But instead he parked his bike and killed the engine.

Climbing off the motorcycle, Tate tugged off the helmet and handed it to Chase with a confused wrinkle between his brows.

"Is your sister home?" Chase asked, feeling like he was back in high school again, and not just because of the man in front of him.

The wrinkle deepened. *Surely,* Chase thought, *he's on the same page I am.* He didn't want to spell it out quite so bluntly—*invite me up because want is quickly becoming an understatement*—but he would, if Tate made him. After all, Tate had already agreed to show him what he wanted to know.

"She texted me about an hour ago, saying she was going out with some friends, and wouldn't be back til much later," Tate said. "Why?"

Chase looked at him. "Do you really need to ask that question?"

"Now? *Now,* I guess," Tate said, all of a sudden flustered. "I guess I didn't know you'd be . . ."

"So eager?" Chase grinned. "I should be offended that you're not."

"No, no," Tate said hurriedly. "I am, I actually . . . well, I guess it was you I didn't think would be so eager."

Chase swung a leg over the seat, and after keying the electronic lock, followed Tate into the building and to the elevator. "Thought I'd be some kind of blushing virgin?" he asked, watching as Tate pushed the button.

"Not a *virgin*," Tate said as the elevator doors opened and they walked in, "but . . . I don't know . . . hesitant."

Chase knew he'd wanted to say *afraid*.

Maybe guys who were about to experiment sexually with another guy for the first time *were* afraid. Afraid they'd hate it or find it gross or unappealing or that they'd be caught out not knowing what to do.

But Chase? Chase felt like he'd been waiting for this moment for ten years and he wasn't about to second-guess his way out of it before it even began.

"I'm not," Chase said, and before Tate could argue, he'd wrapped a hand around his back and tugged him closer, pressing their mouths together in a fierce kiss that he hoped answered all of Tate's questions, and even a few of them that he'd never thought to ask.

Tate's hands snuck around Chase's back and then dropped lower to his ass, palming it firmly before pulling him even closer.

Was he waiting for Chase to panic? Chase didn't know. But all he felt was an overwhelmingly fierce arousal. This was what he'd wanted that day in the pantry. Back then, he hadn't even understood what these feelings were. But he was beginning to understand them now.

Understand that when he felt the brush of Tate's cock, hard in his jeans, that this was what he'd wanted. He'd wanted to feel it in his hand, hard and twitching and wet at the tip, and he'd wanted to make Tate moan and then he'd wanted to make him scream.

Tate's mouth was damp and hot on his, and he could feel each finger as it pressed into his ass. Heat swamped him, and Tate pulled away, just as the elevator doors dinged open.

Chase let Tate take his hand and tug him through it.

He'd never imagined that he'd like *that*.

In the bedroom, he'd always taken the upper hand, let himself drive what happened, but the idea of letting someone else push him, take him, *own* him?

By the time they got to Tate's door, Chase felt his heart thumping hard in his chest, his cock so hard it practically hurt.

"You really . . ." Tate stuttered as his fingers trembled on the keys unlocking the door. "You really like this."

"I fucking *love* this," Chase said, and as soon as the door was unlocked, he was pushing Tate inside, their mouths colliding again with ferocity and purpose.

Tate moaned into his mouth as Chase's hands drifted down his chest. Maybe he should be nervous. Maybe he should be apprehensive. But he'd touched his own cock plenty of times, and he was one hundred percent totally guilty of watching enough gay porn that he at least had an idea of what Tate might like. Because if he *had* nerves, they were all about that: making sure that it was good for the guy he'd wanted forever.

But even the nerves he couldn't quite deny evaporated the moment his palm skidded over Tate's cock, straining at the zipper of his jeans. He bucked once, and then twice, nearly fucking against his hand, and the way Tate's eyes glazed over with pleasure was enough to dismiss every bit of anxiety he'd been hiding.

He could make Tate feel like this. He could make him *look* like this, mouth open, red and wet from Chase's own. He could touch and be touched.

Chase's fingers reached for the button on Tate's jeans, but Tate reached in and held them tight. "Wait," he said, the edge of his voice rough. "Wait. I want . . . let me, okay?"

Chase had assumed that Tate meant he was going to undress himself which . . . that was slightly disappointing, because he'd actually really been looking forward to unwrapping Tate like a present he couldn't wait a moment longer to open.

Except that wasn't what Tate did. Instead of finally getting rid of his pants, he put his hands around Chase's waist, close but not quite close enough to where he was dying to be touched and switched their places. Manhandling Chase, who was six foot four, and who proudly considered himself practically a slab of muscle.

Tate was shorter, but he'd just proven how strong he was. Or maybe how weak Chase was, in his hands.

Chase opened his mouth to say it, to tell him that he *liked* it, *liked* Tate being strong enough to push and pull him and place him right where he wanted him—but before he could, Tate's fingers were unbuttoning his own jeans, trembling a little as they pulled down the zipper.

"If I'd thought I could do this, all those years ago," Tate mused as he moistened his lips. Chase's stomach erupted into a million butterflies as he sank to his knees.

"You could've," Chase said, his own voice as breathless as he'd felt.

"Wouldn't have been like this," Tate said.

"No?" Chase choked out as Tate's fingers closed around him, hot and hard in his briefs, his breath just ghosting over the damp fabric.

"No, this is gonna be so much better." Tate paused. "You said you hadn't done this before."

Chase didn't think he could actually *learn* while Tate's mouth was an inch away from his cock, but he nodded anyway. Anything to make sure he didn't stop.

"Alright," Tate said. "First thing . . ." He tugged down Chase's briefs, and Chase muttered a curse as his cock bobbed, hard as a rock, and brushed Tate's cheek, just enough to leave a wet spot on his skin.

Chase stared at it, transfixed, and knew that one smear of pre-come would be enough to fuel his fantasies for a week. For a *month*.

He'd been getting by on so many tiny scraps: pieces of memory, wild imaginings, fantasies from porn he'd seen, with Tate's face superimposed over the actors'. But nothing was as good as this.

"First thing?" Chase murmured. His fingers were curled against the wood of the door. He wanted to reach down and touch, to pull Tate's hat off, to dig his fingers through his hair, tug him close, but if he did any of that, he'd probably come untouched.

"It's easier on your knees," Tate said. "Angle's better. At least to do this," he added, licking a stripe up the underside of Chase's cock.

It was just a split second, the barest impression of *warm* and *wet* and *mine*, but it was enough. His cock twitched, eager for more.

"Second thing," Tate said. "There's no reason to kill yourself taking it all. I mean, it feels great just like this, right?"

That was all the warning Chase got before Tate's mouth was on him again, and it was so much hotter than merely *warm*, and then Tate was sucking and his fist closed around the bottom half and he wasn't wrong, it was so goddamned good that he was going to come way before he wanted to.

"That's so fucking good," Chase groaned.

"See?" Tate said, and he was grinning, and then diving back in, mouth and hand working together gloriously. Chase wanted to keep looking, to imprint this vision on his brain forever, to never stop seeing Tate like this, to never stop experiencing the staggering pleasure, but his eyes fluttered shut, trying to prolong it for another few seconds.

"But you can always work up to this," Tate added with a sly edge to his voice, and *oh god*, Chase nearly cried out loud, as Tate's mouth met his hand and then sank lower.

"Fuck, fuck, *fuck*," Chase said, and couldn't help it then, his hands were on Tate's head, tossing away the cap, cradling his head, fisting his hair in his fingers as he exploded down Tate's throat.

After a long moment, Tate stood, wiping his mouth with the back of his hand. "And that," Tate added, Chase barely following along in the aftermath of the most mind-blowing orgasm he'd ever had, "is also optional, by the way."

"What is?" Chase stuttered. He should return the favor. He should use what Tate had just taught him, but before he could, Tate was unzipping his own jeans.

"Swallowing," Tate said, like this was something he discussed every day. Those gray eyes looked up at him, searing and trusting, all in the same moment, and Chase felt flayed to the bone by them. How could Tate think these were just lessons and this was all fake? How could he, when it felt like this? Like he'd been waiting his whole goddamned life.

"Can you touch me?" Tate asked quietly, softly, suddenly unsure. "Will you touch me?"

"Yes," Chase said, batting Tate's hands away, and it was his turn to manhandle Tate against the door as he carefully pulled down his pants, and then his gray boxer briefs, running an experimental finger up the underside of Tate's cock, loving the way it twitched in response. "Yes, I definitely can."

"Do you . . ." Tate exhaled loudly as Chase wrapped his hand around Tate's cock and gave it an experimental stroke.

"I know how to do this," Chase said, finishing his sentence. "Don't worry, I'm gonna make you feel so good."

Tate groaned as he began to move his hand faster, trying a few different grips until he found the one that made Tate actually wail out loud. "Yeah," Chase said, a deeper satisfaction than his own orgasm settling inside him. "Yeah, you really like that, don't you?"

"Yes." The word felt practically ripped out of Tate's body. Those gray eyes pinned him again. "Kiss me."

Chase didn't need to be asked twice, and worked Tate through his orgasm as his mouth moved over Tate's. And maybe the floor didn't shake and the earth didn't move, but afterwards, he still felt changed.

Maybe not a new kind of man, but a different one all the same.

Tate bashfully grabbed a few tissues, handing them to Chase so he could wipe the come off his hand.

"So," he said, voice unsteady.

"So," Chase said. Maybe it wasn't right, but the more unsure Tate seemed, the more confident Chase felt. Because the uncertainty definitely wasn't because Tate didn't seem to want him anymore; maybe, Chase thought, it was because he wanted him *too much.*

Of course, just when he was about to ask Tate when they could do this again—hopefully in the next twenty-four hours—his phone vibrated in his pocket, then his ringtone blared.

"Shit," Chase said. "It's probably my agent or my mom. Those are the only contacts on my emergency list and that's the only reason it rings . . ."

Tate waved. "It's fine, I've got stuff to do anyway . . ." He looked around, still unsure, and Chase felt deeply sure that he'd wanted him to stay.

He'd *wanted* to stay. But he knew he needed to take care of this first.

"I'll see you tomorrow, at the truck?" Chase asked, pulling his phone out of his pocket. It was indeed Alec calling.

Tate nodded. "Yeah, why don't you just come for the evening shift? I'll text you the address. We can manage for the lunchtime crowd, I think."

"You'll text me if you can't, though, right?" Chase said. His phone was ringing again. A bad sign.

"Yes, of course."

Chase was almost certain he was lying, and decided he'd swing by tomorrow around lunch, just to make sure.

"You'd better take that," Tate said, and reached up, brushing a kiss across his cheek. "Hopefully, it's not anything bad."

"Alec probably just has his panties in a twist about something," Chase said. He leaned down and kissed Tate thoroughly this time, before opening the door up. The cheek kiss had been nice, but not nearly what he'd wanted. "I'll let you know."

"Okay," Tate said.

Chase called Alec back when he got back out on the sidewalk.

"Hey," he said shortly. "This better have been important."

Alec's resigned sigh told Chase everything he needed to know—it was important, and Alec hadn't even wanted to make this phone call, either. Chase's stomach cramped.

"I was trying to deal with this, and not tell you," Alec said. "But there was a leak, maybe from the team, and I don't want you to find out when you turn the TV on in the morning. But before I tell you, I'm going to repeat that *I'm still dealing with it*, okay?"

Chase leaned against the side of Tate's building and squeezed his eyes shut. Like not seeing could mean that he wouldn't have to hear what Alec was going to say.

"What is it?" he asked.

"You know the Riptide has been working on Sam's new deal," Alec said. "They're looking to make some cap space room, and so they've quietly put around that they're willing to listen to trade offers for you. *But* before you freak out, I want you to know the price the Riptide wants is probably not a price that any team is willing to pay. And I'm working on convincing them that it'd be crazy to trade you away. They should just restructure your deal, instead."

"That's what you've been working on?"

"When I told you to keep your head down? Yeah, this was what I was worried about. I knew Sam's contract negotiations were heating up. I didn't want to give the Riptide any extra reasons to do what they're doing now."

"Shit," Chase said. He felt sick, like he might throw tacos up all over the sidewalk. How had this day, so fucking amazing only ten minutes ago, turned to utter crap?

"Yes, you should've listened," Alec said, but his voice was kind. Probably *too* kind.

"You think you can still fix it?" Chase knew that Alec wouldn't have said so if he didn't believe it. He might be tough, but he didn't lie. *Wouldn't* lie.

"I'm not going to make any promises," Alec hedged, "I can't promise they won't trade you. If they get the kind of offer they're looking for, yeah, you're going to be traded. But there's a good chance they won't, and there's also a good chance I can persuade them to restructure your contract instead. They don't really *want* to trade you, Chase."

"I mean, wouldn't it be stupid to trade me?" Chase knew how egotistical he sounded but he also knew just how good he was. "I was the leading receiver in the whole NFL last year."

"They don't *want* to lose you, Chase. But they also want to make sure they have Sam under contract for the next few years.

That isn't going to be cheap. The trick is gonna be to make sure they can have both of you."

"And you think you can do that?" Chase knew he kept asking for guarantees when Alec had *just* said he couldn't make any promises. But the idea of having to start over, in a new city, with a new team, when he'd just . . . *oh god*. It hit him then. If he was traded, he'd be starting over at the worst time. He'd just come out of the closet because at the time it hadn't seemed so scary. His friends were here. He knew the Riptide wouldn't judge him for it. It had felt *safe*.

But even though coming out wasn't all that unusual anymore, not every team had a player who'd done it. He could end up on a team where he'd be the *only* out and proud queer guy on the team. He'd have to navigate it without Sam or Heath or even Coach R, who was quietly, steadfastly supportive.

He'd have to do it without Tate, who he'd finally reconnected with.

Fuck.

"Did you hear what I just said?" Alec sounded annoyed, and it suddenly occurred to Chase that he'd been talking this whole time, and Chase had missed it during his freak-out.

"Uh, no?"

"I said you know I can't make promises, but I'm going to try my hardest."

"I wish we'd gotten right of refusal," Chase said, referring to the option that very few players had written into their contracts where they could refuse to be traded to certain teams.

Alec sighed. "You knew that was going to be impossible. We discussed it. Wide receivers don't get that kind of power."

And it had mattered a lot less to Chase when he hadn't really thought the Riptide would trade him away, and it had mattered even less before he'd come out of the closet on a whim.

You shouldn't have done it, a voice inside of him said firmly. *You could still have enjoyed everything you just did with Tate, even if you didn't tell everyone you were doing it.*

Yes, Tate had been the reason he'd finally set foot outside the closet, but he'd also come to realize in the last few years that everyone's voice counted. Had he *needed* to do it? No. But he'd wanted to.

At least he'd wanted to until suddenly the ground underneath him wasn't as steady as it had been before.

"Yeah," Chase said. "I know."

"I just didn't want you to freak out when you saw the news, tomorrow," Alec said. "And I wanted you to know it's as under control as I can make it, right now."

The possibility had always existed that Chase could be traded. There were very few guarantees in the NFL. But the Riptide actively looking to move him? That was a whole lot more than a fucking vague possibility; it was a new potential reality.

Away from his friends. Away from everything he knew. Away from the safe bubble they'd made here in Los Angeles.

"I know you're doing everything you can," Chase acknowledged.

"Then why do you sound so panicked?" Alec wondered.

"Because this is happening at all," Chase said, the words exploding out of him. "I . . . I don't want to leave. I really, really don't want to leave."

"Is this about that guy?" Alec wondered.

Chase squeezed his eyes shut again, but nothing could dull the cold, hard truth. "No. Not entirely. But yes. A little bit."

"You're rich. You can live wherever the fuck you want," Alec pointed out. "You could move *him* if you wanted to."

It was hard to explain how little that mattered. "It's not just about where I live," Chase said. "I'm . . . I'm . . . I'm exposed now."

Alec was silent for a long moment. Chase was afraid he was going to be subjected to one of his agent's annoying *I told you so* lectures, but instead, his voice was kind. Definitely kinder than Chase deserved, because Alec had *warned* him. Keep your head down, he'd said, and Chase had very deliberately *not* done that.

"You're worried about coming out and being on another team," Alec said. "A different kind of team."

"They're not all like the Riptide. You know that." Alec would, because not only was Alec an agent for various other players across the country; he was also gay. He knew how that impacted things.

"I do know that. And we'll cross that bridge when we come to it. I promise. But I don't think you're even going to have to deal with it. I really think they *want* to keep you, Chase. I do."

Chase could hear the panic mounting in his agent's voice, even as he tried to stay calm. Was he worried about what Chase would do? *Chase* was worried about what he was going to do.

"I would play for them for free, even," Chase said, recklessly.

Alec laughed. "Let's not get crazy now, okay? But I was going to remind you—restructuring means that you might make less."

"I don't care," Chase said. He had lots of money. More money than he could spend in his lifetime. "Whatever it takes."

"Alright," Alec said. "I'll keep you posted, okay? Just when I say it this time . . . do it, please? While I deal with all this shit, *keep your head down*. Or if you're going to lift it, clear it with me first, okay?"

"I will," Chase promised. Actually meant it this time. If he'd known what was at stake . . . but he couldn't have. He'd never have guessed that Sam's contract was going to impact him so directly.

Alec hung up and Chase contemplated another wrinkle.

Any other time, when something like this came up, he'd go and hang out with his friends. Let their experience and their affection wash over him and at least dull the sick anxious feeling at the pit of his stomach. But he couldn't. Not now. Because as much as he didn't want to admit it, he felt a thread of something that was undeniably resentment winding its way around his heart. He didn't think he could go to Heath and Sam's house and let Sam try to comfort him. How could he, when this wouldn't be happening if it *wasn't* for Sam?

He could always go back upstairs and explain the whole thing to Tate. There was a part of Chase—a strong, difficult-to-deny part of him—that really wanted to. If he and Tate had really been dating, if this whole thing hadn't started out on the wrong, *fake*, foot, he would've.

But fake dating someone didn't mean sharing all your problems with them. Chase wasn't exactly familiar with the whole "fake dating" thing, but he did know that much, and the last thing he wanted was to ruin whatever they did have by over-sharing.

That meant . . . Chase inwardly groaned . . . there was nothing left to do but go home, and try to deal with all of this shit by himself. Because he handled stuff like this *so well*.

Except . . . Chase dialed a number instead. "Hey," he said. "Yeah, I need to see you. Are you free tomorrow? In the morning? That early? Okay." He took a deep breath. "We can meet then."

Then he hung up, feeling like he had just dodged a bullet. And maybe that might have made Chase feel better, but he had a feeling that it was just the first, and there would be more to come.

CHAPTER TEN

Ever since Chase had suggested that he come help out at Say Cheese, Tate had been sure it was a bad idea, doomed to fail. Even though Chase had been excited yesterday, and he'd been eager to learn, Tate had still been sure, deep down, that it was a mistake.

And not only because he had a feeling that if he and Chase spent several hours cramped in a small space together, they were absolutely going to do something that was going to drive Rachel wild.

Prep was uneventful, but despite getting to the truck at an ungodly hour, he and Rachel were still pressed for time. There was just too much to do, and not enough hands to do it.

"You're going to have to do interviews this week," Rachel had said as they barely finished up in enough time to head to the spot where they were scheduled for the lunch hour. "We need help. And not just during lunch or dinner, but for prep, too. We can't do it all, anymore. Not if this volume keeps up."

Tate wasn't sure if it would. That was why he'd held off. "I could always ask Lucas to help out more," he said.

Rachel rolled her eyes. "He's already busy. We need *help*, Tate. And not just your overgrown football player 'boyfriend.'"

"He's not my boyfriend," Tate said as he put out the condiments and napkins in the front bins. "You know that."

"But you wish he was, *and* you're fucking."

Tate was beginning to regret confessing that particular tidbit to his sister. But he was in a habit of sharing everything with her, and it had felt wrong and weird not to tell her the direction the afternoon had taken. And how good it had been. How *right*.

He should've known that telling her would only give her more ammunition in her persistent, "Chase is going to break your heart" argument.

"It doesn't matter," Tate said firmly. "Everything is under control."

But everything wasn't under control. Not by a long shot.

Lunch had also passed fairly uneventfully. Not that they weren't busy—they were. Insanely busy. Busy enough that Tate regretted not telling Chase to come by early. But then, he had wanted to ease the guy into it. He wasn't used to working twelve-hour days—not like Tate and Rachel were. And if Tate forced him to, before he was acclimated to the idea, then *that* help might also potentially disappear, and where would they be then?

Not in a good place, that was for sure.

They got to the distillery they were scheduled at for the evening early so that they could hopefully get some additional prep work in, and, as Rachel had suggested longingly, maybe they could actually take a break.

Chase was waiting for them when Tate pulled the truck up, sitting at one of the empty picnic tables in the field next to the distillery's parking lot.

"Hey," Tate said, approaching where he was sitting after he'd parked.

"Hey," Chase repeated dully, but unlike every time before, he didn't sound happy or excited. He sounded . . . apprehensive was the best way Tate could put it. He wondered if it was because of the phone call he'd gotten yesterday.

Surely, it wasn't because they'd had sex?

"Are you okay?" Tate asked. "You seem . . . not okay."

Chase shrugged. His bright light, which Tate had almost never seen dimmed, was definitely a bit worse for the wear today.

"You can tell me, you know," Tate said. Maybe they weren't quite boyfriends, and they weren't really friends, *yet*, but he could still be there for Chase.

That was one of the things he'd always wished he'd been able to do, back in high school. Because unlike everyone else, he'd never believed that Chase was shallow. He had depths. He just didn't reveal them to everyone.

He'd always wanted Chase to reveal his depths to *him*.

"It's just . . . you didn't see the news?" Chase looked surprised by this. "I thought . . ."

"We've been a little busy today," Tate said. "What happened?" He really should get back to the truck, and help Rachel, but instead, he sat down, right next to Chase.

"I thought you'd have seen the news, and I wouldn't even have to tell you," Chase admitted. "The Riptide are trying to trade me."

"No way," Tate said incredulously. "Seriously? Well, that's shitty."

"Sam is looking to sign a long-term deal, and to do that, the Riptide need to make room to pay him. And right now? I'm making the most money on the team."

"But you *should* be," Tate said. "You were the top receiver last year. Not just on your team, but on *every* team."

"Yeah, well." Chase's voice hardened. "Signing big contracts doesn't always pay off, in the end."

"That was what your phone call was about yesterday," Tate guessed.

Chase nodded. "It was Alec, warning me that the news was going to come out. He wanted me to hear it from him first."

Tate reached over and put a hand on Chase's jean-clad knee. Gave it a reassuring squeeze. "I'm so goddamned sorry," he said. And he really meant it. He knew that Chase's friends were here, and they played for the Riptide. Knew he didn't really want to leave. Knew he might not have much choice.

And that wasn't even taking into consideration the sick feeling Tate got at the base of his stomach when he thought that Chase might leave Los Angeles, and when he left, any possibility of a future they might have would go with him.

You can't be selfish right now. He's struggling. You can't make this about you.

"Yeah," Chase said, clearing his throat. "It sucks."

"Do you . . ." Tate couldn't believe he was about to ask this, because he and Rachel were depending on Chase's help today, but somehow being insanely busy didn't feel like the worst thing in the world. Not now that Chase had admitted what might happen.

"No," Chase said firmly. "I can work. I gave my word to you and Rachel that I would. It's fine, it'll maybe even help, take my mind off it, you know."

"Okay," Tate said.

"Trust me," Chase said, flashing him a smile, even though it was only a shadow of his normal bright grin, "this will be good for me."

Having Chase work at Say Cheese was predictably a huge success. People swarmed the truck in droves. Despite stocking up, they ran out of half of the menu items by seven, and despite Tate's concerns, Chase kept up.

He was *almost* his normal charming self, and if Tate hadn't started to get to know him better over the last week, he probably wouldn't have noticed that anything was wrong. But he was beginning to see through Chase's charismatic act to the soft, vulnerable underbelly, and now that he had, it was impossible to miss that something was deeply wrong.

Was it just the possibility of leaving Southern California and all his friends? The only team he'd known since he was drafted? Or was it something else? Tate didn't know. Wasn't sure if he could get Chase to tell him, but clearly it was eating him up inside.

He *should* tell someone.

The dinner rush finally ended and Chase took a break, wolfing down a sandwich at one of the now-empty picnic tables scattered over the distillery's back patio.

"Hey," Tate said to Rachel, as he did an inventory of the fridge, "can you hold down the fort here? I think there's something I need to do."

Rach raised an eyebrow as she ticked off items on her list. "Does it have something to do with Chase?"

"Yeah," Tate said.

"Good. Because he's . . . well . . . I think he's off? But it's hard to say, because he's really good at pretending everything is fine."

Tate was not surprised that Rachel had managed to see beneath Chase's jovial exterior, either. She was extremely observant, which he resented most of the time because she saw through all the little white lies he liked to tell himself. But for once he was grateful because it wasn't just him who could see that Chase was suffering.

"Yeah, he is," Tate agreed. "But it's not fine, and I'm not going to let him just sit there by himself and stew about it."

"Of course you aren't," Rachel said, patting him on the shoulder. "Even if you didn't have a ten-year-long crush on the man, you wouldn't let him do that to himself. I know you."

"It wasn't . . ." Tate tried to argue. It hadn't lasted *ten years* because that was ridiculous. It had started ten years back, *yes,* but there was a period of time when . . . Tate gave up the mental argument. Okay, it had probably been a ten-year-long crush.

Rachel rolled her eyes. "That's right," she said with a sharp nod. "You know what's up."

"I do," Tate grumbled. "Okay, I'll be right back."

He skirted around the side of the truck, mostly out of Chase's field of view, and went into the distillery, ordering and picking up the sampler they were most famous for. When he came back outside, Tate headed straight for the table Chase was sitting at, setting the lineup of plastic cups down between them.

"What is this?" Chase asked, putting down his half-eaten sandwich as Tate took the seat opposite him.

"It was a hard day," Tate said.

"It wasn't . . ." Chase started to say, but Tate shook his head decisively.

"Yes, it was," Tate disagreed. "It was hard. Don't try to lie to me. I know you better than that."

Chase shrugged. "I've had better days, but it wasn't . . . but I meant it. It was good to work. To not just sit at home and, well . . ."

"Mope?" Tate finished his sentence. "Yeah, I get that. But still, a hard day, and on a completely separate note, you did great, so you might as well enjoy some of the rum this place is famous for."

Chase reached out and fingered the plastic shot glass. "Are you trying to get me drunk?"

"I think it would take more than a couple of shots to accomplish that," Tate said, but plucked one from the tray anyway, and sipped, relishing the burn, and also the dark spice on his tongue. "Still, it's not a bad way to relax."

"Is that what you're doing, then? Trying to get me to relax?"

Tate shot him a glare. "I'm trying to get you to *talk* to me."

"You could've just asked." Chase actually sounded sulky, and Tate knew he was making some kind of progress.

"I did. You didn't seem particularly forthcoming. And then there was the whole 'let me pretend everything is totally fine' act."

"That wasn't . . ."

"Yeah, no," Tate interrupted again. "It was an act. I saw through it. I don't think anybody else did, because you're good at it. Drink up, and tell me what's got you so freaked out."

"It's . . ." Chase took a deep breath. "I don't want you to think I regret it."

"Regret what?"

"Coming out," Chase said. He picked up the shot of rum, and tried it. "I don't regret it, but I also didn't think I'd be doing it and then immediately be traded to another team. I . . . it's not the same on every team, like it is on the Riptide."

"You felt safe doing it, because the Riptide is safe," Tate guessed. He knew how terrifying coming out was, even if you had supportive parents and friends. He couldn't imagine doing it when there might be a whole fan base who hated you for it.

Chase nodded.

"And now you're freaking out, because you might go somewhere not safe," Tate said. He leaned back. "Yeah, I can see that being difficult."

"I've talked to someone. I mean, I used to. I . . ." Chase flushed, and Tate did a double take because he didn't think he'd ever seen him so hesitant, so *scared* before. Because that was exactly what this was, wasn't it? Chase was fucking *terrified*. "I used to talk to someone, about my anxiety and how to handle my emotions when they overwhelmed me. And I called her up and we talked this morning. It was good. It helped. But I just feel so goddamned helpless. I can't even control my own future."

Tate thought of everything Chase had done for him. He'd taken Chase's name and invoked it without his permission, and instead of coming down like a ton of bricks, Chase had taken in the situation and done everything he could to help Tate. Going above and beyond. Even coming out, not necessarily *for* him, but he'd had to know that it would cause a sensation and that sensation would only help Tate more.

He'd done all of that, rather selflessly. Maybe he hadn't really thought through the consequences, but that didn't eradicate the selflessness of his actions.

Tate wished, not for the first time, that he could give something back.

"Is there nothing you can do?" Tate wondered.

"My agent is working to restructure my deal, but I'll be honest, I haven't exactly made it easy for him," Chase said with a heavy sigh. "He told me to keep my head down, and I'm fucking terrible at doing that."

"What do you mean?"

"He wanted to make sure that if I made the news, I did it for 'good' reasons, and not, well . . . attention-seeking or negative reasons," Chase admitted. "And well, coming out like that? Not great."

"But not bad on its own," Tate said. A kernel of an idea was beginning to form in his head. "Would the Riptide like that you had a boyfriend?"

Chase looked confused, as he finished off his rum. "I don't know what you mean?"

"Would it improve your image if we got out and did things together? Things that made you look good? Made you look settled down? Made you look responsible and all that shit?" Tate waved his hands, not sure what *would* work but living in Southern California as long as he had, he realized that he was basically describing a public relations job. "We could make you look good. Make you a bigger, bigger part of the community. Might make the Riptide reconsider."

"It's really about the money," Chase said wryly. "But I can't imagine it would hurt. Truthfully . . ." He hesitated. "Truthfully, I was hoping to change my image anyway. Wanted to be more *myself* instead of that stupid party guy who says dumb shit and throws up in the end zone."

"Wouldn't that fix both of these problems, then? At least a little?" Tate said. He wasn't even thinking of what it might be like to pretend *more* like they were together. Like they were falling in love. When a thread of panic wound its way through him at the idea, he pushed it away. Chase had done so much for him; the very least he could do was to give something back to Chase.

"It might," Chase said thoughtfully. Like he was really considering the suggestion. "Alec might have some ideas."

"I'm sure he would," Tate said. Alec had struck him as a really sharp, knowledgeable guy. Who would also probably want a heads-up. And this way, Chase would give him one.

"I'll ask him," Chase said. "But you really think we should do this?" He sounded uncertain. "You didn't even want to do this, at first."

"I didn't," Tate admitted. "But it helped me a lot, and I think it could help you, too. Why not use something we've already established?"

"Why not?" Chase mused. "Don't you think it's a little unfair that a single queer guy is not responsible but a coupled-up one is?"

"I won't argue with that logic," Tate said, taking another sip of rum. "But maybe try taking on the world's disparities when you're not already fighting a battle you might not win."

Chase smiled at that. Not quite as brightly as Tate had ever seen it before, but it was still a decent version of the smile that had captured his heart all those years ago.

"Alright," he said. "I'll talk to Alec."

"You should," Tate said firmly, because he definitely didn't want to get on the agent's bad side, suggesting that Chase go off half-cocked again. And speaking off going off half-*cocked* . . .

"Do you want to come over tonight?" Tate asked, even though he shouldn't. But drinking three shots of rum on an empty stomach was a terrible idea. All the alcohol buzzing through his system made him want to press his lips to Chase's and take all his clothes off. In a bed. Where he could finally enjoy all that smooth skin and those undeniably ripped muscles at his leisure.

"Is your sister going to be home?" Chase asked.

"Well, yeah, she lives there," Tate said.

"Then you should come to my house, instead," Chase said.

Tate understood why Chase wanted privacy—he was a famous professional athlete, and a lot of people thought he owed them a part of his private self, which he *didn't*—but at the same time, Tate didn't know how he felt about taking their hookups to Chase's house. It would be huge and intimidating, and remind him all over again that the chances of this continuing, even if Chase didn't leave LA, were slim to none.

At some point, Chase was going to find someone who was like *him*, and not anything like Tate.

But privacy? Not having to be quiet? Not worrying that Rachel might blare her weird techno music in the middle of the night and ruin the mood? There were definite benefits in avoiding all of the above.

"Okay," Tate finally said. He left the final shot for Chase—after all, he was eating, and could use all those greasy carbs to soak up the liquor. He should eat something himself.

Chase grinned, and there was that carefree, happy-go-lucky edge that had always left Tate breathless. "I'll text you the address," he said. "And the gate code."

Tate couldn't stop his eye roll as he stood.

"Hey, there's nothing wrong with security," Chase said. "Pays to be cautious." He smiled slyly. "Wouldn't want anyone to interrupt us, right?"

"It'd be a real shame," Tate agreed. He turned to go, but Chase caught his hand, and with an embarrassing lack of effort, reeled Tate close to him, until he was caught in the vee of Chase's legs.

"You're runnin' away again," Chase said softly.

He *had* been, a little bit, because the rum had made him horny and emotional and, ultimately, vulnerable, and he'd wanted to find something to sober him up before Chase took advantage of any of those things. Tate tilted his head. "How do you know that?"

"You afraid I'm gonna do this?" he asked and pulled Tate's head down towards his, the fierceness of his kiss taking Tate's breath away.

He tasted like the dark spiciness of the rum, and something deeper, darker, almost dangerous. It wasn't like Tate hadn't *known* Chase was dangerous. He'd been compromising Tate from that first day in Home Economics, and he was wearing him down now.

The one thing Chase did not need to learn was how to kiss. He was really good at it, and Tate forced himself not to think about how many people Chase must have kissed over the years. How many people would have seen him and wanted him. Thought they could *have* him.

Maybe, Tate thought rebelliously, *he's been a little bit yours, this whole time.*

Maybe you could make him a little bit more *yours,* he added thoughtfully.

"What did you want to do tonight?" Tate murmured as his hands swept over Chase's broad shoulders. "Would you let me do whatever I wanted to you?"

Tate had gotten the impression yesterday that Chase had really enjoyed it when he'd taken over, and the way his eyes glazed over now made it even more obvious. Yeah, he was going to enjoy this a *lot.*

Chase's tongue flicked out, licking his bottom lip. "Yes," he said. "Anything you want."

Reluctantly, Chase let him go, and Tate stepped back, hoping that nobody was watching them practically maul each other in public. Alec probably *wouldn't* be thrilled about that development of their fake relationship.

But the only problem with Chase putting the decision into his hands like that, Tate thought as he returned to the food truck and to (semi) sanity, was that it wasn't all that easy to decide what it was he wanted most. The list was far too extensive. He was going to have to really *think* about it, and figure out a way to narrow it down.

Or, he thought as he began helping Rachel clean up, he could do it *all*.

CHAPTER ELEVEN

It had been impossible to miss Tate's apprehension at coming to Chase's house. The eye roll when he'd mentioned the gate code had confirmed his suspicions.

And watching as Tate's eyes grew wide and worried when he got out of his car, parked in the semi-circular driveway in front of his house, Chase realized that maybe he shouldn't have pushed.

But he hadn't wanted to ask Tate to fuck him when his sister was in hearing distance either. Not for the first time. Chase hoped that was something Tate wanted, because he'd put himself in his lover's hands for the evening—and wasn't that a fucking trip just how much he goddamned loved that?

"I've got to go," Chase said over the phone to Alec.

"Ugh," Alec said, "he's there, isn't he?"

"Yeah," Chase said. "He just got here."

"I'll send over the idea list," Alec said. Then his voice grew concerned. "Don't overdo it, okay? There's no guarantee that this'll work."

"Yeah, but it's better than sitting here, doing nothing," Chase said.

"Good night, Chase," Alec said firmly.

Chase hung up the call and walked out the front door, still watching intently as Tate's wide eyes took in the enormous Mediterranean-themed estate he'd bought a few years back, after he'd signed his rookie contract extension.

Ironically the same contract extension that might end up leading to his departure from Los Angeles.

"Hey," Chase said. "You find the place okay?"

Tate shot him a look. "It'd be hard to miss it," he said. It might be full dark, but the landscape lighting made it easy to see Tate and everything he was trying to hide.

"Are you saying my *house* is big?" Chase teased.

"Yes," Tate said. "And that's all I'm saying is big." Tate shifted uneasily from foot to foot, eyes darting around, like he didn't know where to go or what he should be looking at.

"That's what you're telling me *now*," Chase said, reaching out and pulling Tate into a tight hug. He was surprised at how Tate just melted into him. Like Chase had answered a question that Tate didn't even know how to ask.

That was something, Chase realized as they stood there for a long moment, just holding each other, that he was learning about Tate. Whenever he began to feel uncomfortable or awkward, he got mouthy and defensive. Like the first time they'd met back up again, and Tate had acted like he didn't even want to see Chase, couldn't wait for him to leave—Chase was beginning to wonder if that wasn't what he'd felt at all.

"You wanna see my house?" Chase murmured into Tate's hair. He'd left off the beanie again, and Chase reached up, tangling his fingers in the soft strands, tilting his head to the side so he could brush a kiss against his neck, relishing the scratch of Tate's scruff. It was incredible that at one point, Chase had been nervous that he wouldn't like it. Instead, he couldn't get enough.

"Is that supposed to be a sexy metaphor?" Tate wondered, moaning as Chase tugged him closer, pressing their bodies together.

"It could be, if you wanted it to be," Chase said. Hoping that Tate would agree with him that a tour headed straight for his bedroom was exactly the right kind of tour.

Tate pulled back, the uncertainty gone from his gray eyes. "I want to see *everything*," he said, grinning. "If you'll show me?"

"Of course. I want to," Chase said. Reminding himself that this wasn't all about sex. Even as he felt a particularly potent combination of nerves and anticipation skitter along his skin, making it feel too tight.

"So this is how the other half lives," Tate said as they walked, hand in hand, into the foyer, with its soaring ceiling and hand-painted mural on the back wall and the chandelier that he'd heard had been imported from Italy, all wrought iron curlicues. "Well," he corrected with an embarrassed glance in Chase's direction, "maybe half isn't quite right. Maybe this is how the other *half a percent* lives."

Chase laughed. "It's ridiculous, nobody should get as much money as I do, just for catching a ball really well."

Tate's expression morphed from slightly overwhelmed awe to something harder. Tougher. He squeezed Chase's hand, insistently. "You are the best at what you do which, by the way, isn't just *catching a ball*. Even if that *was* all you did, you're literally the best person in the whole world at doing it. I think that deserves adequate compensation."

Chase shrugged. "And you make the best grilled cheese sandwich in the world. Why aren't you buying mansions and hiring dozens of workers, expanding your empire?"

"Maybe I don't want to," Tate said lightly. "That wouldn't be very fun. Just as much work, probably more, in fact, and I wouldn't get to do any of the fun parts, anymore. Sounds terrible to me."

"Do you want to see the kitchen?" Chase asked. "I barely use it . . ."

He didn't even get the rest of his sentence out before Tate was nodding enthusiastically. "Yes, that. I definitely want to see the kitchen."

Chase tugged him in the right direction. "I feel a little bit like that beast guy in that one animated movie."

Tate looked at him in confusion. "That beast guy?"

Chase caught himself. He'd almost given it all away. This wasn't supposed to be some epic love story—two guys finding each other after so many years apart. *You're faking it, remember?* Chase reminded himself. *You're not wooing a hot guy with a kitchen the way the Beast wooed the pretty girl with a library.*

But before he could figure out what he should say instead, they'd walked into the kitchen and Chase flipped the lights on. Tate let out a little gasp.

Yes, it was cavernous. Yes, it had about a million miles of creamy gold-flecked marble. About a hundred cabinets, the gloss of their wood finish shining under the lights. But Tate passed between the side counter and the gigantic island, not stopping until he came face to face with the enormous gas stove. "This," he murmured, fingers gently brushing the knobs and the burners, "is totally wasted on you."

"Yep," Chase agreed. "Absolutely, totally wasted."

Tate glanced back at him, gray eyes glittering with amusement. "Have you set anything on fire in here yet?"

"Believe it or not, after I lost you as a partner, I didn't try much cooking," Chase said. Wondered if Tate would realize just how true that was on several different levels.

"Probably safer," Tate agreed. "Wouldn't want to hurt this sweet baby here," he added, cooing at the stove like it was a living, breathing organism. Chase pushed aside jealousy—for a *stove*, he thought to himself, *You are seriously fucked if you are feeling envious over a goddamn stove*—and walked over to where Tate was standing.

"So I take it this is a nice stove, then," Chase said.

Tate rolled his eyes. "It's fucking gorgeous, that's what it is. This whole place is . . . well, you know how incredible it is."

"I like it. It's big, but Alec and I talked about what a good investment it is. I've got to keep an eye out for my future, when I can't play football anymore."

"Yeah, I can't imagine living here all by myself," Tate mused.

"It's not so bad," Chase said. Sometimes it did feel like too much house. Like he could walk and walk and keep walking and he'd never come face to face with another living creature. He'd thought sometimes he should get a dog, but then that'd be one more thing he'd have to figure out how to deal with during the season.

But still, it *did* get lonely.

"It's not so bad now that I'm here," Tate teased him. "Is that what you're saying?"

He had no idea how right he was. How much his words warmed the place in Chase's heart that felt like it had been cold and dark for the last ten years.

"That," Chase murmured, wrapping his arms around Tate's waist, and pulling him close, "is exactly what I'm saying."

He was no longer quite as surprised when Tate pressed his mouth to his own. Relished the fact that it was Tate, seeking him out. Tate, kissing *him*.

Maybe we're on the same page, after all . . . but then abruptly, Chase's brain went fuzzy, his train of thought completely derailing as Tate pushed him against the counter, his tongue delving deeply into his mouth.

"Fuck," Tate breathed out between kisses. "Feels good, doesn't it?"

Chase didn't know how Tate could've missed his rock-hard cock, pressed up against him, the ultimate evidence that it felt good. Felt even *better* than good.

"Yeah," Chase murmured, his lips seeking Tate's again. "Yeah, let's make it feel even better. Come upstairs."

Tate's face tilted up towards his. "But what about the rest of the house tour?"

"Fuck the tour," Chase said, "and fuck me, instead."

Tate's eyes went wide with shock. "You want that?"

"More than anything," Chase said, and meant every word. He'd only wanted it, and wanted it to be Tate who did the fucking, since watching his very first gay porn, just after high school graduation.

"I thought . . ." Tate stuttered. "I thought . . ."

"That I wouldn't want it? That I'm such an uber-manly football player that the idea of being fucked instead of doing the fucking would turn me off?" Chase chuckled. "Yeah, *no*."

"You," Tate murmured, coming in so close that Chase thought he could see every single shade of gray in his eyes, the flecks of green and blue, "are *not* what I expected."

"Is that a compliment?"

"Yes," Tate said. "Now, where's your bedroom in this gigantic place?"

Chase wrapped his arms around Tate, slipping them lower, right along the gorgeous curve of his ass. "Hop on," he said, giving Tate a boost. His legs went around his waist and Chase wasn't surprised to discover, as he moved towards the back staircase, that Tate wasn't really all that heavy.

"You are a freakish piece of work," Tate said, nibbling on his earlobe as he took the stairs.

"But you love it," Chase pointed out.

Tate could only laugh. "I kind of do," he admitted. "I bet . . ." He trailed off, and Chase, who'd just reached the top of the stairs, pinned him hard against the opposite wall.

"What do you bet?" Chase wondered, their gazes meeting and locking. "You can't go teasing me like that."

"Why?" Tate said, a little recklessly—recklessly because Chase was currently the reason why his legs were not on the ground. "Don't like a little teasing?"

"I want to know what you were going to say," Chase said stubbornly, his mouth only a breath away from Tate's. "Tell me."

"I was thinking . . ." Tate took a deep breath. "I was thinking you could even fuck *me* like this."

"I could," Chase said thoughtfully, giving a test thrust with his hips. "Yeah, I definitely could."

Tate groaned, biting his lip. "Next time, okay?"

"Won't get an argument from me," Chase said and stumbled, his knees suddenly weak, into his bedroom. Depositing Tate on the bed, he shed his shoes, and socks, and when he turned back,

Tate already had his shirt off and their mouths met, the kiss suddenly turning ravenous.

Was it because of what Tate had been thinking about? Because Chase was thinking about it, too, just as he thought about what it was going to feel like when Tate slid those capable, skilled fingers into his ass and took him apart one perfectly aimed thrust at a time.

Tate tugged on the bottom of Chase's shirt, groaning when Chase pulled back, yanking it off.

"Fuck, you are so hot," Tate said, hands suddenly everywhere—on his pecs, his abs, his biceps, tracing every single muscle that he'd worked so long and so hard to hone. "You are an absolutely fucking work of art."

The truth was, Tate wasn't as ripped as Chase, but he was hardly a slouch either. Chase found himself mesmerized by the trail of reddish hair that disappeared under his waistband and traced his fingertips down it, pressing his palm against the hard bulge in Tate's jeans as he groaned, thrusting against his hand.

Tate took a deep breath, shimmying away from Chase's touch. "Take off your pants," he said. Chase did, sliding his jeans off, fingers catching at the waistband of his boxer briefs.

"Those too," Tate said, voice breathless, and Chase held his gaze, his hands trembling as he pulled them down, hissing as his hard cock hit the much colder air.

"Get on the bed," Tate said. "Do you have . . ."

"Drawer," Chase said. Tate had said he was going to take him apart, that he was going to love everything he gave him, but at the same time, he hadn't really anticipated that Tate would be so *in charge*.

Or that it would heat his blood and his skin and his nerves so much. But it did, everything firing so hard and fast that it made him clumsy as he stepped out of his boxer briefs and climbed on the bed, bending over and giving Tate a little wiggle as he went.

"Touch yourself," Tate said, his voice morphing from firm to something made of iron. Chase nearly moaned as he heard it. Why was this turning him on so much? Why did it even matter that he didn't *know* why? It was, and it was working. He should just let it happen. So he did, carefully gripping his own cock, not wanting to get too carried away before they got to the main event.

There was a breathless sense of expectation in the air. Chase couldn't see Tate as he bent down to the comforter. Could only vaguely sense him behind him, still standing next to the bed. Squeezing his eyes shut, he tried to rely on his other senses. He heard the drawer open. He heard it close. He strained to hear anything else. To feel the touch of Tate's fingers, right where he quivered with anticipation.

"Do you know how sexy you are like this?" Tate wondered. "I could look at you like this forever."

Forever. The word clanged around in Chase's fuzzy brain. It sounded good. *So* good.

Then, before he could contemplate what Tate really meant by that, he felt the first wet fingertip press against him, just as Tate's other hand brushed wide, reassuring strokes along his back. "Yeah, baby, just like that," Tate murmured as the first bit of his finger slipped in. Chase arched against it, knowing he liked it, knowing he wanted more. He wondered if Tate had seen the collection of toys in his drawer. Had noticed that the tube of lubricant was half-used.

"Yeah, I know, baby," Tate continued. "I know you need more. I'm gonna give it to you."

Chase let out a shuddering breath as that single finger worked its way inside, and then a second one followed. He wasn't being overly gentle, but he wasn't going as fast as he wanted either. He was taking his time, *savoring* Chase. And that sent a wave of fiery need washing over him. He knew what it felt like to fuck himself. Knew how good it could feel. But had always wondered, what if it was flesh and blood and not silicone? What if it wasn't just a toy, but it was a *man*? An encounter that was more than just pressing the perfect button inside of him?

"That's so good," Tate cooed. "Fuck, you look . . ." Tate muttered an oath under his breath. "I gotta get in you."

He pushed Chase further onto the bed, his fingers still working deep, and the pleasure bloomed hot and deep inside of him.

"Now," Chase begged, his fingers just barely slipping over his rock-hard dick, precome slippery as he rubbed up and back.

"We're gonna go slow, no matter how wild you like to get on your own time," Tate said his tone cautious, but there was a rough, wild edge to it, and Chase wanted nothing more than for him to push his head down, prop his ass up and just *take* him, the way he clearly wanted to.

The way they both wanted him to.

But before Chase could form the words, even in his own brain, there was the feel of Tate's cock, covered in latex, snubbing right up against his hole, beginning to press in.

He'd wondered, so many times, would it feel all that different?

Instantly, as Tate's cock began to slide in, he knew the answer. It was everything he'd loved about fucking himself with the vibrators but so much more. Tate was warm and real against his back, heart beating as hard as Chase's own, and the rhythm of his breathing matching his thrusts as he slipped further and further in, until he was fully seated.

It was warm, too. So goddamned warm. Nothing like cold plastic.

"Fuck," Chase ground out as Tate bottomed out. "Fuck, you feel so good."

Tate's fingers gripped his hips and then he began to thrust, and Chase realized right away that he *wasn't* going to be gentle. His thrusts were sharp and staccato, hitting him right where he wanted it, and he found himself bracing against the comforter as Tate fucked him just as he always imagined he would, rough and hard and somehow soft, all at the same time.

Chase could hear someone muttering, someone moaning, and he realized that it was *him*. He was the one begging and pleading and groaning, the pleasure making its way through him in a hot, endless rush. He was barely touching his own cock, but he knew it wouldn't matter, he was too close, and the feel of Tate's cock was too perfect inside of him for him to last much longer, even as he tried to prolong the dirty joy of his first fucking.

Hopefully, not his last.

Then Tate gave a particularly sharp thrust, aimed just right, and it undid him, his orgasm washing over him in a big, blinding wave, as he felt his cock jump and streaks of come hit his fingers.

"Fuck," Tate wailed behind him, and Chase's own orgasm stretched as he felt Tate's come begin to fill the condom, so hot inside of him.

It was everything he'd ever wanted from sex, and he'd always wondered if he was asking for too much—but now he knew he wasn't. That kind of all-consuming rush was possible, and not only was it *possible* with Tate, it was better than he'd ever imagined it could be.

Chase slumped down on the bed, feeling Tate's cock slip out of him.

"Goddamn," Tate muttered. Like he couldn't even quite believe what had just happened. Then Chase felt a warm, reassuring hand on his back. "You good?" he asked.

Chase's heart flipped and then flopped. It was too much. All that fucking incredible sex, and then that sweet caring nature that Tate had always possessed. He didn't just want part of it; he wanted it all.

Chase squeezed his eyes shut and nodded. He was in *deep*. It was impossible to even deny it any longer.

"Okay, I'm gonna get cleaned up . . ." Tate said, and Chase's heart beat faster. Was he going to run again? Like the time he had when they'd had their first kiss? But he'd just gotten here. Chase wanted more.

He pushed himself up and rolled over, definitely aware of the mess they were making. "I'll come with you, show you the bath-room," Chase said, wincing a little as he stood up. Tate glanced over at him.

"I'm . . ."

"Don't you dare apologize," Chase said, leaning down and kissing Tate firmly. "It was the best sex I've ever had, in my whole goddamn life."

"Okay," Tate said, smiling as they walked into the adjoining bathroom together.

There was a very vocal part of Tate that could not believe what had just happened. Sure, he'd only been dreaming about doing it for the last ten years, but even after Chase had come out, he'd still never really expected it to happen.

But Chase had not only asked for it, he'd enjoyed every second of it. He'd wondered if Chase would, after not only asking for it, but after Tate had found evidence that he had clearly been experimenting on his own.

Tate found himself lying there, spread out across Chase's chest, feeling very smug about practically everything. Say Cheese was doing great and was now in the Food Truck Warriors, officially, after Rachel had sent over the signed paperwork yesterday. He and Chase were enjoying some *very* fine sexual benefits to their fake relationship, and even if it never became real, he thought he could live with it, because at least he'd discovered what being with Chase Riley was really like.

Stupendous. Amazing. Life-altering.

Based on those adjectives it didn't sound like he *could* get over any of it ending, but he would, he knew he would. He pushed that thought aside, because he was being smug right now, and future panic was not allowed.

He'd even come up with a good idea on how to save Chase's career with the Riptide. Maybe it wouldn't work but he'd have tried—and Tate would have done everything he could to give back to the guy who'd nearly singlehandedly saved their business.

It was a good day. *No, scratch that,* Tate thought with satisfaction, *it had been a very good day.*

"I talked to Alec," Chase said sleepily, shifting underneath him slightly. "He thinks you might be insane or a genius. It's hard to say which yet."

"Genius. Absolutely genius," Tate said. "There's really not even a question."

Chase chuckled, Tate feeling the rumbling of it through his body. "Feeling yourself, eh, Ward?"

It had used to bother Tate when Chase had called him by his last name—and only his last name. Now, he rarely did it, and it was, Tate decided, rather adorable, now that he wasn't constantly worried that Chase's nickname meant he didn't care about him after all.

"Maybe I am, Riley," Tate teased back. He reached down, gripped some of that incredibly muscular ass. The one he'd just fucked. The one that *he'd* just fucked. *Oh my god.* That would be an ego trip basically from now until the end of goddamn time. "After all, I just got a piece of this. And a fine piece it was."

Chase laughed outright. "Trust me, it was an ego boost for me too."

"Seriously?" Tate scoffed. He was about to offer his opinion that if Chase had ever opened up his house and potentially his bed to offers, he'd have had a line around the block. Around the next *ten* blocks. But then Chase tucked a hand around Tate's back and trailing up his spine, ruffled his hair.

"I only got the guy who made me *want* to be fucked, to fuck me for the first time. Why wouldn't I be pretty damn happy with myself?"

Maybe it was not cool to be so, well . . . *uncool*, but Tate found himself absolutely fucking flabbergasted. "Really?" he said, craning his neck so he could look Chase in the eye. His eyes were dark in the dim light of the room, and they were absolutely one hundred percent serious.

Chase meant what he was saying, and that was a truth bomb that Tate didn't quite know how to deal with.

"Yeah," Chase said, nodding. "You should be feeling yourself. You just fulfilled a dream of mine."

"You really mean that," Tate said, incredulously. "Because it was . . ."

The corner of Chase's mouth quirked up. "A dream of yours, too? Huh, I had no idea."

Tate smacked him in the arm, and then settled back down into Chase's arms. Because they were really damn nice arms, and moving was still overrated. "I wonder what our high school selves would say to us right now?" he wondered.

"High school Chase would definitely be high-fiving me right now," Chase said seriously. "He'd want to know how I sealed the deal, and I'd have to tell him, I impressed you not with my on-the-field prowess or my charm, but my goddamn *kitchen*."

"Well, those things weren't exactly hurting you," Tate admitted. "But yeah, it was probably the kitchen."

"What would high school Tate say?"

"He wouldn't know *what* to say," Tate offered wryly. "He'd probably be speechless. Then he'd probably want to make sure that I didn't come in point five seconds, a problem he was dealing with back then, every time he so much as *thought* of you when he had a hand on his cock."

Tate felt *another* cock begin to stir to life underneath him, and it wasn't his own. "Like it when I say that, huh?" he teased.

"Do I like it when the word cock is in your mouth?" Chase wondered. "Yeah, I really fucking do. But I'd like it when my cock is in your mouth, more."

"That could be arranged."

"Yes," Chase said. "But not . . . not just yet. I'm comfy."

"Me too," Tate agreed. He hesitated. "So what else did Alec say?"

"He said he'd send over a few things we could do right away, and said he'd consult with one of his friends that's in PR to put together a more extensive list. You know," Chase warned, "this probably means you're going to have to take some time away from the truck."

Tate had already figured that out. "Yeah," he said. "I can call in a few favors, with Lucas and Tony. Rachel also put out a job posting today, and we're going to be interviewing this week."

"Replacing me already?" Chase teased. "I thought you said I did a good job today."

"You did, but sooner or later, you're going to be destined for bigger, brighter things," Tate said regretfully. And if those things happened to be away from LA, he was going to have to come to terms with having this much of Chase Riley, and nothing more.

No matter what he told himself, he knew, deep down, that it was not going to be easy to adjust to that new reality.

Even though he shouldn't have, and it had only been a little over a week since Chase had come into his life again, he'd begun to get used to him being there.

The separation, when it inevitably happened, was going to hurt like hell, but until then? Tate resolved that he was going to enjoy every second of this.

"So what's on the short list?" Tate asked.

"I don't know," Chase admitted. "He's probably sent it over but I don't know where my phone is . . . oh, it's probably still in my jeans pocket." Tate felt him shift underneath him, felt the muscles he was plastered against strain, slightly. "There," Chase said with satisfaction. "Got it."

"Do you know how *not* to be a physically impressive specimen?" Tate wondered.

"Nope," Chase said. "Okay, here's the email. Um, well, it's not a long list. You're probably going to hate the first item on it."

"What is it?" Tate told himself that this was the *very least* he could do.

"He says we need to establish ourselves as a couple, and that includes more than just tweeting about my boyfriend's food truck and more than me working at it. He wants us to . . . *ugh*," Chase said. "Really?"

"What is it?" Tate didn't know what could possibly be so bad that would make Chase sound so disgusted.

"O'Connor is having a charity benefit in LA this Friday. He wants us to go. Together. As a couple."

Tate froze. "Does that bother you?" he asked, trying to keep his tone carefully neutral.

"Going together as a couple?" Tate felt Chase shake his head emphatically. "No, no, not at all. It's . . . *ugh*," he repeated. "No. It's Colin O'Connor. His foundation. The one he runs with his husband."

Tate did not really follow football—or even sports—with the exception of Chase and the Riptide. "Colin O'Connor, the quarterback?"

"Yeah," Chase said shortly. "Well, not anymore. He retired. After he won the Super Bowl."

Suddenly it occurred to Tate why Chase might not like Colin O'Connor. "His team beat the Riptide in the Super Bowl last year."

"Yes," Chase said flatly. "And a very good friend of mine—well, you've met him. Neal. He missed a field goal that would've won that game and he got all kinds of shit for it. Gave himself even *more* shit for it. And just . . . it's not O'Connor's fault, I know it isn't, but seeing him? Makes me kinda see red."

"But I'll be there," Tate said. "Maybe it won't be so bad."

"Maybe it won't," Chase said, but he didn't exactly sound sure of that fact.

CHAPTER TWELVE

Tate did not have any idea what to expect when Chase picked him up to go to the benefit a few nights later. However, he was not surprised, after remembering Chase's words, to see that this time Chase had decided that subtlety was overrated and had shown up in the custom bright turquoise Audi roadster that he was so well-known for.

Chase had been tense from the moment he'd picked Tate up, almost silent in the car, even as Tate tried to make small talk, mostly about Say Cheese and the work they'd done that week.

"The new sandwich is selling great," Tate said as Chase merged onto the freeway. "Though that might be because you posted about it on Instagram." The new Philly-cheesesteak-inspired grilled cheese had originally been Chase's suggestion, and Tate had thrown it together with none of his usual obsessive recipe testing. He'd hoped it would sell well, and people would like it, but he hadn't had high expectations. However, like everything Chase touched, it turned to gold and they'd sold out of it three days out of five this week.

"Maybe it was a good idea, but you're the one who created it," Chase said, neatly deflecting the compliment. He hadn't been as morose about his trade situation this week, though Tate could tell that he wasn't quite himself either. He'd worked at the truck several days during the week, and while not everything had gone smoothly, Tate was being forced to face the cold, hard truth: they definitely needed the extra help, even if the extra help was Chase.

"We have someone we're trying out next week," Tate said, trying a new subject on for size, hoping that the fact he wouldn't be working every single day next week might improve Chase's mood. "I think she's going to be a good addition to the truck."

"Replacing me already?" Chase asked wryly, his glance over at Tate swift as he changed lanes.

"You know we need the help. Now, and definitely when we move to the lot," Tate said. "If we had the space, we could probably use all four of us on some of the busier shifts."

Chase nodded, but didn't reply.

Tate knew he needed to figure out what was bothering Chase. Showing up at this big gala, their first significant public outing since Chase had tweeted about his boyfriend's food truck, looking like they were already on the outs? Not good.

"So tell me about this guy," Tate said.

"Guy?" Chase deflected—even though he must know perfectly well who Tate was talking about.

"The quarterback guy who runs this charity."

"You mean Colin O'Connor?" Chase raised an eyebrow. "You know who Colin O'Connor is," he added.

Of course Tate knew who Colin O'Connor was. He'd been the first player in the National Football League to come out of the closet as queer when he'd announced that he was bisexual. He'd dated the gay journalist, Nick Wheeler, who'd written his coming out profile, and then had eventually married him.

On a quick break yesterday, Tate had even looked up what Colin O'Connor had been up to since retirement—and it was mainly charity work, using his name to bring money and prestige to events like the gala they were about to attend.

It seemed odd that Chase disliked him so much; even though O'Connor and the Miami Piranhas *had* defeated Chase and the Riptide in the Super Bowl.

"I know who he is," Tate said. "I want to know why you dislike him."

"I don't *dislike* him," Chase claimed, but Tate knew him well enough to hear the lie in his voice.

"Uh-huh," Tate said. He was not even remotely convinced.

Chase sighed. "He's just so . . . just so *good*," he said, with vehemence. "He's like a walking public service announcement, and it gets old."

"He was the first football player to come out of the closet," Tate pointed out. "He made it possible for you and a lot of your friends to be honest about yourselves."

"I know," Chase said, and now he sounded guilty. "I *shouldn't* get annoyed with him, but I do. His husband is fun, though, sometimes."

"The journalist?"

"Yeah. Nick. I think he retired, too. God knows they have enough money."

"And now they run a charity."

"So many charities," Chase grumbled. "They make the rest of us look like selfish brats."

Ah, so that was the problem. Tate realized that what Chase was afraid of was O'Connor making him look bad. He'd taken his platform and done something with it. And what had Chase done? Nothing remotely close to the same thing.

"You don't have to be some kind of paragon to be worthwhile, you know," Tate said.

"I know," Chase agreed, but that false note was back in his voice, and Tate knew he didn't really believe him.

"You've done good things," Tate said. "You helped *me*. You go to charity stuff, I saw . . ." He stopped abruptly. Afraid, like he almost always was these days, of giving something of himself and his feelings away. Maybe that wouldn't be such a bad thing, but he wasn't convinced that their "relationship" was going to last past the point they'd agreed. Some days, Tate didn't know if it would even last *that* long. He had to keep reminding himself they weren't some big epic love story, so he *couldn't* say shit like, "I've seen everything that you've done because I've had a Google Alert on your name for ten years." He'd had it before Google Alerts were even a thing. Practically made a career out of digging obscure Chase Riley stories out of the depths of the internet.

"You saw what?" Chase asked as he pulled the car up to the large building. There were twinkly lights in all the trees, rainbow silk swags lining the front of the entrance, and valets wearing Pride t-shirts under their dark jackets.

"Wow, this looks amazing," Tate said, changing the subject.

"It looks like just the kind of over-the-top bullshit that O'Connor would like," Chase grumbled as the valet opened his door. Another valet followed suit on the passenger side, helping Tate out of the car.

"Come on," Tate said as he and Chase faced the entrance together. "It can't be that bad."

Chase chuckled darkly. "Or it could be worse."

"On the upside, I think we both look *very* handsome," Tate said, nudging Chase with his hip as he reached down and took his hand. Grasped it tightly. "Especially you."

"You like my shirt?"

The invite to the gala, which Chase had forwarded over to Tate, had specified that unlike most big charity balls, the dress code for this event wasn't black tie or even semi-formal—the request was to wear "a shirt that best expresses your sexuality."

"I *love* your shirt," Tate said. Knew that Chase wasn't quite feeling as comfortable as Tate was. But the "I play for both teams," with the faux sports logo on it, fit him to a tee (*literally*, Tate thought with an internal chuckle), and he should wear it with pride.

Tate looked forward to LA Pride every year, and liked to collect the t-shirts with the most ridiculous sayings. For this event, he'd pulled out one of his favorites. It had "I support the homosexual agenda," emblazoned on the front in rainbow lettering.

"Yours is great too," Chase said. Squeezing his hand back. "I'm . . . I was afraid I didn't really . . . that I shouldn't . . ."

"You should," Tate interrupted firmly. "You absolutely should. Own it, okay?"

But Chase still looked unsure, and Tate decided that wouldn't do. There was nothing he'd done or hadn't done that should make him feel ashamed. It was especially hard for Tate when he remembered how absolutely perfectly shameless Chase had been when he'd fucked him. Except that hadn't been in public; nobody else knew what had happened.

Tate tugged him over to the side, near one of the potted trees dotted in twinkle lights. "Listen," he said softly, "if you don't want to do this, we don't have to."

"Do you think I don't want to?" Chase sounded mildly anguished. "I *do*. I'm fucking jealous as hell of Colin O'Connor, who believed he could just say *fuck it* to everyone who disapproved of who he was. I thought I could do the same, but then, I hear I might be traded, maybe to some place that isn't quite so safe, maybe not so protected, and what do I do? I *freak the fuck out*."

"You're really blaming yourself for being afraid?" Tate supposed he shouldn't be surprised. This was Chase, who had seemingly waltzed through life without many obstacles. Yes, he'd worked his ass off, but he'd been born with an insane amount of inherent skill. He'd been a golden boy before he even knew what being a golden boy meant.

And fear? Fear was a huge fucking obstacle. Still, Tate had never really considered Chase to be particularly cowardly. He'd always turned aside criticism and judgment like it just didn't exist. But now? Tate could see him practically trembling with it.

"Fuck yes I am," Chase said. "I'm . . . I should be better than this. I should have . . ."

"I think you should cut yourself some slack," Tate said honestly. "Coming out isn't something that's ever going to be easy. Especially when you're a public figure. It *means* something. And every time you do it—and yes, I am using the plural here, because unlike the way 'coming out' sounds, it's something you sometimes have to do every day of your goddamned life—it takes guts. I know you've got guts, Chase, but it's also okay to admit you're afraid. Sometimes admitting *that* takes the most guts of all."

Chase looked at him in disbelief. "Seriously?"

"Seriously," Tate said with a sharp nod. "It's okay to be afraid. It's a fucking frightening thing. And"—he hesitated, because while he didn't want to give away that he'd been watching Chase for the last ten years, he also didn't want him to live in fear, either—"and I've gotten the impression from your behavior that you've been trying to hide *you* from the world. And now you're walking into the light and that *is* fucking terrifying."

"Yeah," Chase said. His hand was still gripping Tate's hard, but his eyes were clearer. Less cloudy. He looked more determined. "Yeah, it is. But that isn't all of it . . ."

Tate watched as Chase took a deep breath, and he realized that this was blind panic. Chase didn't just need a friendly shoulder to support him, but maybe some *real* help. "Are you okay?" he asked quietly.

Chase stared at him, deer in the headlights. "Uh," he said.

"What do you need to be okay?" Tate didn't know what all of Chase's issues were, but he knew the least he could do was to offer that shoulder. Even if it wasn't enough.

"This . . ." Chase took a deep, shuddering breath. "Just this. Talking. Focusing on what's real, and what isn't exaggerated by my stupid brain."

"Alright," Tate said and held his gaze. "Look at me. Just at me, okay?"

"Okay."

Tate held Chase's hands tightly, and felt him squeeze back. Saw the wild look in his eyes begin to fade.

"Listen to my voice, okay? You're not a fraud. You're not pretending. You're *you*, and unique and amazing, and you don't have to be like anyone else for me to see you that way, okay?"

Chase's gaze was still wide, but his breath wasn't coming in short pants anymore, and he looked calmer. More put together. More like Chase.

"Do you want to still go in?" Tate asked carefully. "We don't have to do this."

Chase's tongue flicked out, and he licked his lips. "I want to, though. I . . . I just get overwhelmed sometimes. And usually that's when I fuck up, but you helped. Thank you."

"Of course." Tate's fingers tightened on Chase's. "I'm happy to be here for you. Whenever you need it."

"Even when I'm afraid?"

"Especially when you're afraid," Tate told him with conviction. He wanted to tell Chase that there was nothing sexier than a man who was willing to be vulnerable.

Chase looked surprised. "You mean that."

"Of course I do," Tate said. He squeezed Chase's hands again. "Come on, you've got this. What do you do when you're afraid?"

Chase smiled, the expression on his face growing brighter and brighter, dwarfing the terror that had been there, only a few minutes before. *This* was the Chase that had captivated Tate in high school. The Chase that had never let go of his heart. Not once, not in ten long years.

"I tell fear to fuck off," Chase said firmly. With confidence. "I guess I was afraid I didn't deserve to wear this," he said, gesturing to his chest. "I haven't always been as honest as I could be with everyone. Not as honest as I wanted to be."

"Everyone doesn't *deserve* to know your truth. You don't owe anyone anything. The only one you need to be honest with about it is *you*," Tate said. "And I think you've known for awhile now how you feel."

"I have." Chase's eyes were dark and serious. Tate's breath caught in his throat. *He's not talking about you. He can't be talking about you.* Except he could be. Maybe Tate had known he was gay before Home Economics their senior year, but Chase had been the first big crush he'd ever had.

Sometimes Tate thought he'd be the *last* big crush he'd ever have.

"We should go in," Tate said, hating to break the moment, but at the same time, wondering how many of these moments they could have, before it became impossible to walk away. Moments when everything felt real and nothing felt fake.

"Should we?" Chase's eyes sparkled. "I'm tempted to take you right back to the car."

Tate was tempted too, even though every night they spent together was going to make it harder to leave, when the relationship inevitably ended. "But what about the plan?" he said. "You want to stay in LA? We need to make you look good."

"Are you saying I don't look good?" Chase teased gently.

Tate rolled his eyes and tugged on their joined hands. Knew that while *yes*, maybe Chase wanted to have sex, what he was really doing was putting off the inevitable. "Come on," he said. "The party awaits."

Chase had never imagined that coming tonight would bring on one of those fucking annoying panic attacks—or he'd never have agreed to come at all. But Tate, *Tate,* had talked him right through it, acting like he wasn't even the least bit ashamed or disgusted by Chase's emotions.

Chase knew he was hanging on to Tate's hand like it was a lifeline as they walked in. And he decided that was okay. If Tate thought it was, who was Chase to argue with him?

He'd gone to plenty of these fundraisers when he'd been comfortably occupying the role of "ally." Had thought, in that faraway, hazy future when he'd be out and proud, that it wouldn't feel much different. Had imagined that maybe it might even feel better, like he finally, really belonged.

But it didn't. Instead he'd felt like a fraud. He'd been a chickenshit, watching and waiting on the sideline, while these guys—Colin and his husband and Heath and Sam and Neal and Jamie—had changed the game. Changed the goddamn *world.*

"I can feel you thinking too hard again," Tate muttered under his breath as they passed under another set of rainbow swags at the entrance to the ballroom. "Just relax, okay? Everything's gonna be fine."

Together, they walked through a series of multicolored balloons that made up a series of rainbows.

Then they emerged into the room itself, and Tate laughed in delight. "They made *Pride*," he said, his smile dazzling as he took in the mini floats, covered in glitter and sequins and a thousand different sizes and shapes of rainbows. The main stage was hung with shiny gold and silver tinsel, sparkling with the light reflected off about twenty or so disco balls hanging from the ceiling.

It was a *lot*, but then Colin O'Connor had never done anything halfway in his entire life. Whatever he committed to, he threw himself into completely.

"I guess I expected some kind of stuffy event, with, like, boring speeches and music that was twenty years old," Tate said, and his eyes were practically glowing with excitement. "But this looks like a lot of fun." He pointed to a glittery sign that advertised, *Drag Show at Nine.* "And look!" he added. "They're even going to have a drag show. That is so cool."

"O'Connor does like to pull out all the stops," Chase said, amused, even though there was part of him that wanted to be annoyed.

"Good evening," said a woman with a purple and pink stripe in her cropped white-blonde hair. "Welcome to the annual fundraiser for the Rise Foundation."

"I'm Chase Riley and this is Tate Ward," he said, watching as she noted their names on the list she was carrying on a rainbow-emblazoned clipboard.

"Great," she said. "The buffet starts in about an hour, and the drag show about forty minutes after that, but until then, feel free to mingle. There's also the silent auction table, on the other side of the ballroom." She pointed in the direction of several long, rainbow-swagged tables. "So many of our local businesses have donated incredible prizes. You should definitely check them out."

You have lots and lots of money, Chase translated, *go buy something with some of it.*

"Awesome," Chase said and tugged Tate in the direction of the silent auction tables.

He could see Colin and his husband holding court on the other side of the room. Neal had told him that he and Jamie had been invited, but that he had an important meeting. "I sent a big check instead," Neal had texted. Which Chase was pretty sure meant, *I don't want to go there and deal with all that field goal crap again, I'm done with it.* Sam and Heath were snorkeling in the Maldives, so they wouldn't be here either.

But then, Chase reminded himself, the point of this wasn't to hang out with his friends, it was to announce to the Riptide and to Los Angeles and the greater sports world in general that he and Tate were together now and he was going to be using his position to contribute to worthwhile causes that he cared about.

"Look at this," Tate said. He pointed to one of the gift baskets. It was tastefully decorated with a subtle gold ribbon, and as Chase looked closer, he saw several bottles of wine, and a restaurant gift certificate.

"Isn't this the same place we went with your agent?" Tate wondered. "And the wine? I think it's the same, too."

Sure enough, Alec Kaufman was listed, in small print, as the donor of the basket.

"Alec's gay too, you know," Chase said, wishing that itch wasn't back at the base of his skull. Wishing that his mind would stop telling him that he didn't really deserve to be here. "He's the one who got me the invite. I'm sure he was invited too. Maybe we'll see him."

But Chase didn't really think so. Alec had given him strict instructions for the night—*stick close to Tate, and make sure everyone knows you're together. Spend some money. Write O'Connor a big check.*

"Should we bid?" Tate wondered, chewing on his bottom lip. He was probably agonizing over the neat script that offered a base "suggested bid."

"No, we'll find something else. Besides, we've already been there, right?" Chase said, and they moved on to the next basket.

It took him a second to take in the brightly colored card, and the even more brightly colored silicone objects in the basket.

"They aren't joking around here," Tate murmured under his breath as he leaned in, peering at the different dildos and butt plugs that were artistically arranged in the basket. "Hey, you might . . ."

Chase felt his face flame red, even though Tate hadn't spoken nearly loud enough for anyone to hear him. "What?" he stuttered.

"We should bid on this," Tate said, glancing over at him, his gray eyes amused and also calculating. "If we do, everyone's gonna know the truth."

The truth. If only the truth wasn't buried under way too many layers of lies. Chase took a deep breath. "You think so?"

Tate looked speculatively at the basket, and then at Chase. "Of course, they might think it'll be *me* who'll use them, and I might, but you'd love them."

He really would. Chase grabbed the pen and signed his name and a bid about a thousand dollars over the minimum before he could change his mind.

"You really aren't fucking around," Tate said with a chuckle. "I like it."

They turned to go to the next basket, and Chase realized that there was a couple walking towards them. He recognized them and realized this whole conversation was probably inevitable. Ryan Flores reached them first, as his husband finished writing down a bid for a basket.

"Hey," Ryan said, reaching out and shaking Chase's hand. "I thought I might see you here." There was no judgment in his voice, but a bright curiosity in his gaze. "And Tate, right?" Ryan said, turning towards him. "Wyatt tells me that your food truck is going to be in our lot."

"Yes, it is," Tate said confidently, shaking Ryan's hand next. "I'm thrilled to be included."

"You've met my husband, right?" Ryan said casually as Wyatt approached.

"Never been that lucky," Chase said. "But it's great to meet you."

Wyatt Flores had kind eyes, a handsome face, and a firm handshake. "I can't believe we haven't met before, especially now . . ." He smiled, crinkles forming by his eyes. "Well, especially now that you've taken such an interest in the local food truck community."

"He's been a godsend," Tate said, throwing a fond, adoring look his direction that hit Chase right in the solar plexus. Did Tate really mean that—and *why?* Also, was that look real, or was he just a fantastic actor?

But Chase didn't think so. Tate didn't have that kind of acting in him.

He was beginning to believe that his whole plan—to win Tate over—had been pointless from the start. If he'd just found the guts to be honest that first night, when he'd let himself get carried away on Twitter, they could've been dating *for real* this whole time.

"I hear he's even working shifts for you," Wyatt said. "I can't get Ryan anywhere near our trucks, but that's probably for the best."

"He tries really hard, and honestly, the people who come to see him? It really adds that little bit of extra *oomph*, you know?" Tate said. And Chase, who definitely would've felt like a piece of meat, if just about anyone else had said that about him, found himself flattered and thrilled that he'd been able to make such a difference in Tate's life.

"Oh, it's definitely better all around that I stay away," Ryan inserted smoothly into the conversation. "But, I actually had a proposition I'd like to discuss with you, Riley, if you've got a second?"

Chase nodded, hating that he felt wary. What was Flores going to say to him? This was a guy who, just like Colin O'Connor, had been the first "out" player in his particular sport. He'd done it before he'd even been drafted, and then after the Los Angeles Dodgers had taken him, he'd proceeded to prove that no matter what he was, he could play the hell out of the game.

"Well, you know, the new food truck lot is opening in a few weeks," Ryan said, drawing Chase to the side, leaving Wyatt and Tate to their conversation. "I thought it'd be fun to hold a pre-opening fundraising event for my own charity. It's got a carnival theme. I'm inviting a diverse group. Make-a-Wish kids, lots of adolescents and teenagers from the local LGBT shelter, all kinds. I thought you might want to help me."

"Help you?" Chase hated how incredulous he sounded, but it was the truth. Who would ever think of putting on such a great community event, and then think, *oh, hey, I should invite Chase Riley to help me—that guy who danced drunkenly by himself on stage when he lost the AFC Championship?*

"Yeah," Ryan said enthusiastically. "I thought, you've got a great connection to the food truck community, and I'd like to reach past my baseball friends, and get some of the Riptide involved. You'd be perfect."

"You really think so?" Chase found himself asking. *He* wasn't even sure he'd be perfect.

"It's not easy doing what you did. I've been there, and I know," Ryan said. "But I find focusing on helping others, others who need it way more than we do, it helps. What do you say?"

"Count me in," Chase said firmly. Because he was willing to sign on for anything that might help silence all those unpleasant voices inside of him. Besides, after the food lot opened, he might not even *be* part of the Riptide anymore. He might as well do one last really good thing, before he was forced out.

"Great," Ryan said.

They exchanged numbers, and then wandered over to where Wyatt and Tate were talking excitedly. It sounded like the subject was the food truck lot, and all the big plans they were making for it.

Chase felt a pang of something that might be envy. He wanted to be making plans for next season, for mini camp and for the preseason games. But instead, he was caught in limbo, not sure where he was going to end up playing next year. It was frustrating and Chase didn't like it at all.

"We should get a group chat going," Tate suggested, smiling as Wyatt nodded with excitement.

"Yeah, totally. And I love that theme night idea," Wyatt added.

"It sounds like you've got lots going on," Ryan said, and they both nodded. Tate looked about as thrilled as he had when Chase had told him that the line for the truck stretched around the block.

Or the night they'd gone out to dinner. Maybe, Chase thought, hope rising inside his chest, maybe even as excited as the time that he'd asked Tate to fuck him.

"We do," Wyatt said.

A fan approached then, asking for Ryan's autograph, which he gave with a smile and a nod, and a quick flourish. He and Wyatt wandered off after that, leaving Tate and Chase still examining the different gifts up for auction.

"This looks fun," Tate said, pointing to a certificate for a full week on a Key West fishing trip on a luxury yacht. Chase thought it sounded a lot like the trip that Heath and Sam had first met on, and remembered how much fun they'd had on it. *Less the fishing, and more the company,* Heath had said, shooting his boyfriend a warm, immensely fond smile.

"Yeah, it does," Chase said, and signed a bid for that one too. If he won it, it'd be a good present for his friends.

Tate raised an eyebrow. "You want to go fishing for a week?"

"Not for me," Chase offered. "But Heath and Sam? They'd love it."

"You're a good guy," Tate said, patting him on the back. But instead of his hand sliding away, it stayed, feeling warm and solid. Chase refused to let himself think that he was just touching him more than usual because they were supposed to be giving the impression that they were a super loved-up couple. He wanted to believe that Tate wasn't doing it for *only* that reason, anyway.

"Really?" Chase knew he sounded skeptical.

"Really," Tate said firmly. "And I'm not saying that, really. I . . . well, I'll admit, I followed you. Pretty closely, in fact." He blushed. "Closer than I should have, considering we weren't really friends."

"But we're friends now."

Tate's gray eyes simmered with something—Chase wanted it to be affection and care. For *him*. "More than friends, I'd like to think," Tate said softly. "Anyway, I know you aren't doing all this shit just to make sure you look good. You *are* good. Maybe you can fool other people, but you've never been able to fool me."

It was the truth—bare, brutal honesty. And it filled him with a little bit of anxiousness, but mostly, it felt like the world was opening up in front of him. Could he have Tate, and not just for four weeks?

Chase glanced out onto the central dance floor, where several couples were swaying to a slow, sweet song. "We should dance," he said. If Tate felt like they should be touching, he was going to take that idea and run with it.

Maybe in the end, even if he convinced Tate to date him for real, it wouldn't matter, because they'd end up separated by thousands of miles, but Chase wasn't the giving-up kind. The idea of a long-distance relationship was awful, but after losing Tate once, Chase wasn't sure he could face losing him again.

"We should, huh?" Tate said, his smile lighting up his eyes. The hand on his shoulder pressed in, fingertips digging affectionately into the cotton of his t-shirt. "I didn't know you were the dancing type."

Chase raised an eyebrow. "I'm sure you heard about the post-AFC Championship debacle," he said.

"Oh, I did," Tate said. "But I meant more of the *romantic slow dancing* type."

Normally he wasn't. He was very much the *drunken, stupid dancing around* kind, which was surely what Tate had meant and had decided not to say out loud. But with Tate? He wanted to be better. And, he also wasn't averse to touching him as much as he could.

Maybe even sneaking a kiss or two.

"Maybe there's lots you don't know about me," Chase said, reaching down and tangling their fingers together. Tugging him in the direction of the dance floor.

As they reached the dance floor, Tate raised an eyebrow as Chase pulled him close. As close as he dared, considering this was supposed to be a charity event. They probably wouldn't be too happy if he started grinding on Tate's leg in the middle of the ballroom.

"I doubt that," Tate said.

"Oh, you're an expert on me now, because you've been stalking me for years?" Chase teased.

Just like Chase had expected, Tate flushed a bright red. "Maybe," he said.

"I think," Chase said, swaying to the music, enjoying the hell out of the way Tate felt, and pulling him even tighter against him.

"I think that I really like that you had such a big crush on me in high school that you kept tabs on me after, Ward."

The sudden panic in Tate's gray eyes made it clear he'd just landed squarely on a truth that Tate didn't want to talk about. Which meant that Chase *really* wanted to talk about it. Was it possible that Tate had been crushing on him, from a distance, this whole time? For ten long years? Same as Chase?

He thought it might be true, and he wanted Tate to say it, more than anything.

Wanted this date to be more than just improving his reputation. Wanted them both to be here because they couldn't stand to be anywhere else.

"That's . . . that's a theory," Tate finally stuttered.

"Yeah, it is," Chase said, humming to the music as he cradled the man he was beginning to think he'd never get over in his arms. "It's a theory I really like."

"Really?" Tate's voice sounded hopeful—so hopeful that Chase could feel his own heart leaping with the possibilities.

"Yeah," Chase said. "You were lucky. It was easy to keep tabs on me. But you? Not quite so easy."

Tate stopped moving abruptly and stared at Chase's face, wonder and disbelief dawning in his eyes. "You wanted to keep tabs on me?"

"Yeah," Chase said. Wondered why he hadn't just been this honest, back when he'd first tweeted about Tate's food truck. Frankly, he should've been this honest *before* tweeting about the food truck. He should've been honest back in high school, and if he hadn't been, he *still* should've been honest when he'd first come to see Tate about using his name.

Tate's fingers were trembling on Chase's neck as they began to dance again.

"I hoped," he finally said. "I hoped, a lot, but it's something to keep that hope alive for ten years."

"It's extraordinary." Chase looked down into Tate's eyes. Hoped, like he'd never hoped before that they were on the same page. "I'd even call it a miracle."

"Really?" Tate's voice wavered. He still sounded the tiniest bit unsure. And that, Chase realized, wouldn't do. He needed to be honest. He'd been honest, finally, about who he was. Now he needed to be honest about how he felt.

"None of this has ever been fake for me," Chase admitted. "None of it. There's nothing I want more than you."

Tate stared at him for one long moment, and just when Chase was beginning to become afraid that he'd said the wrong thing and stuck his foot in his mouth, Tate reached up and pressed his lips to Chase's.

It was too quick by half, especially for their first honest kiss, but when Tate pulled away, he murmured, "You have to know, I've hardly been subtle about it, but I've wanted you for the last ten years. Never really stopped. I'd take you like this—rich and popular and famous—or I'd take you if you were just like me."

And Chase believed him.

CHAPTER THIRTEEN

Tate had known this evening would be surreal—it was hard to imagine going to Colin O'Connor's fundraiser with Chase and actually feeling like he belonged there, both at the party, and by Chase's side—but as it happened, things were even more fantastical than he could've ever imagined them.

Chase *liked* him. For real. They'd kissed on the dance floor, and twice more, during the drag show, and Tate was pretty sure, as they stood at the entrance, waiting for the valet to bring Chase's car, that *none* of it had been for show.

He was *dating* Chase Riley.

Finally. After all these years.

It felt . . . *well,* Tate thought, *it feels too good to be true.*

But it was true, because he'd seen the brutal, honest truth shining in Chase's eyes, and he'd known that he wasn't lying.

"You look . . ." Chase gave him a fond look. Now that Tate knew the truth, it was rapidly becoming obvious that Chase had felt this way from the beginning, and he'd just . . . missed it somehow. *More like, believed it was impossible,* Tate's brain pointed out.

Tate held up the basket they'd won. They'd won *more* than one, actually, but the others had been envelopes full of gift certificates, easy to stuff into Chase's pocket. But not this one. "I look like I'm shamelessly holding a basket full of dildos?" he suggested.

Chase laughed. Free and easier than he had in a week. *You did that,* Tate's brain also pointed out, *and you helped him feel like he belonged in a place like this.*

Tate still couldn't quite believe it, because he'd imagined that this was the kind of thing Chase was innately comfortable with—big gala events with other famous people, where he was expected to throw his money around. Where the bar was open, and the only time Tate had to pull out his wallet was to drop a tip into the discreet jar.

The valet pulled up with the car, and Tate swore he gave him a wink and a nod of approval. Yeah, like *anyone* wouldn't be fucking thrilled to death, walking out of here with Chase Riley on one arm and a basket full of sex toys on the other.

He *was* lucky, and he knew just how much, because for so long he'd fantasized about this and then forced himself to conclude it would never happen.

But it was definitely happening.

"No," Chase said, throwing him another lopsided grin as they slid into the car, "though, believe me, that's fulfilling a few fantasies I didn't know I had."

Tate raised an eyebrow, feeling his skin prickle with the realization—for the second or tenth or hundredth time—that Chase wanted him just as much as he wanted Chase. "A few?"

"Oh yeah," Chase said, and Tate's body temperature jumped, like Chase and Chase alone was responsible for regulating it. "But, really, I wasn't talking about sex. As fun as that is," he added with a wink. He pulled out of the parking lot. "Actually, I was going to say that I thought you looked happy. Really happy. But kind of shell-shocked too."

"Well, to be honest, I kind of am," Tate admitted. "I did not think that my feelings were mutual. Either ten years ago, or today."

"Really?" Chase sounded like he couldn't believe it.

"Ten years ago, I was pretty sure I was imagining things, hoping that you felt the same way I did, or even worse, that you had no idea that what we were doing was flirting."

Chase's expression was amused. "You thought I didn't know? I did, and I didn't know what to do about it, and then we almost kissed, and then, I'll admit, I freaked out a little."

"You weren't the only one," Tate said.

Chase's hand was resting between them, draped over the gear shift, and before tonight, Tate would have wanted, desperately, to cover it with his own. He'd have cautioned himself that this was private, and they were only supposed to be together *publicly*—but now? He could do whatever he wanted. Whenever he felt like it.

He reached over and gave Chase's hand a squeeze, resting his own lightly over it.

"I thought you were going to tell everyone I was some kind of creepy gay freak," Tate continued. It felt good to get all of this off his chest.

"No," Chase said. "Never."

"Don't say never when you have no idea how fiercely I stalked you online." Tate laughed. Incredulous that he could actually confess all of these secrets now. He'd never felt so free in his whole goddamned life. It hadn't even felt like this when he'd come out, probably because there'd still been secrets he was hiding.

I want Chase Riley more than I want to breathe.

"I *tried* to stalk you, but the world sucks, and it turns out that there's way less about that guy you had a massive crush on in high school when he isn't famous," Chase teased.

"Sorry?"

"You can make it up to me. Later." Chase's voice was dark and rough and *yes*, Tate definitely wanted to do that. Maybe he'd even use an assist from some of the items he'd deposited in the back of the car.

"Count on it," Tate said.

"And you really didn't know how I felt . . . like *this* time around?" Chase wondered. "I mean . . . I practically threw myself at you. I didn't even sue you!"

"And I am *so* grateful for that, trust me," Tate said. "But no, it never occurred to me that was why. I thought maybe . . . you might have felt a tiny remnant of what we'd shared ten years back? But no, I just didn't think it was possible. Honestly."

Chase shook his head. "You don't see yourself very well."

"Maybe." Tate thought he'd been realistic, and there was nothing wrong with that.

"No, you don't," Chase said, flipping their hands and giving Tate's a squeeze. "Maybe someday you'll see yourself the way I see you."

Chase told himself that things would be different once he knew how Tate felt and he'd finally confessed his own feelings to Tate.

And they *did* feel different. He felt settled and sure and confident—at least where Tate was concerned. The rest of his life? Still felt like a big mess.

He still didn't know where he was going to be playing next year.

He still felt . . . *jumpy* whenever he thought about participating in Ryan's fundraiser.

And when he showed up at the truck on Monday morning, ready for his shift, Chase didn't know how to feel when confronted by the new employee that Tate and Rachel had hired.

He'd known they had to do it; they were busy enough, and obviously he wasn't going to be able to be their long-term help. But still? Chase felt weirdly excluded as they walked Harmony through the point-of-sale system.

"Chase will still be helping out sometimes, and he can take orders, too," Tate said, glancing over at him. Like he was just remembering that he was there.

It was their first work day as a *real* couple, and it felt like Tate didn't even know he was there. Chase told himself that Tate finding success and *needing* more help was the end result he'd wanted the whole time. But instead he felt . . . *left out*.

Tate had even told him that he didn't need to come today. "I'm sure you've got other very important things to do," he'd teased early this morning when they were lying in bed together. "You don't have to come to the truck today. Harmony should be able to handle it. She's got experience."

But that had felt even worse, like somehow Chase was already irrelevant, so he'd come with Tate anyway, determined to put in a full day's work, even if he wasn't needed.

Maybe if he knew what he was doing next year, he could feel better about leaving the food truck to people who actually knew what they were doing.

Instead, he was hanging around, like Say Cheese was the magical answer to all his problems. Spoiler alert: it wasn't. He knew it, and he knew it couldn't be because the food truck wasn't *his* thing anyway. Football had always been his thing, but now football felt so unsettled and nothing like the positive force that it had been his entire life.

His phone rang in his pocket, and since Tate was already occupied with training Harmony, Chase decided that he could definitely step outside and take the call.

Like he'd hoped, it was Alec. And maybe, he thought optimistically, his agent might even have good news.

"Hey," he said, leaning against the side of the truck. "How are the negotiations going?"

"They're going," Alec said, and the reservation in his voice made Chase's heart beat a tiny bit faster.

"Good? Bad? Hard to say?"

Alec sighed, which was an even worse sign. "It's not that they don't *want* to keep you, Chase. You know that. But money is money, and they only have so much of it to go around."

"So no news, then," Chase said, trying not to sound dejected and failing, utterly.

"There's news," Alec said. "It's not really good *or* bad. But they are willing to talk about restructuring, and I'm meeting with the VP of Player Personnel today, to talk about it. However, I want to give you props for your idea, because she mentioned to me that she'd seen pictures of you at O'Connor's fundraiser. You were right. It *might* help."

"Good," Chase said. "And I'm doing another charity event, too. Maybe it's going to be too late to be relevant, but Ryan Flores asked me to co-sponsor a pre-opening fundraiser for that food truck lot that Tate is joining."

"Tate, your fake boyfriend?" Alec asked.

"Tate, my *real* boyfriend," Chase said, and it was impossible to keep the smug satisfaction out of his tone.

"Even better," Alec said. "Good work, by the way. Though anyone could've seen *that* coming from about a mile away."

"Everyone but me," Chase grumbled.

"Hey, you made it happen, that's worth celebrating. You finally got the guy. Just . . . ten years later than you expected."

"Thanks," Chase said.

"Really, it's a good thing. Fake relationships tend to blow up spectacularly." Alec paused. "Though real ones do, too. But he's a small business owner and a great member of the community here in LA. That's only going to help you."

"Well, it can't hurt," Chase retorted. "I just want to feel like I've got a place, again. Technically, I'm still a member of the Riptide but am I, really? I don't know anymore."

"You're a member of the Riptide, Chase," Alec said firmly. "You're a Riptide player until the moment you're traded, and I'm going to do everything I can to make sure that doesn't happen. You just keep doing your thing. Call up Flores. I want to see that new fundraiser up on your social media in a few days."

"That's not why I'm doing this," Chase said. Did Alec think he was only doing good deeds for selfish reasons? Did Tate? The thought was horrifying. He *wasn't* that self-centered. He'd seen plenty of guys in the NFL who only did charity work to further their own careers, and he'd never wanted to be one of them.

But maybe he was.

"I know it's not, but it sure doesn't hurt," Alec said. "It's giving me a place to start the conversation besides, *Chase is willing to accept less money.*"

"Okay," Chase said, but truthfully, he was less than convinced.

What if he really *was* that horrible and he'd just never realized it?

A wave of frustration washed over him. He just wanted this to be over. He'd told Alec last year that he was willing to dig deep to figure out who he was and what he wanted his image to be, but he'd never imagined it would be so hard. So uncertain.

He wished he'd done all of this before the trade had even come up.

"Just trust me, you're doing everything you can," Alec said. "I'll keep you posted. Oh, and *call Flores.*"

Alec hung up and Chase stared at his phone for a long second. He *should* call Ryan, because it had been a few days and he hadn't heard from him. Maybe Ryan was waiting for him to show that he was really interested, and not just giving lip service to the idea.

He dialed the number Ryan had given him and waited impatiently as it rang.

Ryan picked up on the fifth ring, right before Chase was sure that he was busy and it was going to go to voicemail.

"Hey, Riley," Ryan said. "Good to hear from you." He sounded enthusiastic, and like he really meant it.

That quieted some of Chase's fears, but not all of them.

Chase didn't know what *would* quiet them. That was the whole problem.

But maybe this would.

"I just wanted to touch base and see where we're at with planning," Chase said. "Maybe you might want to meet for lunch?"

"Sure. How about today? I want to get things going," Ryan said. "Believe it or not, I was actually just about to call you myself."

The problem was that Chase *didn't* quite believe it. He wanted to, but a voice in the back of his head kept saying that Ryan was full of shit. Which wasn't fair to Ryan, but Chase couldn't get it to shut up, even though he wanted it to. Desperately.

"Sure," Chase said. He could absolutely duck out on Tate today. He already had Harmony, who had effectively replaced him better on her first day than Chase would probably ever be—but he still worried about it, anyway. "I'm helping my guy out today, though. Maybe you could stop by the truck and I could take a break around one-ish?"

The lunch crowd died out around then, or shortly after then, and with Harmony around, Chase knew he could take as long of a break as he needed to.

"Sure," Ryan said. "Just text me the address, and I'll be there."

"Will do," Chase said, and hung up.

Ryan showed up ten minutes early, but Chase looked at the line, which was still at least twenty people deep, and decided that the baseball player would have to wait. When he finally stepped out of the truck fifteen minutes later, Ryan had claimed one of the picnic tables, sitting under the shade of a trio of straggly-looking palm trees.

"Hey," Chase said as he approached the table. "Sorry to keep you waiting."

"No prob," Ryan said with a shrug. "You guys were slammed. I get it."

And he would, Chase realized. He was married to a guy who ran multiple food trucks. Ryan probably knew the culture better than Chase did.

"Yeah, we really were. You want something to eat?"

"Yeah, that'd be great," Ryan said. When Chase opened his mouth to ask what he wanted, Ryan just waved a hand. "Whatever is hot and ready," he said. "Don't make a big deal on my account."

"Okay."

Chase went back to the truck, asked Harmony to ladle up some soup, and even made the two grilled cheese sandwiches himself. Balancing the two plates on a tray, he made his way back outside. "Sometimes," he said, setting the tray down on the table, "you're just craving a classic."

Ryan bit into one of the grilled cheese wedges and moaned around it. "This is fucking delicious," he said. "Wyatt said you guys knew what you were doing, and I didn't think he was lying, but holy fuck."

"It's not me," Chase said. "The genius is all Tate."

Ryan's gaze narrowed. "You are *whipped*."

Chase tried not to squirm. "Maybe a little," he admitted.

"Don't fight it," Ryan advised. "It's a good place to be, no matter what anyone says. I've been whipped for years. Zero shame."

"You guys seem really devoted to each other," Chase said, taking a bite of his own sandwich after dipping it in the soup. "But Tony said you started out fake dating?"

Ryan laughed. "Yeah," he said. "But was it ever fake? God only knows. Anyway, it turned out right, in the end." Ryan smiled, slowly. "Tony mentioned to me that you were *also* doing that fake thing."

"Eh," Chase said. "Not really. Not anymore."

"You never really were, right?" Ryan said conspiratorially.

"Probably not," Chase said. "But don't tell Tate that."

"It's okay. I get it." Ryan paused to twist open the bottle of water Chase had brought him with lunch. "So, this charity event at the food truck lot, I'm excited about it. I think we can bring a lot of happiness to a lot of kids who don't have much."

"Who're you inviting?" Chase asked.

To his surprise, Ryan pulled out a bunch of folders and spread them over the table. "I brought all the planning materials my PA is working on," he said. "I'd have brought her, but she had a meeting this morning, so we're going to have to manage, just the two of us."

Chase laughed nervously. "I'm not a great planner," he admitted.

"That's okay. Neither am I. We'll just have to muddle through together. Emily will handle a lot of the logistics. She's already contracted with the food trucks to cover their expenses and has hired a band and some circus performers for entertainment. Even got some kind of balloon animal guy."

"Oh, cool," Chase said. "I want to help contribute."

"Of course." Ryan smiled. "I want you to help invite some of the guys on your team and maybe on some of the other teams in the area. Can you do that? I know you've got lots of connections."

Chase did, and he was happy to have Ryan exploit them. "Sure. Did you have any particular guys in mind or . . .?"

"Yeah, actually, I wanted to start with the ones who've donated before, and expand from there. The idea is, they'll come to the event and mingle with the kids. Maybe we'll even throw some kind of quick pickup game together. That'd give the kids a real thrill."

"And the kids?" Chase wondered. "How do you know which ones to pick?"

"Wyatt and I have been making connections with a lot of the local shelters," Ryan explained. "So a lot of them come from the shelters, or from the drop-in centers. We're focusing on kids from either LGBT backgrounds or that we've connected with through my LGBT charity. We just want to give them a really fun, carefree afternoon. A chance to get some autographs, meet some of their heroes, eat some delicious food, make a balloon animal, etcetera."

"That sounds awesome," Chase said. "I can definitely help with that. Is this the list of players?" he asked, as Ryan pushed a paper towards him.

"Yep," Ryan said.

Chase glanced down. Almost all the players he knew personally. Most of them really well. Sam and Heath and Jamie and Neal were all on the list. And a few players from the other Los Angeles team, the Rams.

"This shouldn't be a problem at all," Chase said.

Anyone that Chase didn't know, he knew he could get the number for, and meet with. It paid off being one of the most popular NFL players, and definitely one of the more high-profile players in the LA area.

"Great," Ryan said. He passed him another paper. "Here's the details, for the guys you talk to. Let me know if you run into any roadblocks, okay?"

"Sure thing," Chase said.

He studied the names on the list as Ryan finished his lunch.

"Seriously," he said when he was done. "That was fucking delicious. My trainer is going to be *on* me if he ever finds out what I'm eating, but it was worth it."

"Yep," Chase agreed, "it always is."

Ryan left a few minutes later, after Chase had promised that he would call everyone in the next few days and set up meetings to gauge their interest, though in some cases, Chase already knew they would be happy to participate.

Heath and Sam especially did a lot of charity work, and he knew Neal and Jamie were looking into expanding their own charity reach as Neal came more to terms with what had happened when he'd missed the field goal two Super Bowls ago.

"Looked like you guys were discussing important stuff," Tate said, dropping down onto the bench next to Chase. "What's this?" he asked, pointing at the paper with all the names.

"Some guys that Ryan wants me to ask to join us at the food truck charity event," Chase said, finishing up his soup.

Tate read the list and then glanced up. "These should be pretty easy asks for you," he said.

"Yeah," Chase agreed. "I know most of them."

"And the ones you don't know?"

"This guy," Chase said, pointing to a name towards the top of the list, "he plays for the Rams, and Alec knows his agent well. They used to work together. So that should be easy enough. And the others? Heath or Sam probably know them. Or Neal."

"You don't want to ask Neal," Tate said, proving to Chase just how observant he was.

"I try . . . I try not to put too much burden on him," Chase tried to explain, even though he knew he wasn't doing a very good job of it. "He still struggles sometimes with crowds and lots of fans in one area. I'll ask him to come to the event, and he probably will, because deep down, he does *want* to—but it's still hard."

"The field goal?" Tate asked.

Chase nodded. "We never blamed him. Well, most of the team didn't. But it's a hard thing to deal with. Even two years later. Jamie helps, and sometimes I feel like every kick he makes exorcises Neal's demons a little bit more, but will they ever go away? I don't know."

"You guys deal with a lot of shit," Tate said, leaning in and resting his head on Chase's shoulder. Chase's heart beat a little faster. He still wasn't quite used to this. Didn't know if he would ever get used to it. It felt like a miracle every damn time Tate got close because he *wanted* to—not because he was obligated to.

"Sometimes, yeah," Chase said. Took a deep breath. Wondered for a brief second if he should share, and then, reminding himself that sharing was what partners *did*, forged on ahead. "I talked to someone for awhile. Heath did, too. And so did Neal, after the Super Bowl."

"Talked to someone? Like a therapist?" Tate asked. His hand had made its way to Chase's thigh and he had to push down the automatic sexual reaction he felt every time Tate even got close to his dick. *Tate's just being sweet*, he told himself, *stop being such a perv.*

"Yeah," Chase said. "Like you said, we deal with a lot of shit. A ton of scrutiny. So much pressure. Sometimes it gets to be too much."

Tate shot him a knowing look.

"And yes," Chase added, "sometimes we are complete dumbasses and we bring a lot of that scrutiny on ourselves."

"By tweeting about our boyfriend's food truck?" Tate teased.

"Not my finest moment," Chase admitted. "But I was trying very hard to impress you."

"It worked," Tate said simply, and his hand squeezed Chase's thigh. "But then it's always worked."

"Really?"

"Uh, *yeah*," Tate said, leaning in and pressing a quick kiss against his mouth. But Chase reached up, tangling his fingers in the soft hair at the base of his neck and pulled him back in for a much longer kiss. How could he do anything else when Tate kept touching his thigh like that? It was practically an invitation to drag him back to his car and debauch him thoroughly during their quick lunch break.

"What was that for?" Tate asked dazedly after Chase lifted his mouth from his.

"Because you're wonderful and understanding and you turn me on without even trying," Chase said with blunt honestly. *I probably love you. I've probably loved you for a long-ass time, I'm just now beginning to realize how much. And for how long.*

But even Chase knew it was way too soon to make that particular confession. They had just left the fake dating behind. The last thing he wanted to do was scare Tate off with the seriousness of his feelings. But he knew they were absolutely, one hundred percent *real,* and he hoped that in time, Tate would develop the same kind of feelings for him.

There was a part of him that *very* much wanted to be just like Ryan when he grew up. Happily and utterly whipped for his husband.

And wasn't that a thought? *Husband.*

"Seriously though," Tate said, "I'm proud of you. You're doing this great event, and you're making all these strides on showing everyone who the better man is inside you. The one I've always known about." Tate hesitated. Squeezed his thigh again. "The one I care so much about."

"It was time," Chase said. It was still terrifying to think that he might be forced out into the unknown—to a new city and a new team and a new group that might not treat him the way he'd been lucky enough to be treated in Los Angeles. He might have to leave Tate behind, just now that he'd found him again.

All you can do, his therapist's voice reminded him, the cautionary wisdom she'd always shared with him, *is control your own actions. Control your own emotions.*

"Yeah, I won't disagree with that," Tate said. "In other news, I think Harmony is really going to work out."

"Yeah?" Chase told himself that he was the bigger person. That he could be happy that Tate had found someone he could rely on long-term. Even if he felt like he'd just been replaced. "She did seem on top of things."

"She's great," Tate enthused, and Chase thought grumpily that his boyfriend had *never* been that enthusiastic about his own admittedly minuscule skills in the kitchen.

"I'm glad," Chase grumbled.

"You don't *sound* very glad," Tate teased, pushing himself upright and away from the table, even as Chase fought the urge to grab him back. He knew Tate's break would be short. "I thought you'd be happy to not have to work all these long shifts, anymore."

"I'll miss you," Chase admitted. Didn't want to *also* admit that he didn't know what he'd do with himself. What had he even done in the off-season before he'd met Tate? He didn't know anymore.

"I think you'll just miss the free food." Chase loved how Tate never failed to give him a hard time. Probably a *deserved* hard time.

"It's okay," Chase said. "I know this great guy. Hot as hell. Absolute fire in bed. A bit of a firecracker all the time, actually, and he'll make me anything I want."

Tate grinned. "Is that so?"

Chase nodded. "I already know he's going to come over tonight and make me something special."

"I think that could be arranged," Tate said, tilting his head, his smile so bright that it put the sun overhead to shame.

CHAPTER FOURTEEN

"YOU'RE SPENDING AN AWFUL lot of time over at Chase's place recently," Rachel said as they finished cleaning up the truck after another long day.

Admittedly the days felt *less* long because Harmony was working out great—she'd been with them for a few days now, and even though he'd sensed Chase's disappointment at being told he wasn't needed any longer, they'd transitioned to a team of three.

"We've got privacy there," Tate said, trying not to sound defensive. He'd told his sister about the development in their relationship after Colin O'Connor's fundraiser, but even though she'd been happy for him, he could tell that deep down, she was still skeptical of Chase's motives.

There was a part of Tate that didn't want her to be right, but was afraid she was, anyway.

"I'm sure it's also pretty amazing," Rachel said as she put the last of their stock back in the fridge. "Probably not a hardship to spend time there."

"Yeah, it really is. You should see the kitchen," Tate said. But the truth was, Chase could've lived in a shack, tiny and run-down, and Tate wouldn't have given a shit. He wasn't going over there to spend time at the house; it was the *man* he was interested in.

"Tate," Rachel said, turning towards him, a serious expression on her face. "It's not that I don't approve or that I don't like him. I *do*. Probably not as much as you do . . ."

"I get it," Tate said. "I really do. It's . . . I'm in the middle of it and I can barely believe it's happening. Chase Riley and *me*. I never even dreamed it could happen."

"Yes, you did," Rachel said. "You've dreamed about it for ten years. Even when you thought you'd never see him again, you never let go."

Tate tried not to squirm. He loved his sister. But *god*, she could be unapologetically blunt. "When you put it like that," he said, trying to make a joke but it fell flat.

"What I'm trying to say," Rachel added, "is that you spent all those years not letting go. Don't do it now."

"I wasn't . . ."

"Yeah," Rachel said shortly, interrupting him. "Yeah. You kinda are. You're already thinking, *what the fuck am I doing with Chase Riley?* I can see it in your face. You won him, after all these years. *You* did that, nobody else."

There was a part of Tate that wanted to say, *but* . . . but he didn't. Because Rachel was right. Chase could've spent the last ten years dating anyone he wanted, including men. But he hadn't. He certainly hadn't stayed single and celibate, either, but Tate was pretty sure that he was the only guy that Chase had ever really wanted.

Maybe he didn't see himself as particularly special, but Chase did—and maybe that was all that mattered.

"You're right," Tate said.

"Could you say that again, and slower this time?" Rachel said, grinning. "I want to record it for posterity."

Tate laughed. "No way."

"Get out of here, already," Rachel said, giving him a playful shove. "You've got a hot date, and *I've* got a slightly less hot date with Netflix."

"I think you're overestimating how hot Netflix is," Tate teased as they headed down the stairs. Rachel turned and locked the door. "Because I can guarantee you that Chase is *way* hotter."

"Rub it in, why don't you?" Rachel laughed. "You are *so* gone for him."

Later, after Tate had gotten to Chase's house, and he was in the shower, washing away the sweat and the grime from a day in the truck, he thought about Rachel's words.

He *was* gone for Chase. Had been, from almost the first Home Economics class, and nothing had ever really changed.

Was he falling in love?

Or had he been in love this whole time?

Tate flipped the water off and reached for the towel, not quite used to finding it warm. Of course Chase would have a towel warmer at his house.

"Your house is way too fancy," Tate said, after drying off, and wrapping the towel around his waist.

But his voice died in his throat, because Chase was waiting for him on the bed. Naked. Absolutely, totally, completely, gloriously naked.

His hair was spread across the pillow in a golden swath, reflecting the light from the corner lamp, his eyes crinkled up in an irrepressible smile, and his body?

God, his body.

It was a fucking work of art.

"Has anyone ever told you," Tate said, walking up next to the bed, "that all this"—he gestured to all the long, lean, perfectly sculpted muscles on display, his cock, already hard and wet at the tip—"should be illegal?"

"No," Chase said, a dimple forming. "But they should."

"Well, I'm telling you now," Tate said, reaching down to stroke one bulging pectoral muscle. Chase groaned a little as his finger strayed downward, tweaking one pale pink nipple. "You are too goddamn sexy for words," he said softly.

"Can't think of any?" Chase teased, reaching up, his own hand drifting down Tate's still-damp chest, causing Tate's heart to stutter and his own cock to harden, underneath his towel. "I can think of a couple. Why don't you fuck me now?"

"I can think of another idea I like even more," Tate said. It nearly killed him to pull away from Chase's hand. It wasn't much, just a light brush against his skin, but it was enough to make him burn. Still, he'd had a great idea in the shower—something that could give both of them exactly what they wanted. He turned and grabbed the basket, sitting on the low couch against the other wall. It had been sitting there, untouched, since the night they'd come back from the fundraiser. Despite the fun possibilities, it had felt like an embarrassment of riches just to touch Chase and be touched in return. But tonight, he felt like he was vibrating inside his skin, so turned on by the way Chase watched him with that dark, fierce intensity, that he wanted something more.

"Look at you," Chase said in a low, rough voice as Tate brought the basket to the bed. He rifled through it, looking for something specific and finally finding it, in the form of a black silicone butt plug. "I like the way you're thinking."

"Yeah?" Tate said, raising an eyebrow. "I'm going to put this in you, and then you're going to fuck me."

Chase's eyes widened, his mouth going slack. Any fear that he wouldn't want to do it evaporated. His cock, hard as Tate had ever seen it, smeared a drop of precome across his abs and Tate wanted to lean down and lick it up.

"Like that idea, huh?" Tate said, reaching into the drawer and pulling out the lube they'd been using for the last week.

"I like *you*," Chase said, and unlike his usually sparkling smile, he looked serious, almost solemn. "Doesn't matter what we do."

Tate's heart thumped once, then twice, and then landed on the floor, right at Chase's feet.

You thought you loved him before, but no. This is what love is.

He leaned down, and kissed Chase, pouring all the building, growing feelings into the kiss, letting him know without words that he liked him too. That he *loved* him. Because Tate already knew, despite what Rachel had said, he couldn't be the one to speak first.

"Fuck," Chase groaned into his mouth. "I want you so bad."

"Yeah," Tate said, and ran a hand down Chase's leg, glorying in the muscular flank. "Yeah, you're gonna get me, okay? Just be a little patient. Want this to feel good."

Chase's eyes were huge and full of trust. "Always feels so good with you. The *best* with you."

If Tate's heart wasn't already tucked inside Chase's chest, it would be now.

"You're just trying to butter me up," Tate said. Even as he hoped that what Chase was saying was the truth. Even though he wanted to believe it more than he wanted his next breath.

"No," Chase said, staring at him steadily. "Not even close." He reached up and his kiss took Tate's breath away. His knees went weak, and when Chase pulled him onto the bed, on top of him, he went willingly, pressing his body against Chase's. They kissed passionately, Chase's hands running through his damp hair, tilting his head at just the right angle for his tongue to delve into Tate's mouth.

It was hot and wild and Tate felt unsteady when he finally pulled away, his cock brushing hard and leaking against Chase's thigh.

"Come on," Chase breathed out, his own voice wobbly around the edges. He laughed roughly. "I'm gonna come before you even get it in me."

"No way," Tate said, but he felt on the edge too as he slid down Chase's body, crouching between his legs. His fingers shook as he opened the lube, and after slicking up his fingers, he didn't even bother to tease. They'd both teased each other a little too much, already.

"You're gonna be good for me," Tate reminded him firmly. "'Cause you still have to give me that cock." Tate slid a finger inside of him, and Chase's groan as he pushed it inside, opening him up for the toy, was almost his undoing. He looked so fucking gorgeous like this, unwound and losing it, just from Tate's finger. He nudged a second one in, and it was Tate's turn to moan as Chase took them like he'd been born to fuck.

The toy was slippery in his hand, but from the moment he slid it in, Chase's back bowed and his cock twitched, and Tate thought he'd never seen anything so fucking gorgeous in his whole life.

He slid one finger, and then another into his own hole, giving himself the most perfunctory prep of his life. He knew it was going to hurt a little, but it was a hurt he wanted. A hurt he craved.

After he grabbed a condom with shaking hands, he twisted his lubed-up hand around Chase's cock, listening to him groan, deep and hard. "I'm gonna . . ." Chase warned him, eyes wild. "It feels so goddamned good."

"No," Tate said, straddling his body after he'd put the condom on. "No, you're gonna fuck me. Make me feel it tomorrow, okay?"

He slid the first little way down onto Chase's cock, breathing through the stretch. Chase's back bowed, clearly feeling overwhelmed as he felt the pleasure bear down on him from two directions. Tate braced his hands against the broad chest underneath him, and let gravity do the rest of the work.

"Fuck," Chase moaned, his head thrashing as he tried to hold on. "Fuck, you feel so goddamned good."

"Yeah," Tate agreed, squeezing his own eyes shut as he moved a hand to his own cock, stroking it as Chase bottomed out. He gave himself a brief moment to adjust and then began moving, up and down, as steady as he could.

He knew neither of them was going to last long—it was probably a miracle that Chase had lasted as long as he had. He *loved* being fucked in the ass, and came almost as soon as Tate got in him every time. But this time, Tate thought with the pleasure beginning to crash through him, he was going to get a little for himself. That big, thick cock, the one he'd been dreaming about fucking him for all those years.

"Goddamnit," Chase panted. "I'm gonna come. I can't . . . I can't . . ."

Tate wrapped a hand around himself and felt his cock jump as ecstasy began building. "Fuck, me either," he cried, every nerve ending straining as he felt himself pulse once, and then twice, and fall head over heels into the best orgasm of his life.

He could feel Chase writhing underneath him, feel the condom filling with come when Chase finally let himself go.

"That," Chase said, after a long moment, when they both tried to catch their breath, "was the best thing we've ever done, and might *ever* do."

Tate leaned over and brushed a kiss across his lips, bright red from Chase biting them, trying to hold back. "It was pretty damn good," he agreed, "but I always like to be an overachiever. I think we can do better."

Chase laughed unsteadily. "Can't just be satisfied, huh?"

"With you?" Tate thought his heart must be in his eyes, in his face, all his love absolutely undeniable, but at the moment he couldn't bring himself to care. "Never."

"Good," Chase said with a happy sigh, his arm wrapping around Tate's back. "Let's never move, okay?"

Tate chuckled. "We might have to, sometime. To clean up, at least."

It was at that moment that Chase's stomach grumbled. "And," Tate added, "you might get hungry. Which would be a real problem."

"Fine, fine," Chase said, and Tate carefully sat up, his cock slipping out of him. He slid off the bed and went to reach for the toy that had driven Chase so insane, but he batted his fingers away. "No," Chase said. "Let me leave it in a bit longer."

Tate raised an eyebrow. "Really?"

"You think you'd have the energy to fuck me later?" Chase asked, eyes crinkling with amusement, naked want obvious on his face.

"Why don't I feed both of us?" Tate said, heading towards the bathroom to wash up. "And then I think I might be able to do something about that itch you still want scratched."

Every step that Chase took downstairs felt like a live wire, lighting him up and making him crave more. He'd thrown on a pair of loose sweats, but the plug inside of him felt huge. Both agonizing as he was oversensitive after coming, and still the best goddamned thing he'd ever experienced.

"*You,*" he said, gingerly leaning against the counter and watching as Tate pulled together ingredients for late-night pancakes.

"Me what?" Tate asked, his mouth tilting up in an amused smile. "You're the one who wanted to keep it in."

"Maybe I've been watching too much porn, and I want you to fuck me bent over this counter," Chase said. Which was true. Though, not the porn part so much. Who needed porn when he had *Tate* around?

Having hot sex was one thing, but when he was with Tate, it felt like so much more than brain-melting orgasms.

There'd been a point tonight, when he'd been so deep inside Tate, he hadn't been quite sure where he ended and Tate began. Like they were melding together, becoming better and stronger and smarter and way more awesome than they ever had been on their own.

Chase knew without a single doubt that Tate had made *him* better. He'd given him opportunities to embrace desires that had sat dormant forever, and he'd offered to help Chase be more like himself.

Tate grinned. "I think that we could arrange that. But I'd better feed you pancakes first, then dick. Because we can't have you getting hungry and deciding to bite mine off."

"Nope," Chase said. "Can I help with anything?"

"For pancakes?" Tate shot him an incredulous look. "I think I can handle this. You just sit tight and try not to go out of your mind."

"Yeah, yeah," Chase said, rolling his eyes. But truthfully, he kind of *was* going out of his mind. The plug felt like it was pressing right against his prostate and he couldn't find a position where it wasn't constantly tormenting him.

He tried to focus on Tate's process, because maybe he might want to try reversing their positions one day. He could make pancakes, right? He'd learned how to make a grilled cheese. How hard could pancakes be?

But he'd only ever experienced pancakes made from a box, and Tate was definitely not using a mix. He even separated the eggs, and Chase enjoyed the view of his surprisingly firm biceps as he whipped up the whites.

"I should've suggested you cook shirtless for me in high school," Chase said, watching as he folded the fluffy whites into the batter.

"Yeah, that would've been a sight," Tate said. "I was a silly, scrawny kid."

"You weren't *scrawny*," Chase said. "Trust me, I wanted to do lots of things to you. I didn't really understand what they were, back then, but you were definitely the motivation for me to figure it out."

"Thanks?" Tate's tone was wry as he heated up the griddle he'd found. Chase hadn't even known he'd owned it when Tate had unearthed it. But then he possessed a lot of various pieces of kitchen equipment, from all the private chefs and caterers he'd hired over the years.

"I should be thanking you," Chase said, still squirming as he tried to find a more comfortable position. Sitting was totally out of the question, and even standing was beginning to get dicey. His cock was already three-quarters hard, and getting harder, even though he'd come less than half an hour before.

"Probably," Tate said, ladling pancake batter onto the hot griddle. "I'd ask if you have maple syrup, but I saw your pantry. It's bare bones."

"I could order some?" Chase said. He realized he'd left his phone upstairs.

"You had some honey," Tate said with a shrug. "It'll be fine. But seriously, next time I am bringing a whole bag of groceries over. I can't keep pulling magic meals out of my hat."

"We could've ordered in," Chase said. "You don't have to . . ."

Tate's glance over at him was incredibly fond. "I know," he interrupted. "But I like to feed you."

"Trust me, I like it when you feed me," Chase said. "But next time? Text me a list of what you'll need and I'll take care of it."

"You'll go to the grocery store?" Tate raised an eyebrow. He flipped another pancake onto the plate and passed it to Chase.

"I do that sometimes," Chase said, grabbing a pair of forks from the silverware drawer and handing one of them to Tate. *Though not for a long time,* he amended mentally.

Tate watched with amusement as he sat down on one of the barstools. "Gonna eat standing up?" he teased. "You know I can . . ."

"No," Chase said. "I'm going to eat these pancakes and then you are going to fuck me over this counter, or I'm not going to be responsible for my actions."

Tate laughed. "Alright," he said. "Just checking on you."

"*Please* check on me in about five minutes," Chase said, between big bites of pancake. They were the best, fluffiest pancakes he'd ever tasted, but he couldn't really enjoy them because he felt one unexpected movement away from coming untouched in his sweatpants.

"Don't worry, baby," Tate said, patting him on the shoulder, "I'm gonna take real good care of you."

Like in everything else, Tate was true to his word, and the moment Chase was done eating, bent him over the counter and fucked him so good that even forty-eight hours later, he still felt wobbly when he thought about it.

But he shouldn't be thinking about sex *or* Tate right now, because his cock wasn't likely to behave, and Chase was about to meet with the one guy from the list Ryan had given him that he didn't know personally.

Didn't know much about Spencer Evans—he played defense for the other team based in LA—but he'd assumed that Ryan did, which was why he'd been on the list in the first place.

He was the only out player on the Rams, and Chase had to tell himself that he wasn't going to ask how that felt. Maybe it was fine. Also, Spencer was a big, tough-looking guy, so surely if anyone took exception to his gay status, he could punch them in the face pretty easily.

"Hey," Chase said, approaching Spencer in the coffee shop line, holding out his hand. "Thanks for agreeing to meet with me."

"No problem," Spencer said, his voice short. He looked just about as uncompromising as he did in the pictures Chase had seen when he'd googled him, eyes dark and hard, and Chase suddenly wondered if he should be asking this guy anything at all. Maybe he never should have convinced Alec to get his number.

But you're both going through the same shit, right? he reminded himself. *You've got similar life experience.*

"Regular coffee. Short," Spencer said to the barista, and then turned to Chase, waving his hand impatiently as he glanced up at the menu.

"Uh," Chase said, unexpectedly flustered. He was used to meeting football players, but usually they were a touch friendlier. "I'll have the caramel macchiato. Iced. Big one."

He could've sworn that Spencer shot him an annoyed look as he fumbled with his wallet to pay for their drinks.

You're just on edge because this is the first time you've done this, with someone you don't know, he told himself as Spencer went and grabbed a table in the corner while he waited for his own coffee to be made. Chase remembered what Tate had said about coming out, and that it wasn't a singular occurrence, but something that happened all the time, and had to wonder if when camp started, it would be like this every day.

But then he remembered what Riptide camp had been like, how nobody ever offered judgment, and if they did, he and Heath took care of it immediately. Remembered how comfortable Jamie had felt last year when he'd arrived. Comfortable enough to announce he was gay in college and know that if he played well, he'd end up on a team.

But Chase hadn't come out in college. He hadn't come out when he'd first been drafted. He'd waited, and put it off, and eventually wondered if he wouldn't have to do it at all.

Spencer's just a little unfriendly, that's all, Chase told himself, *he doesn't judge you for waiting. He couldn't possibly.*

"Riley!" the barista called out, setting his coffee on the counter, flashing him a bright smile.

He took it, thanking her, and trying to push his trepidation down, walked over to where Spencer was sitting, sipping his plain black coffee without much interest.

Yeah, his uncooperative mind added, *because it's plain and black and probably boring as hell. Not like the caramel whipped cream confection in your hand, which is going to taste absolutely fucking delicious.*

It seemed Spencer agreed with this assessment because he gave Chase's coffee a suspicious glance as he shoved a straw through the lid.

"You said this is about a charity event that Flores is throwing?" Spencer said, not even bothering with small talk. "I don't do many of those."

Yeah, I can't imagine why, Chase thought. *You're a serious buz-zkill.*

"Yes," Chase said carefully. Not wanting to give Spencer any reason to be any more unpleasant than he already was. "It's taking place at a brand-new food truck lot, before they open. He's invited a lot of disadvantaged kids, thought it would be nice to give them a fun evening, with the food, and a band, and some carnival performers."

"Food trucks?" Spencer said suspiciously. "Isn't that your *boyfriend's* thing?"

Chase took a deep breath. "Uh, yeah. I guess. He owns one of them," he said.

"So this isn't really for the kids at all, huh?" Spencer asked. He'd crossed his arms over his chest, his plain coffee abandoned on the table. "You just want more attention for you and your new boy toy. You must think this all looks real good for you."

"What?" Chase choked on his macchiato. "What do you mean?"

Spencer leaned forward. "You *came out* in a tweet about your boyfriend's food truck. Do you take *anything* seriously? Is that guy even your boyfriend? Are you even gay?"

"I'm . . ." Chase stuttered. Hating that this guy had reduced him to speechlessness. "This is for the *kids*, and this wasn't even my idea, it was Ryan's."

"Sure," Spencer said. He didn't sound convinced.

"Why did you even come here if that's what you think?" Chase said. He thought of what Heath would do to this guy. He'd definitely have punched him in the face, gay or not gay, and Chase found he was contemplating it, despite the fact that Spencer looked like he could take him apart with his bare hands.

Some things were just *not* okay to voice out loud. Not when they were too similar to what Heath had wondered, before he'd talked to Chase about it. Especially when they were everything that voice inside Chase worried about.

What if you're not gay enough?

What if you waited too long?

What if you came out wrong?

What if people think you did it for the wrong reasons?

For attention?

To make yourself look better?

To look like more than just the silly, pretty, party boy that the world thinks you are?

The voice had morphed into one uncomfortably similar to Spencer's.

Chase squirmed in his chair. Felt his emotions begin to roil inside of him.

"I came because I wanted to tell you that you're making all of us look bad," Spencer said unapologetically. "We take this seriously. This is our fucking lives, and we've worked hard, way too hard, to take you making us look like a joke."

"It's not a joke." *I'm not a joke.*

"Yeah," Spencer said. "Not sure that's true. We're all over trying to get people to take us seriously even though we're queer, and you're just . . ."

"I'm just *what*," Chase retorted.

Spencer waved around Chase's head. "Making us look bad. Making us look like we just woke up one day and said, *hey I think I'll come out, might as well kill two birds with one stone and promote my boy's food truck while I'm at it.*"

"That wasn't . . ." Chase stopped. Bit his lip. He couldn't say that was a lie and *mean* it. Because he hadn't thought it through. *Had* hoped that it would help Tate's food truck.

Spencer stood. "I thought so," he said with horrible finality and walked off.

CHAPTER FIFTEEN

"It's not always going to be like that." Sam put his arm around Chase's shoulders and pulled him into a half hug.

"It should never happen like that *at all*," Heath said as he paced back and forth in front of the couch Chase had landed on after that horrible, painful meeting with Spencer Evans.

He hadn't known what to do. Where to go. He hadn't been able to confess the truth to Ryan. He *respected* him, and the last thing he wanted was to give the guy a reason to believe he shouldn't. And Tate? He'd have offered his sympathy but he wouldn't really understand. He'd been honest about himself long ago. He'd come to terms with his sexuality long before Chase had.

And when he'd come out, he hadn't done it on Twitter, to spite some woman who'd wanted to hook up with him.

He hadn't tried to promote his own food truck when he'd done it.

Chase buried his head in his hands.

"I'm gonna go take Spencer fucking Evans apart with my fists," Heath continued.

"Let me help you, *please*," Sam said.

"Absolutely not," Heath said, voice inexorable. "You're still playing. You'll get punished. Benched. Suspended by the NFL. They don't give a fuck what I do."

"No," Chase interrupted. His voice was painfully unsteady. He wasn't in any kind of control of himself, and knew it. He'd thought if he came here, it would help silence all those voices who kept believing everything Spencer had said. But it hadn't helped. In fact, he felt *worse*.

Out of control and desperate and reckless.

He knew what happened when he felt like this. And in the chaos of his brain, he decided he didn't give a fuck.

"No?" Heath and Sam chimed in together.

"He wasn't wrong. He was . . . okay, he was a real asshole about it," Chase said. "But he wasn't wrong."

"He was," Sam said, defending him staunchly. One of the reasons he'd come here in the first place. Because he'd known that Sam would offer him the balm of outraged sympathy, and Heath would go wild and make threats and offer to beat Spencer Evans up.

But none of this was right, because Spencer *was* right.

"There is no way that he should've said any of that to you," Heath said, kneeling before him. His eyes were dark and very serious. "There aren't any rules. God knows I didn't follow any of them if there were."

"Yeah," Sam said, "but Spencer Evans wouldn't ever dare to say any of that shit to *your* face."

Chase couldn't agree more. And that was the difference, wasn't it? Heath was earnest and had made an entire fucking career out of doing the right thing, at the right time. The only time he'd ever gone "off book" for an NFL quarterback was when he'd fallen in love with Sam Crawford and kissed him at the Super Bowl. But Chase? He'd never given a single fuck about the rules, and now that had come back to bite him.

Nobody took him seriously. There might be people out there who thought he was just saying he liked guys as a joke. Like his feelings for Tate could ever be reduced to meaningless nonsense. Chase felt sick, like he might actually puke.

"No, he wouldn't dare. Which is why it's total bullshit that he said it to Chase," Heath agreed.

"He should've said it," Chase said, shucking Sam's arm off him, and standing up. "He was right to say it."

"What?" Heath demanded, incredulous. "What the fuck, Riley? You don't deserve any of this."

Chase wiped his damp palms on his jeans. "I appreciate you guys both taking my side, but I've . . . I've really fucked up, I think."

"You didn't fuck up," Sam argued, but even if Chase didn't know him as well as he did, he'd have known he was lying.

"I sure did," Chase said, and started to walk towards Heath and Sam's front door. "Lots and lots of times."

"Listen," Heath said, trailing after him. Sam had apparently given up, which, Chase thought despairingly, felt a little too right.

As did Heath trying to save a situation that was unsalvageable. "Listen, I don't want you . . ."

"Blaming myself?" Chase rested a hand on the front door. "Too late for that. I fucked this all up. I should take the consequences, right?"

Heath put a hand on his shoulder. "Not what I was going to say. I don't want you taking what he said to heart. There *are* no rules. There is no right or wrong way to come out. It's a personal choice. You aren't obligated to do it a certain way, or at a certain time, or anything. You know Moira would say the same thing I am. In fact you should talk to her. Listen to what she has to say about it."

But Chase knew he couldn't. Because if he called her up and she agreed, as diplomatically as she could, with Spencer, Chase wasn't sure he'd ever get over it.

He didn't think she would, but even the thought of it made everything inside Chase freeze up.

"Maybe," Chase said.

"What are you going to do?" This came from Sam, who had appeared next to Heath.

Chase pulled open the door. "I don't know," he said.

But that was a lie, because he already knew.

He was going to burn everything down.

For a moment he'd considered heading to where Tate and Rachel had the food truck set up for the lunch crowd, but at the last second, he knew he couldn't. They had Harmony now, and Tate had said, as kindly as he could, that he wasn't really needed anymore. They needed to figure out how to survive on their own, without Chase, because that was the future.

Even though logically it made sense, it had still stung.

Instead, he drove home, and after wandering around his huge, empty house for way too many pointless minutes, then spending an hour on the couch, flipping through hundreds of channels, nothing was distracting him from the churning of emotions in his brain. In his heart.

He felt wretched, and nothing was helping to distract from it. The total blankness of his brain made Spencer's words stand out even clearer. Made them even more undeniable. Chase felt like he was unwillingly seeing himself far more clearly than he had in years. Even clearer than when he'd gone to Moira.

Speaking of Moira, there was a part of him yelling that he should call her. That voice sounded suspiciously like Heath's. Then it morphed into Tate's. He ignored them all.

Instead, he turned the TV off, pulled the sound system remote off the coffee table and, after switching on one of his favorite music channels, pulled himself off the couch, and walked over to the bar setup in the corner of his living room. He was going to do what he always did when he was feeling like this—despondent and sad and completely fucking useless. He was going to dance.

He poured himself a shot of tequila. Then another. Then a third.

Felt the familiar fuzziness as the emotions finally began to dull.

This was why he didn't drink very often—he'd always known that if he let himself, he would drink away the chaos in his head.

He'd done this at the "victory celebration" only a month or so back, and it had helped at the time. Of course, the aftermath had been horrible, and maybe this aftermath would be equally as terrible, but right now, with the bottle in his hand, and the bass pounding along with the rhythm of his heartbeat, all he knew was that he felt *better*. At least he couldn't hear all those voices yelling at him.

The voices that all belonged to him.

He danced for the next few minutes, feeling the music surging through his blood, right alongside the tequila, and the noise inside of him didn't quiet exactly, but it was drowned out, and that was all Chase cared about right at that moment.

Reaching for his phone, he knew it was a mistake to open the Twitter app. A mistake to stare at the screen, at the keyboard, at the letters as they seemingly miraculously appeared in the little white box.

Spencer Evans didn't think he was gay enough? Thought he was faking it? Didn't believe that he took shit seriously enough?

Well, now he was gonna prove that he fucking *didn't*.

"Have you talked to Chase today?" Rachel asked as she scrolled through her phone.

The dinner rush had finally ended, and Tate was leaning by the front counter, making sure that nobody came up unnoticed. But they'd sent Harmony on a break, and Rachel was clearly taking one of her own.

"No," Tate said. "I know he was meeting with some guys for the charity event he and Ryan are pulling together at the lot. You know, the one right before it opens? But I haven't talked to him since this morning."

"You should call him," Rachel said, her voice grim, and when she glanced up, there were several worried lines etched in her face. "Better yet, you should go over to his house."

"What?"

Rachel walked closer to him, and shoved her phone's screen in his face. It took Tate a moment to realize what she was showing him.

It was a tweet, from Chase, and all it said was "Let's have a real gay party, guys." Followed by his address.

"Oh my god," Tate said, exhaling abruptly. "What the fuck is he doing?"

"I don't know," Rachel said, "but I think you need to go find out. Not in an hour, when we close, but *right now.*"

Tate was already pulling his apron off, his mind going a mile a minute, worry piling upon concern piling upon absolute complete fucking panic.

Had something happened? Chase had seemed so happy and carefree just this morning. He'd been looking forward to meeting that other football player for coffee. He'd talked about hanging out with Heath and Sam. Going to the gym. Then meeting up much later tonight.

Nothing had seemed drastically wrong. At least not wrong enough to cause Chase to tweet his address to the millions of people who followed him.

Or to invite them all for a "very gay party."

"He didn't get traded," Rachel said. "That was my first thought, but no. Nothing happened. I just checked ESPN."

"Okay," Tate said. He'd forgotten about that possibility completely, in the utter panic of the last minute. "That's good. That helps."

"But something else . . ." Rachel trailed off.

"Yeah," Tate agreed. He pulled out his own phone, hoping to see a text from Chase. A missed phone call. A voicemail. Something. *Anything.* But there was nothing. Nothing to indicate what had gone so drastically wrong.

He'd gotten a notification that Chase had tweeted. There were about ten texts from various people—Tony, Wyatt, even Jamie, who'd exchanged numbers with him after the taco lunch a few weeks back—but nobody seemed to know anything.

His car was back at the regular storage lot they regularly parked the truck at during off hours, so he pulled up the Uber app and requested a car.

Dread began to build as he exchanged texts with Tony, who was just as clueless as he was.

Finally, his car pulled up and Tate got in it, hoping that they could make it over to Chase's house quickly.

"Hey," the driver said, "this is a popular address tonight." Dread began to coalesce in a sick, heavy ball in Tate's stomach.

"You've seen a lot of requests for it?" Tate asked, even though he really, *really* didn't want to know.

"Yeah," the guy said, somewhat puzzled. "I haven't taken anyone there, but it's got lots of traffic for some reason."

"Yeah," Tate said grimly. "For some reason."

He wished he knew what had gone wrong. For a split second, he considered trying to call or text Chase, to demand answers, but if there were that many people at his house, there was very little chance of getting any kind of response.

Ten minutes later, the Uber was almost to Chase's house, and Tate was about to go out of his mind with worry. He wished he had Alec's number, so he could call him, even though he likely had his hands full dealing with what Chase had just done.

"I think we might have a problem," the Uber driver said, just as Tate looked out the window and realized there was a *very* big problem.

The street just outside Chase's gated driveway was crowded with people and cars. He could see other ride share cars dropping off people, a lot of whom looked to be guys, dressed fairly flamboyantly, which Tate guessed shouldn't have been a big surprise. After all, Chase had just invited the greater Los Angeles area to a "big gay party" at his house. It wouldn't come as much of a surprise that the gays would show up. In droves.

"You can just drop me off here," Tate said, and the driver shot him a grateful grin.

"Gonna make it a lot easier to turn around," he said. "Appreciate it."

"Thanks for the ride," Tate said, and got out, making sure to give him a great tip, before taking off towards Chase's gate, trailing another group who'd just arrived.

Music was blaring; so loudly he was surprised that the cops hadn't shown up already, and through the gate, standing wide open, he could see an enormous crowd of people surrounding the house. Lights were spilling out of open doors and windows, along with the thumping bass of the music, and Tate couldn't help but feel sick at it.

What was Chase playing at? He couldn't just invite all of queer Los Angeles to his house?

Except he could. And he had.

Tate didn't know where he could find him, only that he knew he needed to. Right fucking now. As he made his way up to the front door, and then through it, one of the first people he saw was

Heath Harris, standing with his hands on his hips, surveying the chaos surrounding him with deep frustration and an even deeper concern.

"Heath," Tate said, walking over to where he stood. Heath glanced over at him and sighed. "What the fuck is going on? Have you seen Chase?"

Heath shook his head. "Sam is here too, looking, but . . ." He hesitated and looked down at his phone, shaking his head. "Nope. Nothing so far."

"He has to be around here *somewhere*," Tate said. "And you don't know what brought this on? I mean, I know sometimes Chase can do crazy shit, but inviting everyone to come party at his house? That's a bit extreme."

Heath's eyes grew darker. Even more worried. "Yeah," he said shortly. "I know what happened but . . . I'm not sure it's my story to tell."

Tate had gotten to the point where he couldn't hide his own frustration. "Oh." Then another realization hit, hard and fast. Chase had gone to his friends and had told them what happened. He hadn't called Tate. Hadn't even told him that something was wrong. Yes, Tate had been busy working, but he'd have made the time if Chase needed him. And there was no way that Chase hadn't needed him.

But maybe he didn't really want you, that insidious voice inside him wondered. The one he kept trying to get to shut up. The one that Rachel had probably fairly predicted would be the downfall of their relationship. Fake or otherwise. *All he wants is for you to fuck him. That's all you're good for.*

Heath put a reassuring hand on Tate's shoulder. "I'm sure he's going to tell you. I think he probably wanted to, but . . ."

Sam walked up then, interrupting his boyfriend in the middle of his sentence. "I found him."

"Thank God," Heath said. "Where?"

"Outside, in the back garden, dancing like a maniac around the fire pit."

Heath sighed. "Of course he is. Let's go."

"Wait," Tate said. "Wait. I think it should be me that talks to him."

Sam looked at him with confusion, but Tate was pretty sure that Heath's expression contained at least a little bit of dawning comprehension.

"You really care about him, don't you?" Heath asked quietly, his voice barely audible over the loud music and the rest of the partiers.

"Yeah, I do," Tate said.

"Wait a minute," Sam said, still looking lost. "I thought you weren't even together for real."

Heath shot his boyfriend an incredulous look. "And you bought that?"

"Well," Sam admitted. "I guess not really. No offense, but I kinda thought that the 'fake' part was for you." He shrugged his shoulders. "I knew how Chase felt."

"Apparently I'm the only one who didn't realize it sooner," Tate said. "But we worked it out. Or I *thought* we'd worked it out."

"No," Sam said with a headshake. "This isn't about you. This is . . . this is Chase's baggage to deal with."

"But," Heath added, rather forcefully, "that does not mean you should not absolutely call him out on every bit of his shit. He wants to stay in LA and stay on the Riptide. And this stunt? May have permanently killed his chances."

Tate had thought of that, during his interminable ride over to Chase's house. He'd already tried to come to terms with the worst possible scenario—if Chase was traded to a team three thousand miles away—but he'd struggled with it, because *goddamn it*, it just wasn't going to be fair. Not after they'd found each other after all this time.

"I know," Tate said miserably. "I don't know why he'd do this, then. If he wants to stay. If he *wants* to be with me."

"Because he doesn't feel like he quite deserves it," Heath said softly.

"That's . . ."

"Bullshit?" Sam answered for Tate. "Yeah, I know. And you should absolutely tell him that."

"Don't worry. I will." Tate pressed his lips together. Mad, even as he tried to be understanding. "Any other advice?"

Heath lifted an eyebrow. "I know," Tate said, by way of explanation. "But you guys have known him longer. Well, not *longer* but better than I do, in some ways."

"Don't worry," Sam said supportively. "You've got this."

"Yeah, seriously," Heath added. "But don't let him get away with any of this bullshit about not being 'gay enough,' okay?"

"Not gay enough?"

Heath rolled his eyes. "I know. It's ridiculous. But why else do you think he'd try to prove to the world that he could throw the world's gayest party?"

Tate didn't know why, but Heath's reason was as good as any he could come up with.

"Okay, I'm gonna go track him down," Tate said.

"Good luck," Heath said.

"You're gonna need it," Sam added.

Tate found Chase, as Sam had, outside in the backyard, dancing maniacally around the fire pit. His shirt was off, his chest gleaming with sweat in the firelight. Someone must have given him a rainbow bandanna, and he'd wrapped it crookedly and ridiculously around his head.

"Hey!" Chase said, and wobbled over to where Tate was standing.

He looked surprisingly happy—or maybe surprisingly drunk—considering that he was currently hosting the biggest house party in LA.

"What are you *doing*?" Tate demanded.

Chase shrugged his shoulders. "I'm dancing," he said, and Tate remembered something he'd said when they'd first met back up again. That whenever he felt sad about something, he liked to dance.

"Couldn't you have just danced alone, in your house, with your five-figure sound system?" Tate asked. Didn't even try to hold back the judgment in his tone, because *yeah*, he was definitely judging. He loved Chase, he knew that now. But that didn't change the basic fact that he'd just made an enormous error that could cost both of them a price they didn't want to pay.

"Yeah," Chase drawled with exaggeration. He stumbled two feet closer, and yes, he'd definitely been drinking. He smelled like a Miami street corner during spring break. "That's no fun."

"You should tell me what happened today, that made you do all this," Tate said, "because I don't fucking *get* it. You were trying to stay in LA. Trying to stay with the Riptide. And that meant trying to do good shit."

"This isn't good shit?" Chase asked, smiling dopily. "C'mon, Ward, let down your hair a little and dance with me."

Tate stepped back, out of Chase's reach. "You're drunk," he said.

"A little," Chase admitted.

"More than a little." Tate tried to take a deep breath. Tried to ignore all the half-naked people prancing around. Tried even harder to ignore the geysering keg on the corner of Chase's back patio. Or that from very far away, he could hear the beginnings of what might be police sirens.

This party shouldn't have ever happened in the first place, but it was definitely almost over, now.

"What I mean, is that *you said* you wanted to stay in LA. Wanted to play for the Riptide. Wanted . . ." Tate ignored the stab of pain in his chest and forged on. "Wanted to stay *with me*. And I was helping you do that, but then you let yourself get carried away and blew it all to hell with this stupid stunt."

"It's not *stupid*," Chase said sulkily.

Tate threw up his arms in frustration. "I can't reason with you when you're drunk and stubborn and difficult. I wish you'd just tell me what the fuck happened so I can stop guessing."

"I met with the guy," Chase said. His gaze dropped to the ground. Tate saw him nudging an abandoned rainbow party hat, half-sunk into the dirt, with his sneaker-clad toe. "And the guy was an asshole. But he wasn't a *wrong* asshole."

"What did he say?" Tate asked. He reached out on Chase's arm and tugged, and discovered that a drunk Chase would do just about anything, because he followed happily, as Tate dragged him to a much quieter part of the garden. Chase might not care now that anybody could hear, but he might care in the morning, when he was sober.

"He thought . . ." Chase cleared his throat. Still couldn't look Tate in the eye, and suddenly he wasn't just pissed off, but his heart was breaking. "He thought I was a bad guy. And a bad gay."

"What?" Tate couldn't believe that Heath had been mostly right. But then Heath knew Chase very well. Still, it stung that Tate had never suspected that Chase was sensitive about this. He should have been paying attention. Looking for vulnerabilities. Should have given Chase more than just basic lip service when he'd felt worried before O'Connor's gala. But then that conversation with Ryan had set Chase more at ease, and Tate had assumed that he was working his way through it.

But it sounded like it hadn't been a matter of *if*, but *when*.

"He didn't even think it was *real*," Chase complained. "Like I was trying to be gay just to look good, and *wow*, that kinda blew my mind. But when he found out I wasn't joking, he thought I was making him look bad. All the guys who had to work for it." He shot Tate a look full of shame. "He was right. I just *did* it. I didn't agonize. I didn't even think about it. I just …" Chase trailed off.

"It doesn't *have* to be anything. I told you. There is no right way, and there is no wrong way. It doesn't have to be serious, but it shouldn't be a joke. And I don't think it was ever a joke to you."

Chase's eyes were surprisingly serious. "It wasn't. You were never a joke. And," he added, with one of those lopsided grins that had always set Tate's heart aflutter, "it was always you, you know."

It was hard not to take that confession and let it smooth over his frustration and his anger.

But Tate remembered what Heath had said. *You should call him out on every single bit of his shit.* He'd known Heath was right, both because Tate was so angry, and also because he knew Chase deserved better for himself. But Tate couldn't control Chase's emotions for him. He'd tried and succeeded in helping him at O'Connor's charity event, but now? When Tate was busy working? He'd let himself get carried away all over again.

"And I've been trying to help you," Tate said calmly, but feeling the rage building inside him. So *what* if it had always been him. He couldn't keep going through this drama. He had a business he was building. A *life*. He wanted Chase to be in it, but in a second, Chase could go nuclear and could bring it all down with one tweet. "But I can't be there to help you every second of every day, *and* I can't help you if you won't help yourself. This sure as fuck didn't help you."

"It proved I was gay," Chase said. "I thought about what you said, about a line of guys around the block wanting to fuck me, but I only want it to be you."

And I only want it to be me, Tate thought with resignation.

"So you invited them all to party instead?"

"What, afraid a little partying is going to hurt *your* reputation?" Chase flung at him.

"No, I'm afraid your tendency to go off like a drama queen wide receiver is going to hurt *yours*," Tate hurled back.

"I'm just fine over here," Chase said, even as he wobbled on his feet. Clearly, he was not seeing things right.

"Yeah, you seem really fine," Tate said. "I'm blinded right now by all your fineness."

Chase rolled his eyes.

"You should have called me," Tate said, even though it was already clear that there was no reasoning with Chase right now. Not when he'd decided to close off his mind and indulge in . . . what? His emotions? Tate remembered what he'd said at the fundraiser. How sometimes they overwhelmed him, and he didn't know what to do. Clearly, he hadn't known what to do tonight.

"I don't always need you," Chase retorted. "I could handle it."

"This is you handling it?" The frustrated anger was back, and it was surging inside Tate. He wanted someone who was a functional adult, he'd always believed that was Chase, despite his reputation. Believed that he could be better, if he chose to be.

Tate was beginning to realize that Chase wasn't always going to make that choice. Maybe he *couldn't*. Not right now.

He threw up his hands. "I'm done here. You're an idiot, and when you stop being an idiot, maybe we can have a rational conversation."

"What are you doing? Are you leaving?" Chase sounded wounded and part of Tate—a huge part, that was centered in his chest—wanted to take him in his arms and comfort him. And he would, he absolutely would. When Chase sobered up and kicked all these people out of his house.

"Yes," Tate said, "I'm done here." And he turned and walked away.

Heath caught him on the way out of the garden.

"Hey," he said, "where are you goin'? Did you find Chase?"

"Yes," Tate said bitterly. "He's not . . . he's not thinking right now. I can't talk to him."

"I probably won't be able to either," Heath said with a resigned sigh. "I just . . . I guess I hoped that maybe having you around would be a good stabilizing influence, you know? That he might handle shit like this. But maybe . . ."

It was too close to everything Tate had been thinking. He couldn't *be* there every time something terrible happened. Chase needed to learn how to handle his own emotions. His own shit. Tate wanted to handle it for him, even if it wasn't what Chase really needed. But the painful hard truth was he *couldn't*. He actually, literally, *couldn't*.

No matter how desperately he might want to.

"Maybe?" Tate asked.

Heath looked pained. "I thought you might help him get his crap together, but I'm not sure anything's going to work. Not until Chase decides that he's done."

The bottom dropped out of Tate's stomach. "You don't think he's done, not after this?"

"Every single time," Heath said, "every single time he does this, he says it's the last. He says he's learned his lesson. But has he? I'm not sure, because it keeps happening. He has to want to fight for control. To learn how to be better. Until he makes that decision, this is who he is."

Tate nodded slowly. It was his worst fear, voiced aloud. He wasn't sure he could trust himself to respond, but before he could, Sam appeared, expression concerned, and waved Heath over.

"I gotta go," Heath said, clapping him on the shoulder. "But it's gonna be okay, you know?"

"Yeah," Tate said shortly, and knew neither of them believed the little white lie.

CHAPTER SIXTEEN

It was not the world's greatest party.

It was not even the world's *gayest* party.

It definitely wasn't a party on par with the one Colin O'Connor had thrown.

"You okay there, Riley?" Chase looked up and Neal was standing there, Jamie trailing behind him, a concerned expression on his face. Heath and Sam were further back, hovering. Like a pair of worried old gossipy aunties.

Chase groaned and gripped his tequila bottle a bit more firmly in his hand. "I'm *fine*," he said, even though he was very clearly *not fine*.

"You don't seem very fine," Neal said. "I just finished talking to the cops. They're getting everyone out, and we're going to get you to bed."

"Where's Tate?" Chase thought that if he was going to go to bed, that was who he really needed. *Tate*.

"He left, man," Jamie said, coming up and standing next to Neal. He looked horrified, like he'd seen something he couldn't explain. "You're going to have to hire a cleaning service or . . ." He shuddered. "*Something.*"

Chase couldn't find it in himself to care that someone—or maybe even multiple someones—had defiled his house. He hoped they'd had more fun than he had at this party. He hated that Tate had been right. Even more than he'd hated that Spencer was right. And he really hated that Tate had left.

Left him? Or just left.

Chase didn't know, and he wanted to keep crying into his tequila bottle about it.

"You have got a shit load of explaining to do," Neal said. Glanced over and his expression went blank. "And you can start now."

"Ugh," Chase groaned. "Alec's here, isn't he?"

"Yes, Alec is here," Alec himself said, walking up, a thundercloud on his face. "What the ever-loving fuck have you just done?"

"I just threw a party," Chase said. "A *gay* party, because in case anyone missed it, *I'm not straight.*"

"Hey, I think we got that memo," Jamie said, with a nervous chuckle.

"Everyone got that memo," Sam muttered. "Everyone with Twitter, anyway."

"You, my friend, are in very deep shit, but," Alec said with a reluctant sigh, "I also come bearing good news. Which will hopefully hold, after all this hits the fan. The Riptide have restructured your contract. You're staying in LA. Though," he added with a mutter, "I don't know why the fuck they want you."

"Because I am very, very good at my job," Chase said primly, raising his bottle in a mock toast. It was a relief. He couldn't deny there was a part of him that was very relieved. He wouldn't have to start over someplace else. Someplace that might change him. Make him more like Spencer.

But then he thought of Tate. He was going to have to do something. *Say* something. Confess all his worst fears. Apologize. *Grovel*. Anything to win back the only guy who had ever mattered.

"You are also very, very good at being a total pain in my ass," Alec said. "Why the fuck did you even do this?"

"Because Spencer Evans is a prick," Heath said.

"Well, I could've told you that," Alec said. "Seriously. What did that guy say, and why did you listen to him?"

"He was right. I'm a bad gay," Chase said, crying into his tequila bottle.

"Did he say he was a bad guy?" Alec asked, mystified.

"I think," Sam said with a chuckle, "he said it was because he was a bad *gay*."

"Oh my god," Alec said. "Someone help me get this idiot to bed."

"Bed?" Chase said. "I need *Tate*."

Alec groaned. "No, he left, Riley. And I can't say I blame him," Heath said.

Heath grabbed him by the arm and was starting to drag him—not very carefully, either, towards the door. "Come on, dude, use your legs."

Legs? What were legs? Chase didn't know what legs even were. He definitely couldn't feel them. Were they those things attached to his torso? That were dragging along the ground?

He thought they might be.

"I need to call him," Chase said with conviction. "I need to call him *right now*."

"Trust me, you do not need to call him." Alec plucked the bottle from his fingers. "You need to dry out and sober up and get some sleep. Maybe give him a chance to be less pissed at you."

"Pissed at me?" Chase wasn't sure he even believed it. How could Tate be pissed at him?

Oh. Suddenly it hit him why. They were heading up the stairs, Heath's arms a solid iron band around his waist, and Chase spied a bra and several t-shirts hanging from the chandelier in the center of the foyer. *Oh.* And was that . . . Chase couldn't identify the substance on the stairs that Heath was giving such a wide berth, but it definitely might be vomit.

"That's why he's pissed," Chase said. "Because I threw a party."

"Not *just* because you threw a party," Sam chimed in. Chase hadn't realized he was following behind them. "I don't know the guy all that well, but I'd probably guess it's because you threw a party and then posted the invite to Twitter."

"I just wanted to dance . . ." Chase said mournfully as Heath pushed open the door to his bedroom.

"Maybe next time," Heath said as he pushed Chase down onto his bed. The bed he'd shared with Tate, just last night. Chase felt like crying again. "Maybe next time ask your boyfriend to dance with you. Don't invite all of LA."

"He's not wrong," Alec added. "I've called that security company we use, to post some guards at the gate. I don't want anyone just walking in because they don't know the party's over."

"The party's over," Chase repeated, and this time, he realized as he put a hand to his face, he *was* crying.

"And," Alec added. "I called Moira. You're going to want to talk to her in the morning."

The truth was, in the harsh light of day, Chase did not want to talk to *anyone*.

He was embarrassed. He was humiliated. He had done immeasurable damage to his reputation, *again*. And this time, even worse, he had pissed Tate off.

Chase groaned and rolled over in bed, almost instantly regretting that, because his stomach lurched unhappily.

He'd drunk way too much last night—technically way too much *yesterday*, because he certainly hadn't waited for evening to get the party started. He'd let Spencer tie him up into knots, and he'd done nothing to control the emotional fallout afterwards. Spencer's words still hurt in the harsh light of the morning, not any better or any worse than they'd hurt yesterday, but what had possessed him to take that hurt and do the craziest possible thing?

He was sure Moira would have something to say about that.

He really should start talking to her again. Not just because of this, but because he knew he was still failing at controlling his emotions. Sometimes, they still controlled him.

It was hard not to groan again, thinking of the phrase *coping strategies* and how Moira was going to ride him over his total lack of for the next fifty sessions, at least.

There was a knock on the door and Chase gingerly raised his head off the pillow. "Yeah?" he called out, his voice gravelly.

Alec pushed open the door. He was dressed pristinely, in one of his perfectly pressed three-piece suits, complete with tie and coordinating pocket square. "You're awake," he said.

"Sort of," Chase said.

"I'm happy to report that we turned everyone away who showed up after closing time last night. I took the liberty of giving the security guys a big tip."

"Thanks," Chase said. He could feel his face flaming red, at the realization that Alec had been forced to post security at his house because he'd been dumb enough to tweet his address.

"The tweet has also been deleted, but as you know," Alec said, "the internet is forever."

"Yeah," Chase said. He was probably way more intimate with that concept than he should be. What he really should do is just delete Twitter off his phone. Instagram, too. No good had come of him having easy access to either of those apps. He had a feeling that was going to be the bare minimum Moira demanded of him.

"The cleaning crew has been here since five," Alec added. "Your house is no longer a demilitarized zone."

"Since five?" Chase asked. "You didn't . . ."

Alec sat on the edge of the bed. "I had to make sure things got done. I wasn't convinced the security was going to do their jobs. I wanted to be on hand in case anything bad happened."

Chase looked him up and down. His agent looked like he'd just stepped out of the pages of *GQ*. Not like he'd been up all night, making sure that Chase's messes were cleaned up.

He felt that wave of acute embarrassment hit him, yet again.

"Thanks," Chase said, and hoped Alec knew just how much.

"I'd say, *don't do it again*, but . . ." Alec trailed off.

"It won't happen again," Chase said with absolute conviction.

"You'll forgive me if I don't quite believe that," Alec said kindly. Probably too kindly. "But I know you mean well, Chase. We'll figure it out, together."

"I need . . ." Chase cleared his throat. "I need to talk to Tate. I owe him a big apology. I owe a lot of apologies, actually. Though, I should really start with you." His eyes burned. "I'm so sorry. I don't know what got into me. I know how hard you've been working to get the Riptide to restructure my deal. And then I go and do . . . that."

Alec smiled. "You might be the only client who's ever apologized to me. Actually, no, I do think Neal did as well. When he missed the field goal."

Chase scoffed at that, and Alec nodded. "I agree," he said. "But I appreciate the apology, even though I get where you were coming from."

"You do?"

"I talked to Heath. He told me what happened with Spencer." Alec took a deep breath. "Listen, Chase. This is never easy. There are no right answers. There aren't any wrong ones. And there isn't ever a way to do this *right*. Maybe you didn't come out until you were twenty-eight. Maybe you did it on Twitter, by telling everyone about your boyfriend's food truck. That's your prerogative."

"But . . ." Chase said, but Alec held up a hand.

"No," the agent said firmly. "No, there are no *buts*. We don't get to judge someone else's behavior when we haven't been in their shoes. Even Spencer Evans doesn't have the right to do that."

"He was right," Chase said, staring at the edge of the blanket, fingers picking at a loose thread. "I was careless. I wasn't serious about it. And you guys . . ." He swallowed hard. "You and Heath and Sam and even, god, that asshole O'Connor. You were serious and courageous and I was just . . ." He made a disgusted noise. "I fucked it up. Like I always do."

"Heath wasn't serious. He kissed his boyfriend over the Vince Lombardi Trophy. Just because he's a serious guy doesn't mean everything he does is serious. And this doesn't have to be serious. It *shouldn't* be serious, really. Do non-queer people agonize over how they're going to tell people they aren't queer?"

"No?"

Alec nodded sharply. "No. They don't. Spencer Evans is full of bullshit, and I'm going to make sure he knows it."

"You don't think . . ." Chase took a deep breath. "You don't think I fucked it up?"

Alec stood, slowly. "I think that every day is a new one," he said. "And the beginning of a new set of choices. You can decide, every single morning, who you're going to be, and what you're going to stand for."

"Is that what you do?" Chase asked.

Alec rolled his eyes. "I'm not a fucking saint, Riley. Just a man. I fuck up just as much as anyone else. The difference is you're dwelling on your mistakes and letting them define you."

It was undeniable. That was exactly what he was doing.

"I think I can be different," Chase said cautiously. "I want to be. I *need* to be."

He wasn't dumb enough to believe everything could be fixed overnight. But he *could* be better.

Alec smiled. "Then you can." He paused. "Clean up and eat something, before you call Tate."

While he was in the shower, Chase realized that calling wasn't going to be enough. He'd behaved insufferably, and Tate was probably understandably pretty pissed.

He needed to talk to him in person.

Which, Chase realized as he dressed, had been why Alec had suggested that he get dressed first. He'd known, better than Chase had, what kind of groveling he was going to need to commit to.

Alec was sipping an espresso in the kitchen, reading something on his laptop, when Chase walked in.

"Much better," Alec said, nodding in approval. "This afternoon, we'll have to go to the Riptide offices and sign the new contract. I want to get it done as soon as possible, before they decide you're a liability and let you go after all."

Chase made a beeline for the coffee machine. "Can they do that?" he asked with a wince, even though he knew perfectly well that they could. They could still decide to trade him.

He was never truly going to be safe, not until he retired. He was going to have to figure out a way to cope with that. *Moira,* Chase thought, *I really need to call her.*

But Tate first.

Chase poured himself a cup of coffee, gulping it in three big swallows. Then poured a second one.

"He's downtown today. I'll text you the address," Alec said, like he knew what he was going to ask next. Like he already knew that Chase didn't want to even *touch* the Twitter app on his phone. "I'm not sure he's going to be happy to see you."

"I'm not sure either," Chase agreed. "But I need to apologize, either way."

"You do," Alec agreed. "Meet me at the Riptide offices at four. I'll let them know we're coming. And . . ."

"I should call Moira?" Chase asked wryly. "Yeah, I was already planning on it."

"Good." Alec smiled. "I sent her an email last night and let her know to expect your call."

As Chase poured a third cup of coffee to go, he realized he didn't know how he'd ever gotten so lucky in having Alec as an agent.

In having Alec as a *friend*.

On his way out of the kitchen, he stopped and wrapped his arms around the guy in a big bear hug. "Ooooph," Alec exclaimed. "You're wrinkling me!"

"You'll live," Chase said, and paused, clearing his throat. "Thank you for being here for me."

"It's my job," Alec pointed out.

"This is not *all* your job," Chase said. "I know that much."

He'd appointed himself the protector of the queer guys on the Riptide, and really, throughout the NFL. He'd done it, and not really thought about it. He'd had so many guys' backs, and not once had he considered who had his.

But it turned out that Alec did, unequivocally. And Sam and Heath, and Neal and Jamie did too.

"Maybe, maybe not," Alec said with a small smile. "But I'm happy to do it, anyway."

"*Happy* to do it?"

"Okay, not *happy* about it," Alec said. "I could do without any more cleanup for some time, but you're a good guy, Chase Riley. And you make me a lot of money."

Chase laughed, knowing that Alec was so rich, the percentage he got from Chase was hardly a good reason to put up with his shit, if he didn't want to. "Fair enough."

"Get out of here," Alec said. "Go make your apologies. I'll see you at four."

"Wish me luck," Chase said.

"You're going to need it," Alec said.

Alec was not wrong.

When Chase pulled up at the parking lot of the high-rise Say Cheese was scheduled at for lunch, he could see Rachel in the window, and she gave him a frosty glare.

When he walked up, her shoulder didn't get any less cold.

"He doesn't want to see you," Rachel said firmly.

"I can't blame him for that," Chase said. "But I want to apologize."

"Is it an apology if you're just going to do it again?" Rachel asked archly.

Ouch.

"Any time my ego needs taking down a peg, I definitely know who to come to," Chase said. "But I still want to talk to him." He hesitated, not sure that Rachel's stony expression boded well for that possibility. "Please."

Rachel regarded him for a moment or two longer. "He cares about you, you know?" she said. "Probably too much, if I have anything to say about it."

"I guess it's lucky for me that you don't?"

"Probably," Rachel said. And then sighed. "Fine," she said. He saw her turn away from the front window, and a minute later, the door opened and Tate walked out.

He was wearing his trademark beanie, and his eyes were shadowed with dark circles. Clearly he hadn't slept well, either.

Of course, Chase had brought it on himself, and on Tate too, for that matter.

"Hey," Tate said shortly. "I've got . . ."

"I know you're busy," Chase said. "And I thought about calling you, because of that, but this is the kind of thing that's better to say in person."

"Yeah," Tate said, before Chase could continue. "I think so, too. I don't think . . ." He took a deep breath. "I don't think we should see each other anymore."

The abruptness of it took Chase's breath away, the impact of the worst-case scenario happening before he could even do anything to prevent it. "What?"

Tate shoved his hands into the pockets of his jeans. "We're just . . . we're really different, you know? Maybe at one point, but now? I realized last night, even back in high school, we were always on different paths. Maybe it's better that those paths don't intersect."

"You don't really believe that," Chase said.

"Yeah, I actually think I do." Tate looked away, like it was too much to say it. "I don't *want* it to be true, but this isn't the first time this has happened with you. I can't keep going on like this, expecting the worst."

"Is that really what it's like?" Chase asked. Breathless and pained with the possibility that being with him was the way Tate described. *Expecting the worst.*

"There's good too. So much good . . ." Tate trailed off. "But . . ."

"Then I fuck it up," Chase said in a hard voice. "That's what I came to say. I'm sorry I fucked it up last night. I let that guy get into my head and maybe I hadn't really dealt with a lot of stuff, before that, and well, I know it wasn't pretty. So I'm sorry."

"I know you're sorry." Tate's voice went soft. His eyes were anguished, pale gray and huge in his face. Chase's heart contracted.

This couldn't be the end. He'd worried that it might be, but he hadn't really expected that Tate would resist him. They'd never been able to resist each other. Not from the very beginning.

But maybe . . . maybe Tate had finally figured out how.

"But it's not enough," Chase said. *You will not start crying. Not right here. Not right now.*

"I . . . I don't think so. Not right now. I . . . maybe you should deal with some of that stuff you talked about. Talk to your therapist. I can't . . . I can't always be there for you. Especially when you don't let me in." Tate looked awkward, as he shifted his weight from foot to foot. Nothing like the joyous way they'd come together so many times over the last few weeks. Nothing like the sweet tenderness he'd caught in Tate's gaze more than once. He'd been sure that Tate was falling for him, same as he'd fallen for him. But maybe love wasn't enough.

It definitely wasn't enough for Chase to fix himself. He had to do it because he *needed* to—not because Tate wanted him to.

"I understand," Chase said. Even though he wished he didn't.

"I'm grateful for everything you did for me," Tate said.

Chase thought of the way Tate had encouraged him to embrace his sexuality. Had taught him more about who he was than he'd realized in ten long years. "It was nothing," he said.

"Okay," Tate said, and then turned away.

Chase squeezed his eyes shut. Forced himself to stay in place. Told himself that it was probably good for him to get his heart really broken once. He was a rich, immensely successful football player who had every single thing he'd ever wanted, handed to him on a silver platter.

Except one.

And it turned out that was the one thing that mattered more than anything else.

"You sent him away?" Rachel asked as soon as Tate climbed back into the truck.

"Not like you weren't trying to do it," Tate retorted. Wished he felt slightly better than absolutely fucking horrid. Wished he hadn't felt like he had to say any of that to Chase. Wished he didn't believe that it was the best thing.

"He looked terrible. Maybe as bad as you do," Rachel said, her voice taking on a surprising edge of sympathy. "And I didn't try to get him to leave because I actually *wanted* him to leave. I wanted to give you time to reconsider your stupid-ass decision."

"It isn't a stupid-ass decision," Tate said. Even though it kind of felt like one. What was he doing? He'd only wanted and dreamt of and fantasized about Chase Riley forever. And now he was pushing Chase away?

What the *fuck* was he thinking?

He was thinking that Chase was a hurricane in human form, and that he couldn't let himself get caught up and destroyed.

He had too much to lose. And while Chase had a tendency to land back on his feet, Tate knew he'd never possessed the same kind of luck.

Or the money to get himself out of any possible scrape.

He needed to be smarter.

"Maybe he'll get the help he needs," Rachel said optimistically. Which, really, said it all. Because optimism wasn't exactly Rachel's default setting.

"I hope so," Tate said. Wondered if that would make any difference ultimately, but knew it probably wouldn't, because this was Chase Riley. And while Tate might have scratched a long-time itch for him, there was no way Chase was going to wait around, pining for him.

He'd move on and find someone new, someone else to blow his mind in bed, and laugh with him, and feed him, and … *ouch*. Tate's heart contracted miserably.

Not once in all those long years of distant crushing had he ever expected that he could do any of those things, all he'd ever had was pipe dreams. But then he'd unexpectedly gotten to do all of them, and now he didn't know how he was supposed to go without.

He and Chase had gotten tied up together before he'd even known what was happening.

Or maybe they'd always been that way, he just hadn't realized it before.

"Do you need me to call in Harmony?" Rachel asked. It was her day off, because their schedule was lighter today.

"Why?" Tate asked.

Rachel shot him a knowing look. "Because it looks like you want to go cuddle up on the couch in front of a terrible rom-com and stuff your face with ice cream, that's why."

"No," Tate said, straightening. The idea of doing nothing, of letting himself actually *think* about what he'd had and what he'd lost—*what you turned down,* his uncooperative brain added—sounded so terrible that he couldn't face it. "No, I don't want . . . honestly, I'd rather work."

Rachel rolled her eyes. "Of course you would," she said. "Why am I not surprised?"

"Besides, we're taste-testing the new sandwich, with the new soup," Tate said. "And I wanna see how it goes."

With their newfound popularity quadrupling sales, and their residency at the food truck lot looming, Tate had decided a menu revamp was in order. He'd gone through their sales numbers and had kept the things that sold well and was experimenting with a few new menu items.

"One rule, then," Rachel said as she hefted a big hotel pan of chicken out of the oven. "No whining. No moping."

"What?" Tate couldn't quite believe it. Rachel had been undeniably more sympathetic than he'd expected, but now this? He was going to get whiplash.

"You're making *me* feel bad that it's over, and that's just . . ." Rachel shook her head, pragmatic to her core. "It's not going to happen, okay? We'll just go back to how it was. It was good back then, right?"

CHAPTER SEVENTEEN

Two weeks later

"I say this with all the love in my heart," Rachel said, leaning against the counter, "but you have *got* to take Chase's Google Alert off."

"What?" Tate looked up from his phone. That sweetly bitter combination of regret and love was swamping him as he watched Chase's TV spot that he must've recorded since they'd broken up, because he couldn't remember Chase ever mentioning being a spokesperson for "Happy Health," which was a mental support network of counselors. Tate had seen their marketing materials around, had noticed that Heath Harris had done a whole series of ads for them, talking about his own mental health journey, and now Chase was joining in.

Tate wanted to think it was a good sign. Maybe he was talking to his counselor again, or maybe this was just something he was doing because it paid well.

"You're seriously pathetic, and I say that with all the love in my heart," Rachel said. "You either have got to move on or call him up.

You can't just keep mooning after him, even though *you* dumped *him*."

"I didn't . . ."

"But you did," Rachel said bluntly. Tate couldn't really fault her for the painfully harsh delivery. Despite that she'd warned him that awful morning two weeks before, Tate could admit that he'd done plenty of whining. And probably even more moping. "And you *can* change your mind, you know. I know you've reconsidered. That maybe you were a little overly judgmental."

Had he been judgmental? It was hard to deny it.

But then there was also all that fear Tate had felt that day. What if this kept happening? What if Chase kept melting down and Tate couldn't stop him? What if Chase pulled him in with him?

Tate knew now that it wouldn't happen. Chase wasn't that guy. But how to say so? Tate still didn't know. He was ashamed. Embarrassed. Just plain fucking sad.

"Just because I . . ."

"Miss him?" Rachel challenged. "Love him? Want to spend the rest of your life with him?"

Tate sighed. "You are really pushy, you know."

She grinned. "And you love me, anyway. And you love *Chase*, too, by the way. In case you didn't realize."

"Trust me, I realized," Tate said moodily.

"Then you should tell him. Tell him you're sorry. You were a judgmental prick."

"I wasn't . . ."

"Just because he's a famous football player doesn't mean he has all his shit figured out. And yeah, when it hits the fan, because he *is* a famous football player, everyone knows about it. It's way more public than any meltdown you're used to. But that doesn't mean he deserves any less of your support."

Tate couldn't help but nod miserably.

"Listen," Rachel said, "the guy came out. Yes, he came out in a way that . . . we'll say charitably was not the most stable way of doing it. And then he panicked because it got real after that. Well, remember when you made that post on Facebook? And you called me after, laughing and crying, because you'd actually done it? And then you went out and got drunk and hooked up with some random guy? Some random guy with *long, blond hair*?"

"Yes," Tate said. "But it's not . . ."

"Not the same." Rachel made a disgusted noise. "Right. Of course not. And you're not afraid of what being in love with Chase Riley would mean, either. *Never.*"

She went back to her prep, and Tate put his phone away and tried to do the same, but her words haunted him all the way through lunch.

Had he judged Chase too harshly because his meltdown over his sexuality had happened so publicly? Or had he judged because it had happened at all? It wasn't easy to come to terms with the fact that you weren't what the world considered "normal," even when you were already considered freakishly gifted at catching footballs.

When they had their break between their lunch and dinner crowds, Tate stared at his phone for a long time. He watched Chase's Happy Health commercial twice. Then three times. Wishing that he could just call up Chase and ask him if he was doing okay. If he was getting the help he needed. Desperately wanting to know that everything Chase was saying in the ad wasn't just lip service for his sponsorship.

Was he getting the help he needed? Was he talking to someone who both understood and understood *him*?

It had been easy enough—though never *easy*—to keep those thoughts contained before he and Chase had met up again. He'd always worried about him. Hoped that he was doing okay, no matter what he said on social media or what the sports commentators said. But now, it was so much harder. He *knew* Chase now. And he could, if he swallowed his not-inconsiderable pride, actually call him to make sure.

But if he did, what would happen then? Chase would either be glad he called and maybe they could be friends again, or maybe even more, or Chase would still be pissed off about Tate's judgmental behavior, and he'd brush him off. Tell him he'd moved on. Tell Tate that he *wanted* to move on.

Tate didn't know which he'd get, even as he knew which response he'd deserve. So he didn't call, and didn't check in. Because the idea of Chase brushing him off? It hurt too damn much.

Besides, the food truck lot was opening in two days. Tomorrow was the charity event, and Tate had already committed to the truck being there. Chase would be there, with all his friends, and the kids they were bringing in to enjoy the food trucks before the lot officially opened to the public. He'd see Chase then, and he'd know how he was doing, just by looking at him. Maybe Chase could present a false front to the rest of the world, but Tate had always been able to see through it.

See right through to the man underneath.

"Hey!" Tate glanced up and saw Wyatt Flores walking towards him, a big smile on his face. He'd gone outside ostensibly to get the last of the condiments and plasticware set up in the bins outside of the truck. But in reality, he was avoiding Rachel, because she wouldn't stop harassing him about Chase.

For a split second, the voice sounded *almost* like Chase's, and Tate hated the panic that sprang up inside of him. He knew he *should* apologize. Chase certainly deserved one. But Tate didn't know how, because he still hadn't figured out how they could possibly move forward.

In his mind, he'd always just fantasized about dating Chase Riley, the man. But he knew that wasn't all he was dating. He was also dating Chase Riley, the superstar wide receiver for the Los Angeles Riptide. It turned out that dating the latter came with a lot more complications than he'd anticipated.

Maybe a better man wouldn't care as much. Maybe a better man wouldn't be so scared.

But Tate wasn't sure *how* to be that man.

"Hey," Tate said. "How's it going?"

"Everything looks great," Wyatt said with enthusiasm, and then his expression turned more serious. "Except maybe you."

"You heard?" It was inevitable that he would. It seemed gossip traveled faster in their food truck circle than Tate had ever anticipated.

"Yeah," Wyatt said, and patted him on the shoulder. "You know, I never wanted to date someone famous either."

"You didn't?" So many people talked about that being the end all, be all of dating life. Finding someone who was rich and famous and hot.

But Tate had only ever wanted Chase, not the trappings.

"When Ryan hired me to be his personal chef, I told myself that nothing was ever going to happen," Wyatt said wryly, as he leaned against the side of the truck.

"A vow destined to be broken," Tate said, trying to make a joke, but all too aware of how flat it fell. His heart just wasn't in it. Wasn't in much these days, if he was being honest with himself.

"Nobody would blame you for being afraid of being with someone like Chase," Wyatt said seriously.

"I'm not . . ." Tate argued, even though, deep down, he *was*.

Chase had the ability to torch his entire universe. And Tate? He was just *Tate*.

"You are, and that's okay," Wyatt said. "That's sort of what I came over to say. But also that . . . Chase seems like a really great guy, and I don't want you to regret anything later, because you let him get away."

Tate didn't want to experience that kind of regret either. And he knew he would.

"How did you . . ." Tate took a deep breath, and his hands, busy before with the napkins and the plastic forks and knives, stilled. "How did you deal with it?"

"I reminded myself that I knew *him*. Yeah, he might have enough money that he could buy and sell me a few hundred times over. He could fix anything, with just a phone call to the right person. He could leave me tomorrow for someone who was richer and more famous and way, way hotter. But when I thought about it, when I really considered who Ryan was and what he wanted and how he'd behaved since I'd known him, I realized that I trusted that he wouldn't hurt me. Deep down, I knew no matter the trappings that surrounded him, that he was a good guy. Acted like an idiot sometimes," Wyatt added with a knowing grin. "But that was part of who he was, and I knew I couldn't live without him."

Tate thought, suddenly, of how many times he'd absently or purposefully thought of how well he knew Chase Riley. Better than anyone else, he'd always believed. Knew how he was, deep down. Knew everything that he'd been privileged enough for Chase to share with him. And until his idiotic behavior a few weeks back, Tate had never doubted him.

Not for one moment.

"Thanks for the advice," Tate said. Wondering when he would see Chase. Wondering, now, *again*, how he could possibly apologize. Because he knew now that he could never let Chase get away again.

CHAPTER EIGHTEEN

CHASE HAD DREADED AND anticipated this day for the last two weeks.

Tate's words the morning after his complete gay meltdown had been harsh. Too harsh? Chase still wasn't sure. He was trying this new thing where he didn't just accept everyone else's judgment on him without thinking it through first. But it had been two weeks—two insanely long, painful weeks—and he'd had four sessions with Moira, and they were no closer to figuring out if Tate's attitude was right or wrong or, frankly, anything else, either.

But he could say this—he *did* feel better.

More in control. Less controlled by his own errant emotions.

He remembered feeling this way when he'd seen Moira the first time. When he'd first started going to her, it had felt like he was about five seconds away from flying apart.

Back then, she'd taught him ways to deal, and he'd gotten better, and now they were revisiting all of those coping mechanisms, refining the ones that worked, and chucking the ones that didn't.

But even Moira Rogers couldn't hand Chase a method for dealing with today.

Today was the big charity event that he and Ryan were throwing at the new food truck lot, and Tate was going to be there. Chase wouldn't be able to avoid him—and even worse, he wasn't sure if he could even resist him, even though he knew he *should*.

"It's not about making him grovel," Moira had said yesterday, "though that would feel good, I'm sure. Tate has to decide that he wants this level of scrutiny in his public life. If being with you is worth being under the microscope."

The problem was, Chase didn't know if that was even a decent exchange. What if it wasn't? What if Tate decided that he was better off without Chase in his life?

It would be the worst possible outcome, and Chase hadn't even begun to figure out how he was going to deal with it. How could you, when ten years of fantasies and pining resulted in . . . *nothing*? Technically, Chase thought as he stared moodily in the mirror, giving his hair one last once-over, it would be *worse* than nothing. Heartbreak and disappointment. Even disillusionment. Definitely worse than nothing.

"You can do this," Chase said, giving himself a pep talk. "It's gonna suck, but you can still do it."

But just like Chase imagined it would, it did suck.

The first person he saw when he parked on the street and walked onto the lot was Tate.

He was standing with Tony, the breeze riffling through his hair, for once not wearing his regular beanie. He looked . . . *so good*.

Smiling and laughing like nothing was wrong. Like he hadn't broken Chase's heart two weeks ago.

Chase turned and ran right into Ryan.

"Oh, good, you're here," Ryan said, clapping him on the back. He'd been a good friend the last few weeks, once Alec had encouraged him to tell Ryan what had happened with Spencer Evans.

"I'm here," Chase echoed. Considering, despite how embarrassing it might be, that *not* being here might be a better option.

"It's going to be fine," Ryan said, giving him a supportive smile. "Trust me."

Chase wanted to believe him, but he wasn't so sure.

"In any case," Ryan continued, "there's plenty to keep you busy, if you'd like to help me set up."

"Sure," Chase said. And turned away from where Tate and Tony were still laughing together.

He'd schlepped four loads of supplies and decorations from the van Ryan had rented when Rachel appeared in his path, a worried frown on her face.

"Oh good, I found you," Rachel said.

"You found me?" Chase answered, confused.

"Yeah," Rachel said. "I need your help *now*."

"I really don't think..." Chase hesitated. It wasn't like he didn't want to help Rachel. He did, because she was a good sport and he'd always liked her. But the chances of running into Tate *while* helping Rachel seemed high. He'd been hoping to get out of this without any direct contact.

That way, it might hurt a little less.

But really, Chase reconsidered, who was he kidding? It was going to hurt like a bitch, regardless.

"Sure," Chase said. "Let me just get this stuff over to Ryan first."

"Good," Rachel said. "Meet me at the truck."

It was pointless to ask which one she meant, because of course she meant the truck she owned with Tate. Chase inwardly groaned as he dropped off the final crate for Ryan and his PA.

It'll be easier if you just get it over with, Chase told himself as he walked over to where Say Cheese was parked. Tate and Rachel had gotten a prominent, good spot on the lot, centrally located, and despite all his conflicting opinions about the man, Chase couldn't help but be happy for him. He *loved* him, right? That didn't just go away. Even if he was angry and hurt and ashamed and *dumped*.

"Here," Rachel said, gesturing to the open door on the front of the truck. "I'll be in shortly."

Chase climbed in, hating how many good memories were flashing back through him. The first time he'd ever been in here. The afternoon they'd spent "training" and he'd kissed Tate up against the back counter.

Then he spotted the very last thing he'd expected to see. Tate, staring at him like a deer caught in the headlights. Like he'd hoped, despite every indication otherwise, that he could avoid Chase for the entire afternoon event.

"Hey," Chase said nervously. It was weird to be cooped up in this small space, after Tate had told him that he didn't want him anymore. He fought against his urge to apologize for insinuating himself into a place where he didn't belong. Where he wasn't welcome. "Rachel said she needed help with something?"

Tate frowned. "Rachel told *me* she needed help with something . . ." Then suddenly he was pushing Chase out of the way and making a beeline for the door. Which, taking into account Tate's muttered curse words, was now locked.

"Did . . ." Chase took a deep breath. "Did she lock us in here together?"

Tate was still on the narrow set of stairs, in front of the door, jiggling the handle like it was miraculously going to open. He didn't turn and look at Chase, who was hovering a few feet away.

"Yes," Tate finally said in a clipped and annoyed voice. "Yes, she did."

"Oh." Chase couldn't figure out what was happening, but he did know one thing: he did not like this development. At all. How on earth was he supposed to deal with all of Tate's careless rejection when he was forced up against it?

"It's okay," Tate said, pulling out his phone from his back pocket. Chase absolutely did not look at how absolutely fucking amazing his ass looked in those tight jeans. Nope, he definitely did not. Because even though they were trapped in a tight place, he already knew where Tate stood.

And it was not next to him.

"What are you doing?" Chase asked as he dialed.

"Calling Tony. Getting him to unlock this goddamn door," Tate said. He still hadn't turned around and looked Chase in the eye. Chase was trying not to take it too personally, but it was hard.

"Yeah," Tate said, after Tony answered. "Yeah, she's insane. We have to prep and get set up and . . ." There was a long pause, and even though Tate was silent, Chase could practically *hear* his incredulity. "What? You want me to do *what?*

"No," Tate retorted after Tony must have made some non-persuasive argument. "Absolutely not. This is not, you can't force me to . . ."

After a long moment, Tate pulled the phone down from his ear. Slowly he turned around. "Well," he said, still not looking at Chase, "it seems we're in here together until they decide that we're allowed out."

"What?" Chase couldn't believe that this was happening. "Why?"

Tate's shrug was tight, like he didn't want to give anything away. "I guess they don't like that we're not talking."

"That's rich," Chase grumbled under his breath. He pulled out his own phone. If Rachel and Tony wouldn't let him out, then he knew someone who would, because he'd know just how much this hurt, to be locked up with the man who didn't want him anymore.

He picked the contact name and hit the "call" button on his phone.

Heath picked up on the first ring. "Sam and I just got here," Heath said, sounding out of breath. "Neal and Jamie are with me, too."

"Good," Chase said. "Then you can do me a favor."

"Oh?"

"You can get me out of this goddamned food truck," Chase said. "It's the one that says Say Cheese on it. If anyone's in front of the door, and won't get out of the way, I trust you know what to do with them."

"Huh," Heath said. Chase swore he could almost hear him from the other side. "You mean *this* truck?" he asked, and Chase heard a rhythmic echo as he gave the side a sharp smack.

"Yeah, that's the one," Chase said. Thrilled that his enforced imprisonment was about to end. "Just unlock the door, okay?"

Heath was quiet for a moment. Too many moments. "I don't think I can, Riley," Heath said and actually sounded *sorry*. "I think you need to have this conversation, even if you don't want to."

"Trust me, I *don't*," Chase said vehemently. "What I need is to get out of here!"

"Talk to him," Heath said. "Trust *me*. You want to."

"But I . . ." And then, *worse-case scenario*, Heath hung up the phone.

"Well, fuck," Chase said savagely. He kicked the metal baseplate and it echoed with a lot more force than Heath's little love tap had. "*Fuck*."

"Let me guess, he decided not to help you," Tate said.

"I think your crazy sister got to him," Chase said.

"It seems likely," Tate said. But he seemed less upset than he had only a few moments ago.

Chase sulked against the counter. Tate climbed up the stairs and skirted by him so carefully, like he was terrified to even *touch* Chase. It was too terrible to even contemplate that they had gotten to this place after all the incredible pleasure they'd shared together.

Tate was still looking at his phone, and Chase decided that if he could be silent, then there was no reason to talk.

But just when he'd settled in for a very long, very quiet afternoon, Tate asked softly, "What did your friend tell you about getting out?"

"Heath?" Chase hesitated. "He said they wanted us to talk."

"Yeah," Tate said. "That's what they told me too. I guess they can't stand that we aren't friends anymore. That we aren't talking."

"You . . . you . . . *dumped* me." The words practically exploded out of Chase's mouth. "Did they think I was going to want to be friends with you after that?"

Tate looked at him now, something akin to shock in his face. "Well, I didn't . . ."

"You *did*," Chase said. "And maybe you were right. Maybe we were a disaster together but . . ." He didn't want to be the one to say, *but you were wrong, we weren't a disaster, that was just me, and I'm getting better, I promise. You'll see if you would just . . .* but Chase cut that voice off hard and fast.

"We weren't a disaster together," Tate said softly.

"Oh," Chase said.

"I think we were pretty great." Tate leaned against the bulkhead at the front of the truck. "I . . . I shouldn't have said some of those things. I was a judgmental asshole, just when you needed someone in your corner the most."

"I think if anyone is apologizing it should probably be me," Chase said wryly.

"No," Tate said firmly. "You came over that morning so you *could* apologize, and I never really let you. I never listened, anyway. Because I was so busy being afraid of what kind of chaos you might bring to my life. What kind of chaos you were bringing to your own."

"Chaotic destruction?"

Tate chuckled, shaking his head. "No. Not even remotely close. I mean, I'm not thrilled with what you did. I'm worried about you. Worried you won't get the help you need, because I *know* you don't want to be that guy, Chase. I know who you are. I've always known. And honestly?" Tate smiled, his expression amused. "You're all I've ever wanted. Baggage and therapy and bad Twitter habits, and all."

It was everything that Chase had wanted to hear, but he still didn't understand. "Then why did you . . ." He wasn't even sure how he wanted to end that question. Why had Tate dumped him? Why hadn't Tate called him in the last two weeks? Why had it taken their friends locking them in together for them to actually *talk* about this?

"I was so fucking afraid, okay?" Tate admitted. "I wanted to apologize. I wanted to tell you that I didn't mean it, but what if you were sick of me already? What if I was just an itch you wanted to scratch and then you'd done it and you were done? What if I was just an experiment? I couldn't . . . I couldn't deal with being just that, not with you. But then I realized, I know you, the *real you*, and if I trusted you like I thought I did, I should really *trust* you."

"Come 'ere," Chase said roughly, and Tate fell into his arms like he'd never left. Like he'd been waiting this whole time for the invitation. He felt so good. So fucking *right*. How could something he'd wanted for so long be wrong? Chase knew that if anything was wrong, it was denying their feelings.

"I love you, you know?" Chase said, resting his forehead against Tate's. Loving the way his gray eyes warmed, just for him. "I want you to know that. I'm not ever just going to . . . move on. Or think of you as an experiment. That was never what it was about, for me. I liked you a lot. I missed you when we didn't talk anymore, after high school. And now? It's definitely more than that. I know how serious my feelings are."

Tate's eyes were wide and amazed, gleaming in the dim light of the truck. "Really?" he said with wonder. "I didn't . . ."

"I do love you," Chase said and added in a faux stern tone, "and you are *not* allowed to question that anymore. It's *you* I want. It's always been you."

"Funny," Tate said with a dreamy smile, leaning into him like there was nowhere else he wanted to be, "it's always been you, too. I've loved you, *well*, I won't even tell you how long. But it's been a long time."

"I want you to know, I'm getting some help," Chase said, after a long moment. "But it's a process. I'm not going to be perfect. I can't . . ."

"No," Tate said firmly, pressing a finger against Chase's lips. "I know that. I was a dick, okay? I don't want you to be perfect. I just want you to be Chase."

"I want to be that guy, too. The one in your head, on that pedestal," Chase said, hearing the longing in his own voice. "I'm gonna get there. I know it. I just can't get there right now."

"I think together we can do anything," Tate said, and the look in his gray eyes was a promise and a vow. "Anytime you need me, I'm here for you, okay?"

"What if its too much? What if I need too much?" That was something Chase worried about. A concern he'd actually confessed to Moira. Tate had been absolutely fucking amazing at talking him down before O'Connor's fundraiser. But what if he couldn't do it on his own? Not ever? Wouldn't Tate get frustrated and annoyed and eventually leave him because of it?

Moira had been firm that there was no way that was going to happen. That Chase had all the weapons he needed to fight his own demons. *And if Tate helps you out sometimes, because he cares about you,* she'd said, *then that's just more ammunition.*

"You can't be," Tate said. "I *want* to be there for you. I was hurt that you didn't call me when Spencer was a dickhead."

"I wanted to," Chase admitted. "But being your burden . . ."

Tate looked like Chase had just hit him over the head with a new set of truths. "You don't want to be *my* burden," he said, eyes widening. "And here I was, worried about being *your* burden."

"How about we agree to be each other's burdens?" Chase asked softly, pulling Tate more tightly against him. Hoping that they never had to leave this moment. Wondering how everything could be so terrible one minute, and so wonderful the next.

"I think I could get behind that idea," Tate said, gray eyes filled with wonder. And *love*, that was what that look was. Chase had been seeing it for so long, he had never been able to pinpoint it, but it was love.

Tate loved him.

And he definitely loved Tate.

"Hey, you think we can get out of here, now?" Chase wondered, his heart full to bursting. Maybe he'd fucked up, but in the end, he'd done *one* thing that was absolutely, perfectly, brilliantly *right*. He'd won the man of his dreams.

"Yeah, probably," Tate said, linking his hands behind Chase's neck and tugging him down, their lips nearly meeting. "But first we should make them sweat a little."

Chase raised an eyebrow, his own hand reaching back and squeezing Tate's incredible ass. "How about you make *me* sweat a little first?"

"I like the way you think," Tate said, and kissed him.

When Rachel had admitted to locking him and Chase up in the food truck and refused to let them out again until they talked things out, Tate knew when he eventually walked out the door he'd either be on top of the world, or dragged so low he wouldn't be able to hold his head up.

There was part of him that wanted to ask Rachel how she'd known it would be the former and not the latter, but he knew if he did, Rachel would just give him one of those mysterious, knowing looks and say, "Well, it all turned out for the best, didn't it?"

And Tate couldn't deny that she was right. It *had* turned out, better than he could've ever imagined.

They'd had a great afternoon—once they'd finally emerged, somewhat disheveled, from the truck. Tate had served the kids all the grilled cheese and macaroni and cheese they could fit in their stomachs, alongside the fresh squeezed lemonade from Sean's truck, and the baklava cheesecake from Alexis's and meatballs on a stick from Gabriel's. The band had played, and they'd all done the chicken dance, together, Tate laughing alongside Chase as he couldn't get the moves quite right.

Chase had thrown together a quick pickup game of flag football in the empty lot next door, and Ryan had scored the winning touchdown on a deep pass from Heath.

It had been a wonderful day; one of the best days that Tate could remember. They'd given something amazing and special to these kids, hopefully something they could hold close during the difficulties of their lives—and he also knew, because Chase had told him, that he'd tucked five-hundred-dollar gift cards in each of the goody bags they were taking home.

It was extraordinary that he was in love and loved back by someone who cared so much about other people. Who was generous and kind and funny and irreverent and definitely the most gorgeous man that Tate had ever seen.

All it had taken was him discarding the fear that had held him back, and believing, despite all the logic that said otherwise, that he deserved this.

That he deserved Chase.

"It was a good day, huh?" Tony walked up next to him, slinging an arm around Tate's shoulders. "You can thank me later, in detail, for that assist, by the way."

"It could've turned out terrible," Tate pointed out. Even though it hadn't.

"Yeah, I don't think so," Tony said with a smile that echoed Rachel's own. "You guys were crazy about each other. Everyone saw it but you."

Tate scuffed his shoe in the gravel. "And you saw all this before anyone else did," he said, waving around at the lights crisscrossing the central seating area, the trucks clustered together like good friends, and the stage at the far end, where the band was just wrapping up their cover of "Born this Way."

"Yeah, it's gonna be great," Tony said with satisfaction, and all that boundless confidence. "What's going on now?" He pointed at the stage, where the singer had left, followed by the instrumentalists, and Ryan and Chase had commandeered the microphone.

"I'm not sure," Tate said. "But I wasn't exactly invited to the planning meetings the last few weeks, so maybe they're doing something I don't know about."

"It looks like your boy is about to give a speech," Tony said slyly.

"Chase doesn't give speeches," Tate said. He couldn't remember one time that Chase had given a speech in all the years he'd been following him.

"Maybe he does now," Tony said, patting Tate on the back. "And we all know who we can thank for that development."

Tate rolled his eyes. "I'm sure it has nothing to do with me."

"You sure about that?" Tony retorted. "The guy upended his whole life for you. I think that might be enough to persuade him to give a speech."

"I guess we'll see," Tate said. Ryan had tapped the microphone, grabbing everyone's attention who was still milling around the food truck lot. There was a big cluster of kids in the corner, with the balloon animal guy, and they all turned towards the stage.

"Hey, everyone," Ryan said, "I just want to say thank you for coming and I hope you had a great time. I couldn't have put this on without the help of my good friend here, Chase Riley. I'm going to give this over to him, because he has a few things he wants to say."

It seemed that Tony was right, and Chase *was* going to give a speech.

They'd only had a few hurried minutes after their love confession, and most of those minutes had not involved talking, so Tate told himself that Chase hadn't had the time or the chance to confess his plans.

"Hey, guys," Chase said, taking the microphone from Ryan, "you might know me, I'm Chase Riley." There were scattered pockets of applause throughout the assembled group and Chase grinned. "Yeah, maybe not for the things I want to be known for, though," he continued, his voice going unexpectedly serious. "And that's what I wanted to talk about briefly today. Accepting yourself and letting others accept you. I'm lucky enough that I have the resources to talk to people who can help me with that. Who can walk me through every step of the game plan. That's part of why I'm partnering with Happy Health—I want you to know that it's *okay* to get help. And okay to need it. I did, when we lost the Super Bowl, and I needed it this year, too. It doesn't make you weak to ask for help; it makes you *strong*. So I want to help all of you guys get strong, are you with me?" There was an even louder cheer this time and Tate realized that he was transfixed. Not just because he loved the man who was up on stage, doing what he could to help take care of these kids that nobody wanted, but because he'd had to overcome his own demons to do it.

"Part of the goody bag you're getting today," Chase continued, "is a free voucher to any Happy Health clinic or online resource. It's good for your lifetime. I want you to know that you can *always* get help, whenever you need it. Even when it feels like you don't deserve it."

Chase paused.

"That's something else I want to talk about," Chase said. "Because sometimes we *don't* feel like we deserve it. I didn't, I didn't for a long time. I'm still working on that. I'm not perfect. Sometimes I still mess up. Sometimes I tweet things I shouldn't." The audience laughed there and Tate looked around, proud and happy that they were listening. And Tate knew then, though he'd already begun to think that he'd been wrong, that Rachel was right, and he'd judged Chase unfairly.

"I was struggling with accepting who I was. I thought I needed to be someone I wasn't. But what I've learned in the last few weeks—and hopefully will *keep* learning—is that there is no right way to be queer. We're all different. We all love differently and share differently and we're permitted to *be* different. And that's okay. I want you to know you have blanket permission to be whoever you want to be. Me? I'm gonna stick with my guy over there." Chase pointed to him, and Tate couldn't help the flush creeping up his neck as everyone turned to look at him. "He's the best thing that's ever happened to me."

Chase's speech ended with rousing applause, and it took him a few minutes to get back to where Tate was standing. Tony had left to deal with closing the trucks up for the night, but Tate lingered, wanting a minute of Chase's time. But it seemed everyone else wanted a minute with him too.

Alec had arrived, and Tate realized it was the first time he'd seen him wear jeans. Tate even thought he spied some telltale powdered sugar dust on his sleek gray button-up shirt. He was with another man, big and bulky, with a Los Angeles Rams hat on.

Tate watched as Chase turned to say something to his agent and stiffened, his head rearing back when he caught sight of the other man.

And Tate knew then who he was.

This must be Spencer Evans, the guy who had insulted Chase. Told him that he wasn't gay enough. Had made him feel about two feet tall with his shitty words and his judgmental behavior.

Tate found his fists clenching, and he desperately wanted to go over to the much bigger man and give him a piece of his mind. But then, Spencer dipped his head and Chase's expression went from hard, to much, much softer, and Tate had to wonder if maybe things weren't quite what they seemed.

Alec wouldn't have *brought* Spencer unless he knew Spencer wouldn't continue to fuck with Chase's head. Maybe . . . Tate wondered if maybe Spencer was actually here not to continue causing problems but to apologize.

Chase's conversation with Spencer only took a minute, but he seemed contemplative when it finished and when he walked over to Tate, finally, he wasted no time in asking.

"So, did Alec drag that guy here to apologize to you?" Tate asked, reaching down and intertwining their fingers together, squeezing Chase's hand tightly.

"Actually," Chase said, sounding just as surprised himself, "I think he came because he *wanted* to apologize."

"Then it's all good now, between you?"

"I don't want to punch him in the face, anymore," Chase said, a sudden grin breaking over his face. "So yeah, I think so?"

They began to walk towards Tate's food truck. He still needed to clean up—or help *Rachel* clean up, and she'd be pissed if he spent any more time out here, mooning over his hot, accomplished, *thoughtful* boyfriend.

"So, you give speeches now, huh?" Tate asked, his mouth curling into a smile. He knew just how proud he looked; he could feel it radiating out of him. "It was really good. I'm so proud of you."

"I wanted to be better before we ever met again," Chase confessed. "I wanted to be a better man, because someday, I thought I might meet someone who deserved that. But then I realized it was you, all along."

"The first, and the last," Tate said, and reached up, pulling Chase in for a fierce, loving kiss.

"I'd say it feels like fate . . ." Chase said, reaching up to brush Tate's hair back.

"But it's more than just fate?" Tate nodded. "It really is more. Because you know what? I'm always going to *choose* you."

EPILOGUE

Six months later

"I just checked the guest list," Tate said, hopping onto the counter next to where Chase was carefully flipping a sandwich on the gigantic stove.

Chase was never going to be a chef—not even *close*, as far as Tate was concerned—but it was really nice to come home some nights and have someone else cook.

Even if it was a grilled cheese sandwich.

"You checked the guest list?" Chase repeated as he grabbed a plate from the counter next to the stove.

"Well, yeah, Alec sent it over to me, so I figured I should take a look," Tate said. "I had some time after the lunch rush, so I pulled it up on my phone."

"Oh," Chase said.

Tate had thought he knew Chase Riley really well six months ago, when they'd gotten together for real, and for good, but now? Tate knew Chase better than he knew himself.

"*You* didn't send it over to me," Tate said, still smiling. Chase was looking anywhere but at his face. Which meant that he'd figured out the source of Chase's unease.

He'd kind of hoped that Chase would tell him, but he'd also learned to trust his boyfriend, and trust that if it had been something big, he'd have told Tate immediately.

But this? This was just Chase being silly. And now they both knew it.

"I see you were trying to avoid me realizing that you invited Colin O'Connor," Tate said conversationally, reaching over to the plate and grabbing the sandwich, taking a big bite out of one corner. He chewed slowly and then swallowed. "That's big of you."

"It's . . . it's not a big deal," Chase said. Even though he was definitely trying to hide a smile now. "He's part of our community, right? And rich. Really, really rich. Why wouldn't I invite him to our fundraiser?"

"Maybe because you keep claiming you don't like him?" Tate said slyly, taking another bite of the sandwich. Maybe it wasn't quite as good as one of his, but Chase was doing a damn good job in front of the stove these days.

Plus it really didn't hurt that he was just wearing one of those flimsy aprons and a pair of loose athletic shorts.

And he was absolutely doing it on purpose. Probably hoping to distract Tate from learning his big secret.

"Claiming?" Chase raised an eyebrow, moving over to the sink and stashing the pan in it. "I . . ."

"Really have zero issues with Colin O'Connor," Tate said, smiling. "And we both know it."

"I could have issues with him," Chase grumbled.

"Yeah, but you don't," Tate said kindly. Reached out and cupped the back of his neck, tangling his fingers in his soft, loose hair. Tugged Chase closer. "It's okay to think that you're not chopped liver in comparison. Really."

Chase squirmed. "I . . . I guess I'm not. He's a great guy, and . . ."

"You're also a great guy?" Tate said. "The Riptide certainly think so. Or so Alec tells me. Already re-negotiating your contract. Extending it, even. That's not just because you catch a ball really well."

"Fine, fine," Chase grumbled. "I guess I can also be . . . sort of great."

Tate pulled him the rest of the way, until his legs were wrapped around Chase's waist and he was so close he could see every shade of brown in his gorgeous eyes. "I think you're absolutely fucking fantastically awesome, okay?"

Chase couldn't contain his smile at that. "I love you too," he said.

"Even if I didn't love you," Tate argued. "I'd still think that. The things you've done to bring attention to mental health? The work you've done with your new foundation? You're a beacon of hope for a lot of people out there, and evidence that change is possible."

"Once an idiot, not always an idiot?" Chase said, the edge of his mouth quirking up. "Yeah, it feels good to know that. To really believe it." His expression softened. "I really couldn't have done it without you."

"Well," Tate drawled, letting his hands drift up Chase's defined biceps. Still, after all this time, it kind of blew his mind that he could touch like this. That Chase wanted it as much as he did. "It wouldn't have been as fun, that's for sure."

"Speaking of fun," Chase teased. "I didn't just make you dinner."

"Oh?" Tate usually loved it when Chase got creative. He'd not been disappointed yet.

"I made dessert too," Chase said and pulled his apron off, lowering his shorts.

"Fuck," Tate swore when he saw the telltale purple silicone rim of Chase's favorite plug peeking out from between his muscular cheeks.

"You like?" Chase asked, gasping as Tate reached down and tugged on it. Not hard enough to dislodge it, but just enough to make him feel it.

"Yeah, I *love* it," Tate said. "You know this is my favorite kind of surprise."

"The kind of surprise where you fuck me bent over the kitchen counter?" Chase wondered, his voice so innocent it was a miracle that he was as filthy as he was. Tate thanked God, fate, anyone who would listen, for it every single day.

"Yes," Tate agreed, hopping off the counter. "And it's definitely mine too."

He reached for Chase and their mouths met in a sloppy, desperate kiss. It occurred to Tate that horniness might explain a lot of Chase's behavior as he gently maneuvered his boyfriend over by the island—they'd tried various positions for the kitchen fucking, and this one was definitely the best, with no obtrusive knobs or handles or the potential for setting themselves on fire—and pushed him down. Unbuckled his pants and pulled down his briefs and crowded up against Chase, reveling in the feeling of skin on skin as his boy buckled beneath him, desperate and wanting.

"Don't worry," Tate said, leaning down and brushing Chase's hair aside so he could press a hot, wet kiss to his neck. "I've got you."

"Ahhhh," Chase moaned into the marble as Tate twisted the plug out, tossing it on the floor and losing no time in sliding inside. Chase was wet and slick and just loose enough, but still a hot vise around his dick. He felt so good that Tate was afraid—like he always was—that he might come too soon. It was more than just the incredible pleasure of being inside Chase. It was being inside, as close as he could ever be, to the person he loved most.

Tate pushed himself a bit higher on his toes, making sure the angle was as good for Chase as he could make it, but in only a few strokes, Chase was crying out, come splattering all over the floor, moaning as Tate worked him through his orgasm.

His own was not far behind, and he groaned, fingers tightening on Chase's hips as he let his orgasm overtake him.

Tate slumped against Chase's big body, reveling in a little bit of closeness, before he had to pull out and clean up the mess they'd just made.

"That was great," Chase murmured into the marble countertop. "Ten out of ten, highly recommend."

"Maybe don't recommend it on Twitter," Tate teased him. A joke he could make now, because Chase had deleted his app from his phone and had learned better ways of communicating with his fan base.

"Don't worry," Chase said. "If I did, you'd have a line a mile long, and I don't like to share. Especially you."

"Only you," Tate echoed. "Always you."

To read a bonus scene about Chase and Tate returning to high school for their ten year reunion, click here.

To continue the Food Truck Warriors series with *On a Roll*, Gabe and Sean's story, click here.

To check out the Riptide series, with books about Heath & Sam, Neal & Jamie, and Alec & Spencer, click here.

INTERESTED IN READING MORE OF
BETH'S BOOKS?

CHECK OUT A FULL LIST OF TILES
BY SCANNING THE QR CODE
OR VISITING HER WEBSITE

WWW.BETHBOLDEN.COM/BOOKLIST

WANT TO FOLLOW BETH?

MAKE SURE YOU NEVER
MISS A RELEASE?

SCAN THE QR CODE BELOW
OR VISIT HER WEBSITE
FOR A SOCIAL MEDIA LIST,
NEWSLETTER SIGNUP,
AND SO MUCH MORE!

WWW.BETHBOLDEN.COM/ABOUT

9 781964 691091